AN AFRI

David Barnes,

with best wishes,

David

An African Romance

David Willington

Ashgrove Publishing
London

For Mary, who shared the Africa bug with me

By the same author:

History

Alumni Montium: *Sixty years of Glenalmond and its people*

St John's Episcopal Church: *The History of a Worshipping Community*

Fiction

In Search of the General

George's War

A Palestine Affair

A Polish Adventure

Historical Note

It is easy to forget how recently, compared with other parts of the world, Central and East Africa were penetrated by Europeans. David Livingstone had begun his explorations in 1841, though these lay mainly to the south of Lake Victoria. In 1862, Speke had discovered the source of the White Nile. When my grandfather was born in 1878, Disraeli was Prime Minister and the 'Scramble for Africa' had only just begun. The territory later known as Uganda was the prize of Central Africa because of its fertility and because it lay on Lake Victoria; the White Nile flowed north through it. It was therefore more accessible than lands to the east, facing the Indian Ocean. However, between 1896 and 1901 a railway was built from Mombasa on the coast to Kisumu on Lake Victoria, a distance of 660 miles. Much of the intervening territory was hostile, either because of climate, disease or native tribes. A depot was established in 1899 at milepost 312 which became Nairobi. Thereafter the Highlands of Kenya were gradually opened up to white settlers.

Johann Ludwig Krapf was the first European to sight Mount Kenya, *Kirinyaga*. He had been sent out to Mombasa by the British Church Missionary Society. In 1848 he travelled into the interior with a view to establishing mission stations. He described the sighting as follows:

'It happened that on leaving Kitui on 3rd December 1849 I could see the Kegnia most distinctly [it was 87 miles away], and observed two large horns, or pillars as it were, rising over an enormous mountain to the north west of the Kilimanjaro, covered with a white substance.'

Geographers back in England could not believe that there could be snow on the Equator, and thought that the white substance was 'calcareous earth'.

Joseph Thomson was sent out in 1883 by Lord Aberdare, the new

President of the Royal Geographical Society, to establish the truth of the matter. He was the second European to see Mount Kenya as he explored the high plateau, 12,000 feet, which he called the Aberdares.

'[Fifty miles away] there rose…a gleaming snow-white peak with sparkling facets, which scintillated with the superb beauty of a colossal diamond... But now, even while I stood and gazed, a moisture-laden breeze touched the peak, wove a fleecy mantle and gradually enshrouded the heaven-like spectacle. In a few moments there but remained a bank of clouds over the wood.'

He could not get closer because of the hostility of the Maasai.

In 1887, Count Teleki reached the top of the valley that was later named after him, at a height of about 15,000 feet, the base of the two peaks.

The mountain is protected by a thick band of forest and bamboo between 7,000 and 10,000 feet and this made the approach to the peaks very hard-going, as Dr J Walter Gregory, a professor of Geology, described in his attempt to climb Mount Kenya, in June 1892 (*The Great Rift Valley*):

'Through the dark and dismal forest we had to force our way. Occasionally an elephant path would run in our direction and we could then make comparatively rapid progress. The elephants, however, did not obey the rules of mountaineering, and their tracks soon ran down into valleys, so that most of the way we had to cut a path step by step. Every blow of the matlocks upon the bamboos shook the sodden canopy overhead, and continual showerbaths of water kept us wet and miserable. My clothes were soon soaked through, while the raw, damp cold chilled the porters to the marrow. We had to stop every hour to light fires to warm them, and even then they found the climb almost unbearable, and one or two cried like children…So far the work had been simply miserable. We had not once seen or felt the sun since we left the meadows of Laikipia…[On the fourth day] the forest gave place to scattered clumps of trees, and the rank undergrowth to a firm, rich turf; the long monstrous slope broke up into a bed of undulating ground, which, with its numerous swampy, mossy hollows, its irregularly scattered boulders, and its stiff, greasy clay reminded me of a glacial moraine. The men threw down their loads and basked in the sunshine...He [Fundi] had often asked me about the great white fields he had seen with Teleki, and how bitterly disappointed he had been at not reaching them...I therefore waited for him to pass me, that he might be the first man to set foot on the glaciers of Kenya.'

The altitude was measured at 15,580 feet.

The twin peaks, later named Batian (17,058 feet) and Nelion (17,022 feet), were first climbed by Halford Mackinder in 1899. Not till 1930 was a second attempt to climb the mountain successful.

'Kenya is God's own country with the Devil's own problems.'

(James Griffths, Labour Secretary of State for the Colonies, 1950.)

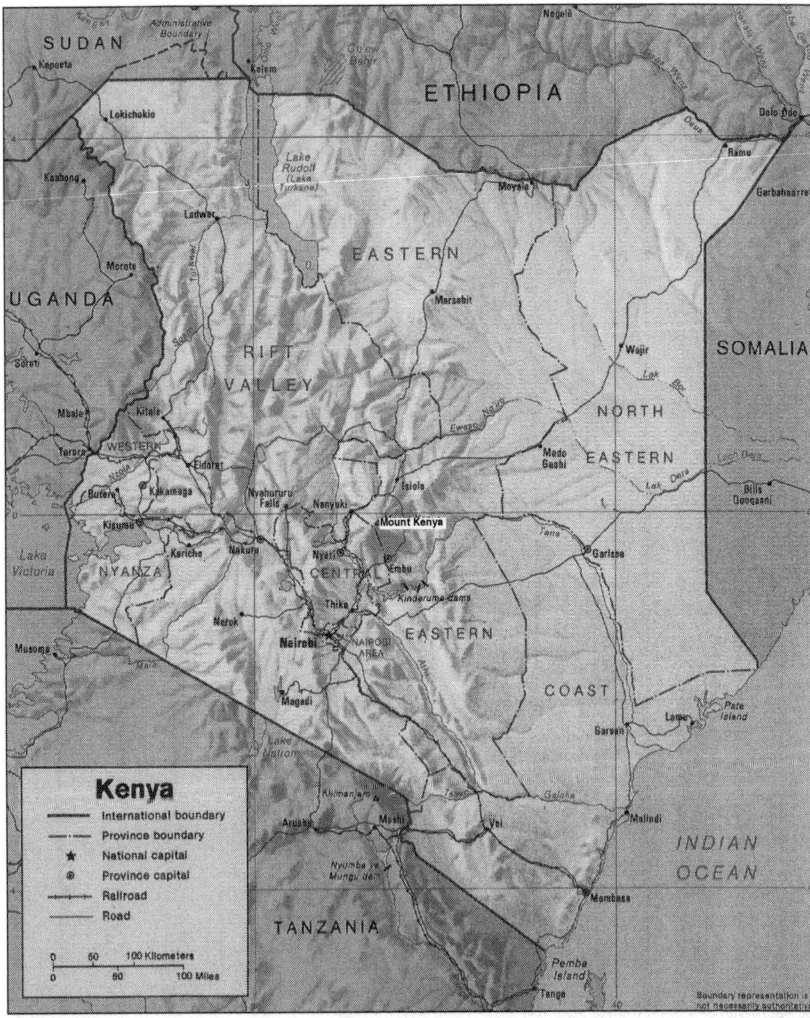

Kenya
International boundary
Province boundary
National capital
Province capital
Railroad
Road
0 50 100 Kilometers
0 50 100 Miles
Boundary representation is not necessarily authoritative
SUDAN
ETHIOPIA
UGANDA
SOMALIA
TANZANIA
INDIAN OCEAN
Administrative Boundary
Kapoeta
Kelem
Nagelē
Ch'ew Bahir
Dolo Odo
Lokichokio
Kaabong
Lake Rudolf (Lake Turkana)
Moyale
Ramu
Garbahaarrey
Lodwar
Moroto
EASTERN
Marsabit
RIFT VALLEY
Soroti
Wajir
NORTH EASTERN
Mbale
Kitale
Tororo
WESTERN
Eldoret
Mado Gashi
Butere
Kakamega
Isiolo
Nyahururu Falls
Nanyuki
Mount Kenya
Bilis Qooqaani
Kisumu
Kericho
Nakuru
Nyeri
Embu
Garissa
Lake Victoria
NYANZA
CENTRAL
Kinderuma dams
Thika
Narok
Nairobi
NAIROBI AREA
Musoma
Magadi
COAST
Lamu
Pate Island
Garsen
Lake Natron
Kilimanjaro
Arusha
Moshi
Voi
Malindi
Nyumba ya Mungu dam
Mombasa
Pemba Island
Tanga

Chapter One

February 1951

Michael Charteris awoke not long before dawn. He had not slept well and he felt heavy-headed. At first he could not remember where he was. It was cold and he threw back the bedclothes with reluctance. He padded over to the bathroom, shaved and dressed. Others were moving around in the house and he went along to the dining room.

'Morning, Mike,' said Patrick Howarth.

'Morning, Patrick,' he replied.

'Sleep well?'

'So-so.'

'Coffee?'

'Please.'

'We should be ready to go in about ten minutes. Bring a warm pullover and a hat. But it shouldn't be windy.'

The sun came up with tropical suddenness. Between the trees at the end of the garden, Michael could see the two peaks of the mountain.

'How far are we going?' he asked.

'Through the forest and onto the plateau.'

Just then Patrick's wife, Annabel, appeared.

'Everything's ready,' she announced.

They went outside. The Land Rover's engine was running.

'I bought it last year; it's one of the first in the country,' said Patrick. 'Very pleased with it. Why don't you sit on the back with Thomas? His real name is Ndegwa, but he answers to Thomas.'

Michael got on the back, which carried three camp chairs, two frying pans, a kettle, a hamper of food, plates, mugs and eating irons.

'*Jambo*, Thomas,' said Michael.

'*Jambo, Bwana*.'

Michael noticed a twin-barrelled rifle and a box of ammunition.

'Buffalo, *Bwana*. Just in case.'

A mile from the house they came to the track and soon entered the forest. The track climbed steeply in places but Patrick used the crawler gear; the murram surface was dry and smooth.

'It gets rougher higher up,' said Thomas.

The forest was dense and it was not possible to see more than five yards on either side of the track. Colobus monkeys called out from the trees.

'What's that?' Michael asked Thomas, pointing to a bird with a dark head and greenish body.

'Turaco. And we should see some parrots.'

At one point the Land Rover stopped and Patrick and Annabel got out.

'There is one very steep bit here - about a hundred yards. The three of you can walk up it and give me a push if necessary.' He looked about him. 'Look, Mike, elephant droppings.' He inspected them. 'Not recent though.'

The Land Rover made it up the slope unassisted and they climbed back in. Fifteen minutes later they emerged onto the plateau. By now the sun was nearly overhead and very warm. Ahead of them the moorland sloped gently up to the base of the peaks.

'How far away are we?'

'About ten miles.'

'I could almost reach out and touch them.'

'The track peters out after three miles, so we will find a breakfast spot soon.'

The moorland was intersected by deep ravines but the track kept to the top of a broad ridge. It became very rough and tested the Land Rover's springs.

'I think we'll stop here. Thomas and I will prepare breakfast, while Annabel takes you for a nature walk.'

'How high are we?'

'About 11,000 feet. If you get a headache, we have some pills.'

Annabel led off smartly up a short slope and strode on for two hundred yards. Michael followed, breathing heavily.

'I didn't realise I was that unfit.'

'No. It's just the effect of altitude.'

She pointed out some vegetation. 'Tropical gigantism. Those are lobelias, like the ones in your garden, only twelve feet high. Over there, *Erica Arborea*.'

'You mean heather?'

'Just as you have in Scotland, only bigger.'

'What are those trees?'

'They are not trees, but giant groundsel, *senecio johnstonii*. It takes about two hundred years for them to grow that high.'

They walked on a little further. 'Cabbage groundsel. It shuts itself up at night and opens up with the sunrise.'

She put her hand on his arm and pointed. From behind a large clump of grass emerged a bird with brown and grey plumage, with a reddish neck.

'A big partridge?' Michael whispered.

'Montane Francolin. They make good eating.' The bird ignored them as it walked past.

'They have no fear of humans as few people come up here.'

She handed him binoculars. 'Up there.'

Michael searched the sky and saw a large bird soaring near them. 'What's that?

'Is it white underneath with a red tail?'

'Yes.'

'Augur's Buzzard. They're fairly common all over the country.'

'What do they find to eat up here?'

'Rock hyrax, and smaller creatures, like mice. They will also go for carcasses, provided they are reasonably fresh. If they find a dead buffalo, they have a feast.'

They walked on a little way.

'I say, Annabel, that splash of colour. What is it?'

Annabel examined the red flowers on a thin stalk. 'Well, aren't you lucky! This is quite rare: *gladiolus watsonioides*, only found on Mount Kenya and the Aberdares.'

'Who was Watson?'

'Dunno. Beautiful though, isn't it?'

'You know, what at first sight appears a monotonous landscape is full of interest. And those peaks, what are they called?'

'Nelion and Batian. Ngai lives on them. He's the chief god of the Maasai and Kikuyu. We have to treat his mountain with respect.'

'I'm sure. Do we make sacrifices to him?'

'We have done already, as a thanksgiving in advance. Patrick shot an impala yesterday and we will be cooking it today.'

'Talking of food…'

'Let's wander back and see if breakfast is ready.'

Patrick and Thomas had lit a fire with dried heather shoots as fuel and rashers of bacon were being cooked in one frying pan and eggs in the other. A kettle was coming to the boil and beside it a pan of milk.

'Smells good,' said Michael.

'Help yourself.'

They all tucked in. Thomas was persuaded to have an egg on a slice of bread.

Patrick poured tea, and added hot milk and sugar. The brew tasted insipid, and he noticed that Michael frowned as he sipped it.

'It's just hot liquid, Mike. Up here water boils at about eighty-eight degrees and the full taste of the tea doesn't come out. But drink up. You mustn't become dehydrated.'

Just then Michael noticed a creature about the size of a rabbit approaching the food hamper. Thomas picked up a stone and threw it; the animal scurried away.

'Rock hyrax. Cheeky buggers. We'll leave one or two bits when we go. Have some mango.'

They ate the fruit and tossed the skins and some bacon rind onto a bare patch of earth. Thomas and Annabel packed up while Patrick and Michael lit their pipes.

'I won't forget this breakfast in a hurry. Thank you for bringing me up here. Have you ever climbed the peaks?'

'Only to a lesser top, Point Lenana. I am not a rock climber. Still it's a respectable height, sixteen and a half thousand. If you ever try it, start out from your last camp at three o'clock so that you get to the top at dawn. The light is so clear you can see Kilimanjaro, two hundred miles away. If you leave it till later, the cloud comes up the valleys and by midday it will be misty on the tops. Fancy a walk?'

'Of course.'

'Annabel and Thomas will take the Land Rover down and we will follow the track. There is a short cut to the house. We should be back for lunch.'

Patrick took a rucksack from the car and the rifle and a box of ammunition.

'Water and some spare food if you get hungry.'

'Can I carry something?'

'You can take turns in carrying the rifle. It gets damned heavy after a while.'

'Do you expect us to meet anything?'

'There are elephants in the forest, and a few rhino. We would be very lucky to see a leopard. The most dangerous animal is the buffalo.'

'Would you shoot it?'

'Only to save a life.'

'What do we do if we meet one?'

'Buffalo are cunning creatures but they are short-sighted. The approved wisdom is that you should throw down your pack on one side of the track and hide behind a tree on the other side. If that doesn't work, climb the tree.'

'Have you ever had to do that?'

'Once, when I didn't have a rifle. And it did work. But since then I have never gone without.'

The car was loaded up. Annabel took the wheel and Thomas jumped onto the back. Michael waved and started to get up, but Patrick held him back.

'Just wait a moment. Over there.'

Once the car had moved off, four hyrax emerged from the scrub, at first hesitantly, then with confidence, to nibble at the bacon and mango skins. Sunbirds picked at crumbs of bread. Another small brown bird tried to join the feast but was jostled out of the way.

'Mountain chat.'

They watched for a few minutes. Then the hyrax disappeared

suddenly and the birds followed suit. Michael looked up and there was the buzzard circling not far above them. Disappointed in its prey, it eventually moved away.

Patrick knocked his pipe out and got to his feet.

'Time to move. You can carry the rifle for a bit.'

'You are right; it is heavy.'

'Fourteen pounds. It takes point five ammo. If you hit it in the right place at a hundred yards, it will drop a charging buffalo or lion. If they still come on, you fire the other barrel.'

'And if you miss?'

'You drop the rifle and climb a tree. One of our *watu* was killed by a buffalo last year and I had to go out and deal with it. The village feasted on the meat for days.'

They strode on in companionable silence. At the edge of the forest they stopped to remove sweaters, as it was getting very warm.

'Here, you take the rucksack,' said Patrick. 'I'll have the rifle. If for any reason we get separated, just follow the track down. About just over the hour there is a fork. Take the left hand one. That's the way we came up. Another hour and you will be at the road and it is fifteen minutes back to the house.'

'Interesting that you refer to time, not distance. It was the same in Burma. Thick jungle, deep ravines, jagged mountain ridges. Something that looked no distance on the map took hours. Besides, the maps were unreliable or had blank spaces.'

'What unit were you?'

'King's African Rifles. Which is a little odd, since I have never been to Africa before now. I was with the Royal West Kents and spent two years waiting for a German invasion which never happened. I got fed up and asked for a transfer to see some action. The man at the Military Secretary's Office hummed and hawed. Then he said that the KAR needed some officers on secondment. A month later I was in Dimapur as a captain pretending I was ready to face the Japanese. I had a crash course in Swahili. Fortunately my company sergeant-major took me under his wing and taught me how to deal with my askaris. It helped that I am tall, though some of the chaps were big men; they could carry a bren for miles along with the rest of their kit. We beat the Japs off Imphal and chased them across the Chindwin. Just before Mandalay I got hit and invalided out. Back in India, they patched me up roughly and sent me home.'

'Where were you hurt?'

'Left leg mostly. It took some time to put it together again.'

'Are you sure you can manage the walk back?'

'I'll be fine.'

'Good.'

Patrick filled his pipe and lit it. 'Let's move on. Remind me why you are here. Two days ago Annabel told me that you were coming. Don't get me wrong. We are very pleased to have you. Round here we see the same old faces time and time again, and even when we go down to Nairobi. So it is a pleasure to talk to someone new. Tell me more about yourself.'

'It's quite a long story.'

'Well, we have some way to go.'

'I was born in 1918. My father was a solicitor in Devon. I disliked the idea of the Law, too stuffy, so I went to Sandhurst instead. My older brother is the intellectual; he went to Oxford, became a Whitehall warrior because of his poor eyesight. Now he is a civil servant. I've told you about my wartime soldiering...'

'You didn't tell me about your Military Cross.'

'How do you know that?'

'Ah. There are ways and means.'

'OK. It was for a company action that went well, for once.'

'How modest. What happened after you got home, and were patched up?'

'I could speak Swahili and had experience in jungle warfare. So the Army put me on garrison duty in Germany, which was interesting for a while, but I wanted more adventure. Three years ago I tried to get out to Malaya, but I was considered too valuable checking food distribution in the British Zone of Germany. Two years on staff courses and then came the opportunity to take long leave – six months. So I thought I would use it to see where the KAR comes from. There is another reason for getting away. I was married in

1945, but it didn't work out. We didn't see each other for weeks on end and she got bored with officers' quarters in Camberley. Not an unusual situation in the military. Fortunately there were no children and we were able to make a clean break.'

'How did you make contact with us?'

'My nephew, Simon, is at Sherborne, in the same house as your boy. When I mentioned I was thinking of coming out here, he spoke to your son - Charlie, isn't it? - and he volunteered you. I wrote to a contact in Nairobi and he said I must visit you. I arrived a fortnight ago and found a room at the Norfolk Hotel. I called in at KAR HQ and was given several introductions. Pottered around Nairobi, played golf, was invited to dinner at the Muthaiga Club. I was taken round some local sights, then I took the train to Gilgil, where Charlie had been at school, I think. I stayed a couple of days with the Headmaster. I talked to the boys about my wartime adventures. Then I scrounged a lift to Nanyuki, and here I am. I arrived rather later than I intended. You had been out somewhere. But a cold supper and a glass of whisky was very welcome. I was dog tired and crashed out as soon as soon as I hit the sheets.'

'You must stay with us for a few days. There is plenty for you to see and do round here, and I have an old army jeep you can use. Practice your Swahili on Thomas, though his main language is Gikuyu.'

'What does he do for you?'

'He's a sort of major-domo on the farm. A bright chap, good NCO type, stands no nonsense from the *watu*. He is also a devout Christian, scrupulously honest.'

'Has he a wife?'

'Oh yes, just one. And five children. They live in a *banda* not far from our house. In due course I will take you round the estate in the jeep. And this evening, Annabel has arranged a little dinner party, just neighbours, but you should get a feel for the place from them.'

'Are we eating the impala you shot?'

'Yes. It takes hours to cook, but it is delicious. What we don't eat will go to the *watu*.'

They fell silent. On either side of the track the forest was dark and impenetrable with tall trees and thick undergrowth. It wouldn't do to wander off, Michael thought. And it would be difficult to see even an elephant unless it was very close. Most animals would slip away if they heard or smelt humans.

Just as they were coming round a corner, he saw a small buck disappear into the bushes ahead of them.

'Dik dik,' said Patrick. 'You don't often see them; they usually don't break cover.'

Colobus monkeys started screeching.

'Something's on the move.' Patrick stepped off the track and motioned Michael to join him. He loaded the rifle. They waited and soon heard snuffling – like a giant hedgehog, Michael thought – and the crashing of foliage trodden underfoot.

Patrick put his finger to his lips.

Thirty yards ahead of them a buffalo emerged onto the track. Michael's heart thumped. Patrick brought the rifle up to his shoulder. The buffalo swung his head from side to side and pawed the ground. After a minute it stood still, defecated loudly, and moved off into the forest on the other side; the noise of its passage died away. Patrick lowered the rifle, but signalled to Michael to keep absolutely still.

They waited for ten minutes but there was no further disturbance.

'They're cunning beasts. It could be lying in wait for us, but I think it has moved on. It realised that there were foreign bodies around, but it wasn't threatened. Sometimes they come in pairs, but this was an old bull, and they are usually loners. Come on.'

They walked briskly past the spot where the buffalo had entered the forest, but there was no sign of its passage; the foliage had closed behind it.

At length Michael asked: 'What about you, Patrick? How did you come to farm in Kenya?'

'As you said, a long story. Family tradition has it that Grandfather took the farm as the settlement of a gambling debt back in 1910. It's a good story and may have a modicum of truth in it. He died fairly soon afterwards, so I never knew him. My father expanded the farm and sent me to the school in Gilgil, which had just opened. Apparently I was a feral child and needed knocking into shape before going off to boarding school in England. There I was considered rather exotic. My first language was Swahili and I spoke English with a clipped colonial accent. I came back in '34 and was given a section of the farm to look after. When Abyssinia blew up in 1935 I joined the Kenya Regiment, a territorial battalion; gentleman soldiering. In 1939 we were given the option of signing on for the KAR, but I had a young family and there was no one else to run the farm. My father had had a stroke and was in a home in Nairobi. So, unlike you, I have never fired a shot in anger.'

'Do you regret that?'

'I have about 200 workers on the farm. I built them a school and a medical centre. I am the biggest employer in the area. You could say I have battalion-sized responsibilities.'

'That is certainly true.'

'Before the war we were mainly ranching, but then we concentrated on food production. The top soil round here is surprisingly fertile, being volcanic in origin. So we grow vegetables and a lot of maize, some of which goes for export. I'll tell you more when we go round tomorrow afternoon.'

'What about Annabel? Where does she come from?'

'Old settler stock, near Nakuru. We met at a polo match. She is very practical and can turn her hand to anything, whether looking after the *watu* or sewing up an injured dog. And all the outdoor pursuits. We have Charlie at Sherborne; Naomi is only six and we employ a tutor for her. We had another child between them, but it died at birth.'

'I'm sorry.'

'Obviously a great shock, but it turned out that it would have been severely handicapped. So we were much relieved when Naomi came along. She's the splitting image of Annabel, not only in looks; they are both strong characters, and I foresee battles ahead. She is a very engaging child; you'll like her.'

'I look forward to meeting her.'

They came to the fork. Within a few minutes the forest began to thin out and they felt the full force of the sun. Alongside the track were small *bandas* with tiny plots of land beside them.

'They are starting to encroach on the forest. There is some illegal logging but the land is needed for cultivation; Kikuyu are farmers by nature. I can sympathise, but we have to be careful.'

'Do the people here work for you?'

'Most of them. They are happy to walk three miles to us for work, if this means they have their own patch of ground, which the women work as well as bringing up lots of children, fetching water, washing clothes and cooking food.'

'What do they live on?'

'Vegetables, *posho* porridge, eggs. Pretty basic. It is a very narrow line between daily living and penury. Especially when you have five or more children to feed.'

As they walked past, Patrick called out greetings to women who were working their plots. At one point he stopped for about five minutes to chat. The woman seemed upset about something. Michael could not make out the details but some words came back to him.

'It seems that one of her *totos* is rather ill,' said Patrick. 'I'll send Annabel to see her later today. Apparently the witchdoctor has been, muttered some incantation and made the child drink some potion, which caused him to be violently ill. He hasn't kept anything down for two days.'

When they reached the house, Patrick poured beers and Naomi was brought in to see Michael. She shook hands gravely. Michael asked her what she had done that morning. 'Lessons,' she replied, 'with Simmie.'

'Simmie?'

'Miss Simpson,' explained Patrick. 'She is a governess from England. You'll meet her later.'

'I have had my lunch.' said Naomi. 'Can I go and play now?'

'Of course.'

On the verandah a snack lunch was laid out. Annabel joined them and Patrick told her about the sick child.

'Hm. Could be anything.'

'Where is the nearest doctor?' Michael asked.

'Nanyuki. Our own medical centre deals with small injuries and dishes out basic pills and refers them on if necessary. It's difficult to persuade people to go and see the doctor, since that means paying money which they don't have and taking time off work. No National Health Service here. We give hard cases a little discreet help.'

'Where do you go if you are ill?'

'Nanyuki. If that doesn't work, there is a good hospital in Nairobi. If the worst comes to the worst, we go to London. Fingers crossed, we haven't had to do that.'

Whether it was because of the early start or the heat and the exercise that morning, Michael began to feel sleepy. He couldn't help yawning.

Patrick sympathised. 'Go and have some Egyptian PT. Annabel and I often sleep after lunch for an hour; makes all the difference.'

'I had better see this woman,' said Annabel. 'Can I have the Land Rover?'

'Are we set for tonight?'

'Everything is in hand. The impala is turning on the spit.'

'As usual, I will leave it all in your capable hands. I have some paperwork to look at.'

Michael retired to his room, took off his shoes and lay on the bed. Within a minute he was fast asleep.

He woke two hours later with a knock on the door. A maid came in with a cup of tea. 'Four o'clock, *Bwana*.'

'Oh. Thank you.'

He sat up and sipped. It wasn't very hot. There must have been three spoonfuls of sugar in it. Nevertheless he drank it and soon felt restored. He went out onto the verandah and found Patrick smoking his pipe.

'I've just had Annabel on the radio from Nanyuki. The *toto* has appendicitis and they are going to operate. The mother is there too and distraught. So Annabel is going to stay with her for a bit. I've sent Thomas to find the husband.'

'Does this sort of thing happen often?'

'Fortunately not. But we have the means to help and when someone's crisis arises we must swing into action. Look, can you potter about for an hour or so. Go where you like. Our guests are due at 6.30, though time is flexible round here. We don't dress.'

'That's just as well. I haven't got a suit.'

Patrick went off and Michael lit his pipe. Naomi came onto the verandah, followed by the governess.

'Hello, I'm Jane Simpson, charged with looking after Madam here.'

Michael stood up. 'Michael Charteris.'

They shook hands.

'Naomi has things to show you. Can I leave her with you?'

'Of course.'

'When you get back, Rosie, one of the maids, will give her supper and a bath, so that she will be scrubbed up to meet the guests.'

'Er...Will you be there tonight?'

'Yes, and I hope we can have a chat. I've met everyone before, several times, so a new face will be welcome.'

When she had gone, Naomi whispered to Michael: 'She's pretty, don't you think? All Daddy's friends admire her.'

'You're right, she is pretty. Now, what have you got to show me?'

Naomi did not take his proffered hand but led off smartly to the end of the garden and into a paddock. Beyond the paddock was some open bush, the grass turning brown.

'When the rains come it will all be green again,' she said. She climbed onto the top rail.

'Come up beside me. I am not allowed outside on my own, so I sit here and look out for my animals.'

Michael climbed up and sat beside her.

'What are we looking for?'

'Shh!'

Nothing happened for a few minutes. Then she tapped his arm and pointed.

'Just there, under that acacia tree.'

Michael could see nothing at first.

'What is it, sharp eyes?'

'Just watch.'

To his delight a warthog emerged into the open, its tail vertical with a black tassel on top. Behind it came six little warthogs, their tails in the air and trotting briskly to keep up.

'There's a stream down there and they go to drink while it is still light. Then they come back to their den for the night. I try to see them most days and I count the little ones. There were eight, but two have gone. Something ate them.'

'They are delightful,' said Michael, 'even though they are so ugly.'

'Daddy says that only one or two will survive to grow up. That is very sad.'

'Yes, it is.'

Michael was about to say something about Nature red in tooth and claw, but thought better of it.

'Do you see lots of animals out there?'

'Lots. I have seen all the big ones except leopards. I like the little ones best, though. Tomorrow night, if I am allowed to stay up, I will show you my bush babies. They only come out at dusk.'

'What about snakes?'

'They are all around us but they keep out of our way. I am not allowed to run around in bare feet, so I have to wear these boots outside. They can get very hot.'

'I understand.'

'The vibration of my footsteps frightens them away, so Simmie says. Did you see the golf club by the door? Daddy uses it to kill snakes that get into the house.'

'I must tell you. I was in Burma during the war and we came across very big snakes. Pythons. They could swallow one of your little warthogs.'

'Golly.'

'The soldiers caught and cooked them. I tried one and it was quite tasty.'

'What did it taste like?'

'Sort of rather like chicken with a hint of fish, without being too strong. Made a change from army rations.'

'I don't think I would like that. What about the venom?'

'You don't eat the head.'

'I see.'

Naomi jumped down. 'I am taking you to my special animal. I help look after it.'

She headed back to the garden and round to the other side of the house. There was another paddock with one section of it cordoned off. Naomi opened a small gate and beckoned him through. Inside were a cow and its calf.

'This is Begum and her calf is Lakme. They come from India.'

She went up and patted the calf.

'Sihiwal cattle. See the hump on the shoulder. And they have long slim faces. They are good for meat and milk. They are a bit thin just now, because of the shortage of green grass and we have to feed Begum on banana leaves. Daddy wants to introduce more of them into Kenya.'

She took a bottle of milk from a box. 'I put this out every day for Lakme, because Begum is a bit dry. It's time for her drink.'

She stroked the calf and put the teat into its mouth. The animal gulped eagerly and the milk was soon gone.

'There. That will do till tomorrow.' She patted the calf and the mother.

'Goodbye, Begum, goodbye, Lakme.'

'Er…Goodbye,' said Michael.

As they walked back to the house Michael reflected on the child's directness. He hoped she would not lose it when she was sent off to boarding school.

They came to the back of the house where a *watu* was turning the handle of the spit. The impala was being roasted gently over an open fire.

'Smells delicious,' said Michael.

'Must be a very boring job,' said Naomi. 'He's been at it for three hours. I hope he gets some of it to eat.'

'What are you having for supper, Naomi?'

'I don't know. Rosie cooks something for me, usually with baked beans. I eat it because I am hungry, not because I like it.'

Michael could say nothing to that. Just then Rosie came out and called for Naomi.

'Coming, Rosie. Tomorrow night, Michael, don't forget the bush babies.'

Chapter Two

Just after 6.30 Michael came along to the verandah where Annabel was laying out the drinks. 'How is the *toto*?' he asked.

'They will operate first thing tomorrow. Fingers crossed.'

'Indeed.'

'Drink?'

'Please. G and T.'

Annabel made drinks for both of them.

'Patrick will be here in a few minutes. Let me tell you about the people coming. Hugh and Melanie Frampton are on the other side of Nanyuki, about three quarters of an hour away. The family has been here since the earliest days. You'll find them - dare I say it? - rather dismissive of blacks in general, but they are good farmers. The other couple are more recent. Andrew is a District Officer and Charlotte works in the medical centre at Nanyuki. They are younger than us and have rather different views of the natives from the Framptons. It should be a lively evening.'

'I look forward to it. Naomi showed me her animals today and she promised to show me the bush babies tomorrow.'

'I think we can let her stay up a little for that. Have you met Simmie – Jane?'

'She brought Naomi to me this afternoon.'

'She's a good soul but I think she gets a bit lonely out here. Please chat her up.'

They heard the noise of a car in the drive. Patrick emerged from his office.

'Looks like the Framptons. Have you got the whisky there? Hugh drinks whisky every night from five o'clock onwards,' he explained to Michael. 'He makes do with beer during the day.'

Hugh and Melanie came in. He was white haired and sunburned, with a large moustache. Melanie was tall and slim, her hair dyed with henna. Michael judged them to be in their late sixties.

Introductions were made.

'And what is it you do, Charteris?' asked Hugh. 'Cheers, by the way.' He took a large gulp from his glass.

Michael explained that he was on long leave from the Army.

'Had a good war, did you?' Hugh barked.

'Quite a tough one, as it happened, but I survived more or less in one piece.'

Hugh grunted. 'Did my bit in the first show. Brought a KAR battalion to France, while Melanie ran the farm. Made a much better job of it than me.' He nudged her. Melanie made no reply but sipped her drink.

Just then Jane came in with Naomi to say goodnight to her parents.

'Ah, the lovely Jane,' said Hugh.

Naomi was kissed by her parents and offered her cheek to Melanie.

'Good night, dear.'

Naomi then shook hands solemnly with Michael.

'Good night, Naomi. Sleep well. And I haven't forgotten the bush babies.'

Jane took the child off to read her a story.

Another car drew up. 'That will be the Holmes'. See their driver gets something to eat, Patrick.'

Patrick went off.

Introductions were made. Andrew and Charlotte were about Michael's age, Andrew tall and wiry, Charlotte rather plump.

Drinks were offered, but Charlotte declined. 'I have just discovered I am expecting again.'

'Congratulations.'

'Is that number three?' Melanie asked.

'Yes, and we hope it will be a boy this time.'

'Would you like to sit down?' asked Annabel.

'I'm not that far on, yet,' she replied. 'Mr Charteris – Michael – what brings you to Kenya?'

Michael explained as briefly as he could.

'KAR? How interesting. You must know of a lot of people here, then.'

'Not really. Most officers and senior NCOs were seconded from other regiments. I found the askaris were generally formidable fighters, good men to lead in battle. And they really knew their jungle craft. Better than the Japanese. And our Geordies got on very well with them, as did the Scots. They respected each other.'

Patrick returned. 'That's your man fixed up, Andrew.'

'Thanks.'

During the general conversation, Michael asked Andrew about the duties of a District Officer.

'Know everybody. Speak the language. Settle disputes. Magistrate supervising criminal investigations. Support farmers, and not just the whites. Take the lead in emergencies, like floods or bush fires. See that taxes are paid, and punish those in arrears. And numerous other things. Quite simple, really. The most important thing is to keep the chiefs and the village headmen onside. I seem to spend a lot of time talking. Land is very important to the Kikuyu. To own and work even a small plot is their ambition.'

'What about the workers on the white farms?'

'The so-called "squatters"? A wise farmer like Patrick pays them well, looks after them and their families and gives them a *banda*. Some of them have a *shamba*, which the wife works.'

'But what if they lose their jobs?'

'The *banda* is in effect a tied cottage. But that doesn't prevent them from having land elsewhere. They have to be prudent and save. Otherwise it is the shanty town in Nairobi and day-labouring.'

'How did you come to be a District Officer?'

'By mistake, as it happens. I read Classics, tried for the Diplomatic, failed, tried the Colonial Office. I received some basic training in London and was all set to go to Malaya, when I was told that I was going to Kenya instead. Apparently they had confused me with another Holmes. So I have been here since late 1938. Charlotte and I married just before we came, rather against regulations. There was a lot to learn very quickly for both of us, but we survived and now we love it, particularly as things have opened up again after the war. Then there was no chance of getting home leave but now we can go back once every three years. Fortunately our parents are still going strong.'

Michael explained how his jungle expertise from Burma was ignored and he was sent to Germany instead of Malaya: 'Typically perverse British admin. There aren't many other Charteris' to be confused with.'

'I overheard you telling Charlotte how proud you were of your askaris.'

'Yes, I was.'

'I have three men attached to me as general dogsbodies. They are reliable and good company; ex-Army. But they do have some views about the Colony that I am beginning to share, though I would never admit it to them.'

'Such as?'

'These men have been exposed to western attitudes. They have fought alongside us, they have bled beside us, they can respect the British but they are no longer in awe of them. They are aware of a Socialist government in London, they know former colonies such as Australia have long ago become nations in their own right and that India has received its Independence recently. So why not Kenya? And the other factor is land tenure. They resent the fact that the best land in the Rift Valley and the Highlands has been appropriated by the whites. They feel that advantage was taken of them by the settlers when they were still a primitive tribe. The British have imposed many regulations on their farming contrary to traditional practice and I spend a lot of time trying to explain and justify these regulations. Kenyans in general are getting more politicised. Most look forward to Independence at some time in the future and realise that it will take time. The Kikuyu hierarchy is generally loyal and some businessmen have done very well out of the British and don't want the apple cart upset. Others are more impatient and there are the zealots who believe that they can succeed only by making the British occupation as uncomfortable as possible.'

'What about other tribes?'

'The Kikuyu are the largest single unit and are associated with the Embu and Meru. The Kalenjin are much smaller and resent the Kikuyu. The Maasai are a law unto themselves. There is another tribal group, the Luo, by Lake Victoria. And the Indians, of course, and Muslims down on the coast. How far they will unite in concerted political action is anyone's guess, but I think it unlikely at the moment. Loyalty to the tribe is still very strong and trumps other considerations.'

Ephraim the chief houseboy announced that dinner was ready. Jane came in and told Annabel that Naomi was asleep. Michael was put beside her opposite Hugh with Melanie on his other side.

Patrick carved the meat and they helped themselves to vegetables.

Michael turned to Jane. 'This is delicious. I have never had impala before.'

'Kenya is not the place for vegetarians. We, the whites anyway, are carnivores.'

'What exotic creatures have you eaten?'

'Zebra, ostrich, both very tasty when cooked properly.'

'May I ask, were you brought up here?'

'No. I come from Bristol. I was taking a secretarial course, and getting fed up with it. I thought I would try something else, something out of boring England. I have had some experience of child care. Through a friend of a friend I heard about the Howarths. I wrote to them on spec, as it were. My father paid for my passage and they met me in Nairobi. We agreed a trial period of three months and I have been here for nearly a year.'

'Will you stay on here?'

'The Howarths have been very kind to me, and Naomi is a little treasure, albeit a trial at times. I think I will stay on till Naomi goes to school, in about two and a half years. She will have to be a boarder, poor thing; she loves her freedom here.'

'Will that be in England?'

'Not at first. But at some stage she will join her brother. He comes out for the summer holidays.'

'And when she goes...do you have any plans?'

'Travel the world...go home to Mummy and Daddy...try to get a job. I really don't know. I want to settle down sometime, obviously, but I have a few years yet for adventure.'

'Well, I hope you make the most of them. Can I ask? Do you have opportunities to go to Nairobi, or explore the country? It would be a pity not to.'

'The Howarths let me have a weekend off every month and I borrow the jeep and drive to Nanyuki or Nyeri. One of the *watu* comes with me. I stay overnight with another governess and sometimes she comes to stay with me. When Charlie…'

'Charlie?'

'The Howarth's son. When he is home for the holidays there is usually a family expedition up towards Turkana.'

'Have you done Mount Kenya?'

'Indeed. With Patrick, Charlie and another man who has a daughter aged fourteen. We made Lenana. I have always loved walking the hills but this was a tremendous experience.'

'Did you suffer from the altitude?'

'I was fine. We are half acclimatised anyway, living up here.'

'What do you miss most living out here? A leading question.'

'The children here love art; there is so much Nature all around to paint. But there is no music. I used to play the piano and sing, but there are no facilities and, frankly, people are not interested.'

'Do you read a lot?'

'I have read almost all the books the Howarths have. Well, not the farming manuals. Patrick sometimes has taken me down to Nairobi to buy school books for Naomi and I can have a browse for myself. Do you?'

'Do I what? Oh, read. I am into History, especially military and political history. I am a soldier, after all. There is one topic which I have been thinking about quite a lot recently. We had a seminar on it at Staff College. How far should the military go to assist the civil power? People have always been suspicious of the Army, ever since Cromwell, whereas everyone loves the Navy. In other countries the Army has been used to crush political opposition, part of the apparatus of a fascist or totalitarian state. Or overthrow an elected government. That is what happened in Spain. So we are taught to act as the government directs, even if it includes sorting out the messes they have made. Ours not to reason why.'

'But if you are asked to do something illegal or unjust?'

'We have rules of engagement, approved by the Ministry of War. But rules cannot cover every contingency and we have to exercise discretion, and answer for it afterwards if necessary. Sorry, I have been riding my hobby horse.'

'Don't apologize. It's good to talk about something different from polo ponies or what sort of rains we are going to have.'

'I am happy to oblige. I mustn't monopolise you. I hope we can talk again sometime.'

'I'll look forward to that.'

She turned to talk to Andrew on her other side. Hugh noticed that Michael was not in a conversation and boomed across the table:

'Charteris, you said you were with the KAR in Burma. How did you find your African troops?'

'They made excellent jungle soldiers. They were very observant, very patient, prepared to endure hours of discomfort. They could lie still in an ambush for hours on end. They had to be trained, of course; all soldiers do. Once they learnt the business they were extremely reliable. Back in barracks they could misbehave – what soldier doesn't? – but in the field, they were in their element.'

'I found that they were pretty primitive in the…er…niceties of military life. They crapped anywhere despite being ordered to go to the latrines. And when they raided enemy trenches, they often came back with body parts. I won't be specific.'

Michael said nothing.

'When you think about it, they are only two generations down from the trees, so you can't expect civilised behaviour.'

'But you employ them.'

'I do them a service. They take the wages I pay them and I make them work. Actually, they generally do a reasonable job and do what they are told, but I have to punish them for stupidity sometimes. They see that something isn't working but they don't fix it. Result: damage to machinery. That makes me very angry and I have to deal with them. A clip over the ear or a stick across the backside usually does the trick. No more than I had when I was a boy.'

Michael was about to comment when Hugh went on: 'If I let things go, they get very slack and it takes a lot to get them back into line.'

Andrew intervened: 'Hugh, that's old-fashioned talk. It might have been acceptable fifty years ago, but things have changed. We whites are here on sufferance. Sooner or later, the Africans will tire of our rule, and a reckoning will come.'

'Nonsense,' replied Hugh. 'This lot could no more govern themselves than fly to the moon. If it took us centuries to achieve a democracy and sound government, how can they possibly do it in a generation? There would be chaos and mayhem. The only reason they are not at each other's throats is because we are in charge. Before we came the agriculture was primitive in the extreme. People starved when the rains didn't come. Cattle and goats died of all sorts of diseases, rinderpest, for example. Infant mortality was high. In the old days women would have ten children, most of which would die before the age of five. Now they don't, because of basic modern medicine. We are improving their lives immeasurably, and they ought to be grateful. The chiefs and the headmen know this and they won't rock the boat.'

Patrick sought to divert this monologue, as he could see that Andrew was bristling with indignation.

'Hugh, have you had any incidents recently?'

'You mean rustling? Nothing to speak of, though one of my *watu* lost five goats.'

'I have heard of cattle being hamstrung. Andrew?'

'There have been some instances up in Laikipia, but nothing round here so far.'

'What about the Mau Mau, Andrew?' Michael asked. 'What does Mau Mau mean?'

'Nothing. Just a mysterious name, a bogeyman to inspire fear. In fact it is a collection of badmash gangs among the Kikuyu. They have a political aim, of course, to drive the British out by civil disobedience. They were officially banned last year. At the moment they are trying to win over the Africans. They exploit grievances and apply pressure to those who oppose them – chiefs, headmen and Christians.'

'Why Christians?'

'The Mau Mau go in for lurid oathing ceremonies, quite theatrical, in fact, or so I have heard. For Christian believers, that is anathema. You mustn't underestimate the work of missionaries. Many Kikuyu have abandoned polygamy and they realise that the way to get on is to embrace western ideals, like being baptised and learning English.'

'The Mau Mau are communists,' Hugh burst in. 'This fellow Kenyatta may have been to London University, but he also spent time in Russia. The Kenya African Union, before it was made illegal, was just a front for Moscow. The Reds don't give a damn about Africans on the ground; they are just cannon fodder in the attack on the British Empire. It doesn't help that Attlee and his lot are fellow-travellers.'

'Not every nationalist is a communist, Hugh,' said Patrick. 'Stalin hated the kulaks and the Kikuyu are the kulaks of Africa.'

'Kulaks?' asked Jane.

'Small farmers, proud of working their own land by the sweat of their brow, like our Kikuyu. Stalin eliminated them because they resisted communism.'

'Enough politics,' announced Annabel. 'Anything new on your front, Melanie?'

'We have been thinking of buying a place down on the coast for our retirement.'

'We are not retiring yet,' growled Hugh.

'No, dear. But it would be nice to have somewhere to get away from the daily grind. If we like it, we can live there permanently. We have in mind a house at Vipingo, just north of Mombasa. It is right on the Ocean and as there is a reef offshore there is small danger of sharks.'

'What will you do with the farm?'

'My son has no interest in it. If we can find a good manager we will keep it on. Otherwise we will sell.'

'Would you consider moving to England?' asked Michael.

'Our son is in London and he has children. But England is cold and dank. We would have to buy a complete set of new clothes, for a start. The last time we were over, 1936 I think it was, I had a bad attack of rheumatism. We don't know many people there any more.'

'England has had a pretty tough time since the war,' said Michael. 'There is still rationing, though not of bread any longer. It has taken a long time to clear away the bomb damage in the cities. Taxes are high. Industry is antiquated. Nothing seems to work properly. Sometimes it feels as though we lost the war, not won it.'

'Do you have big plans for the future?' Melanie asked.

'Well, keep out of England until Mr Churchill becomes Prime Minister again. Seriously, though, I want to stay in the Army and with luck I should get a battalion soon. The Army has obviously contracted since 1945 but I have a good record, I think, and I have wide experience. I have no personal commitments, so I will be happy to go wherever His Majesty chooses to send me. Within reason, of course. As for the present, I have to be back in London by the first of July. After that, who knows?'

Andrew stood up and announced that he and Charlotte must on their way. 'A busy day tomorrow. Thank you, Annabel and Patrick, for a lovely dinner and good to meet you, Michael.'

The driver was summoned and the Holmes' departed.

Hugh asked Patrick if he could have a word about business and the two went off to Patrick's study. Michael began to clear the table, but Annabel reminded him that the boys would do that.

Michael and the ladies went through to the sitting room, where a log fire was burning.

'It gets pretty chilly in the evenings. Come and warm up.'

'Whisky, Michael?'

'Why not?' He looked at his watch.

'Jane?'

'No thanks. I must get to bed soon.'

'What are you going to do tomorrow?' Michael asked.

'Lessons with Naomi in the morning. Then Patrick suggested that we come with you round the farm in the afternoon.'

'Won't you have seen it all before?'

'There is always something new, and there is a stream for Naomi to guddle in. And animals to look at. Patrick has set aside some ground for wildlife to roam about.'

'That will be a treat.'

Jane said goodnight. Michael sipped his whisky while Annabel and Melanie chatted. Michael felt his eyelids drooping. He got up.

'Sorry, Annabel. I can't stop yawning. I must go to bed. Glad to have met you, Melanie. Please give my apologies to Hugh. Annabel, thank you for a lovely meal and what a busy day!'

'Sleep well.' .

* * *

In the morning, Michael had a leisurely breakfast and wrote letters, one to the headmaster of the school at Gilgil, thanking him for his hospitality, one to his host in Nairobi and one to a friend at the War Office in London:

> ...This last few weeks have been a most welcome respite from soldiering at a desk, and I have seen and done interesting things...

He described his recent activities.

> At the moment I am enjoying myself so much that the last place I want to be is England. I suppose I will have to do a spell at home to be eligible for a pip to my crown. But if there was a chance of a battalion overseas, Cyprus or Malaya, or anywhere apart from Germany, I hope you will put in a word for me...

When he finished he sealed the letters and asked Annabel if he could drive down to Nanyuki to post them.

'Why don't you come with me?' she said. 'I am going to call in at the hospital to see how the *toto* is. You can drive. You must be familiar with American jeeps. I hate the thing myself. The steering is heavy and the brakes are unreliable, to say the least. I don't think it has been serviced for years.'

'I'll have a go.'

The steering was indeed heavy and the clutch idiosyncratic. Fortunately he did not have to test the brakes with an emergency stop.

Michael drove sedately and the journey took half an hour. At one point he had to slow right down in case he bounced Annabel out of her seat as the road surface was ribbed.

'Last year's rains,' she commented. 'Tell me, did you have these jeeps in Burma?'

'We had quite a lot of American kit, but I went most of the way on foot. As far as possible we stayed off the roads, where the Japanese were inclined to set up ambushes. Added to which, in many places there were no roads at all. We were supplied from the air, and there was the railway.'

'Did you meet General Slim?'

'Only at a distance. We all revered him. He had the common touch and natural authority. The greatest British general of the war. I think his campaigns will be studied at Staff College for years to come.'

At the edge of the town was a billboard, announcing that it was on the Equator. Beside it was a small stall selling fruit.

'They are here every day, but I have never seen anyone buying anything.'

He left Annabel and the jeep at the hospital and wandered along the main street. He pottered along past the Settlers' Store and Barclay's Bank until he came to the Post Office. He saw some British soldiers in uniform. At a hotel, the Sportsman's Arms, he saw a notice: 'Out of bounds to Other Ranks.' At a crossroads there was a sign: 'To POW Camp 354'. He followed the road for a little bit and saw huts in the distance. He wandered back to the hotel and asked for a coffee. A white-coated steward showed him into the lounge where some Europeans were discussing farming matters. One was telling his colleagues about an incident a few days previously when a *banda* on the edge of his farm was burnt down. The inhabitants were uninjured but lost all their possessions.

'It was deliberate,' he was saying. 'Must have been Mau Mau. They came after dark, ordered them out and then set fire to the place. They told them that this was a warning to those who collaborated with the colonial power. We saw the blaze and rushed over but the gang had slipped away. Bastards.'

'I have heard of similar happenings towards Nakuru,' said another. 'They target farm workers, not the whites – yet.'

'These guys had firearms as well as *pangas* and clubs. There was nothing the poor people could do. And the Police were hopeless. They came and took statements but that was all.'

Michael sat listening for a few more minutes, paid his bill and headed back to the hospital. Annabel was waiting by the jeep.

'Sorry. I treated myself to coffee at the hotel.'

'No matter. I've only just got here.'

'How is the patient?'

'Less an appendix. It seems to have gone well and he should be back at home in a very few days.'

'That's good news.'

'The mother is much relieved and effusively grateful. When the boy gets home I will visit every day to make sure. Let's go.'

On the way back, Michael asked her about the POW camp.

'From the Ethiopian campaign. At one point there were 80,000 Italians in it. Do you know about the story of three Italian prisoners who escaped from the camp in 1943? They were mountaineers in peacetime and they broke out of the camp and attempted to climb Mount Kenya. Their only guide was a picture of the mountain on the label of an Oxo tin. They reached nearly five thousand metres but could not make the summit. They turned themselves in after three weeks, starved and emaciated. They received only a token punishment from the Camp Commandant because of their "sporting effort". It is a fascinating story. They wrote a book about it afterwards. I think we have a copy.'

'There seems to be some military activity in the camp now.'

'There is always a British battalion there and an airfield. Some people are allowed to use it for light aircraft. Patrick is thinking about getting a private pilot's licence. It will save a lot of time going to Nairobi.' .

⋆ ⋆ ⋆

After a late lunch, Jane and Naomi came through and joined Patrick and Michael for a tour of the estate. Michael asked how big it was.

'Fourteen thousand acres. You saw the *bandas* on the way back yesterday. On the other side are fields for corn and vegetables. And we have started a sideline in flowers. We have four hundred cattle and some sheep in an enclosed pasture and the rest is unenclosed. I leave it as a sort of reserve for wild life. Perhaps in the course of time we can expand it into a tourist venue.'

'Enclosured pasture?'

'Fences and barbed wire. Three miles of it. We patrol the perimeter everyday and it needs constant repair to keep out lions and elephants. And the occasional poachers. It is worth the expense because the herd is protected from outside contact with disease.'

They passed through fields where workers were hoeing vegetables. Patrick stopped to question a foreman and appeared satisfied with the answer. At the cattle pasture he conferred with a herdsman.

'We should have some calves soon. When they are two months old we single out half of the good ones and send them to the market in Nanyuki. The others we keep for breeding. Any that don't pass muster we slaughter for meat. We can freeze them and eat them ourselves or sell them. Same for the sheep.'

'What about water supplies?'

'There are several springs on the farm, pretty reliable though they run lower in the dry season. There is a bigger stream, coming off the mountain, and we draw water from it for the crops. At the top of the farm, near the *bandas*, is a small dam and we pipe water from it for the house and farm buildings.'

They came to a gate in the fence. Patrick jumped out and opened it.

'Out there is the bush. An arm of it comes near the house.'

'I showed it to Michael yesterday,' said Naomi.

'I don't suppose we will see very much this afternoon. Most sensible creatures are having a siesta. There were elephants the other day and there are always some buffalo. Plenty of Tommies.'

'Tommies?'

'Thompson's gazelle. And lots of other buck. Not so many zebra round here these days. During the war they were shot in large numbers to feed the prisoners of war. Oh, look. Over there: reticulated giraffe. And a *toto*.'

They drove nearer. The giraffe and her baby ignored them. Patrick handed binoculars to Michael. He had a good look and passed them on to Jane.

'How sweet!' she said. 'The baby must be seven feet tall.'

'They are normally very placid animals. The males do fight each other by swinging their necks and landing blows. And their kick can kill a lion.'

'What about lions?'

'They are out there. They tend to keep out of our way unless they are hungry, then they will have a go at the cattle. I had to kill one last year. Want to see a rhino?'

'Rather.'

Patrick drove up to a small kopje overlooking the plain. They got out and climbed up.

'Over there by the trees. That's where they usually hang out, if they are around. The black rhino is a solitary beast and pretty grumpy, so it doesn't do to get too close. Their eyesight is poor, fortunately. When they charge they can't change direction very quickly, so it is possible to jump out of the way at the last moment. But I wouldn't like to try it.'

They scanned the ground with binoculars for twenty minutes.

'Sorry. Nothing doing. Another day, perhaps. We had better get back.'

Naomi protested.

'I am giving you time at the stream,' Patrick replied. 'Then you have to feed Lakme, and there is your bath and supper…'

'And show Michael the bush babies,' she added.

They returned to the farm. The stream was in the open ground near the house and had a small pool which Naomi was enlarging by making a dam. Michael and Jane sat down to watch her. Michael produced his pipe.

'Do you mind if I smoke?'

'I'll join you.' She produced a packet and held Michael's hand while he lit her cigarette.

'I justify smoking by telling myself that it helps to keep the mozzies away. Not that there are many up here, anyway. Annabel doesn't like me smoking indoors in Naomi's presence, which is understandable. So I cut down consumption by only smoking out of doors.'

Michael found himself staring intently at her. She was indeed pretty with a lithe figure, 'good bones' as his mother used to say. Jane affected not to notice and asked him about the war.

'Naomi tells me that you ate snakes in the jungle. She is very impressed.'

'I have tried them. Not too bad if you fry them.'

'Tell me about your wound. Sometimes you walk a little stiffly. I am just being nosy.'

'Many people had a lot worse. I had a bullet in the thigh. Another couple of inches to the right would have put paid to my marriage prospects. The bone was badly chipped and the muscles well and truly torn. That is why it took a year to heal properly. But now I am passed A1.'

'Good. Marriage prospects? An officer of your age should be married, especially if you want to be a colonel.'

'I was, briefly, but it did not work out. It didn't survive peacetime, like so many wartime marriages. No children.'

'I too had a war time romance, with an American officer. I was eighteen. He was killed in Normandy. Afterwards I found out that he already had a wife back home. I got over it. Since then there has been no one who has really interested me.'

'No young men out here?'

'The men are either old and vaguely lecherous like Hugh last night, or married and off limits.'

'What about teachers at the prep schools?'

'There are some young men at Gilgil and in Nairobi, but they are too far away for regular contact and mostly they are out on a two-year contract.'

'Have you met any soldiers from Nanyuki?'

'One or two young officers, but they come and go fairly frequently and they don't have much free time.'

'Are you into polo?'

'No, and not agricultural shows either. They bring in people from all over and a lot of drink is consumed. The chat is boringly local, as I told you last night. Patrick and Annabel go along but don't linger. As a rule, if they go out to meet people, they go to their homes rather than the country club. They are very absorbed with the farm. At the moment Patrick does not have any white assistants, so they don't go away for long. All a bit introverted. Just as well they seem to have no vices and get on well with each other. If they do have words, I beat a retreat.'

'Very wise.'

'On the whole, I am lucky to be where I am and to have them as employers. I do have my downs, though.'

'Who doesn't?'

'Sorry to burden you with all this. It's you being a new face.'

'I am delighted to be that new face. Look, Jane…'

Jane stood up. 'Time we were getting back,' she said. 'Come on, Naomi. Lakme needs her milk.'

⋆ ⋆ ⋆

Early in the evening, with twilight coming on, Jane brought Naomi in her dressing gown through to the verandah.

'This way, Michael,' she said.

She trotted round the house to a small hut by a tall tree. She pointed to a bench by the hut and invited him to sit down beside her. Jane sat on the other side.

'Now, hush and wait.'

Nothing happened for ten minutes. Michael ventured a glance at Naomi but she sat stock still. He looked at the hut again. Then Naomi tapped his arm. Along the roof of the hut bounded a tiny creature, like a mouse with big eyes and ears and a long tail. It paused for a moment then leapt into Naomi's lap.

'It's Murata,' she said. 'It means "friend" in Gikuyu.' She produced a bit of mango from her pocket and put it on her lap. Murata picked it up, took a nibble and jumped back onto the roof of the hut.

Michael was enchanted.

Another bush baby took a flying leap from the tree onto the roof of the hut but did not venture further. Instead it sidled up to Murata who showed no inclination to share the booty. So it summoned up its courage and took a leap, landing on Jane's shoulder. She sat very still as it stood up and thrust its nose into her ear, making light hooting noises. Very slowly she took a piece of mango from her pocket and put it on her knee. It ran down her arm, seized the mango and nibbled enthusiastically. Then it jumped back onto the hut to finish it beside Murata. The two turned toward them and seemed to make a little bob, as if to say thank you. Then they leapt back onto a low branch of the tree and disappeared.

'Bush babies always cheer me up,' said Jane. 'They say that when you have been to Africa, a bug has entered the system and you feel you must go back. I am sure I will.'

Chapter Three

Gichuchi was twenty-five years old, or so he reckoned. He lived with Njoka his father in a *banda* on Hugh Frampton's farm. His two younger brothers lived in Nanyuki. Their mother, Njoka's second wife, had died after giving birth to the youngest child. Up to four years ago the family had owned a *shamba* in Rift Valley Province, but had been forcibly ejected by the authorities. Their plot now formed part of a farm allotted to a white settler. This man had come out from England to Kenya Colony after war service. He knew little of farming and even less of local people and customs. Njoka begged that the family should stay and work for him, but he was refused. So they gathered up their few possessions and went off in search of work and a home. After six months of wandering and casual labour they were taken on by the Framptons' foreman. They lived in a makeshift shelter until a *banda* near the farm became available.

Njoka had ensured that his children had elementary schooling but there had not been any money for further education. However, they could all speak English, which made them more employable. The youngest boy, aged fifteen, worked for a *dukawallah* in Nanyuki. The middle brother cleaned the latrines at the Army Camp and did other odd jobs. Njoka was given some responsibility in supervising the farmhands, but Gichuchi himself worked as a labourer. In their own time they worked the small garden beside the *banda*. They had food on the table and a little spare cash. Every Sunday, Njoka marched him off to the local Catholic church. Gichuchi always lived in fear of his father, who had had no compunction about beating his sons if they misbehaved. So he duly went along to church, especially as there was a girl there whom he had eyes on.

Now they were settled, he could turn his thoughts beyond mere survival. Other men his age had wives, some more than one. He wanted to be his own master, to have the self-respect and confidence that his father had. He tried not to quarrel with him but he was given no encouragement to make his own way. Inside him resentment was building up. One day Hugh Frampton came across him erecting a fence. Frampton was in a bad mood. The fence was not straight. Gichuchi explained that there was a rock where he was meant to put a fence post and therefore he had to alter the line of the fence. When told to remove the rock, he said that he had tried but it was too big for him to move by himself. He bent down to show Frampton that he could not move it however much he tried. Frampton, who always carried a stick, told him to put some effort into it and started hitting him about the shoulders. He got up and turned to face the choleric old man. He clenched his fists but let his arms hang down by his sides. If he struck him it would mean instant dismissal and probable arrest. When Frampton had gone, a farmhand called Mutahi, who was rather older than Gichuchi and who had watched the scene, came up with a crow bar and together they removed the rock. Gichuchi thanked him and said that he would give him any help he wanted in return.

'Don't worry about that. Why don't you come along to a meeting tonight? I'll meet you at the road and we can go along together.'

'What meeting?'

'You'll see. But it's about the British.'

Gichuchi rubbed his shoulder. 'I'll be there.'

That evening he slipped away from the *banda* without telling his father and went down to the road. Mutahi was waiting by a tree. Without speaking they walked for a couple of miles and turned aside into a wood. Through the trees Gichuchi could see some lamps and beyond a campfire with figures sitting and standing by it. Gichuchi and Mutahi drew closer and saw that most of the men were young. They joined the outer semicircle at the fire. Behind the fire was a wooden box. From the darkness on the far side emerged a tall figure clad in goatskins and wearing a lion's head cap. He carried a spear. He banged the butt of the spear on the box and stepped onto it. Everyone fell silent. Lit by the fire from below and his stature enhanced by the box he was standing on he made an impressive figure.

He said nothing at first. Then, when everyone had had a chance to appraise him, he began to speak softly in a low voice:

'Brothers. Brothers. Why are we here?' He paused. There was no response. 'We are here, brothers, in this forest, because we have to meet in secret. Otherwise the Police will catch us. The Police should be our brothers but they are simply agents of the *wazungu* who have stolen our land and made it their own. So we are landless labourers, people of no importance. We are deprived of our dignity. We cannot afford wives. We work for a miserable wage and are beaten by our employers. We have nothing to hope for. To add to our woes our chiefs and elders have sold out to the *wazungu* and they have no sympathy for us. The missionaries with their alien creed have turned them into Christians and they are no longer true Africans. Brothers, I could go on but now I invite you to speak what your heart tells you.'

He said no more but glared at them. After an uncomfortable silence, a man stood up and told how he had been dismissed from his job for speaking disrespectfully to a harsh employer; he was now destitute. Others followed. They complained of their hardships in the countryside and some said that they would go to Nairobi where they might find work. A dozen or so voices were heard. Gichuchi agreed with every word that had been said and there was a general muttering of assent.

The meeting was called to order by a sharp rap of the spear on the box.

'Now then, brothers. My name is Njirami Warui. Remember that. If you want to join our society ask for me. If you want to go to Nairobi, I can put you in touch with brothers there. But wherever we are, we must work together to drive the *wazungu* out and win freedom for Africa. Do not tell anyone about this meeting, because we have been declared illegal – illegal in our own country! Come back here soon and we will take you to a place where you can prove your loyalty to the cause. Now go. Do not speak to one another but reflect in your hearts on what you have heard tonight.'

When he got home Njoka was asleep. In the morning he kicked Gichuchi awake and went out without exchanging a word. After eating a few mouthfuls of cold *posho* and drinking some tea he went to work. He was assigned to clearing out a ditch. On the way out with his tools he met Mutahi, his companion of the previous night. They squatted down behind a bush and Mutahi offered him a cigarette.

'Well, brother, will you join us?'

'Are you already a member?'

'Yes. For nearly a year now.'

'What do you do?'

'I look around for suitable people.'

'Are there many here?'

'Many are sympathetic, but only a few have taken the oath.'

'And if I take the oath, what then?'

'I think you will be a fighter. You will have some training in the use of weapons. And then, when they think you are ready, you will join a unit.'

'That's exciting.'

'Yes. But life will be hard. Are you prepared to leave your family?'

'Oh yes. There is nothing to keep me here, save earning a few shillings.'

'Very good. Don't tell anyone about our chat. Just come along with me to take the oath when the time comes.'

'I will.'

Mutahi got up and went his way. Gichuchi started work on the ditch. He did not speak to anyone during the day. Frampton came and made a cursory inspection of his work and merely nodded. When the job was over he handed his tools back in and wandered back along the road towards the *banda*, turning over in his mind his conversation with Mutahi..

* * *

The following Sunday Gichuchi attended Church and sat beside his father as usual. He glanced across at the ladies' pews and to his dismay the girl was not there. The priest and the altar boys processed in and the choir started a hymn. With a deep sigh he resigned himself to an hour of boredom. Halfway through the bidding prayer, there was a disturbance at the back of the church. The priest ploughed on but most people turned round to see what the matter was. Someone had come in and apologised to the doorman for being late. There were whispers of 'Shhh' as the girl tiptoed down the aisle and sat at the end of a pew opposite Gichuchi's. He turned round and saw her looking at him with a rueful smile. He smiled back and lifted a hand in greeting. His father noticed this and gave him a sharp nudge. During the hymns the girl sang with a clear and tuneful voice, and during the homily she took sideways glances at him and held his gaze. Did he imagine it or did she purse her lips into a kiss? To Gichuchi the service seemed interminable. After the blessing he hurried out while his father talked to some other older men. He watched as the women filed out. She came out towards the end and as casually as she could edged towards him and handed him a cap.

'I think you left this behind,' she said.

'I haven't got a cap,' he spluttered.

'By the big tree at the crossroads. We can have a few moments together.'

She passed on, chatting with other women. Gichuchi knew the tree and hurried to it, leaning against it with his back to the crossroads. He forced himself to be patient. He examined the cap in his hand but it gave no clue to its owner. He threw it down on the other side of the tree facing the road. After a few minutes he heard footsteps and round the tree came the girl, carrying the cap.

'Hello, Gichuchi,' she said.

'Hello. I'm sorry, I don't know your name.'

'Mary.'

'Mary? That is not a Kikuyu name.'

'My father and mother are very religious. They wanted me to have a Bible name.'

'Well, Mary, I am very glad to meet you at last. But how do you know my name?'

'Women share information. You live with your father Njoka.'

She came closer and took his hand. She led him into the wood till they were out of sight of the road. She sat down and patted the ground beside her.

'Come and sit here, and tell me about yourself.'

'There is nothing much to tell. I am just an ordinary man. I work, I earn a little bit of money. When my father is not looking I go down to the *duka* and buy some liquor. I have no particular friends to share it with, so I drink on my own. My father disapproves.'

'Would you share it with me sometime?'

'I have a little left in the bottle.'

'Let's drink it tonight. We'll come back here. Meet me by the tree. I have a torch.'

'Are you sure?'

She got up. 'I must get back.' She gave him a kiss and ran off before he could respond.

The rest of the day he spent hoeing the garden round the *banda* while his father went off to talk to friends. When he had not returned by late afternoon, he made a meal for himself. He kept replaying in his head the conversation he had had with Mary. He recalled her features: she was of medium height, not bad looking and had a winning smile and an attractive voice. As far as he could tell from her flowing garments she had a good figure. He wondered how an exchange of glances could lead so quickly to an assignation. He had no idea why she was attracted to him, as he had little to offer her. He doubted that his father would tolerate having her living in the *banda*.

With all these thoughts churning around in his mind he set off with his bottle. He waited behind the tree with eagerness and some apprehension. She did not come for a long time. He has almost given up hope when he heard her voice. He stood up and came round the tree. They embraced without a word and went into the wood to the place where they had talked that morning.

They sat down and he offered her the bottle, a cheap whisky. She took a sip and made a face as it went down. He moistened his lips with it as there was not much left.

'I'm sorry I was late,' she said. 'I had to wait until my parents had gone out to a prayer meeting. And I mustn't be too long. They will be angry if I stay out late.'

'But you are, well, a grown woman.'

'They still treat me like a girl. I am twenty, and I have been married.'

'Married? What happened to him?'

'He was much older than me and he died within a few months. Now my parents want me to marry another older man in the church. He is ugly and I don't like him.'

'I'm just a labourer and do odd jobs on the farm. What do you do?'

'Help my mother in the house. I take in washing which earns me a few shillings. I sometimes cook for other people if they need help. Until I get a good man I can't see what else I can do.'

'I have often thought of going to Nairobi. I might earn more down there.'

'At least up here I have food and shelter and I have friends. Down there it will be lonely and I won't be safe. I have heard of girls who are forced to become prostitutes. Anything would be better than that.'

'I have never been further than Nanyuki, where my brothers work. A big city must be frightening.'

She indicated that she would like another sip. Gichuchi drank some himself and passed the bottle.

'Can we be friends, Mary?'

'More than friends, I hope.'

'Do you mean that?'

'Yes, I do.' She turned to him and slipped her hand inside his shirt. 'You are big and strong. You don't boast. And you have good teeth.'

She ran her hand over his shoulder. He winced slightly.

'What's the matter?'

'The other day Mr Frampton hit me with his stick. I am still sore.'

'What a brute! Had you done something wrong?'

He explained about the fence and the rock. 'I hope other *bwanas* are not like him,' he said.

'Some are, some aren't, or so I have heard. What does your father say?'

'He says that I probably deserved the beating and we have to put up with the situation for the time being. We should be grateful that we have work and a place to live. It suits him. I want something more for myself.'

He passed the bottle across. 'We've nearly finished it. Have another drink.'

She took only a modest sip, so he had to swallow the rest at one go. He coughed and shook his head.

'I don't really like the stuff, but it makes me feel better.' He threw the bottle away and lay back.

'Can I see you again?'

Mary did not answer but bent down and kissed him. He ran his hand down her back.

'I'll be at the river tomorrow afternoon, washing. I have to let the clothes dry in the sun so you can keep me company.'

She got up. 'I'm sorry I have to go so soon. Thank you for the drink.'

'I'll walk you back.'

He put his arm around her and he saw her to the end of the track leading to her *banda*. She faced him, took his hand and placed it on her breast. Then she hurried away.

* * *

Over the next few weeks, Mary and Gichuchi met by the river. While the clothes were drying they lay in some shade. Mary, who had not been cut as a girl, had initiated their love making and guided the inexperienced Gichuchi. In order to meet her at the river he had to slip away from work in the afternoon and once when he had been assigned a task at the far end of the farm he could not get there in time. At first Mary was upset but he managed to see her just before dusk.

Usually he was working alongside Mutahi. When he made his excuses and left, Mutahi grinned knowingly. Very occasionally a foreman came around at the end of the day to see how much work had been done. Mutahi explained that his absence was because of a tummy complaint or a cut that needed attention. Gichuchi always worked hard in the mornings so that Mutahi had little to do in the afternoons. As they worked Mutahi talked about the secret society and its objectives.

'Are you still interested?'

'Yes I am,' Gichuchi replied.

'Are you prepared to become a brother?'

'I think so.'

'Even if it meant being separated from your girl for a time?'

Gichuchi swallowed hard. 'Maybe she will come with me.'

'It might not come to that. You see, there are some who are warriors but they need a lot of support from people who carry on their daily tasks, people like me. In fact, it's the same with all armies. I saw that in Ethiopia. For every warrior in the field there are maybe five people needed to keep him supplied with food, ammunition and information. Their work is very important.'

'I see.'

'I said that I thought you would be a fighter in the forest. You are young and strong.'

'I am afraid of forests.'

'Forests are only a refuge. Our enemies, the British, are in the farmlands.'

Gichuchi seemed relieved by this information.

'There will be a little ceremony soon. Will you come?'

Three days later, Gichuchi joined Mutahi on the road and they walked down to the track which led to the clearing where the previous meeting had been held. They went past it and penetrated deeper into the forest. On the way they were joined by several other men, who greeted Mutahi. No names were mentioned.

They came to a clearing with a group of men and women sitting on the ground and beyond them a large hut. Mutahi told Gichuchi to sit down and went to confer with a man waiting at the entrance to the hut. It was now dark but a rising moon began to illumine faces. Gichuchi did not recognise anybody. Nothing happened for some time. Then some figures emerged from behind the hut; they were armed with *pangas* and clubs and acted as guards. They stood on either side of the path leading to the hut. Three of those sitting on the ground were called and before they entered the hut *pangas* were waved over their heads. A curtain was pulled across after they entered. Gichuchi listened carefully but could hear nothing. Within a few minutes three more people were called forward. The first group did not reappear out of the door of the hut, but Gichuchi later caught sight of people hurrying away from the back of the clearing. He waited his turn, nervously wondering what was going to happen. Finally, with two other men, he was called forward to the hut. The curtain was pulled back and they stepped inside, followed by the guards, who spread out around the walls of the hut. The interior was lit by a hurricane lamp. One of the guards came forward to relieve them of their coats, watches, money and shoes, anything that had a European origin; Gichuchi had neither watch nor money, only a pair of old army boots. In the middle of the hut stood the Oath Administrator; his face was whitened with chalk. He put a strip of goat's flesh on the right wrist of each man. A goat's intestines were used to bind the three together by the feet and shoulders. A man emerged from the shadows, took a swig of beer from a jug and spat it in their faces as a blessing. The Administrator took the right hand of each man and pricked it. Then he picked up a gourd filled with blood and smeared the blood over their foreheads and joints. He stood back a little and held up a hand.

'May this blood mark the faithful and brave members of the Gikuyu and Mumbi Unity. May this same blood warn you that if you betray our secrets or violate the oath, our members will come and cut you to pieces at the joints marked by the blood.'

Each had to lick the others' blood from their fingers and in return repeat this oath:

'If I reveal the secrets of Gikuyu and Mumbi* to a person not a member, may this blood kill me. If I violate any of the rules of the oath, may this blood kill me. If I lie, may this blood kill me.'

The Administrator took a piece of intestine and stood in front of each of the three and cut it. The guards round the walls shouted out in turn: 'May you be cut like this! Let the oath kill he who lies.'

Each man was handed a lump of soil, moistened and formed into

* Gikuyu and Mumbi were, in legend, the ancestors of the Kikuyu tribe.

a ball, and was told to hold it to his navel and face east, towards Mount Kenya. Gichuchi was the first to swear:

'I, Gichuchi, swear before God and those present here that I will be a faithful and true son of Gikuyu and Mumbi and a loyal brother, even unto death.' The Administrator came forward and made a cross with a mixture of blood and fragrant oil on his forehead. The next man swore the oath in a clear voice. The third man began shaking his head, refusing the oath, and attempted to break free. One of the guards stepped up and beat him about the head and shoulders and another pricked him with a *panga*. He changed his mind and was duly sworn. To mark the end of the ceremony, everyone in the room shouted out: 'Forward ever and backward never.'

At the far end of the hut was a table where a clerk sat. He returned their belongings and noted their names, demanding fifty shillings for registration. Gichuchi said that he had no money with him.

'I can give Matuhi the money soon,' he explained.

'Very well,' said the clerk, looking at him suspiciously.

Gichuchi reclaimed his boots. Waiting for him outside the back door was Matuhi.

As they walked home, Mutahi asked him if he was glad he had taken the oath.

'It was very frightening. But I am now a brother, and this gives me joy.'

'Good man. Now don't expect anything to happen for a time. But when the call comes you must obey at once. It is better that your family don't know, for their own protection.'

'What about the girl?'

'You mustn't tell her either.'

'If I go away, then I will have to.'

'We shall see when the time comes. Gichuchi, don't underestimate the force of the oath. The oath is for ever. You will offend the spirits of your ancestors and indeed Ngai himself, if you have lied. They will punish you severely in their anger, and not just you, but your family. Punishment is inevitable. Do you understand?'

'Yes, I do.'

* * *

Once he had paid Mutahi for the registration fee Gichuchi heard nothing more about the secret society for several months. He did not forget the commitment he had made, but it passed to the back of his mind. Life went on very much as before. There was always work to do on the farm and he had no more unpleasant encounters with Frampton. He saw Mary most weeks and even contemplated asking the foreman if he could have a *banda* for them to share.

One Sunday Mary did not appear in church. He was initially cross but then realised that there must be something amiss, because she was a regular attender. Her parents were not there either. He thought of going round to their house but an instinct held him back. That afternoon he was, as usual, hoeing the vegetable patch at the *banda*; Njoka was away visiting friends. Mary arrived weeping, her face swollen, with a cut lip and bruises on her shoulders. He warmed some water, washed away the blood, and made her a cup of tea. When she calmed down she told him what had happened.

Her mother had discovered that she was pregnant. Her God-fearing father had beaten her and thrown her out of the house.

'You are the father, Gichuchi. There has been no one else.'

Gilchuchi nodded. He thought for a moment.

'Then you can come and live with me. We have room here. My father is very set in his ways, but I think he misses a woman about the house. What about your things?'

'I just ran away. They must still be at home, unless he has thrown them out too.'

'Well, we had better go round and collect them.'

'Not today. Tomorrow. I couldn't face my parents just now.'

Late in the afternoon, Njoka returned. He was angry at first, and there was a shouting match.

'Is this the girl you keep eyeing in church?'

'Yes.'

'How long have you been…at it?'

'Several months, Father. She is a widow.'

'Widow? At her age?'

'Yes. Now her father wants to marry her off to an older man. She does not like him.'

'Is that why she got herself pregnant, to escape this man?'

'I don't know. She swears the child is mine. I want her, Father, and I will take care of her.'

Njoka grunted. 'Well, it's about time you took a woman. She is quite pretty, I'll say that. Can she cook?'

'I'm sure. She is preparing a supper for us now.'

They ate in silence. Mary cleaned up afterwards and sat down with them. To Gichuchi's surprise, Njoka thanked her and asked when the baby was due.

'I don't know exactly,' she replied, 'but I have missed for two months now.'

'We must send you to the doctor in Nanyuki, as soon as possible.'

The following morning the three of them walked to Mary's parents' house. Njoka knew the man by sight. At first there was silence.

'We have come for Mary's things,' said Njoka.

Mary's father looked at them stony-faced. Mary's mother appeared behind him, weeping. She stepped forward, only to be pulled back by her husband.

'I will marry her,' said Gichuchi.

'You can have her, the little slut. But you won't get anything for her. I don't want to see her again. She has disgraced us.' He turned around and began to stride away. Over his shoulder he shouted: 'She had better not come to church. She is a sinner. God may forgive her, but I won't.'

Mary wept. Gichuchi put his arm around her and they slowly walked back to the *banda*. Njoka stayed for a moment, in case Mary's father had anything more to say, and then went off to work.

The following morning, Mary went to collect the washing to be done that day, and Gichuchi reported for work. His absence the previous day had been noted and he was docked some of his wages. Mutahi met him and asked if there had been anything the matter. He replied that he would not be slipping away in the afternoons any more and there would be no need to cover for him. Mutahi nodded, and then asked if he would be going to Nanyuki in the near future.

'Yes. We have to see a doctor.'

'Oh dear. Are you or your father ill?'

'No. It's not like that.'

'Come on. Tell me. Is it the girl you mentioned?'

'Er..yes.'

'I have heard something to that effect. Well, look after her.'

'I will. Why did you ask me about Nanyuki?'

'You have a brother who works at the army camp. We need some information about it. Will your brother help us?'

'I am not sure, but I think so. Has he taken the oath?'

'Not yet. When you have finished with the doctor, go to the camp, both of you, and ask to speak to your brother. What is his name, by the way?'

'Njeru.'

'Introduce Mary to him and then say that you would like him to come to your house for a little celebration. I will meet him and ask for his help.'

'My other brother, Karumbi, must come too. He works at the main *duka* in Nanyuki.'

'Will he help?'

'He is only fifteen.'

'Hm. Might be useful. The *duka* is on the street that leads to the camp. He could keep an eye open for things.'

At the end of the day, Gichuchi went to the river to see how Mary was getting on. She was gathering up the dried garments. He carried the basket and with her distributed them round the *bandas*. When they came back to their *banda* there was a large bag by the door. Mary opened it. Inside were all her clothes, neatly folded, and some personal items.

Among them was a bracelet, which was a favourite of her mother.

Chapter Four

A week later, Gichuchi and Mary caught the early bus to Nanyuki. They had a wait at the clinic as it was very busy. Mary was eventually called in to see a doctor and Gichuchi went out to buy a snack. On his return Mary was sitting outside on a bench. She was smiling.

'All is well, he tells me. I'm to come back in four months for another check.'

'That's good. Have you paid?'

'It wasn't much. I'm starving. What have you got there?'

He handed over a paper bag with a slice of bread, a chicken leg and a slice of pawpaw for each of them.

They ate eagerly.

'Now we must go and see my brother Njeru. He works at the camp. I want to introduce you and to invite him and my other brother for a visit. We will have a little celebration. We haven't seen them for some time.'

It was a twenty minute walk to the camp gates and hot in the noonday sun. As they approached the barrier, a British soldier came out of the guardhouse, throwing away a cigarette.

'What do you want?' he asked peremptorily.

'My name is Gichuchi and this is my wife Mary. I want to speak to my brother, Njeru, son of Njoka. He works in the camp.'

'Well, you can't come into the camp.'

'I understand. Please. Is it possible that he could come out to see us? We need not be long. We will wait here.'

Mary flashed him a big smile.

'Njeru, you say?' the soldier. He consulted a list and looked at his watch. 'He is on his lunch break.'

Just then an African came up from the camp to the guardhouse with a package. Having delivered it he was turning away when the soldier called out.

'Hey, Matthew, go and find Njeru. Tell him his brother is here, with his wife. *Haraka, haraka*, there's a good chap.'

Twenty minutes later, Njeru arrived. He was short and somewhat stout. One eye was beginning to cloud over. He greeted Gichuchi with a smile and an elaborate handshake.

'I didn't know you were married.'

'Not yet but we are going to be. Here's Mary.'

Njeru eyed her up and down. 'Hello, Mary.' He turned to Gichuchi. 'It looks as though you have chosen well, brother.'

Gichuchi asked him to come over for a feast at the end of the week. Njeru nodded.

'I will bring a jar of *pombe*.'

A hooter sounded.

'I had better go,' said Njeru.

'Goodbye, and don't forget.'

Njeru scuttled back inside the camp.

'He's not at all like you,' observed Mary

'He's my stepbrother from Njoka's second wife. She died some years ago. I don't really like him,' he went on. 'He always had some scheme on to make a little money and was dishonest, even as a boy. But, poor chap, he is losing the sight of one eye.'

'I saw that.'

'That is why he has to take simple jobs. My little brother is quite different. He is very intelligent, much more intelligent than me. Let's go and see him before we get the bus.'

They called in at the *duka*. Karumbi was behind the counter. He came round and embraced Gichuchi. He was not tall and Gichuchi had to bend down.

'Who is this?' he asked.

'My wife, or rather she will be soon. Mary.'

Mary came forward and Karumbi embraced her as well.

'How are you, brother?' Gichuchi asked.

'I am working hard. Mr Hussein has given me a pay rise. I have been stocktaking most of today but Mr Hussein has gone out and left me in charge.'

'Is he looking after you?'

'I eat with him and his family in the evening. He does not let me drink.'

'I should hope not.'

Gichuchi explained about the forthcoming celebration.

'Will Mr Hussein give you a day off?'

'What will Mr Hussein do?' said Hussein as he came through the door. 'You shouldn't be chatting to customers like that, in front of the counter.'

'This is my brother, Gichuchi, and his bride Mary. They are having a feast at home. Can I have time off?'

'Please, Mr Hussein,' said Mary.

'Very well,' said Hussein reluctantly. 'When?'

'At the end of this week,' replied Gichuchi.

'Right. I am a family man, and families are very important. You can have a day off. Catch the first bus and the first bus back the next day.'

'Thank you, Mr Hussein.'

'And behave yourself.'

He went into the back of the shop.

'Don't let him down, Karumbi. Njeru is coming as well but make your own way.'

'Right.'

'Father is looking forward very much to seeing you again. He doesn't have much time to come to Nanyuki.'

'Is he well?'

'He's fine.'

'Goodbye, Karumbi,' said Mary, and kissed him. He blushed.

Gichuchi and Mary caught the bus and arrived home just as Njoka came in from work.

* * *

As it happened, Karumbi and Njeru travelled on the same bus, but it was so crowded that they could not speak until they arrived at the farm. Njeru was carrying a flagon of *pombe* and Karumbi a bag and a small present for Mary, which he had bought at the *duka*. They exchanged brotherly greetings but otherwise had little to say.

They found Njoka by the *banda*. Gichuchi was working in the garden and Mary was making preparations for the feast. While Karumbi talked to his father, Njeru announced that he was going off to see some friends.

On his way he was accosted by Mutahi, whom he had known in the past. Mutahi had another man with him. They persuaded Njeru to come and have some tea with them. At Mutahi's *banda* they sat down and caught up with news. When they had drunk, Mutahi went inside and produced a box from which he took out a reefer.

'Best quality *bhangi*.'

He lit it and passed it to Njeru. After each of them had had a couple of puffs, Mutahi put it aside and asked Njeru about his work in the camp. Njeru told him in some detail and Mutahi listened patiently.

'There is some information we would like to have. We know where the Armoury is but we don't know who is in charge of it.'

'Sergeant Protheroe. He sits in the office by the door and checks weapons and ammunition in and out.'

'Do you have any dealings with him?'

'I clean the office and sweep the Armoury floor. I am searched when I go in and when I come out.'

'We don't want you to steal anything. Can you tell us what weapons there are there?'

'.303 rifles and sten guns, mostly. The ammunition is kept in a large safe.'

'What sort of man is this Protheroe?'

'He is an unpleasant man. He is harsh to his corporal as well as to me. I think he is not very popular around the camp.'

'Does he ever leave the camp?'

'When there is firing on the ranges, that's Tuesdays and Fridays usually, he takes a lorry with the weapons and the ammunition follows in a jeep. I have watched it all being loaded.'

'Is there a guard with the lorry?'

'A soldier sits in the back. The corporal drives the jeep which follows the lorry closely.'

'And when the firing is over?'

'He comes back with the weapons. If they have used all the ammunition the jeep does not wait but comes back earlier.'

'And have you seen him in town?'

'Several times. The soldiers go to one or two bars and there is a brothel. The Red Caps keep an eye on it. Just in case there is any trouble. For the sake of the girls.'

'Have you ever seen Protheroe at the brothel?'

'No. But I followed him once, out of curiosity, and he visited a house on the edge of town.'

He described the location. Mutahi looked at his companion who nodded.

'Thank you for all this information.' He relit the reefer and passed it to Njeru.

'Can we rely on you not to mention this conversation to anyone?'

'Of course.'

'Do you swear?'

'I do. I am willing to do more for you if you want.'

'No. It is best that you don't know anything more.'

When the shared reefer was finished, Mutahi gave Njeru another one to take with him.

He went to visit other friends and the meal was ready on his return. When he had eaten he lit his reefer, smoked half of it and fell fast asleep in a corner.

* * *

Mutahi and his companion went into the forest where the oathing ceremony had taken place. There they found Njirami Warui sitting outside the hut and repeated to him the information they had received from Njeru.

'We need guns and ammunition, as much as we can get,' he said. 'How should we go about getting them? You, Mutahi, have been in the Army. What do you suggest?'

'We won't be able to break into the camp and raid the armoury. It is too heavily guarded. Rifles and ammunition are carefully accounted for. It is a grave offence for a soldier to lose his rifle or steal ammunition. The punishment is a court martial, jail and dishonourable discharge. That would probably deter most people. It is not unknown for British soldiers to sell equipment to civilians, but we wouldn't be able to buy rifles, not even old ones.'

'But somehow we have to persuade this Sergeant Protheroe to part with some rifles. Could we bribe him?'

'It is quite likely that he would take the money and not hand over the rifles. If we took our revenge and killed him, the British would arrest everyone they could lay their hands on, and we would still not have the rifles.'

'From all of what you say, if we are to get hold of rifles, it will have to be by force outside the camp. Any ideas?'

Mutahi's companion, who had said nothing so far, indicated that he wanted to speak.

'I have an idea. It may not work, but it is worth looking at. Njeru said that he had followed Protheroe to a house on the edge of town. I know that house. It is used as a private brothel. Very few people go to it and they dare not speak of it. The owner has one or two young boys there. He kidnaps them and after a while sells them back to their parents.'

'That's appalling. How do you know this?' asked Njirami.

'A boy's father confessed this to me once when we were drinking. He said that if the parents did not pay, or if they told anybody, the boys would be killed. He said that when he got his son back he was badly hurt, and not only physically. But he did not take him to a doctor. The parents and the boys themselves are too ashamed to tell anyone.'

'Do we know when Protheroe goes to that house?'

'Njeru said that it was in the evening. The soldiers are off-duty then and are in civilian dress, what they call mufti. Protheroe went into town with the rest but then, after a drink, left on his own.'

'What are you suggesting?'

'That we catch Protheroe there and threaten him with exposure unless he supplies us with rifles and ammunition.'

'How will he do that?'

'That is for him to work out. We'll tell him where to take them. We will need a camera. Can you get hold of one?'

Njirami pondered this. 'It might take some time,' he said at last. 'In principle it sounds a good idea.'

'Do we have any brothers in the camp?' Mutahi asked.

'Only Njeru and he has not yet sworn.'

'But he can give written messages to Protheroe. He doesn't have to know what's in them. And we must decide what to do with the man who owns this house. He is an abomination. I can understand doing it with girls but this… I think we had better kill him, anyway.'

⋆ ⋆ ⋆

Planning the operation took several weeks. Four brothers from the forest were brought into town. A camera was obtained from Nairobi and someone agreed to develop the film. The route from the camp to the ranges was surveyed and a place was found where a lorry could be ambushed and driven out of sight of the road itself. Meanwhile a watch was kept on Protheroe's visits to the house. He was always alone.

When all was ready, the house, which was little more than a large hut with a corrugated iron roof, was surrounded. Mutahi and his friend were there along with the men from the forest. They were armed with knives and *pangas*; Mutahi had the camera. They saw Protheroe go in. They waited until they could hear a scream from inside and rushed in by the front door and the back. In a room they found a naked boy lying face down on a bed with Protheroe on top of him, his trousers round his ankles. He tried to get up but he was held down while Mutahi took some flash photographs. His hair was pulled back so that his face was clearly visible. One man had stayed outside at the back and caught the owner of the house as he attempted to escape. He was brought in to witness the scene in the bedroom and his photograph was taken.

With a *panga* at his throat, Protheroe was told to get dressed. His clothes had been searched and a purse and revolver removed. Then he was led to the front door and pushed out. He ran away as fast as he could. Meanwhile Mutahi had wrapped the boy in a blanket and took him into another room, where he found a second boy tied to a bed. He released him and took the boys outside. He had brought some food and let them eat a little. The other men came out after a while. They picked up the boys and carried them to a house in town where they were looked after.

Mutahi asked his friend what happened to the owner of the house.

'We tied him to the bed, gagged him and cut his balls off.'

* * *

Njeru took an envelope to the Armoury office two days later. Protheroe was in the Armoury itself and did not see Njeru enter and place it on the desk. He called round in the afternoon to sweep the floor and tidy up. He found Protheroe sitting at his desk looking very white and staring at the window.

'Can I clean, *Bwana*?' he said. 'It is the usual time.'

Protheroe made no reply. Njeru asked again. Still there was no reply

'Are you going to the range tomorrow, *Bwana*? I could wash the outside of the windows then. They are dirty. I wouldn't be in your way.'

Protheroe slammed his fist on the desk and got up. 'Bugger off. *Haraka, haraka.*' He picked up a walking stick and waved it threateningly at Njeru.

'Sorry, *Bwana*. What is the matter?'

'Just go, you black bastard.'

Njeru walked away. Protheroe shouted at his retreating back: 'I want those windows clean when I get back tomorrow.'

In the evening, Njeru reported this exchange to Mutahi.

'Good. Thank you. It is better that you don't know what is going to happen, so please don't ask.'

At the end of the range exercise, Protheroe dismissed the soldier and told him to go back with the corporal in the jeep, ahead of him. Protheroe drove the lorry slowly and out of sight of those in front until he came to the designated spot where he was to turn off. An African got up from behind a bush and waved him in. The four men were waiting for him. Mutahi was there with the camera. His companion had the revolver, which he kept aimed at Protheroe, who sat in the cab.

Within a very short time, ten rifles were unloaded with a box of cleaning kit. The men searched the back of the lorry, but could not find the ammunition. Meanwhile Mutahi had taken a photograph of Protheroe in the cab.

'Where is it?'

Protheroe refused to say.

'Remember the photographs we took with the boy, *Bwana*. Your colonel would not like them.'

With great reluctance Protheroe brought out a box from under his seat. Mutahi opened and inspected the contents.

'All correct. Two hundred rounds of .303.'

Protheroe drove off at speed. The whole operation had taken less than three minutes. The four men waited until it began to get dark, and then set off for the forest with the booty.

* * *

Njeru was unaware of the hijack of the rifles but he noticed that Protheroe was even harsher in manner than before, not only to Njeru but also to the corporal and private assigned to the Armoury. Over the next few days, officers visited the Armoury, examined lists and counted weapons. Security seemed to be tightened. African workers were checked and searched at the gate instead of being waved through. Around the camp, they were greeted with suspicious looks instead of cheery smiles. Njeru was interviewed by the Military Police but could not tell them anything. He said that he was never in the Armoury building without the close presence of a British soldier. He had no access to keys. When he had swept the armoury last he had noticed that there were fewer rifles on the rack but he did not know why; it was none of his business.

'Can you read, Njeru?'

'Yes, a little, but my eye is not so good.' He pointed at his cloudy eye. 'I am afraid the other one might go the same way. I don't really see very well.'

'Do you tell other people about your work at the camp?'

'I have a friend I drink with occasionally. He used to work here and he asks me how I am getting on. There is nothing much to tell. I sweep, wash floors and clean latrines. I must say, I don't like the pictures the soldiers draw in the cubicles.' He shrugged. 'Sometimes I complain that *Bwana* Protheroe has been nasty to me.'

'Who is this friend of yours?'

'Kibira. He works at the garage in town. Has done so for two or three years.'

'I see.'

Njeru was dismissed, and heard no more of the matter.

There were changes afoot in the camp. The perimeter fence was strengthened. Several lines of huts, unused since the war, were reopened and Njeru was sent in to clean them. Of Sergeant Protheroe there was no sign. One day, on Armoury duty, he asked the corporal where he was.

After an embarrassed pause, the corporal told him that Protheroe had gone away and that he was now in charge.

* * *

When Mary was seven months, she and Gichuchi went to the doctor at Nanyuki for an examination. Gichuchi went along to see his little brother Karumbi at the *duka*. Karumbi asked permission to leave the shop for a while. They sat in the shade of a tree by the road. Karumbi told him more about his work. Mr Hussein had said that he was very happy with Karumbi's work but thought he should look for something more in keeping with his talents; he had suggested a clerkship with a lawyer, or something in local administration. At the *duka* there was nothing for him in the long term; his own son would be taking over in due course. Besides, Indians were generally unpopular and it would be better for Karumbi to be with his own people.

Gichuchi said that he was pleased for him and he should start looking around at once.

Just then a convoy of Army lorries passed by, heading for the camp.

'Another one,' said Karumbi. 'There was a big one yesterday and the day before. I mentioned it to Mr Hussein, who said he hoped there would be more business for the *duka*.'

'How many lorries?'

'I started counting. At least twenty. Each one had twelve soldiers with all their kit.'

'You are observant. Say two hundred and fifty soldiers in each convoy.'

'And jeeps with officers. Altogether it must be a whole battalion.'

'Is that unusual?' Guchuchi asked.

'We see lorries every day, but not so many in a convoy. I wonder why they are coming.'

'Perhaps they are here for training. So I have heard. And then they go home after six months. I know because I look out for their badges.'

'Could you keep a record of traffic to and from the camp? Just convoys. Not for me, but for a man called Mutahi.'

'Is he in the society?'

'Yes.'

'And are you, Gichuchi?'

'I have sworn an oath.'

'Tell this Mutahi that I will keep a record, but I will not swear an oath. I am too young to be a fighter. And I am too small. But I will help a friend of yours.'

'Thank you.'

Gichuchi patted his shoulder and they parted. He walked back to the clinic where Mary was waiting. She was looking worried.

'The doctor says that I must be very careful. The baby might come early and might not be fully ready for the birth. I must avoid any awkward movement. I mustn't lift things.'

'I'm sorry. Are you in any pain?'

'No. I just feel heavy.'

They made their way slowly towards the bus stop. Gichuchi told her about his conversation with Karumbi and how well Mr Hussein thought of him.

'That's good,' she said. 'I hope he will get away from the sort of life we have to lead. I know you work hard for your money,

Gichuchi, but we deserve better. Maybe this Mau Mau will make things better.'

'Maybe.' He changed the subject. 'Is there anything you want to buy while we are here. Something for the baby?'

They went to a shop on the main street, but even simple baby clothes were too expensive.

'We could ask Njoka for some money,' he said.

When they returned to the *banda*, Mary set about preparing a meal. Njoka came back at dusk in a bad mood. Frampton has sworn at him for some dereliction on the part of one of the farmhands and had threatened him with a stick.

'I wanted to swear back at him but he is quite capable of throwing us out on the spot. Mary and her baby need a home just now.'

Gichuchi told him about his conversation with Karumbi about his future and Njoka nodded.

'He is the brightest of you.'

In the following days Mary carried on washing clothes but an unexpected pain in her back gave her a warning and she told her clients that she could not do the washing any more. Instead she did some light work in the garden and cooked meals. She spent some time chatting to the mother in the next *banda*. Gichuchi was most solicitous in looking after her and when she complained that she could not sleep he made a back rest for her so that she could sit up during the night and ease the pain. One day her mother came to the *banda* when the men were away and sat with her. Mary told her about the cost of buying clothes for the baby and she promised to have a look in a box at home.

'Does Father know about me?'

'He never speaks of you.'

'Will you say a prayer for me in church?'

'I do. Every Sunday.'

'When the time comes, will you come over to me?'

'Of course. Send Gichuchi at once.'

A day or so later Mary was coming back from visiting a neighbour. She was feeling a little dizzy and, not looking where she was going, she tripped over a tree stump a few yards from the *banda*.

She felt intense pain in her belly and crawled to the door. With great difficulty she hauled herself onto the bed. Her screams alerted the neighbour who rushed over. She took one look and shouted for her son, a child of nine, to run and find Gichuchi.

Gichuchi and Mutahi were not far away digging a ditch for a drain. The foreman was standing over them, giving instructions. The *toto* shouted at Gichuchi that he must come at once.

'Not till this job is finished,' said the foreman.

Gichuchi ignored him and climbed out of the ditch. The foreman made to stop him but Gichuchi angrily threatened him with a spade and pushed him aside. When he reached the *banda* Mary told him to fetch her mother. She came at once bringing some clothes and wraps.

By this time, Mary was bleeding badly and there was no sign of the baby's head. Gichuchi was frantic with worry and he was told to boil some water. Mary's screams died away because she was lapsing into unconsciousness. All the women round the bed could do was to wipe away the blood and pray. Suddenly Mary gave a loud cry and the baby's head began to appear. However, she was so weak that she could not push, leaving the head barely exposed. The blood continued to flow and soon she became deeply unconscious. An hour later she was dead.

Other neighbours gathered round. Mary was wrapped in a shroud and laid on the floor. Njoka returned from work at the usual time. He held the distraught Gichuchi in his arms before going off to see the priest.

The next morning Mary was buried in the garden with a short ceremony. The priest rattled through the text with unfeeling haste and annoyed Gichuchi by referring briefly to the wages of sin. The few neighbours who had attended went away after expressing condolence.

Njoka returned to work. Gichuchi sat outside the *banda* staring ahead but seeing nothing. Frampton drew up outside in a jeep and angrily stood in front of him.

'Why are you not at work? And you have threatened the foreman. You have always been trouble.'

Gichuchi said nothing but pointed at the mound which marked Mary's grave.

'Stand up when I speak to you.'

Gichuchi made no reply but for the first time a tear ran down his cheek. Frampton stepped forward and raised his stick. But when he saw the look in Gichuchi's eyes he drew back.

'Consider yourself dismissed. Don't let me see you on my farm again.'

With that he turned away and drove off.

Late in the afternoon Mutahi came to the *banda*. For the first time that day, Gichuchi spoke.

'I have lost my girl. I have lost my job. There is nothing for me here. I want to go to the forest – now. Tell me where to go.'

Chapter Five

Gichuchi was just one of hundreds of young men who joined the Mau Mau. Few were motivated by the politics of liberation; most sought adventure in their otherwise drab lives as a relief from grinding poverty. They were taught to despise their chiefs and headmen who had thrown in their lot with the British. Indians – *dukawallahs*, clerks and skilled workmen – were regarded as yet another form of alien imposition; they remained aloof from African society and by their presence were accused of retarding African progress.

Fortunately for the British, the Mau Mau revolt was confined to Kikuyuland and did not spread to other parts of Kenya. The gangs of fighters were based in the forests of the Aberdares and Mount Kenya, from where they made descents on white farms and loyalist areas. There were activists in Nairobi. Many thousands of sympathisers in the towns, reserves and farms formed a 'Passive Wing'; they set up committees to organise supplies of food, information and recruits. Guns, grenades and ammunition were taken from Army and Police barracks by force or collusion; weapons were manufactured in secret workshops. This 'Passive Wing' also organised the administration of oaths and did not scruple to kill informers and individuals who opposed them.

The British administration had been aware of the Mau Mau for several years. It became a banned organisation in 1950. Since then its activities had been monitored by the Special Branch, which was composed of white officers and a few loyal Africans. Hit-and-run tactics made the Mau Mau an elusive enemy, and a conspiracy of silence hindered efforts to deal with it.

Despite the insurgency, Princess Elizabeth and Prince Philip visited Kenya in 1952 and stayed at the Treetops Hotel near Nyeri, on the edge of the Aberdares. It was there that she learned of the death of her father, King George the Sixth, on the night of 5th and 6th

February. She returned to London immediately. Thereafter attacks on white settlers and loyalist Africans increased. In the first half of the year sixty attacks on settler property around Nyeri alone were recorded and African workers killed. The settlers argued for tough action and over 500 Kikuyu were taken into preventive custody. On 20th October the Governor, Sir Evelyn Baring, declared a state of emergency. In Operation Jock Scott, 150 members of the Kenya African Union, which was actually a legal organisation, were arrested in an effort to decapitate the Mau Mau leadership; however, the KAU, led by Jomo Kenyatta, was not connected to the Mau Mau. On 3rd of December the trial began of Kenyatta and other politicians. Over the next few months, many Africans were detained, interrogated and interned but there was no diminution of Mau Mau violence. There were two regular battalions of the King's African Rifles already present in Kenya and two reserve battalions were being brought up to strength. A battalion of the Lancashire Fusiliers was transferred from Egypt. The Kenya Regiment, a territorial regiment composed of settlers and a few Africans, was reactivated. Despite the military build-up little progress was made in disrupting the Mau Mau gangs. Tactics were ineffective, intelligence was poor and inefficiencies were readily exposed, not least the lack of communication between the various branches of the security forces.

As in other British colonies, British officials, such as District and Police officers, were spread thinly over large areas. With garrisons round the world and the current insurgency in Malaya, British battalions were used sparingly. The Military relied for the most part on native battalions with British officers. In order to inculcate a local responsibility for law and order and to release soldiers for combat, a Home Guard had been set up. Its functions were to protect chiefs and headmen, to guard schools and patrol local areas. Fortified posts were created. A few rifles and shot guns were allocated to the most trustworthy men; the rest carried *pangas*, spears and other traditional weapons. They were not paid but were given reward money for the recovery of stolen rifles and ammunition. In the course of a year large numbers were enrolled and were deployed mainly in the Kikuyu reserves. As the campaign developed, the Home Guard also provided guides for military operations and assisted the screening process. Kikuyu farmers were accustomed to live on separate *shambas* around the country. In an effort to protect them and exercise greater control, the administration evicted them from their smallholdings, often by force, and settled them in fortified villages. This was also British policy in Malaya. British settlers readily occupied the vacant land. Because of 'villagisation' it was easier for the authorities, assisted by the chiefs and headmen, to screen individuals for Mau Mau sympathies and activities. Suspects were interned in camps and, if necessary, tortured to extract information. As an example of this process, at Limuru in January 1953 1,500 people were screened, of whom ninety-six were arrested. Magistrates were given new powers to seize property and increase penalties for crime. In December 1952 the Governor had approved a new Emergency Tax which was to be levied on all Kikuyu. These measures were very unpopular and revenge attacks were launched on British settlers. At Thompson's Falls Commander Meiklejohn was killed and his wife mutilated. On January 24th 1953 Mr and Mrs Ruck and their young son, who lived at Kinangop, were cruelly murdered in their home; Mrs Ruck was a doctor and well known for her work with the Africans. But most of the victims of Mau Mau violence were Kikuyu themselves, loyalists and those who worked on the settlers' farms.

* * *

Michael Charteris had returned to England in the summer of 1951. He wrote a long letter to the Howarths, thanking them for their hospitality and telling them of his recent visit to Sherborne to see his nephew Simon, and the Howarths' son Charlie. With the permission of their housemaster he took them out to lunch. It turned out that the boys were close friends and shared a study. Thus Michael did not have to say very much but asked a few questions and let the boys chatter happily. His years in the Army fell away when he recalled his own boyhood at school. To his surprise very little had changed in boarding schools since the twenties. Both boys seemed to accept the hardships and occasional brutality with a shrug of the shoulders, to be endured as a necessary evil but not taken too seriously. There were far more important things to be concerned about, such as Latin tests and games; both of them were keen cricketers.

Charlie asked him about his stay in Kenya. He told them of the people he had met in Nairobi, the breakfast on Mount Kenya, his encounter with a buffalo and watching game with Naomi.

'Did you like Simmie? Charlie asked.

'A very nice young lady.'

'Simmie is very beautiful,' Charlie explained to Simon.

When he got back to London he sat down to write to Jane, something he had contemplated for a long time.

> ...What you said about Africa is very true. Yes, I have caught the Africa bug and the longer I stay in drab old England, the more I am drawn back. I know I only spent a couple of months there and that not all is as it appears on the surface. However, I have no special ties in England and if the Army won't send me back in some capacity, then I may as well resign and try other reasons for getting out there. Resignation would indeed be a major step but peacetime soldiering has limited appeal and I am young enough to try something else. I have been in the Army since I went to Sandhurst at the age of eighteen. However, if I can combine Africa with the Army, that would kill two birds with one stone. Or perhaps three, since, if you are still there, I would be able to see you again. If you are so minded, please let me write to you when I know what I am going to be doing...

To his delight he received a letter from Jane a month later:

> ...Things are a little tense round here. There is a gang in the forest not all that far from us. At the moment they carry out raids for food supplies and no one, as far as we know, has been killed. There have been reports of intimidation and oath-taking. All we can do is carry on as normal and just take precautions; we discourage the *watu* from going out at night. Andrew Holmes, the District Officer, the one who came to dinner

when you were with us, is very busy trying to set up these new villages in our area, a policy he disagrees with, but it has come down from on high. The farmers are pushing for really tough measures, but Andrew and others feel that we have to keep the people on side. I don't know the exact figures but in the whole of Kenya there are 40,000 of us sitting on top of five million Africans. We can't govern them unless we can keep their goodwill. The trick is to protect and advance the majority and eliminate the bad guys. It all takes time.

But you know all this. I am busy looking after Naomi. She is a very determined young lady and when she argues with her mother I say nothing if I can get away with it. Most of the time she is very bright and charming. But there are no children of her age round about to play with or even make contact with. Once a week I go down to the local school, about half a mile away, to help with English and reading classes. With Annabel's permission I now take Naomi with me. As a result she has picked up Gikuyu very quickly; I know only a few words and so she helps me out. Three years from now she will go to the school at Gilgil and I shall have to think about coming home.

Of course you can write to me. Quite apart from anything else, we are in a bit of a backwater here and news of the world outside is very welcome. I do hope that you will find a way to come, sooner rather than later, please…

Michael found himself behind a desk at the War Office. For once his job was in line with his experience – jungle operations. He paid a short visit to British Honduras to observe training there and was set to go to Malaya, when his boss came into the office.

'Sorry, Michael, I have pulled rank. I am going to Malaya. However, I have something else for you instead. Kenya. They are bring two battalions of the KAR up to strength. One lacks a CO at the moment. Would you like to go?'

'Like a shot'.

'And there is the possibility of seeing some action, from what I hear. I have to phone the man back this afternoon. Can I say that you will go?'

'Sir.'

Within two weeks arrangements had been completed and in December 1952 Lieutenant Colonel Charteris was met at the airport by Major Bright.

'Welcome to Africa, sir. Is this your first time?'

'Thank you, Major. Actually I had a spell of leave recently and came out here for a holiday. I am glad to be back.'

'Very good, sir. I understand you were with the KAR during the war.'

'Yes, Fourteenth Army. What about you?'

Michael had read the file but wanted the Major to talk about himself.

'Oh, D-Day, the Rhine, a brief stint in Palestine – not very pleasant – and then a posting out here.'

'What do you do when you are not soldiering? Polo?'

'God, no! Photography. I go out into the bush with my servant and take what I can. The Park near the city has most of the big game and I am building up a portfolio. There have been one or two hairy moments, I can tell you.'

'I am sure. What about birds?'

'Those, too. It requires a lot of patience to get a good close up. I use colour but it is very expensive so I mustn't waste a shot.'

'How very interesting. You must tell me more sometime. But we have to discuss military matters as well. Too late today. Let me get settled in. I need a good kip after that flight. Shall we say 0800 in my office tomorrow?'

'Sir.'

* * *

Over the next weeks Michael spent a few days with each of the four companies of the battalion. The Headquarters Company was stationed in Nairobi itself, the others up country at Embu, Nakuru and Nanyuki. He found that Major Bright had a firm grip on things in Nairobi and dealt with matters promptly in his absence. On his travels he took Company Sergeant Major Tickell, who had been recommended by Bright. Tickell was tall, like himself, and well-built. He was a man of few words, but when he spoke they were well chosen. Michael had a good memory and soon got to know his officers. He dined in the Mess and accepted invitations to the Sergeants' Mess. He observed training in progress. He did not address companies all together but spoke informally to as many men as he could. In anticipation of command he had brushed up his Swahili and soon he felt reasonably proficient. At the end of each inspection he reported his conclusions to the officers and CSM Tickell spoke to the NCOs. The company at Nanyuki was in fair order but those at Embu and Nakuru had room for improvement; the officers seemed more interested in polo. He heard about the scandal over the theft of rifles and ammunition, but the men concerned were not from his unit. There were other defalcations which appeared to have been largely ignored. He decided to spend more time with those companies and if necessary replace some officers and NCOs. However, with the Declaration of Emergency, there was little time to organise major changes.

He also made calls upon District Officers to introduce himself and learn their views. In the course of these visits he met Andrew Holmes. From him he learnt that a number of Kikuyu were confessing that they had taken the oaths, but under duress. As they had not been harmed by the mysterious disasters that had been threatened to those who broke the oaths, they and others who had also sworn and who wanted to oppose the Mau Mau were encouraged to come forward. A process had been set up called *kahungwa mubori*, 'to have the lungs cleaned', a cleansing ritual which demanded a full confession. If that were done, then the man would be eligible to join the Home Guard.

The Mau Mau were becoming more and more aggressive. Early in 1953 they attacked the Police Station at Naivasha, which was slackly guarded, and there was a suspicion of collusion. Rifles and ammunition were stolen and prisoners released. Emboldened by this foray, one night the Mau Mau attacked the village of Lari in Rift Valley Province. Lari's chief was openly hostile to the Mau

Mau. Ninety-seven people of all ages were hacked to death or burnt within their houses. Their chief was brutally tortured and then killed. When the security forces arrived all they found were putrefying corpses with horrific injuries. The gang escaped from the area before a pursuit could be mounted. This outrage was well publicised and shocked many Kikuyu as well as Europeans. As a result the decision was taken to arm the Home Guard and provide British officers to lead them. However, it took some time to implement these measures and meanwhile the Home Guard did not trouble to exert itself beyond maintaining a token presence and occasionally inflicting rough justice on petty criminals.

* * *

Towards the end of his travels up country Michael radioed the Howarths and asked to visit them. He had written on his arrival in Nairobi and had sent a separate note to Jane. CSM Tickell he left in Nanyuki to enjoy a bit of leave with colleagues. Driving himself and wearing civilian clothes but with his army revolver, he arrived at the Howarths' farm just before lunch.

'Jane is down at the school just now,' explained Annabel. 'She will be back later. I am sure she would like to see you.'

Over lunch he described his activities since arriving to take up his command.

'There is an awful lot to do in a short time. We have taken in many new recruits during the last year who have to be trained. The existing personnel had got used to a rather easy life. Fortunately, I have a good man in the HQ Company who is gingering things up and I have had to be firm with some of the officers up country. I had a good meeting with Andrew Holmes. He is having a difficult time; he has a lot on his plate anyway and he does not always agree with government policy. He finds the Home Guard a bit of a liability.'

'Thomas, you know, my major-domo - he came with us for breakfast up the hill – he doesn't think much of them. There are some shady characters and at times they seem more interested in their own feuds.'

'I gather they are to have European officers and firearms.'

'We don't have a Home Guard round here. But we do have a direct radio link with Nanyuki, and if they are on their toes the Army can be with us in a couple of hours. By which time, of course, it will be too late. There are many farms more isolated than we are.'

'There is talk of changing the role of the military from guarding the farms to carrying out large-scale sweeps through the forests. You might not get a rapid response from the contingent at Nanyuki, but the Police can send constables fairly quickly and the Special Branch will take a look and see if they can identify any prisoners or casualties.'

'Hm. Not very satisfactory, but we will have to make do. We do have a safe room to which we can retreat, but the *watu* have no safe place.'

'Have you a plan in the event of an attack?'

'I have a few rifles of one sort or another. They are ready to be handed out to Thomas and trusted men…'

'But not before an attack?'

'No. Otherwise they might fall into the wrong hands. We have to rely on an early warning.'

'What will these men do?'

'Take up position round the *bandas*. Hold off the attackers so that the people can get away. I have few thunderflashes from before the war. They might discourage attackers. Also, I have installed a siren to make a loud noise and some electric lights which might catch a few in the open. If there is sufficient warning I have told my people to congregate around the farm buildings and bring their *pangas*. There will be security in numbers, I hope. Thomas has briefed the men. We had a rehearsal a few days ago and most people obeyed instructions. Let's hope it works when the time comes.'

'That seems the best you can do with your resources and manpower. Not an ideal prospect.'

* * *

After lunch, Patrick and Annabel retired for Egyptian PT. Michael decided to walk to the school. He left his revolver in the house; he was grateful that he could forget soldiering, even for an afternoon. From the entrance to the farm he turned onto the road and wandered slowly along, looking at the neat little plots of maize and vegetables. He passed a *banda* with an old man sitting outside.

Michael greeted him: '*Jambo, Mzee*.'

'*Jambo, Bwana*.'

'*Habari yako*?'

'*Mzuri. Asante*.'

The old man continued in English; 'Are you a friend of *bwana* Howarth?'

'I am.'

'I sit here a lot and watch who comes by. Tell him I think there have been some men around, men I have not seen before. They look bad men.'

'Is this recently?' Michael asked.

The old man pondered for a moment. 'Three or four days ago.'

'Have they been back?'

'No.'

'Well, thank you for the information. I will pass it on. *Kwaheri, Mzee*.'

'*Kwaheri, Bwana*.'

Michael went on his way. He came to the school, really just a large shed with open sides. The children sat on benches facing a blackboard on an easel, on which was inscribed the first verse of the National Anthem. The teacher sat at one side and Jane was standing in front of the class with Naomi beside her.

Jane read out the first line while Naomi pointed out the words. She asked the class to repeat it, which they dutifully did. When they had gone through every line, she repeated the whole verse and the class recited it back to her.

A boy who must have been thirteen or more, because his voice was nearly breaking, asked Jane what 'victorious' meant.

'Defeating her enemies.' The boy nodded and then asked: 'Does the Queen live in the sky?'

'Of course not.'

'Then how can she rain over us?'

Jane took a piece of chalk and wrote 'rain' and 'reign' on the board. 'This one means the weather and this one means rule. It is confusing, isn't it? That is why we must get the spelling right, not just the sound.'

The teacher nodded enthusiastically; the children looked puzzled.

'Now we will sing,' Jane announced.

She started off in a clear, tuneful voice and took them through line by line. Led by Naomi they sang the whole verse through twice and then Jane took away the blackboard. She sang the first three notes and then let them sing by themselves; they were word-perfect.

'Well done, everyone,' said the teacher. 'Go into the playground and come back when I ring the bell.' She picked up a football and gave it to the boy who had asked the questions. Naomi had bought a rope for skipping and the girls gathered round her for their own game.

Jane had seen Michael at the back of the class but did not acknowledge his presence until the class was dismissed.

'Hello, Michael. Thank you for coming. But shouldn't you be out soldiering somewhere?'

'I am on an important reconnaisance. Time spent in reconnaisance is never wasted. That is what we were taught at Sandhurst.'

'What are you reconnoitring?'

'Oh, Africa at ground level and…you, perhaps.'

'And what did you find out?'

'That you are a natural teacher and have a lovely voice.'

They went and sat down on a bench. 'It's terrific to see you again,' he said.

'It has been a long time. You haven't changed a bit.' She looked at him closely. 'Well, maybe just a touch of grey by the ears.'

'And you are as lovely as I remember you.'

'Thank you, kind sir.' They were silent for a moment. Then she said: 'In answer to the question you will not ask, I have not met anyone here who interests me. I shall be going home when Naomi goes to Gilgil. By then I will have had enough of Africa and I have to see my parents. It has been wonderful most of the time and I have no complaints.'

'I quite understand. I hope we can keep in touch, wherever we are.'

'I certainly will. What have you been doing since you arrived?'

Michael explained about the difficulties he had had in his new command. 'Nothing that cannot be sorted out. We will be taking the field soon.'

'Will you be leading from the front?'

'The battalion is spread over four areas and I have to delegate. But I will have to be involved, at the front, in some action. Nothing inspires a soldier more than his colonel sharing a foxhole, as I discovered in Burma.'

'Please don't get yourself killed.'

'I'll do my best. At the moment, the Army is preparing to send out patrols at platoon level, just to find out where the blighters are. In due course we will have to to carry out sweeps in full force to drive them towards the guns, as if it were a grouse shoot. It will be a long and tedious process. The thing is, unless the War Office sends out more battalions we won't be able to protect the farms as well That is what I have been talking to Patrick about. Farmers will have to rely on themselves, at least initially. He seems well organised.'

'We have had one or two drills, just the family and house servants. He made me practice shooting a rifle. I wasn't very accurate.'

'No one is when under stress, unless they are trained. But the mere fact of you having a weapon in your hand and pointing it at the intruder should make him pause.'

'I hope I will never have to use it, even for display.'

The teacher rang the bell and the children reluctantly returned to their benches.

'It's time we went home,' said Jane. 'I have to do some reading with Naomi, which she enjoys. She finds sums difficult so we do those first thing in the morning. Will you walk with us?'

Naomi ran up and took Jane's hand. As they walked along the road she took Michael's hand as well and demanded a swing. After two or three goes she skipped ahead. Michael found himself taking Jane's hand and received a squeeze in return.

'Are you staying tonight?'

'No, alas. My sergeant has had a free afternoon in Nanyuki. We will sleep in camp overnight and leave for Nairobi first thing in the morning.'

'Will I see you again soon?'

'Difficult to say. We have an operation in Kiambu and Thika coming up very soon and one of my companies will be involved. It will be the battalion's first operation since I took over, so I will have to be there. Could you come down to Nairobi?'

'I'm due a weekend. I can stay with a friend of the Howarths. What does the Army do at weekends?'

'When not on duty, play football and drink. So I should be able to slip away for a bit. I'll take you out to dinner.'

They came to the turning for the farm. 'Naomi, run on ahead,' Jane said.

She took Michael's arm and led him off the road out of sight of the farm.

She faced him and put her arms round his neck.

'Our first kiss.'

* * *

Jane came down to Nairobi a few weeks later and Michael met her at the Railway Station. He excused himself from watching a battalion football match and they spent the afternoon in the Nairobi National Park; he had hired a Land Rover. The ranger at the gate suggested where they might go to be reasonably certain of seeing game. Jane said that she had never seen hippo or cheetah, and lion only at a distance. They drove slowly for half an hour, during which they saw giraffe grazing and buffaloes in abundance. From time to time they stopped for Jane to take photographs. An ostrich crossed the track. A little further on they saw a secretary bird stalking along.

'Such an elegant creature; those long black legs.'

'I never had a secretary like that,' observed Michael.

'I wish I had colour and a telephoto lens. One of these days I will be able to afford one.'

They came to the pools of the Mbagathi River. Michael parked as close as he could but left the engine running. They got out and gingerly went down to the water's edge. There they watched several hippos basking and snorting in the pool, about twenty yards away. One seemed to catch sight of them and opened its huge jaws in a yawn. Michael noticed large hoofprints where they were standing.

'I have heard that they can outrun humans. Let's go back.'

They retreated slowly to the Land Rover.

'Mind you, it's so damned hot that any respectable creature should be having a snooze.'

The rains had not come and the grass was short; there was little shelter from the sun. At a water hole they saw kudu and smaller buck.

'I wish I could identify them,' said Jane. She was keeping a list of animals observed.

They turned eastwards and came to a small kopje. The track went below it and they thought about climbing up to have a panoramic view. As they came round a corner they saw a lion and lioness lying side by side just off the track. Michael pulled up.

'What do we do?' Jane asked.

'Drive past or stop and hope they won't charge us?'

'Just stop,' said Jane. 'Patrick told me that when they mate they leave the existing cubs and go off by themselves. They are at it for hours on end. No wonder they look sleepy.'

They watched the beasts for some time but no interest was shown in them. Jane took photographs.

'That will impress the folks back home. I will say that we stalked them through the bush.'

They drove on.

'We have yet to see your cheetah.'

'We'll be very lucky if we do, at this time of day.'

They came to some thin woodland and followed the track through. Below an acacia they saw a black rhino about thirty yards away. Michael stopped but left the engine running. Jane took out the binoculars and studied the animal.

'It doesn't look very happy.'

'Rhinos are always miserable.'

'There is something wrong with its left eye. It's clouded over.'

Jane opened the door, stepped out and took a photograph. The rhino started trotting towards them. She swiftly got back in.

'If they can't see us, they can at least hear and smell the car, something intruding on them. Michael, just ease forward and see if it follows us.'

He did so.

'I didn't realise how big they are,' he said. 'We would come off worse if he charged the car.'

The rhino began to move faster, its head down and the horn thrust menacingly forward.

'Discretion, I think,' said Michael and he pressed the accelerator gently.

Jane turned round in her seat. 'Faster, Michael.'

'I don't want to stall.'

The rhino was getting very close. Michael put his foot down, keeping in low gear. The wheels spun and threw up a cloud of dust. This disconcerted the animal for a moment which gave them time to get a fair distance away.

'I like adventures,' said Jane, 'but that was rather too close for comfort.'

They reached the East Gate of the Park.

'Where would you like to go now?'

'I am staying with friends of the Howarths in Langata, the Bensons.'

'I'm going to take you out to dinner.'

'That would be lovely. But I need to change first.'

'And so do I. I will drop you and go back to the barracks and pick you up as soon as I can.'

'There is a restaurant in Karen. I don't know what it is like.'

'Let's try it anyway. The food doesn't matter, the company does.'

After a rapid shower and change, Michael was back and invited in. The Bensons and Jane were sipping gin and tonics. Stanley Benson offered him a drink.

'A small one, thank you. It doesn't do for the CO to come back half-seas-over.'

They chatted for a few minutes. Benson asked Michael about himself but did not mention the Emergency. When it was time to go, Milly Benson told him that Jane was always very welcome to stay with them and she hoped that he would visit again.

The restaurant was busy. The service was slow but the food, basic fare, was delicious and they soon emptied their plates.

'I was starving,' said Jane.

They talked about their families and childhoods. Both agreed that they had been generally happy at home but had grown restless in their teens.

'Same for everyone, I suppose,' said Jane. 'Coming out to Africa was my big break away from the mould, though I was in my twenties. I must have been a late developer. My parents supported me.'

'My father didn't want me to be a soldier. He wanted me to carry on the family business – Charteris and Charteris – but became reconciled to my taking the King's shilling.'

He took a deep breath and asked her outright; 'What will you do when you go home?'

She raised her hands. 'I have no idea. It is in the lap of the gods.'

'Well, unless there is some pressing reason, I hope I might be part of it.'

'I was half hoping you would say that.'

'Only half?'

She took his hand. 'Michael, we haven't known each other for very long but I know enough to want to see more of you, whatever that may bring.'

'Ditto.'

He looked at his watch. 'Sorry. I must be back in barracks soon. Duty calls.'

'A soldier's lot. I have enjoyed today – very much. Thank you.'

They went out to the car without speaking. At the Bensons, he got out and opened the door for her.

'How gallant. For that you deserve a big kiss.'

After a long embrace he watched her go until the Bensons opened the door. She turned and waved. He blew a kiss back.

Chapter Six

Senior officers, brigade and unit commanders were invited to a reception at Government House to welcome the new General Officer Commanding, Sir George Erskine. As well as the Governor and Lady Baring, there were civilian officials, civic dignitaries and their ladies, and some prominent businessmen and farmers. Service personnel were in tropical dress uniform, which Michael had run up by an Indian tailor at the last moment. The Governor was in court dress, but carried his topee. The civilians wore a variety of linen suits. The only black faces were waiters in white coats serving drinks and canapés.

By five o'clock the guests were assembled on the lawn in front of Government House. A military band played in the background. At the front was a dais with a microphone. A functionary got up and called for silence. Then the Governor and the General stepped up. Sir Evelyn coughed and began to speak:

'Ladies and Gentlemen, it is my great pleasure to welcome Sir George Erskine and his wife, Lady Ruby, to the Colony. Sir George has had a very distinguished career and has much experience in many campaigns.'

He consulted his notes.

'He has served in India, he won the DSO in North Africa and was appointed Commander of the Seventh Armoured Division, which he led in Italy and Normandy. He had adminstrative experience at Supreme Headquarters, Allied Expeditionary Force. After the war he served in Hong Kong, and latterly has been GOC Egypt. These are difficult times for us all, but I am sure that Sir George is the man to lead our forces through this emergency.'

Sir George took over the microphone.

'Thank you, Sir Evelyn. I am very proud to have been appointed to this command. I recognise the magnitude of the task ahead, to rid the Colony of terrorism and enable it to flourish freely. My position is different from that of my predecessor, in that I now have the unified command of all security forces, whether military, police or auxiliary troops. In that way I hope we can take decisive action to ensure the safety of all people in Kenya. The measures we are adopting will not bring a swift result but it will be a sure one. I have every confidence that we will succeed.'

With that he stepped down and, accompanied by the Governor and an aide, began to circulate among the guests. His wife was joined by Lady Baring and together they went round the opposite way. Michael realised that he was one of the most junior officers present and kept out of the way of his seniors. He wondered if the Howarths would be present, but recalled their distaste for Nairobi functions. After standing by himself for some time watching the crowd he was accosted by an elderly man in a crumpled suit and panama hat.

'Alone and palely loitering, young man?'

'Just taking it all in.'

'Are you new to the Colony?'

'Newish, sir. Just since the end of last year. But I have been here before, two years ago.'

'Not an old hand, then. Trouble is, there are too many of us old hands. I have been here fifty years. James Ridout.'

'Michael Charteris.'

They shook hands.

'Where are you from, Mr Ridout?'

'I had a big farm near Nakuru but I passed it onto my son. I live in Langata now. I am President of the Farmers' Association. We have an office in the city. It keeps me going and there is a lot to do just now. We try to represent the views of our members to the Government, but, alas, they don't always listen. At the moment we are encouraging people to take steps for their own defence. The Police are thin on the ground and the so-called Home Guard is not reliable.'

'That's interesting,' said Michael. He mentioned his conversation with Patrick Howarth.

'I know him. A good man. The thing is, Charteris, I am sure we will beat the terrorists, but at considerable cost, and I don't mean money or lives. I mean loss of trust between us and the Africans. I have lived and worked with them all my life and I have come to the conclusion that we cannot deny them a share of government. Look at the Administrative Council; only one native, and he is Indian. We made a great mistake in imprisoning Kenyatta. It would have been much easier to isolate the terrorists if we had him on side. And the price of that would have been Independence.'

'Is that a good thing?'

'Good or otherwise, it is inevitable in the long term. I will not be around to see it myself.'

'Are your views widely shared?'

'I am gradually persuading my son, since he will have to cope with the new situation. But most of my colleagues won't hear of it.'

Ridout took another glass from a passing waiter. 'Cheers.'

'Cheers,' replied Michael, as he took a sip from his existing glass.

'Do you know this Erskine fellow?' asked Ridout.

'I have never met him. I know no more than what His Excellency said.'

'Hm. Looks and sounds a businesslike chap. We'll see. Good to talk to you, Charteris, and good luck with your command.'

He shuffled off. Michael looked about him. He was near a group of civilians and was about to introduce himself to them when he saw the General's party heading towards him. An aide came forward and called him over.

'This is Colonel Charteris, sir.'

The General was rather shorter than Michael and for a moment did not meet his eyes. Instead, he looked at Michael's medals.

'Ah. Military Cross. And the Burma Star. We don't see many of those out here. Were you a Chindit?'

'No, sir. KAR. There were three battalions over there. Which is why I am here, I suppose.'

'You must know something of jungle operations, then.'

'I tried to get to Malaya, but my Brigadier went instead.'

'Such is Army life. You will have to make do with Kenya. But I am sure we will need you expertise in due course.'

'Sir.'

* * *

In April a sweep, Operation Anvil, was carried out in Nairobi in the shanty town that had grown up near the Kariakor Market and in the Mathare Valley. The whole area had been sealed off so that no one could escape, and the rest of the city was patrolled. Planning for this operation had occupied several weeks, mainly carried out by Major Bright and his opposite numbers in other units. Security was tight; the soldiers, though they had been trained in this type of search operation, were not briefed until shortly before dawn on the day. In full kit, with rifles but berets instead of helmets, they piled into lorries and were driven into the city, so that they were able to start shortly after sunrise. Once in place they divided into platoons and set off on pre-arranged routes. Michael went with Major Bright initially, then detached himself and followed one of the platoons.

The inhabitants of the shanty town were taken by surprise. There was little resistance, though one or two men who attempted to escape were rounded up quickly. Those who had no identification or could not account for their presence were taken away by lorry; they were allowed only a minimum of belongings. In the shacks a thorough search was made for firearms, ammunition, grenades and other ordnance. Several caches of weapons were found and the premises demolished. Women, children and the elderly were left behind.

By the end of the operation, which lasted several days, nearly a thousand men had been transported or marched under guard to a camp just outside the city. There they were made to sit on the ground in the heat of the day to await screening. A bowser with water and a limited supply of food were provided. One by one they were subjected to screening by Special Branch officers. Some were released quickly but the majority were were detained in the camp and later interned at Thika or transferred to a Kikuyu reserve up country. Michael was unused to this form of soldiering and was not able to judge the overall success of the operation. But Major Bright was pleased with their Company's performance.

Two days later there was a debriefing by the head of Special Branch for army officers. General Erskine and his staff were present.

First of all, unit commanders were asked for their comments. When it came to Michael's turn he said that he hoped that the results were worth the effort. There had been some understandable resentment on the part of the locals at their peremptory treatment. Collective punishments should be used sparingly, and only if the results were likely to justify the means. He concluded by saying that however many troops they put into the field, they could not defeat the Mau Mau unless they had the cooperation of the natives.

His remarks did not go down well in some quarters. One officer stood up and said that the only language the natives understood was force and he would put the whole lot in camps with their women and children as well. That would teach them a lesson. Another said that he agreed with Colonel Charteris in part, but punishments should be exemplary and swift, to deter others. In his expereience the processes of the Law were too slow. Quite often his men had captured terrorists who were definitely guilty, but they had to be kept under guard for days until a magistrate's hearing. In the field this was not always possible and, though he could not be absolutely sure, he reckoned that some prisoners were shot if they refused to give information.

Eventually the GOC brought an end to this discussion. He said that the points raised were very much in the minds of the Governor and indeed the Colonial Secretary, who had to answer to Parliament for the conduct of the administration. He then invited Special Branch to speak.

'Gentlemen. Thank you for your recent efforts. To stifle any doubts you may have, I must tell you that we netted about a hundred activists and two or three hundred suspected of sympathy with the Mau Mau. So it was well worth the dislocation caused to the Africans. We cannot be sure, of course, that we have caught everybody, but we have made a significant dent in terrorist manpower. We believe that Nairobi was used as a base for Mau Mau operations as far away as Thika and Limuru. To deal with the prisoners we have set up a court within the detention centre and we should be able to process them rapidly. Once again, thank you for your efforts.'

He looked across at the GOC, who nodded slightly.

'As a result of the sweep I believe we will be in a position to release several units and move them up country within the next few weeks. With all due respect to the Military, the fewer soldiers seen on the streets of Nairobi, the better.'

⋆ ⋆ ⋆

The Headquarters Company was brought up to Nanyuki. Its arrival was duly noted by Karumbi at the *duka* and the information passed on. The Devonshires were also in the camp. There were worries that there might be friction between the British battalion and the askaris. However, the CO of the Devonshires was of one mind with Michael and those involved in a street fight between members of the two units were confined to barracks and their pay docked. Tensions were eased by joint exercises in the bush where the Africans were able to give a lesson or two in tracking and survival.

There were other concerns. It was reported to Michael that some soldiers in the battalion on patrol had been beating up suspects. With Major Bright in attendance he questioned Captain Symonds about the matter.

'Well, they were being uncooperative,' he explained. 'With these people one must be tough. A cuff over the head or a bang with a rifle butt works wonders.'

'Did you administer these blows?'

'Not personally. But it wasn't torture or anything like that. When we are in the field we don't have time for niceties. We want quick answers.'

'I have heard that one man was held down and severely beaten on the back and buttocks. Is that true?'

'Yes, well, he was truculent and badmouthing our askaris. So I ordered Sergeant Collins to beat him. It did the trick. The other prisoners fell over themselves to come forward with information, information that turned out to be very useful. We soon located a gang and shot them.'

'Did you take any of them prisoner?'

'We tried but they ignored our call to surrender and so they had to be dealt with.'

'How many men?'

'About twenty.'

'What happened to the bodies?'

'Having searched them we left them to rot. We searched their camp as well, removed all the weapons and found some papers which we handed over to Intelligence.'

'I see. Captain Symonds, you have been out here longer than I have and have had more first-hand experience of dealing with these insurgents. But you must be aware that corporal punishment in colonial units was banned just after the war, and that applied not only to soldiers but by soldiers as well.'

'But, sir, other units do it.'

'That may be so, but not my battalion. In case you don't know, Captain, I commanded KAR troops in Burma against the Japanese. I did not allow my men to mistreat the local Burmese people to obtain information, not ever. General Slim would have been appalled.'

'It's not the same here, sir. After all, the local people are the same tribe as the Mau Mau.'

'In Burma it was our job to protect the locals as well as to defeat the Japanese, and they knew this and cooperated. Here, we are protecting the people against the gangs. If you mistreat them, you will send them into the arms of the terrorists and turn them into freedom fighters.'

Michael drummed his fingers on the desk while the Captain stood nervously shifting from foot to foot.

'How do you expect our soldiers to behave well when you countenance or even order them to be brutal? I regard this as a serious matter and it will be referred upwards. There is a limit to my powers, however, so for the time being consider yourself reprimanded. It will go down on your record. Major Bright has taken down the details and he will give you a copy in due course. Have you anything to say?'

'No, sir.'

'Then dimiss.'

When he had left, Michael lit his pipe and put his feet up on the desk.

'No doubt he will claim that he has been following usual practice and I am sure that many of his colleagues will be sympathetic. How old is he?'

Bright consulted a file.

'Thirty-two, sir.'

'Old enough to know better. If this is as widespread as he claims, then it should be brought to the attention of the GOC. I know he has only just got here but this does require an official policy statement, I think. Things have a habit of coming back to bite us, particularly if they get into the British press. I will take it up with the Brigadier. Please let me see a draft before filing it and giving Symonds a copy.' He paused to relight his pipe. 'Actually, I find the whole thing throroughly distasteful. But that's not important. We have to consider the reputation of the battalion.'

Michael took his feet off the desk.

'We both deserve a drink. Scotch?'

'Please.'

'And do have a smoke. There are some other things to chew over.'

He took a sheet of paper out of his desk.

'Have a look at this. It is a plan to clear a mile-wide exclusion zone around the forests, the Aberdares and Mount Kenya. That is where the Mau Mau hide out before making forays. The idea is two-fold: to stop supplies reaching the gangs from the hinterland and to flush them out of the forest into the open where we can deal with them.'

'Big operations, both of them.'

'Now the villages are set up and the population concentrated it will be easier to prevent people entering the forest.'

'What does the exclusion zone actually mean? Not a wall, surely?'

'No. Just a patrolled area with no people in it. That is the theory. Those people who still have *shambas* there will have to move out. No doubt there will be marker posts along the roads.'

Bright pondered this. 'Seems pretty porous to me. We don't have enough men to cover the huge distances.'

'I know. The trouble is that insurgents can slip away as individuals and disappear among the local people. That is why the chiefs and headmen have been cultivated and why we must keep them on side and not beat up their people. They can easily spot an intruder. The Home Guard will help protect the villages.'

'Talk about loose cannons.'

'I suspect that once this is over they will be disbanded pronto. Someone will have to get all the weapons back. Otherwise we will have good old-fashioned banditry.'

'So, sir, what is to be our role?'

'The Brigadier has told me that we will be going into the forests. Two companies, anyway. The other two will patrol the exclusion zone. I would like you to take command of them.'

'I am very happy with that, sir. Frankly, on a personal level, the forests do not appeal. But if duty calls…'

'No, Major. I will be going into the forests. I am supposed to be the one with jungle experience.'

'How soon do we get into the field?'

'About two months. I am going to start jungle training as soon as I can get clearance. The forests will be a pretty hostile environment for the insurgents as well as for us. But we have better communications and the RAF to bomb them and drop supplies to us. If you and the other battalions can deny access to the forests, we might even starve them out.'

* * *

Michael had permission to take over a small stretch of forest on the south side of Mount Kenya, northeast of Nyeri. He himself led a force of two platoons on a preparatory exercise. He brought in two native trackers from the Kenya Regiment. The platoons were ordered to isolate themselves for a week beforehand, as did Michael, the officers, and NCOs, including Tickell, now promoted RSM. They were not allowed to wash, shave or smoke, and were searched for cigarettes before being transported. Each man had to carry a *panga*, rations, water, weapons, ammunition and a sleeping bag. Once they were in the forest they were not permitted to talk except with permission, and to use hand signals wherever possible. In that week they were given instruction in silent killing by hand, knife or rope. Michael called the men together two days before the operation began.

'We may well encounter large game – buffalo, elephant and rhino. Their eyesight may be poor but they have an acute sense of smell, which is, curiously, one of the reasons why we have not been washing. Our smell will blend in with forest smells and will not be threatening to them. Only in a last extremity are you allowed to shoot them. One reason for not talking is that we must always be on the alert and listen to the creatures of the forest. Monkeys and birds make noises to signal the approach of danger. If we are clumsy and crash through the undergrowth they will give away our presence. In return, they will warn us of an approach by animal or human.

'This exercise will last up to a week. Number One platoon, Lieutenant Jamieson, will camp at a certain location and patrol the area in order to find Number Two platoon's position. Meanwhile Number Two platoon with Lieutenant Berkeley will do the same in the reverse direction. The objective, of course, is to carry off as a prisoner a designated man left in the camp. If the operation is successful you should achieve a capture without the other side noticing. But there is to be no rough stuff. We want you all back in one piece. Your officers will brief you in detail about procedure. There will be radio contact available throughout.

'The experience gathered in this exercise will be of great value to our larger operations later on. There will be a thorough debrief of everyone afterwards, and...you will allowed to wash and smoke. I will be leaving my pipe in my office and I will miss tobacco just as much as you.

'One last thing. There is a possibility that you will come across a group of Mau Mau. You are to engage them, kill as many as you can and search them for any documents or intelligence. If any surrender, they are to be brought in.'

* * *

Much to Michael's surprise the exercise went without undue mishap. One man twisted an ankle badly and he was carried down to a track which led through the centre of the area, and left there to be picked up by Land Rover. Both platoons, though starting ten miles apart, found the opposing camp and came within fifty yards without being detected by the men left behind. They carried off their 'prisoners' and returned to their camps. There were no detailed maps of the area, and the platoon commanders made notes of the topography as they went. Both platoons had to cross the track at some point. Michael, RSM Tickell and Corporal Harun, the radio operator, patrolled it on foot. The shrieking of colobus monkeys ahead caused them to conceal themselves and they observed Lieutenant Jamieson handle a textbook crossing of the track. He was leading with two men; they crept across with weapons at the ready and then signalled to the others to follow two by two. Apart from the cracking of a twig they made no sound.

The advance of ten miles across difficult terrain took three days, as Michael had expected. The men had to cross three ridges and numerous streams. No Mau Mau gangs or their camps were discovered, not could the trackers find any other trace of insurgent activity. There were no encounters with large animals. The weather had not been kind, swelteringly hot during the day but because of the altitude the temperature dropped sharply after dark. On two afternoons there were thunderstorms and heavy rain which brought all movement to a halt. When sketch maps were compared it was found that the platoons must have been, at one point, within no more than half a mile on their opposing courses but neither was aware of the other.

At a general debriefing a day after their return everyone agreed that there should be more waterproof pouches. Matches for lighting the hexamine stoves had to be dried out. The smell of the stoves could be picked up from a hundred yards away, so there could be no cooking away from the overnight bivouac. All tins and rubbish, including used toilet paper, had to be taken away and buried later. A common observation was that they were very tired after sleepless nights, which made concentration and watchfulness more difficult to maintain. Tempers were easily frayed and the discipline of silence imposed additional strains. They suggested that, if possible, friends should be assigned to the same patrols. Michael demurred at this, explaining that while he understood their point, a professional soldier could not choose his comrades. Rather, as a unit they must build up an atmosphere of mutual trust and understanding, so that they knew how each man should react in a situation.

RSM Tickell had a separate meeting with the NCOs which elicited useful points, such as the camouflage of rifles with sacking which would also prevent the noise of metal knocking against metal. Soldiers should carry a spare sweater for the cold at night, and there should be a thorough check of kit by NCOs before a unit set out on patrol. Not every soldier was fully equipped, for example with spare batteries for torches, and some had carried unnecessary items, though perhaps a Bible should be allowed; some men read a passage every morning.

Lieutenants Jamieson and Berkeley reported that all their men had found the experience testing but responded to the challenge very well. They felt proud of themselves and sang the whole way back to Nanyuki. However, the officers expressed some doubt that this sort of operation and the demands it made would be feasible at battalion, or indeed company strength. Two platoons, working together and equipped with bren guns, was perhaps the optimum size of unit in hunting down and destroying the guerillas. A company split into units of that size could cover a great deal of ground and respond more quickly to information given by prisoners.

Michael thanked the officers for their efforts and said that he would be sending a report to the Brigadier. The rest of the day was spent in routine matters and composing a draft of his report, which he discussed with Major Bright. After a drink and dinner in the Mess he turned in early and fell asleep at once.

At three o'clock the next morning he was woken by the Duty Officer with the news that a farm to the north of Mount Kenya was being attacked by a substantial force of Mau Mau.

Chapter Seven

Six Months Earlier

After his confrontation with Frampton Gichuchi was tempted to leave at once, but Mutahi dissuaded him.

'Mr Frampton is not going to chase you away today. Even he could not be so hard-hearted. As long as your father is employed by him you have every right to stay in the *banda*. You must have some pay coming to you. Get your father to collect it. And you must think carefully. There is no reason why you should not seek work on another farm, or go to a town or even Nairobi. Labourers are always needed. However, if you decide to join us as an active member, then you will become a soldier and that means being treated as an enemy. If captured you could be tortured and shot, or imprisoned for a long period of time. Quite apart from anything else, you will be cutting yourself off from your family. Do you really want that? I don't know what Njoka thinks, but I am sure he is not a rebel.'

'I don't care what he thinks.'

'Not now perhaps, but in the years to come, when he is getting old. He will need your support; in fact he will be expecting it. And what about your brothers?'

'They can look after him.'

'Very well. Here is something else to consider. Life in the forest is hard. Here there is always something to eat but in the mountains you have to become a hunter. If you get sick, or injured, no hospital will treat you. And if you desert or betray the movement, the Mau Mau will seek you out and kill you. There is no going back.'

Gichuchi said nothing, so Mutahi went on:

'I am not trying to discourage you. I am just presenting you with the facts.'

Mutahi looked at him. Gichuchi nodded, but did not meet his eyes.

'Well?'

Gichuchi remained silent.

'Let me ask you,' said Mutahi. 'Why are the Mau Mau fighting?'

'To get the British to go away, I suppose.'

'Yes. And when they have gone away, what then?'

Gichuchi shrugged his shoulders.

'I don't know.'

'Do you want Kenya ruled by Kenyans, standing on its own two feet?'

'Yes. That must be right.'

'But it is not only the British who stand in our way. There are a lot of Africans who are content to live under the British, or are content to wait for change. These people have to be dealt with as well.'

'Do you mean kill them?'

'Not necessarily. Just discourage them from working for the British. We must take back the land stolen from us by the British and give it to our people to farm, as they did before. You agree with that, surely.'

'Yes. I do.'

'It is not going to be easy to achieve but it will be worth the hardship. And when we win, you will be hailed as a hero, for daring to fight against the odds.'

Mutahi patted his shoulder. 'I will come back tomorrow and, if you are still of the same mind, I will contact the Mau Mau about you. Stay here for a couple of days, gather your things and take the bus to Nanyuki. Say that you are going to look for work in town. Someone will approach you. He will ask if you are a faithful and true son of Gikuyu and Mumbi. You will reply "I am a loyal brother, even unto death". You will be taken to join a group in the forest and given training in weapons.'

Gichuchi nodded.

'See you tomorrow, then,' said Mutahi, and left him sitting on the ground in front of the *banda*.

* * *

Njoka collected the few shillings owed to Gichuchi from the Farm

Office. He did not attempt to discourage Gichuchi from going, because he recognised that a turning point had come in his son's life. He gave him a little money from his own savings. Gichuchi gathered up his few things into a bag slung over his shoulder and was accompanied by his father to the bus stop.

'Go and see your brothers. They might know of someone looking for labour. Wherever you go, keep your nose clean and say your prayers. Please let us know where you are.'

'I am not sure when I will be able to do that. But if you don't hear from me, don't think the worst has happened.'

They shook hands and Njoka, never usually one to indulge his emotions, hugged him.

'Goodbye, son.'

'Goodbye, Father.'

Njoka walked away and Gichuchi was left alone with his bag at his feet.

At Nanyuki he first went to see his little brother Karumbi, who announced that he was leaving the *duka* at the end of the week and going to work at the Local Surveyor's Office. Gichuchi told him of Mary's death and his leaving the farm. Karumbi shed a boyish tear for him, but Gichuchi told him not to be distressed; he was making a new start and he was glad that Karumbi was doing the same. He asked him if he had heard of any jobs going in town, but Karumbi shook his head.

'Not in town but Njeru might know of something available at the camp. Are you going to see him?'

'Yes. I was hoping I could stay with him for a night or two.'

'Come back and see me, Gichuchi.'

'I will.'

Gichuchi embraced his brother. There being nothing more to be said, he picked up his bag and walked out of town towards the camp. He waited outside for Njeru to finish work.

He had some time to wait. He went over in his mind the events of the last few days; he could still not take in how swiftly his circumstances had changed. All his hopes had been centred on Mary and all his working hours had been devoted to providing for her and their child. There were three choices open to him, he reckoned. He could find a labouring job on a farm in the area so that he could still keep in contact with his family; but that would mean doing what he had always done and held out no prospect for improving his lot. He could go further afield, perhaps to Nairobi, where there must be many opportunities of trying different things; perhaps he could learn a trade. Or he could hang around Nanyuki until he was contacted by the Mau Mau and taken into the forest. After some reflection he decided firmly against staying in the area. He would remain in Nanyuki with his brother Njeru for a few days and, if no approach was made to him during that time, he would take the bus to Nairobi. Whatever happened, the prospects were frightening, but he had nothing to lose.

Njeru was surprised to see him. As they walked back to town, he explained why he had left the farm. Njeru said nothing while he told his story. When he had finished, Njeru took his arm.

'Of course you can stay with me. It's just a shed but there is room. I usually eat in town in the evening. The Army gives me something to eat midday.'

Gichuchi asked him about a job in the camp, even for just a few days. He needed some money in hand.

'They have become very wary of taking on casual labour. You will have to provide a reference from a priest or your former employer.'

'That won't be possible.'

'Well, you can try, anyway. I will vouch for you. Gichuchi, I don't know quite how to say this.' He turned to face Gichuchi. 'I am so sorry about Mary. A lovely girl. And I could see that you were devoted to her. She deserved better than to die like that.'

'Don't talk about her.'

'But you must grieve. It's natural.'

'I want to put all that behind me, and that's that.'

'Very well.'

They walked on in silence. Njeru had a small hut in the shanty area near the market. They bought some food at a stall and then repaired to a shebeen; they drank beer and smoked *bhangi*. Njeru tentatively asked him if he was a brother.

Gichuchi did not answer directly but asked him if he remembered Mutahi.

'I gave him some information about the Armoury,' replied Njeru. 'I understand that rifles and ammunition were taken away. There was a lot of trouble in the camp.'

'Mutahi has persuaded me to join the brothers. I took the oath some time ago. And now the time has come for me. I am just waiting for a call. If it doesn't come soon, then I will go down to Nairobi and find work. There are brothers down there.'

'I won't join,' said Njeru. 'I have work here. It suits me and I am paid regularly. There is a woman in the town. I see her from time to time. I can't expect much more in life, what with my eyes.'

'Ah, women,' sighed Gichuchi. He started to become maudlin and wept copiously until Njeru took him home.

* * *

For several days Gichuchi hung around Nanyuki. He visited Karumbi at the *duka*, but he was usually too busy for more than a few words, though one day they had a good talk after Karumbi's work. He warned his little brother that he would shortly be going away, probably to Nairobi, but wherever he could get permanent employment.

'I'm so glad you are getting on, Karumbi,' he went on. 'Make the most of yourself. It would please Father that at least one of us was making his way in the world. I don't have your skills but I can work hard.'

'Are you a brother?' Karumbi asked directly.

'Me? I have sworn the oath, like many others. That was last year. But nothing has happened since. So I must make a living somehow. Where that will lead, who knows? I might get a call one day to go and fight. Look, it is better for you if you don't know what I am doing. For your own protection. Do you understand?'

'I think so. Don't forget us, though.'

'Be sure I won't.'

One morning Kiriba, Njeru's friend, took pity on him and gave him some shillings for cleaning the forecourt of the garage, but as he had no mechanical skills he could not be anything more than an odd-job man. Every afternoon he went to the Army camp to enquire if any labour was needed, but to no avail. Then he waited for Njeru and together they walked back into town. He also spent a day cleaning floors and latrines at the Sportsman's Arms. When he was not employed he meandered round the town, keeping to obvious places. He went to the bus station to ask about fares to Nairobi. He had enough money and some to spare when he got there, but he could not afford any extravagance. He resolved not to drink so much in the evenings with Njeru, or smoke *bhangi*, which, after initial euphoria, left him with frightening dreams and a sore head.

One day he was sitting outside the market, moodily watching people come and go. He was just about to get up and stretch his legs when a young man in a khaki jacket squatted down beside him.

'I am a friend of Mutahi,' he said.

'I know Mutahi.'

'Are you a faithful and true son of Gikuyu and Mumbi?'

Gichuichi was taken aback for a moment.

'Why? Oh, yes. I am a loyal brother, even unto death.'

'Very good, Gichuchi. Are you ready to come to us?'

'I am. There is nothing for me here.'

'This afternoon, take the *mutatu* to Timau. You will be met there and taken to one of the camps in the forest.'

* * *

Gichuchi was met by Mwangi, a man about his own age. From the bus station they walked to the market and collected some produce in the baskets Mwangi had brought. Gichuchi noticed that no cash changed hands and asked Mwangi why.

'It's a form of protection for the stall holders. If they supply us with food from time to time, we leave them alone. It doesn't really cost them very much and they are grateful that their *shambas* are not destroyed.'

'But why should we destroy them, take away their livelihood?'

'Because many of these people are so-called loyalists. They prefer to be subservient to the *wazungu*. They need to be reminded where their true duty lies. You see, we know who are our friends, and those who are not.'

There was still one basket to fill. Mwangi went to the stall at the end of the line selling papaya. Mwangi held out the basket. The stall holder placed two parcels on the bottom and piled fruit over the top.

Gichuchi looked enquiringly at Mwangi..

'There are other things we need beside food,' he said.

From Timau Gichuchi and Mwangi walked along a track for some miles past small *shambas*. In one or two the *banda* was burnt down and the small fields untended.

'These belonged to people who would not support us.'

Their loads were heavy and Gichuchi was glad when they came to the edge of the forest. A man was waiting there. After a brief greeting, Mwangi took out the papaya from the basket and showed him the parcels at the bottom. He took them and put them in a rucksack. Then without a word he set off into the forest along the track.

'Ammunition taken from the Police Station,' explained Mwangi. 'Come on. We have an hour's walk ahead of us and we want to get there before it gets really dark.'

The track into the forest enabled them to move fast at first. Then it began to climb steeply uphill. Where it turned sharp right to follow the contour there was a narrow path leading straight on, difficult to see in the gathering gloom. Mwangi put down the baskets and took out a short length of rope. He tied one end round his waist and the other round Gichuchi.

'Not very far to go now but we don't want you to get lost. Just follow directly behind me. I won't use a torch. The path is well-worn but it is easy to take a wrong turning.'

Mwangi set off at a steady pace. Gichuchi tripped once or twice but came to no harm. They did not speak. Around them were the usual noises of the forest. At one point there was an outburst of screaming from Sykes monkeys and a chattering of *ndete* birds. Mwangi stood stock still. After a few moments the noises calmed down.

'What was that?' whispered Gichuchi.

'Something big. Rhino, possibly. It has moved on. We must be downwind of it.'

'I have never seen one.'

Mwangi resumed the march and having crossed a stream, which was freezing cold, they came to the camp. It was in a small clearing with tents and shelters under surrounding trees. At one side at the edge of the trees was a fire with cooking pots bubbling and a spit, on which a deer was being roasted. Over the fire was a corrugated iron roof, to keep the rain off and conceal the fire from patrolling aircraft. Having deposited the market produce, Mwangi took Gichuchi to his shelter, a canvas affair covered with foliage. Inside were some blankets and a few possessions.

'You will be sharing with me,' he said. 'You can leave your things there quite safely. We respect our colleagues' property.'

Gichuchi dropped his bag.

'Now I must take you to see the Brigadier,' said Mwangi

'Brigadier?'

'Yes. Njirami Warui. He commands this camp. There are about seventy of us. You are the latest recruit.'

Gichuchi was led to a large hut set well back in the trees. Mwangi pulled back the curtain and ushered Gichuchi in. Standing by a table was a tall figure.

'The Brigadier', explained Mwangi.

'Who are you?' the Brigadier asked.

'Gichuchi, *bwana*, son of Njoka.'

'Welcome, Gichuchi, son of Njoka. You look a fine upstanding fellow. Have you ever used firearms?'

'Never.'

'Well, we can teach you. Do you have any weapons at all? A *panga*?'

'No, just a pocket knife.'

'Where do you come from?'

Gichuchi said that he had been working on a farm not far from Nanyuki but had left because he had been beaten by his master. And his wife had died.

'So you hate the *wazungu*?'

'Yes.'

'We don't have many women here, just women brought along by their men. We respect that relationship. I won't have any quarrels about women. And I do not tolerate buggery. The penalty for that is death. Do you understand?'

'Yes, *bwana*.'

'One other thing we are very strict about. Ammunition is in short supply, so there is no firing except when explicit orders are given. We have some grenades, but only certain people are allowed to use them. So for most close fighting we use *pangas*. It is very important that these rules are obeyed. And no smoking. We must be able to smell the *Wa Johnny*.'

Gichuchi nodded.

'I want to hear that you will obey these rules.'

'I will obey these rules and I understand why they are there.'

'Good. Mwangi will look after you and you will be in his squad. Dismiss.'

Gichuchi was uncertain what to do, so he muttered something, bowed and turned away. Mwangi took his arm.

'I'll show you where things are.'

Over the next few days Gichuchi got to know his immediate colleagues. He was given lessons in jungle craft and weapon training, though he only actually fired a rifle twice. But he hit the target both times. His physique was tested by some forced marches, carrying significant loads, and his strength and endurance were noted.

His first operation was a raid on a white-owned farm not far from the forest in the direction of Meru. Ten of them set out, two with rifles and the rest with *pangas*. The objective was to hamstring cattle and carry off some goats for food. The gang, led by Mwangi, set off towards evening and encamped near the edge of the forest overnight. Before dawn, clad only in loincloths, they moved out into the open country, with about a mile of *leleshwa* bush to cover before they could reach the cattle bomas. They spread out and did not concentrate until they were at the farm. Within five minutes they had hamstrung ten cattle with a quick slash on the back of the hind legs. In the next pen were goats. They seized five, slit their throats and carried them off over their shoulders.

The bellowing and bleating of the animals had aroused the guards who came running just as the goats were being carried off. The two men with rifles, who had taken up position at the gate, fired twice each and brought one guard down and forced the others to take cover. Within a minute the members of the gang had scattered into the bush and did not pause until they had reached the forest. Once inside they went to their overnight bivouac and in a stream washed the goats' blood off themselves and put on their outer clothes. The goats were tied to poles, each carried by two men. Then, taking great care to remove all traces of their presence, they made their way back to the camp, where a hot meal was waiting for them.

Mwangi's gang carried out two more similar raids over the next few weeks. Both were successful though, in the second, one brother tripped and fell, and was captured. Mwangi had no compunction about ordering his best marksman to shoot him dead before he could give away any information.

Gichuchi was horrified.

'If we can't carry away our wounded,' Mwangi explained later, 'we must kill them. For the good of everybody. He was a friend of mine but I have spared him from torture at the hands of the Home Guard or Special Branch. No one can hold out for long against torture. He will be always remembered as a hero of the brotherhood.'

When not plundering farms, Mwangi's gang was engaged in carrying food supplies brought close to the edge of the forest by sympathetic supporters from the Reserves. Gichuchi acted as a porter. The supplies were left hidden in the bush, sometimes for several days before they could be collected. On one occasion they found a man on watch beside the cache. He heard them approach and waved. Mwangi thought he might be a decoy and sent Gichuchi up to him while the others remained under cover. As he drew near, the man took off his shirt and trousers to show that he was unarmed. Gichuchi gripped his *panga* tightly and came within a few feet.

'Don't be afraid, brother,' the man said. 'Here are your supplies.' He pointed to a dip in the ground covered by some foliage. He walked across, took away the branches and showed some sacks of flour with an open box containing packets of sugar and salt and some fruit. Beside it was a tin ammunition box.

Gichuchi thanked him and called to Mwangi, who approached cautiously. When he had scrutinised the man and scanned the area carefully, he called up the rest of the gang who loaded the goods onto their backs. Mwangi took the ammunition in a rucksack. The man got dressed again and took Mwangi aside.

'I have a message for the Brigadier. The *wazungu* are forcing more and more of our people into villages and the Home Guard are acting as garrisons. Already many brothers have been killed by them. Anyone they suspect is shot out of hand. It will become more difficult to bring supplies to you. And there is another thing. The British Army is planning to clear a strip round the forest a mile wide. Those who live there will be moved out into villages away from the forest. This area will be patrolled by the Army.'

'I see. We will have to be more self-sufficient.'

'We will do what we can and will keep you informed as much as possible. Our people report that a new squadron has flown into the airfield at Nanyuki. So you can expect more air patrols. Bombs are being brought in by lorry.'

Mwangi did not share this news with the rest of the gang but kept the information to himself until he had spoken to the Brigadier.

A few days later, Mwangi's squad went out on another expedition to bring in supplies. They had further to go than before, and reckoned to be away three days. They went to the appointed place to pick up the supplies but when they arrived, they found that the flour sacks had been cut open and the contents scattered over the ground. From the droppings, it was evident that birds had been helping themselves to the fruit. The ammunition box was filled with pebbles.

Mwangi took in the scene immediately and ordered his squad to retreat to the forest as quickly as they could. Fortunately it was not a trap; there was no one lying in wait. Back in the forest they went back to their overnight bivouac. There was some food left which they finished up. Then they made ready for a rapid march and cleaned the site. After an hour, Mwangi halted and by signs ordered his men to lie down. Gichuchi and the others obeyed without question, but he did not understand why. He looked at the man next to him who put a finger to his ear and pinched his nose. Immediately Gichuchi understood. His heart began to thump and he heard the voices of the *Wa Johnny* and clattering of mess tins. He could smell the hexamine stoves and the smoke of cigarettes.

Mwangi signalled everyone to stay put. He wriggled forward very slowly until he had a view of the clearing where the British soldiers were. They were a patrol of about twenty men brewing tea. Several brushwood shelters were being constructed. In the middle was a radio set with a tall aerial.

Mwangi lay motionless for half an hour. During that time he spotted three sentries between himself and the camp, the nearest about ten yards from him. The British patrol was encamped in the line of their route. There was nothing that his men could do but retreat and take a long detour. Very carefully he turned around and inched his way back. By hand signals he indicated that they should retreat. Gichuchi got onto his knees clumsily and started to move away, snapping a twig in the process.

'*Pole, pole*,' hissed the man next to him. Gichuchi obeyed, slowly crawling forward and putting his knees where his hands had rested.

The movement caused a twittering of birds. Everyone froze. Mwangi, who was bringing up the rear, looked around, but the British had not taken any notice of them, even though they were still less than fifty yards from the sentry. Just then there was a clap of thunder and it began to rain heavily. Mwangi signalled that they should speed up but still keep close to the ground. Within a few minutes they had put a distance between themselves and the British. Mwangi called them all together and whispered that they must keep going, no matter how cold, hungry or wretched they felt.

'As long as we are moving we are closer to base. I know a path not far from here which we can follow for most of the way. When it gets dark we will rope ourselves together in pairs and cut across a valley. There will be a stream to cross but we must help each other. Any questions?'

No one replied.

'Let's go.'

When they got to the path they broke into a trot which they kept up for four hours until darkness came on. Gichuchi was grateful for the exercise, since it kept him warm. At a small stream Mwangi ordered a short rest. Before Gichuchi could stiffen up, they were on the move again and soon came to a stream which the recent rainfall had turned into a river. Now roped together they crossed with great care. One man slipped and was almost carried away, but a concerted effort hauled him back. They reached their camp three hours later, very tired and very hungry.

At dawn, Mwangi went to the Brigadier's hut to report on their expedition. Njirami heard him out in silence.

Then he said, 'Have you eaten?'

'Me? Not yet. The cook is preparing a meal for the men.'

'What you say is worrying, the fact that our supplies have been destroyed. Someone along the line must have given the game away. I will look into it. As for the British patrol, I realise that they are stepping up their jungle operations. We had an aircraft overhead yesterday. Fortunately we heard it in time, and everyone was able to get under cover, and the fire was out. But just in case we are going to move. I have a site in mind towards Nanyuki but not too far from here. I think we can do it in one day, tomorrow. I am going to check it out today. There is another reason for moving in that direction. I am planning a full scale raid on a big farm. It's time we showed General China* what we can do.'

* Another Mau Mau commander in the forests of Mount Kenya.

Chapter Eight

Njirami's force moved camp the following day. Some of the shelters were abandoned deliberately and the ashes from the fire were not removed, to give the impression that the camp was still occupied. One or two items of clothing and a *panga* were left in the open. A roundabout route was taken to the west and a small party brought up the rear and removed as far as possible traces of their passage by destroying footprints and covering the path with loose foliage. Mwangi's squad was sent out in the opposite direction, with instructions to create an obvious path to the east, breaking off branches and leaving the odd item on the ground, until they reached one of the main tracks through the forest, about four miles away. Then they walked backwards the way that they had come. They were not far from the original campsite when they heard aircraft engines and took cover. Three planes from the base at Nanyuki came in very low and dropped bombs onto and around the camp. One bomb went wide and killed two members of Mwangi's squad. Their comrades stripped the bodies of clothing and removed all their gear. Mwangi took charge of their small personal possessions. One of them had a woman in the camp and she would get his things; the other's he would distribute among his squad. Then he led his men by a circuitous route along an old elephant path and reached the rest of Njirami's force by midnight.

Gichuchi and the squad were allowed to rest that day after a substantial meal. Meanwhile Mwangi and other squad leaders planned the attack on the farm. One of the day labourers there was a passive member of the Mau Mau and had supplied a rough sketch map, but he did not know of any defences. The attackers were to be divided into two groups: the larger one would destroy the *bandas* and the dam; the other, led by Mwangi, would storm the main house and then set fire to the farm buildings. All the weapons available to the force were to be taken: rifles, two sten guns, three shot guns and six grenades, as well as the *pangas* that most men carried. The whole force would lie up near the edge of the forest until midnight. Then it would descend at a run, shouting and blowing whistles to create confusion. Any *watu* who resisted were to be killed, and as many *wazungu* as they came across. Gichuchi was given a .303 rifle and six rounds of ammunition, all that could be spared.

'Try to make every shot count.'

A large meal was served in the afternoon, after which Njirami called the men together. He stood on a box to say a few words:

'Now we have a chance to strike a great blow against the British, where it hurts them the most, their farms which are their source of income. They occupy land which they have taken from us. They deserve no mercy. Sadly, some of our African brothers have thrown in their lot with them. We don't have time to persuade them to our cause and therefore those that resist us must be shot. One thing I insist on. Do not be distracted by the opportunity to carry off booty, whatever it may be. We must move fast and we will not have time to linger. We have committed nearly all our resources to this attack. Make the most of it and Ngai will be on our side. Remember: "Forward ever; backward never."'

Leaving a few men and the women to guard the camp, the force moved off in silence to their positions within sight of the farm but under cover.

At the mention of *bandas* Gichuchi was reminded of his father. He was glad he was assigned to the attack on the house, not the Africans. Despite the tough talk from Njirami, he had his doubts about the policy of 'he who is not with us is against us'. If the Mau Mau was to succeed in its aim of driving the British out it would need all the help it could get from the African population. He resolved therefore that if a brother or sister came into his sights he would shoot high, no matter what. He dare not share these thoughts with anyone else, least of all Mwangi, who was a good leader but one who would brook no argument and, as Gichuchi well knew, could be quite ruthless.

At the signal the force moved out of the cover of the forest and in silence trotted down the track that led past the *bandas*. It was very dark and only a few lights peeped out from the line of huts. Just before they reached it, the group assigned to the house slipped past quietly. Only when they were closer to the farm buildings did the other group start shouting and blowing whistles. People came out of their *bandas* to see what the noise was and started screaming when the huts were set on fire and rifles were fired. One man emerged from his hut and started firing at the attackers. He was shot on the spot. The Mau Mau went into the hut and dragged his wife and small children outside. They were hacked to death. Seeing this, other people came out with their hands up and watched miserably while their *bandas* were set on fire. Some tried to escape towards the fields but were killed by sten gun fire.

As Mwangi's squad neared the farm buildings and the main house, suddenly lights came on and they were caught in the open. A siren sounded. Mwangi ran forward and hurled a grenade at the door of the porch but he was shot down immediately. The grenade exploded against the door, which swung open. Gichuchi and others gave covering fire while several men charged through. However behind the door at the back of the porch was a grill that had been drawn across. They tried to break it down by brute force but without success. There was nothing for it but to retreat outside and throw another grenade. Fire from an upstairs window caught them and three men went down. Gichuchi fired at the figure in the window but did not know whether he had scored a hit. He heard the explosion of thunderflashes in the farm buildings and turned to look. He saw two of his colleagues running away from five men armed with *pangas* and a shotgun. One went down and was quickly dispatched. The other threw down his rifle and ran as fast as he could. As he crossed the yard he was brought down by a shot from the house. Gichuchi realised that the attack was losing momentum; at least six men of Mwangi's group were dead or dying. His position behind a water tank was exposed. Without too much calculation he decided that a quick death from a bullet was preferable to being mutilated and hacked. He had three shots left in the magazine. He fired one shot at the window and ran as fast as he could to the side of the house. He found cover behind a small hut. He waited there as the sounds of the firefight diminished. Either he could surrender or rush the back door of the house and create as much havoc as he could before the fatal shot. Remembering the Mau Mau slogan, he charged at the door. It was locked. He fired two shots at the lock, but to no avail. He beat at the door with the butt of his rifle. The wood of a panel splintered and he was able to reach in and draw back the bolt. He pushed the door open and entered the room. He ran across it and into a corridor. He was confronted by a woman and a young girl. The woman was pointing a rifle at him; she fired but the bullet missed him. He realised that he had no more shots in his magazine. He gripped his rifle by the barrel to swing it like a club. But a glance at the girl, looking so small and vulnerable, gave him pause and, throwing down his rifle, he turned to escape. The woman fired again and the bullet grazed his temple. He staggered with the impact, hit his head on the edge of a shelf and passed out.

⋆ ⋆ ⋆

When Michael was woken with news of the attack, he alerted the detail, commanded by Lieutenant Jamieson, which was on duty for a rapid response. Within a quarter of an hour it was on its way to the farm in two lorries; Michael, with Corporal Harun, his radio operator, followed in a Land Rover. One lorry drove up beyond the *bandas* to cut off the retreat into the forest. Following a well-practised drill, the soldiers fanned out and drove the attackers back towards the blazing *bandas*, shooting anyone who brandished a weapon. The lorry returned down the track and a bren gun mounted above the cab prevented any escape on that side. The *watu* were mostly following instructions and running towards the farm buildings. The other lorry was parked by the yard. A loudspeaker called on the terrorists to surrender. Within a few minutes the soldiers had swept through the farm buildings shooting any armed Mau Mau found there and putting out a small fire that had been started. The *watu* began to arrive and they were shepherded into one of the barns. Surviving Mau Mau were herded into an enclosure and kept under guard.

Meanwhile Michael went to the house and made contact with

Patrick, who reported that everyone was safe inside the house, but they had a terrorist tied up on the floor.

'Leave him there for the time being.'

'You came very quickly,' said Patrick. 'Thank you.'

'We have had a rapid response drill going for some weeks, but this is our first big operation.'

'Well, it seems to have worked well. Can we go outside now and see what has happened to the people?'

Michael left the corporal in the house. He and Patrick walked across to the barn. There was a lot of shouting and weeping. Patrick banged with his stick and called for silence. He spoke in Gikuyu.

'You are safe now. Colonel Charteris is here with his soldiers. They will stay here until daylight and check the farm for any intruders.' He produced a list. 'Please answer your names.'

When the roll call was taken, Thomas's family was found to be missing, and seven individuals.

'I want you to remain in here for the time being. There are soldiers to guard you.' He pointed to three men who had appeared at the door. 'When morning comes, we will be able to see what the damage is and locate those who are missing. My wife asks that some women should come to help her provide you with something to drink. Any volunteers?'

Three elderly women came forward and were taken to the house to help Ephraim and the houseboys.

Annabel came out to the barn and asked if anyone was hurt. One man had fallen over in the darkness and had cut his head badly. The wound was cleaned and dressed. No one else came forward, but she suspected that some people were still too shocked to react to her request. And there might well be wounded lying out on the farm, perhaps in the fields, but nothing could be done for them just then.

Michael radioed for another squad to be sent to the farm at dawn, to relieve the duty detail. Two Land Rovers arrived with Special Branch officers. They asked if there were any people in the barn who did not belong to the farm.

'There may have been. I can't be sure.'

'We'll have a look. Maybe your people can identify any strangers. The prisoners can wait till morning.'

As it happened, three terrorists had infiltrated themselves into the *watu*, who were now getting over their shock. These men were soon picked out and were taken aside by Special Branch.

Michael spoke to Lieutenant Jamieson and heard his account of events.

'That was well done. Keep your men in position around the farm buildings. There is nothing more we can do until dawn. Then we will search the whole property. I have asked the relief detail to bring a brew. Any casualties?'

'No, sir.'

'Good. Any ideas of the number of terrorists?'

'We estimate about fifty in all. There are ten dead in and around the farm buildings. We certainly shot a few up by the *bandas*. Maybe twelve prisoners. Some must have escaped.'

Michael looked at his watch. 'It will be dawn in two hours. Keep your men on their toes, just in case they attempt another attack or someone gets excited. Don't hesitate to shoot to kill if they don't respond to a challenge. These men are outside the law.'

'Very good, sir.'

When he was satisfied that the situation was stable, he went to the house and spoke to Patrick.

'Did you use your safe room?'

'It all happened so quickly. The terrorists certainly had the element of surprise. We had no inkling that an attack was imminent. All I could was to hand out rifles to Annabel and Jane. Annabel is a good shot. We didn't have time to barricade the back door which is how our intruder got in. However, the precautions I took, the siren, the lights, seem to have worked. In the end we did not have to use the safe room, thanks to you chaps turning up so promptly.'

'Let's see about that prisoner you have.'

'Here's Jane. She'll tell you all about him.'

In the excitement, Michael had not been able to give her much thought, but she was always at the back of his mind.

'Hello, Michael.' She gave him a hug. 'Thank God for the British Army.'

'I'm very glad you are safe.'

She said that when the attack started Annabel told her to take one of the rifles and go to Naomi's room. When she went in and went to peer outside, the window had shattered by a bullet. She grabbed the child and took her downstairs. She thought that the corridor was the safest place since there were several escape routes off it. The man had burst in through the back door and come into the corridor. He had made to swing at her with his rifle, since he had run out of ammunition (she had later checked the magazine), but then dropped it and started to flee. She had fired again, hitting him somewhere in the head. He fell, hitting his head on the corner of a chest of drawers, and passed out on the floor. She had screamed. Ephraim and the house boys came running. They had tied him up and left him flat on his face. One of the boys watched over him with Jane's rifle.

'Is Naomi all right?'

'I put her to bed in my room, which faces the back, so that she should not see what was going on in the yard. She was sound asleep when I went to her and I had to carry her downstairs. She never really woke up and she is fast asleep again, I think.'

'Well done,' said Michael. 'You were very brave and steady.'

'Maybe. I didn't have time to think. I hope I haven't killed him. He was running away, after all.'

'Let's have a look at him.'

Michael went through to the corridor, unbuttoning his service revolver. He told the house boy to put his rifle on the ground, pointing away from him; Michael had noticed that the safety catch was off.

The house boy did so and went away to the servants' quarters. Michael looked at the head wound, which had bled profusely but seemed to be only a deep graze. The man was beginning to come round, so Michael pulled him into a sitting position and leant him against the wall. Jane fetched a cloth and some warm water and cleaned his face; the flow of blood had dried up. He stank abominably.

'Go and bring some warm sweet tea.' She went away. Then Michael asked, in English and Swahili.

'What is your name?'

The man did not reply at first, so he was asked again.

'Gichuchi.'

'Well, Gichuchi, you are in big trouble.' He took his revolver from its holster and showed it to him. 'Unless you cooperate, I will not hesitate to shoot you.'

Gichuchi trembled.

'Stand up.'

His hands were bound behind his back and his legs were tied at the ankles. He staggered to his feet and Michael took a step back to survey him. He was a tallish man, broad shouldered and with good muscles. A thought began to enter Michael's mind. He pulled a stool across and told him to sit down.

Jane came in with a cup of tea. She held it to his lips while Michael kept the gun pointing at him.

He drank the tea and muttered a thank you.

'Now I am going to bandage your wound,' she said. 'OK, Michael?'

'Fine. I think he is someone we could use, so let's be nice to him.' But he did not put away his revolver.

The bullet had scraped the temple and had taken a little bit out of the top of his ear. It must have hurt a great deal. Another quarter inch and it would have shattered his skull.

Jane put some TCP on a piece of lint and deftly tied a strip of *banda*ge round his head. The ointment stung painfully and he groaned. Jane produced some aspirin and fed him two tablets. Then Michael tied him round the waist to the leg of the chest of drawers which was heavy.

'I must leave him here. But he won't be going away in a hurry. I want to keep him separate from the other prisoners.'

* * *

When dawn came, the *watu* were allowed to return to their *bandas*. As it happened, only four were totally destroyed and Patrick organised a party to rebuild them; the others could be repaired. As the

Mau Mau did not carry off any loot, people were able to gather up their scattered possessions. There were seven bodies to be identified and buried; Patrick sent a message to the local pastor. The grimmest sight was Thomas's family, he himself shot and his wife and children hacked to death.

After the arrival of another detail of soldiers, a search was carried out of the farm property, which took some time. Michael drove Patrick up to the dam at the top. A grenade had been used in an attempt to blow a gap in the wall, but the structure was too solid to sustain any damage. At the farm buildings the dead terrorists were laid out in the barn and were examined by Special Branch, who were able to identify some of them. The bodies were then thrown onto the back of a truck and taken away to be buried. Special Branch also carried out a preliminary interrogation of the prisoners and three were separated from the rest and taken to Nanyuki; the rest went to the prison camp at Meru.

Meanwhile, the first detail was given breakfast and stood down. Before they climbed onto their lorries, Patrick thanked them for their efforts and handed Lieutenant Jamieson some cash to buy beer for them.

Michael was invited to breakfast in the main house. He was waiting for a report from the detail searching the property.

'What are you going to do with the chap tied up in the corridor?' Patrick asked.

'I have in mind using him as a member of a special gang to track down the Mau Mau leaders. I'll take him back to Nanyuki myself and see what our intelligence *wallahs* can get out of him. There are schemes to turn prisoners round and forsake their oaths. This is what we are working on in the tribal reserves. We are patrolling the prohibited areas to catch refugees from the forests. When it comes to the forests, my experience in jungle warfare suggests that big sweeps and bombing can achieve quite a lot, but if we are to crush the Mau Mau completely within a reasonable time we have to go after them using the same skills that they employ against us. We can train the British squaddie in stalking skills but our Africans are much better. For a start they have more natural patience. We should infiltrate small gangs into the forest to track down and kill the Mau Mau leaders or, better still, capture them.'

'But won't they prefer to die?'

'Perhaps. But hunger drives men to desert. When they can no longer be supported by sympathisers in the reserves because supplies cannot get through to the forest, then they will be sorely tempted to throw in the towel and give themselves up. A short spell in detention camp will seem a better proposition than slow death by starvation.'

'I see. Well, I hope it works. I am full of anger at what they have done to the *watu*, people who work for an honest livelihood. Those prisoners…I would crucify the lot. That sounds very silly, but that is what I feel at the moment.'

'I understand. But you have to look beyond this present crisis.'

'I know, Mike,' said Patrick, 'and I will. It's just that at the moment I am very tired and somehow we all have to get through this day.' He took a sip of coffee. 'Ah. Here's Jane. How are you? And Naomi? I am ashamed to say I have been too preoccupied to think about her. But she was in your capable hands.'

'She's fine,' Jane replied. 'I have managed to keep her from seeing the bodies, but she is asking questions. Perhaps you could satisfy her curiosity, Michael.'

'I will do my best.'

'Don't talk down to her. She will be cross with you if you do.'

Annabel came in, grabbed a cup of coffee and sat down.

'How goes it?' Patrick asked.

'Most people are physically unharmed. Just a few need dressings for cuts and bruises, and there is one with a flesh wound. I will take him to Nanyuki later. But they are all very shocked, Patrick. And those who have lost husbands who have been shot are prostrate. There is nothing we can do but let them have their mourning, and see that they are supported with whatever they need. In due course you'll have to decide what to do with them.'

'I know. But I am not going to rush things.'

'Very wise. Mike, your chaps have done a terrific job. I see that some are now helping to repair some of the *bandas*.'

'Many of them have families who still live in *bandas*.'

There was a knock on the door. Patrick went to answer it.

'Lieutenant Havers, sir, for Colonel Charteris.'

'Yes. Please come in.'

Havers reported that the whole farm had been searched and no terrorists had been found. Apart from the *bandas* of the workforce, no obvious damage had been done.

'Very good, Havers. Call your men in and let them have a brew. I will discuss with Mr Howarth if he needs any more assistance. That man tied up in the house. His name is Gichuchi. When you go, take him with you and put him in a cell by himself. And treat him with kid gloves.'

'Sir.'

Patrick and Annabel got up from the table and went out. Michael was left alone with Jane.

'It's lovely to see you again,' she said, 'but in distressing circumstances.'

'I am glad in a guilty sort of way that this has given me a chance for a few minutes with you.'

'Surely you can stop being a commanding officer for a moment.'

He got up, came round the table and kissed her.

'Will that do?' he asked.

'For now. Will you say hello to Naomi?'

Naomi came in.

'Hello, Michael. This is the first time I have seen you in uniform.'

'Well, I am on duty, Naomi.'

'Have you killed many men?'

'My soldiers have, to protect you and the farm workers. It is sad, but there are misguided people who think they can achieve their ends by violence. It's up to me and my men to stop them.'

'Did you kill all of them?'

'No. We have taken some prisoners. Just a few escaped because they ran away as soon as my soldiers arrived.'

'That man in the house. Jane shot at him.'

'I thought for a moment he was going to attack you,' said Jane. 'I am very glad I didn't kill him. I didn't really mean to fire. It just happened.'

Michael put his hand on hers. 'I once told you that it takes training to handle a firearm under stress, training that you have not had.'

'Well, I will never hold a gun again.'

'Let's hope that you never have to.'

'What are you going to do with the man?' Naomi asked.

'He is probably someone we can bring over to our side. I don't think he is a fanatic. In fact, he might be quite glad to be captured and have his wound tended to. You see, Naomi, we won't ever be able to kill all the terrorists. Much better that we should try to win them over. Turn them into good citizens.'

With that Naomi seemed to be satisfied. Jane told her to get her books out ready for the morning lessons.

When they were alone, Jane asked: 'Can I hope to see you again… sometime…and without all this?' She pointed to his colonel's tabs.

'As soon as ever we can. I am based in Nanyuki for the foreseeable future, just down the road. Here is my office telephone number, if you can find somewhere to ring from. You will probably get my corporal initially, but don't worry. He is very discreet.'

'Won't you be very busy?'

'Up to my eyes. But even I can take a few hours off at the weekend, unless the Mau Mau show their ugly face again.'

'Patrick and Annabel will need a lot of help just now. But when things are back to normal, I can come down to Nanyuki. Not far away.'

'I'll look forward to that.'

They got up and went outside.

'Time to go. Look, I must contact Patrick anyway in a day or so. Perhaps we could have a word then.'

They kissed and he went off to find Patrick. He was talking to people repairing their *bandas*. Lieutenant Havers was with him. Michael told him to have his men back in camp by 18.00 hours.

'In the meantime, Havers, keep your men under arms, just in case, but if Mr Howarth wants some help, let him use them. I will be on my way now.'

'Sir.'

Patrick walked a few steps with Michael.

'Thank you again, and your men. They have been terrific.'

'Part of the service. Patrick, can I ask you about a private matter? I would like to keep contact with Jane. If I radio you, as I will do in a day or so to find out how things are, can I speak to her as well?'

'Of course. And she can have some time off with you in Nanyuki, or wherever. She is a great girl.'

When Michael got back to the house a policeman was waiting.

'Inspector Davies, sir, Special Branch. We have been checking the prisoners. I gather you have bagged a terrorist for yourself.'

'Yes. I tell you about him later today. I have something in mind.'

'I see.'

'Don't worry. I will keep you posted.'

'Well, I would like you to know that you have netted quite an important fish, Njirami Warui, the local Mau Mau commander. They call him the Brigadier. We'll take him back to Nanyuki and give him a grilling.'

Chapter Nine

As it happened, Michael himself could not contact Patrick for several days, but asked Lieutenant Havers to drive up and check that all was well. He gave him an envelope to take, which contained a summary of Michael's own report on the attack, and a note for Jane.

> Alas, I must go soldiering again up to Nakuru to deal with a counter-terrorist action by another of my companies. I expect I will be away for a few days. But when I get back I will radio the farm and we can fix a date to meet.
>
> M xx
>
> PS Would love to say more…

When he eventually returned to Nanyuki, he spent a day with Major Bright dealing with battalion matters, and then he was summoned to a conference at Army HQ in Nairobi for battalion commanders. His men were praised by the Chief of Staff, who quoted from a letter he had received from Patrick. Another colonel, Fanshawe, queried why he had not killed more terrorists.

'When it comes to the crunch,' he said, 'prisoners are a nuisance. The detention camps are full. Special Branch can't process any more. The more we kill now the sooner the whole ghastly business will be over. In their most recent engagement my men killed sixty-nine.'

'The body count is not a matter for competition,' replied the Chief of Staff testily. 'We have to tread carefully. Questions have been asked in Parliament about our conduct and that of the Home Guard with relation to suspects. General Erskine is much exercised by this. I would remind you that one of your colleagues is facing an enquiry on just such a matter.'

'Well, we can't be blamed for the actions of the Home Guard.'

'No, but General Erskine has responsibility for all security elements. I agree that the Home Guard can be a liability but they are an essential part of the political campaign, giving the Africans a share in their own defence.'

There being no more comment on the subject, he turned to Michael.

'Michael, you have some ideas to share with us.'

'Yes, sir. Quite soon we will be undertaking large scale sweeps through the forests, to flush the terrorists out by driving them towards the prohibited areas around the forests, where our forces will be waiting for them. However, I wonder how many of us here have had direct experience of jungle fighting, of the difficulties, dangers and sheer unpleasantness of it.' He told the assembled officers of the exercises he had carried out with his African troops on the south side of Mount Kenya. 'We can put whole brigades into the field but the area is so big and the terrain is such that we can't winkle then out of every nook and cranny. These terrorists are skilled in jungle craft and they can simply disappear while the *Wa Johnny* are crashing around, giving away their presence miles off.

'We do need regular troops to drive the terrorists towards the waiting guns and to patrol the prohibited areas so that supplies do not get through to them. But we also need gangs like theirs to seek out and destroy the leadership in the heart of the forests. My African troops have shown that they have the necessary endurance and skills. And we need former Mau Mau to provide us with information about local intelligence and terrorist methods. I am working with Special Branch in our area to pool information.'

'Will you be there, Michael, crawling through the undergrowth?' asked Fanshawe.

'My men will expect it of me and my officers.'

'Rather you than me,' replied Fanshawe, who was of generous build. 'Look, can't we bomb them? The RAF has command of the air. Once we have located their camps we can call down high explosive on them, or perhaps even napalm. It will save a lot of trouble.'

'Quite apart from the political implications of using napalm,' Michael replied, 'the Mau Mau are mobile. They can move camp very quickly and leave virtually no trace of where they have been. And, it must be admitted, our radios don't work very well in that terrain. The RAF mostly relies on visual acquisition of targets. The Mau Mau can hear them coming from miles away. And they are very attuned to the danger signals given off by animals and birds. That is why our troops must live close to nature, as they do.'

'What specific action do you have in mind, Michael?' the Chief of Staff asked.

'In about a month, after a period of training, I propose to put four teams, or gangs, into the forest, first two, then the other two. Each will be commanded by an officer and there may be someone from Special Branch. Each operation will last a week at the most. After these initial operations, we will review progress and report back.'

'Very good, Michael. And the rest of your battalion?'

'Logistical support of the forest teams, of course. Patrolling the prohibited areas, as directed, and protection for farms, as in our latest operation. We will be kept pretty busy.'

'All this sounds pretty positive. But I will have to convince Sir George.'

* * *

Meanwhile Gichuchi had been kept in solitary confinement at the army camp. His wound was dressed and soon healed. He was allowed to take a shower and given Army denims. After a week he was interviewed by a Special Branch officer. The questioning was gentle, firstly to test his command of English and general intelligence. Then, when he felt that Gichuchi was comfortable with the situation and giving direct answers, the policeman asked him about his family and background. Gichuchi, who had had plenty of time to brood on his predicament and was expecting to be shot at any moment, willingly told his story, and when it came to Mary's death, he wept. The policeman was sympathetic, gave him time to recover and asked him about his brothers. Gichuchi said that Njeru worked in the camp and Karumbi at the District Surveyor's Office. At this, the policeman made a note and then looked up at him.

'You will understand that you cannot be allowed to see them just yet, but you will be allowed to in due course, if you behave yourself.'

'I understand.'

The policeman moved onto Gichuchi's time with the Mau Mau. He was reluctant to speak, since he had sworn the oath, and he was afraid terrible things might happen to him and his family if he broke it.

'Don't worry. We can keep an eye on your family. We know all about these oaths. The oath you swore was a sham, a bit of ritual designed to impress you. But it does not count for anything. I have come across many people like yourself who have confessed their part in the Mau Mau or have given us information and have come to no harm. In fact they feel much better for having told us everything. The Mau Mau are simply gangsters and they have nothing to offer ordinary folk like you. If they win, they won't bring peace, just more terror and intimidation. I have a suggestion. There is a village elder here, a much respected man, and he will conduct a little ceremony for you. Once you have admitted your part in the Mau Mau, you will be cleansed, not with blood and goat's intestines, but water and milk, pure things. Do you understand?'

Gichuchi nodded.

'Say it out loud.'

'I understand.'

'Very well. Think about it and we will do it tomorrow.'

Gichuchi reflected on his time with the Mau Mau. He knew its reputation for cruelty; he realised that its cause was failing, and that the hardships of forest existence could only grow worse with supplies being cut off and with the threat of starvation. He had not actually killed anybody, which relieved his conscience. He didn't know what the policeman had to offer him if he confessed, but he had implied an end to his incarceration.

The following morning he was taken by Land Rover under guard to a village just outside Nanyuki. A tall village elder, dressed in tribal clothes, was waiting in front of his *banda*. He greeted the policeman and looked Gichuchi up and down. At his feet were two bowls. Gichuchi was made to kneel down and wash his hands and face and rinse his mouth out. He then repeated the words dictated to him:

'I, Gichuchi, son of Njoka, renounce all my dealings with the Mau Mau and all such evil men. I now cease to be a brother. As Ngai is my witness.'

The elder made him stand up and took a sip of the other bowl, which contained goat's milk. He spat some into Gichuchi's face, took a further sip and passed the bowl over so that Gichuchi could empty it.

The policeman thanked the elder, took Gichuchi's arm and led him back to the Land Rover.

'There. You are free now to talk and help us defeat these evil men. When we get back to camp, I am going to talk to you again and you are going to go through your time with the Mau Mau, from when you were recruited until your capture. Every detail is important. There will be an Army officer listening and he may well ask you questions. But remember, you are now among friends and you must tell us everything.'

Back at the camp, the Special Branch officer and Lieutenant Jamieson, who had led the first detail at the Howarth's farm, interrogated Gichuchi. He had a good memory. With little prompting he gave a detailed account of his experiences, first his recruitment and his meeting with Mwangi, then training and the operations he had taken part in. When he came to his capture, he was asked why he did not try to kill the woman and the little girl in the house.

'I had no bullets left. I went into the house ready to die and first kill as many people as I could. But then, when I saw them, I couldn't do it, even though the woman had a rifle. Our raid had failed and there seemed little point in more killing, just for the sake of it. Then I heard a shot, felt the pain and...I can't remember anything more until I came to and found myself tied up. I felt so very tired, so I just lay there.'

'Very good, Gichuchi. Now tell us what you can about your Brigadier, Njirami Watui and any other brothers.'

Gichuchi said that he had only spoken directly to Njirami once, when he came to the camp for the first time; he repeated what he had been told about rules in the camp. He said more about Mwangi.

'I think he was a good leader. I learned a lot from him about living in the forest and operating there. He took care of his men but he could be utterly ruthless.'

While he was talking, the policeman and the Army officer made notes. The interview had taken most of the morning.

'What happens to me now?' Gichuchi asked.

'You will stay in the camp and you will be given some training. You will not be allowed outside and if you attempt to escape you will go to prison. But if you behave yourself you will be able to see your brother Nyeru.'

For the first time, the Army officer spoke.

'I have listened with great interest to what you have had to say, Gichuchi. We can use your expertise in the forest. Our object is to put a stop to the Mau Mau. This can best be done by capturing or killing the leaders. We already have Njirami in custody and, like you, he has been interrogated. We hope that most ordinary brothers will surrender. We will offer an amnesty to people like you but those who have ordered or committed atrocities will face the full rigour of the law. That is only fair, isn't it?'

Gichuchi nodded.

'You mentioned that Njirami talked about driving the British out of Kenya. And yet, in the raid not one *mzungu* was killed. We know that at least seven men belonging to the farm were killed and one family hacked to death. And *bandas* were burnt down. It looks like Njirami wanted to make war on his own people rather then fight for Independence. Killing Kikuyu was easier than fighting the British.'

'Yes, but...'

'You and I, Gichuchi, are soldiers. Our objective is to bring about peace so that ordinary people can get on with their lives. Once that is done, then the politicians can get to work and decide the future. Do you agree?'

Gichuchi had turned over these thoughts in his mind incoherently before, but he had never heard them expressed so clearly.

'I am just an ordinary man. What you say seems right to me.'

When Gichuchi was taken away, Lieutenant Jamieson told the Special Branch officer that the colonel would probably want to use him in one of his gangs.

'He seems an honest sort of fellow. I think he will work his passage and keep his nose clean, because the last thing he wants is to go to prison. If he does, the other inmates might discover that he broke his oath and would deal with him. So he will cooperate. And when all this is over, he can embark on a new life, with perhaps a little pension or gratuity. And find himself another wife. Poor girl, that was a cruel thing to happen. Something that good midwifery could have easily sorted out. Instead of mumbo jumbo.'

The policeman nodded: 'I can't see the Mau Mau setting up prenatal clinics. I have investigated his brother Njeru. He's a general dogsbody around the camp. A good worker, though. When the rifles were stolen some time ago he played the three wise monkeys but I am sure he was involved somewhere along the line. We can keep an eye on him. There is this other man Gichuchi mentioned, who worked on the same farm – Mutahi. Apparently he acted as a recruiting sergeant for the Mau Mau. I'll put him on our list as a person of interest. I don't want to pull him in at the moment since that might show our hand with Gichuchi.'

'I'll leave Mutahi to you. We need to get cracking with our gangs. Colonel Charteris has told me to take custody of Gichuchi and start training him with the others.'

* * *

Gichuchi was confined to barracks and shared a small dormitory with three other men. All of them were converts from Mau Mau and under threat of prison if they misbehaved. They did not talk much between themselves. A doctor examined Gichuchi and found him to be in excellent physical shape. His command of spoken English was improving by the day and he was making progress in writing it. He had lessons with another Kikuyu; he did not know who he was and did not see him outside the classroom. He was allowed to do some occasional labouring around the camp. He earned a little money but there was nowhere to spend it except in the NAAFI; there was a side door where Africans could buy snacks, drinks and cigarettes. Lieutenant Jamieson and his sergeant, Walters, kept an eye on him. He had to report to one of them three times a day and a chitty was duly signed. Twice a week he was taken out to the range; he proved to be a natural shot. With regular askaris from the KAR he was taken out on runs and other endurance tests, in which he more than held his own. He enjoyed the competitive element and, although he still did not know what was in store for him, he felt proud of his new skills. Lieutenant Jamieson and Sergeant Walters insisted that he report to them at the stated times and made him do press-ups, burpees or star jumps on the spot if he was late. He did not resent these impositions because he recognised that they were designed to instil a sense of responsibility. When he did a good time on a run or a good grouping on the range, he was complimented. From time to time he saw the officer with red tabs, who had spoken to him at the farm.

One day, with one other man called Moranga, he was taken out of the camp in a truck with the canvas cover fastened down, so they could not see out or be seen from outside. After half an hour they left the road and bumped up a track into the forest. The truck stopped and they were let out.

Lieutenant Jamieson and one other man got out of the Land Rover that had been following the truck.

'Half a mile from here is a small clearing in the forest. There you will find Sergeant Walters and two soldiers. The soldiers will be standing sentry around the clearing and Sergeant Walters will be in the clearing itself. There will be a red box there and in it two small parcels. We want you to find the clearing and, if you can, remove one of these parcels. That is, without Sergeant Walters seeing you. When you have the parcel there will be no further need of concealment. By the way, Sergeant Walters and the soldiers are armed with live ammunition and will fire if they detect an intruder.'

Gichuchi and Moranga winced.

'They will be firing about head height. So you must not stand up until you get into the clearing. If you are seen, you will be tied up and marched back to the truck. If you succeed you can keep what is in the parcel. All clear?'

They nodded.

'One more thing. The exercise will finish at sixteen hundred hours, when I will sound this siren. Sergeant Walters will blow a whistle as well.'

He went to the truck, leant inside and switched the siren on. The noise was ear-splitting.

'When you hear that, come straight back to the track for transport back to the camp, where there will be a debriefing. Don't be tempted to disappear to rejoin your old chums. Be sure that we will find you and you will go to prison. Understood?'

'Yes, sir.'

'You will start from here,' Jamieson said to Moranga. 'Gichuchi, get in the Land Rover.'

There was another man sitting inside.

Jamieson took him about ten minutes up the track. 'This is where you start.' Jamieson pointed him in the general direction he was to go. 'Good luck.'

Gichuchi saluted and walked back down the track for about fifty yards till he came across a path he had noticed on the way. There was one on the other side of the track; this was a crossing place for animals. He followed the narrow path very slowly, stopping to listen every twenty paces. The path went up and down but was generally straight and ahead of him was a hill which he could make out through gaps in the trees. On one occasion he stepped off the path and crouched down behind a tree trunk. He had heard loud rustling ahead and the screeching of monkeys. There came a scurry of animals down the path; he recognised a duiker. He didn't see what had caused the disturbance but remained motionless. When all had been quiet for some time, he ventured out and carried on.

He didn't have a map but he had reckoned that he had paused to listen about twenty times. That meant that he had covered perhaps a half of the distance. He checked his bearings on the hill ahead of him and noticed that the path had veered to the right somewhat.

The forest became particularly dense and there was nothing for it but to carry on along the path for the moment. There was a slight breeze. On the tenth pause his nose picked up, to his left, a smell with which he was familiar, a hexamine stove. It was still quite faint. He left the path and went down on his hands and knees, taking great care not to snap a twig on the ground. The smell grew stronger. Suddenly he heard from nearby the crash of rapid fire from a sten gun. He froze. He decided that the burst of fire had not been directed at him. He went down on his stomach and inched his way forward, following his nose. Soon he heard men talking and the lighting of a match, followed by the smell of cigarettes. There was no extraneous sound to cover his approach but no animal or bird cries to give him away. Creatures round about the clearing had disappeared when the soldiers occupied it.

Lieutenant Jamieson had warned that sentries would be posted around the clearing. His pulse began to beat faster and he had to make an effort to control his breathing. Suddenly, from his left, and very close, came a burst of firing. The branches of the trees splintered about him. He froze and did not move a muscle for some minutes. In the heat of the sun insects began to crawl over him and it took all his will-power not to scratch or brush them away. Added to which, he found he needed to urinate. While he was wondering what to do the sky darkened and there was a crash of thunder. It began to rain in large icy drops. The sentry, who was no more than three yards from him, swore loudly and went into the clearing to put on a cape. Gichuchi took the opportunity to turn onto his side and open his trousers. The patter of rain concealed the flow. He buttoned up and resumed his painstaking stomach crawl. He began to feel cold and hoped he would not sneeze.

At last he came to the edge of the clearing. About ten yards away he saw Sergeant Walters with a cape around his shoulders facing away from him. He was sitting on a camp chair. Beside him was the red box. Of the sentry who had fired there was no sign. Sheltering on the far side of the clearing was Gichuchi's companion from the truck. His hands were tied in front of him and he looked miserable.

'So near and yet so far,' Gichuchi said to himself. He turned over in his mind possible ways of covering those ten yards. He could rush into the clearing, but he would be heard. If he crawled, he would be in the open and the chances of Walters not turning round during his approach were negligible. There was nothing for it but to wait for something to distract Walters sufficiently for him to run across to the box.

The minutes passed. The rain stopped and the sky cleared. He noticed that the sun was starting to go down. Time was running out. He was on the point of throwing caution to the winds when one of the sentries in the forest swore loudly and shouted out to Walters that he had tripped: he thought he had twisted an ankle. Walters told him not to move and he would come and examine it. He got up and left the clearing. Gichuchi scrambled to his feet and ran to the red box. Inside was a round parcel. He sat down in the camp chair and opened the parcel. It was a tin of fifty cigarettes. He opened it and took one out. The hexamine stove had been covered over because of the rain and there was a dry box of matches underneath. Gichuchi lit a cigarette and gave it to the other man who was looking at him pleadingly. Then he lit his own and settled down in the chair.

Sergeant Walters returned, half carrying the injured soldier.

'Well, blow me!' he said. 'You are a cheeky bugger.'

He blew his whistle and the other soldier came back. Then the siren sounded.

'Made it just in time. Well done. You deserve some smokes. We'd better be getting back.' He untied the other man. 'Perhaps you two could help this chap back to the main track. It's not too far.'

* * *

Back at the camp they were given time to change and have a meal, and then summoned to the Company office for a debriefing. Michael sat in on the meeting.

Lieutenant Jamieson spoke.

'Both of you, Gichuchi and Moranga, did very well. We had two experienced trackers from the Kenya Regiment following you at a discreet distance. They have said that you chose suitable routes, though, you, Moranga, went too fast and made too much noise. You were allocated up to four hours to cover half a mile, a distance you could walk in ten minutes. Stalking takes a lot of time and care. However, the sentries and Sergeant Walters did not notice your approach. It was bad luck, Moranga, that you sneezed two yards from a sentry and he promptly captured you. Luck does play an important part in an operation like this, no matter how carefully you proceed. For example, we don't expect you to lie there passively when a buffalo comes charging out of the forest. And in a real situation you would be armed.

'Now you, Gichuchi, did all the right things. You couldn't help tearing your trousers on a bush and leaving a little thread attached to it. In a real situation your oppo following behind would remove it. It is a compliment to you that at times the tracker had to close up to within a few yards in case he lost you. He followed you to twenty yards from the clearing. When you got near the clearing you did not react to the burst of gunfire or rush out but waited for your chance. When it came you took it without hesitation.'

Gichuchi held up his hand. Jamieson gave him permission to speak.

'Sir, I don't know what I would have done if the man had not twisted his ankle and called for help.'

'I realise that, Gichuchi. But the point is, you acted decisively. He who hesitates is lost. Do you understand?'

Gichuchi nodded.

'Very well,' said Jamieson. He turned to Michael. 'Do you want to say anything, sir?'

'Not much.' He looked at the two men. 'I have had a lot of experience in fighting in jungles and forests and I know how uncomfortable and unpleasant it can be. You have to have a lot of patience and be constantly on the alert. As Lieutenant Jamieson has said, you have done pretty well, both of you. I am sure that you have learnt the lesson about moving slowly, Moranga. We will give both of you more training and practice. I think that you will be up to the task that lies ahead, challenging the enemy on their own ground. But remember that these operations are secret and must not be divulged even to your friends and colleagues.'

He got up and everyone got up and stood to attention.

'Carry on, Jamieson.'

'Sir.'

* * *

As a reward for his efforts, Gichuchi was given an evening pass out of camp. He was reminded that he must not talk about his training to anyone, upon pain of imprisonment. His brother Njeru was instructed to accompany him and see that he returned by 22.00 hours. They met at the camp gate and walked into town.

Njeru remarked that he was looking very fit.

Gichuchi paused to think what to say. 'I have lots of physical labour to do. And you, Njeru, what are you up to?'

'Still cleaning bogs and doing odd jobs. I earn enough for my food and drinks.'

'What about Karumbi?'

'He is getting taller by the day. He has bought himself a smart jacket and trousers, quite the man about town. He will go far. I wish I had his brains, but I don't and my eyesight is getting worse. So I have to be content with what I do have: work and a woman.'

'Will I meet her?'

'Not tonight.' Njeru looked up at him. 'What happened to your ear? You have a scar on your head.'

'I was shot. Fortunately, only a graze but it bled a lot and hurt like hell.'

'Are you going to tell me about it?'

'No. What about Father?'

'I haven't seen him for months.'

'Well, why don't you go and visit him? It's only a bus ride away.'

'Well…I suppose I can.'

'Tell him that I am alive and well, but I can't see him just now. But I have not forgotten him.'

They went to the shebeen that Njeru frequented. Gichuchi was very conscious that he must not reveal any information and did not drink or say very much.

Njeru rattled on about this and that, drinking heavily. Eventually he tired of doing all the talking and asked Gichuchi directly why he was in the Army camp. 'I thought that you were going off to the Mau Mau.'

'I changed my mind.'

'Why?'

'Because...because I realised that they could never win the battle against the British.'

'I see. But don't you want your country to be independent, not ruled by faraway people in London?'

'I suppose I do. But the Mau Mau are killing their own people, not the British. They are bad men. I have seen what they have done.'

'You are talking nonsense, brother. They are fighting for our freedom, and they are prepared to die for it. When they have driven the British out, we can claim the land that has been stolen from us. Think of what happened to our father.'

'I do. It makes me angry but he will never get his own land back. He has work. I am sure he hopes that the three of us will make a better living.'

'Did he tell you that?'

'No, but, knowing him, that is what he would think.'

'The trouble with you is that you joined the Mau Mau because you had nothing else to do and you were sore about your girl. And when you found the life as a freedom fighter too tough for you, you chickened out and joined the other side.'

'Not true, Njeru, and may God forgive you for thinking that.'

'God doesn't come into it. You are really a traitor to the cause.'

'Why do you call me a traitor, if you work for the British yourself? All you do is clean bogs, as you said, drink and cosy up to this woman friend of yours. You have no ambition. You have absolutely no idea of what the Mau Mau really is. All you have is a vague dream of freedom, which is not going to happen. You are just a slob.'

Njeru pulled out a knife and lunged for him. Gichuchi easily caught his wrist and twisted the knife from his grasp.

Njeru shouted that he had better look out because the Mau Mau would be after him as a traitor.

Gichuchi said nothing. He got up and left, jogging his way back to camp.

Chapter Ten

Over the next few weeks Michael was always on the road, visiting outposts of his battalion or driving down to Nairobi for more conferences. Whenever he got back to Nanyuki he had a day's work at his desk. About six thirty each evening he walked across to the Mess for a gin and tonic and dinner. His young officers respected his leisure time and did not bother him on these occasions with too many military concerns. He preferred to listen to their chatter rather than lead a conversation. After dinner he returned to his office to work and once in a while Major Bright dropped by for a nightcap. About ten he retired to his quarters and picked up a book, of which he managed two pages before falling asleep. All the while he felt guilty for not contacting Jane, but the opportunity simply had not arisen.

One day, he had a radio message from Patrick to say that he was coming to Nanyuki on business the next day and was bringing Jane. They would be at the Sportsman's Arms mid morning. He looked at his diary and found that for once there was nothing specific written in and no routine duties that could not be delegated. Having made the necessary arrangements he changed into civvies and drove into town. Patrick and Jane were sitting in the lounge over a pot of coffee. He greeted them and sat down opposite Jane. Patrick poured him a cup and then announced that he had to attend to business at the bank.

'We don't need Jane today,' he said. 'Bring her back whenever.'

'That would be very kind. Jane, can you put up with me for a whole day?'

'I think I might, if you twist my arm.'

'Consider it twisted.'

Patrick went away and Michael and Jane started to speak at the same time.

'You first,' she said.

Michael explained that he had been desperately busy since the raid on the farm and that this morning was literally the first occasion when there was nothing on his plate.

'But I have been thinking of you,' he said lamely.

'I should hope so,' she replied. 'Sorry, that's not fair. I have been very busy as well, helping Annabel and Patrick with the *watu*. All of those we have spoken to are very loyal and deeply upset at what has happened, and not just because of any personal loss. They regard the Mau Mau as bandits who are giving the Kikuyu a bad name. And their physical security has been threatened and they feel very anxious. Fortunately the school was not attacked and the children's routine has not been disrupted. The dead have been buried and Patrick has set up a memorial stone with their names inscribed. *Bandas* have been rebuilt and money has been given so that people could replace household items they had lost. All this will be covered by general farm insurance, Patrick hopes, but the bank and the insurance company have been dragging their feet. Apparently, war damage is like an act of God, something not catered for in the small print. Patrick says that it isn't a war, just civil disturbance.'

'No doubt the lawyers will argue it out.'

'And it will take years.'

'So, what would you like to do?'

'Well, I have given the matter some thought and I have come equipped for an outdoor venture.' She pointed to her boots. 'What about you?'

'I keep a pair in the Land Rover, and binoculars, and I always carry a revolver, though so far I have never fired it in anger.'

'I hope you won't have to, today. There is a family, the Unwins, who have a ranch towards Laikipia. When I first came out I was given an introduction to them and I visited them once. They are quite isolated and I got Patrick to radio them this morning. They would be delighted to see me any time.'

'And me?'

'I think you would find them an interesting couple, rather older than us. They have had the ranch for many years. She is also a good artist, mainly wildlife.'

'Do you think they would give us lunch?'

'I am sure of it.'

The farm was seventeen miles northwest of Nanyuki along a murram road. Jane fished out a piece of paper on which she had written down directions that Geoffrey Unwin had given her over the radio.

'After seven miles we take the left fork and that leads slightly uphill until, after another four miles, we come to a right turn beside which is a large baobab. We take the right turn past a water-hole and after five miles we come to a sign beside a track leading to the farm. We can't miss it.'

'You are the navigator. I'll watch the milometer. But just in case, here is a military map. I am breaking protocol in showing it to you, but I will make a special case. Between us we should get there.'

As they left the environs of Nanyuki the country changed from *shambas* to open plains. On their way they passed close to a *zareba* enclosing Maasai huts. A little further along were herdsmen with their cattle; they were armed with spears and one had a shotgun. Michael had to wait while the herd crossed the road in front of him. In return he received a wave.

Jane explained: 'They bring their beasts up here after the rains, so that they can fatten them up before returning south along the Rift Valley. The Unwins regard them as a damned nuisance because they think they have grazing rights wherever it suits them. But they look very splendid.'

'From what I gather, they steer clear of politics, because they despise other tribes. They have a reputation for fierceness. I wouldn't like to meet one on a dark night.'

Further on they saw a herd of zebra and in the distance a solitary giraffe. They came to the top of a rise with a panoramic view. Jane asked Michael to stop the Land Rover.

'Just look at that.' The open bush stretched ahead of them, gently undulating, as far as the eye could see. In the distance there was a line of purple hills.

'I looked at a map yesterday.' said Jane. 'If we carry on in the direction we are going, after a thousand miles we come to Khartoum, with nothing much in between.'

'They call it Mamba.'

'Mamba?'

'Miles and miles of bloody Africa, or bugger all.'

Michael lit his pipe and Jane a cigarette.

'Makes one feel small,' he said. 'Those early explorers, they must have been a tough lot. The immense distances they had to cover on foot with hostile tribes, wild animals, not to mention diseases.'

'From what I have read, many of the missionaries who set out from Mombasa were dead within months.'

'No wonder the Europeans came to the Highlands, a much more equable climate. And more like home. It can get damn cold in the forest overnight.'

Jane took the binoculars and swept the horizon. 'Some antelope over there. I wish I could tell what they were.' She passed the binoculars to Michael.

'Grant's Gazelle, Tommies, impala?' he asked. 'Whatever they are they are very beautiful. Look, they are jumping up as they run.' He passed the binoculars back. 'Before I leave Kenya, I must go on a proper safari with an expert.'

Jane watched the beasts as they fled out of sight. 'I wonder what has spooked them.'

She turned round to look at the view behind them.

'Golly. From here, it looks as though we could stretch out a hand and touch Mount Kenya. The air is so clear.'

Michael looked at the map. 'It's forty miles away. Before I came out I read a little history. The mountain was seen for the first time just over a hundred years ago. One of these days, I want to climb it.'

'Take me with you, won't you?'

'Of course. You have done it before. You can be my guide.'

They did not speak for a minute or so, contemplating the twin peaks.

'You know,' said Michael, 'my grandfather was born the same year as Johann Krapf set eyes on Mount Kenya. Although the country is old – a century is but a hand's breadth – once we got hold of it, change has been so rapid. No wonder people wanted to come out here, with so much virgin territory to exploit. Not quite a gold rush, but a change from tired and shabby old Britain.'

'That is partly why I came out,' said Jane.

They drove on. The heat increased as the sun crept towards noon and the water-hole was deserted. Within a few minutes they came to the turning for the farm. Geoffrey Unwin was working in the yard.

'Jane, how lovely to see you again.'

'Geoffrey, this is Michael Charteris.'

They shook hands. Geoffrey looked at the Land Rover.

'Army?'

'I'm afraid so.'

'You are very welcome just the same. Come on in. Memsahib is making lunch.'

Michael judged the Unwins to be in their sixties.

Geoffrey poured beers.

'I have to ask,' said Michael. 'Have you had any unpleasant attentions from the Mau Mau?'

'Like everyone else, we worked out a plan in the event of an attack and we have firearms. As you saw, it is pretty open round here and there is no cover. I have night watchmen in the bomas. They have been instructed to fire off their shotguns if they detect any intruders. And that includes lions. The *watu* as a whole are loyal and have been with us for some time.'

'You may know that the Howarths' farm was attacked recently. My unit got there in good time and dealt with the terrorists.'

'Yes, I heard over the blower. Well done. What unit are you?'

'KAR.'

'I was with the Durham Light Infantry in France, till I copped a blighty. I still have a piece of German shrapnel in my backside. Doesn't bother me too much but it can ache at the end of the day.'

'The Japanese had a go at my left leg. Not that you would notice now.'

'Fourteenth Army, eh? Did you ever come across that bounder, Wingate?'

'He was killed just before my time.'

Doris interrupted: 'No more war reminiscences, you two. Leave those for tonight.'

'Tonight?' asked Jane.

'You must stay, having come this far. Michael, can't you radio your colonel and tell him you have been unavoidably delayed?'

'I am the colonel.'

'Give yourself permission, then.'

'That is very kind of you to have us.'

'We don't have guests all that often.'

'Then I must use the radio, Geoffrey, to leave a message and tell them where to get hold of me if there is a crisis.'

'And I must speak to Patrick to let him know where I am.'

'We'll do that after lunch.'

Over the meal Michael and Jane learnt some family history. Geoffrey had been working for an engineering firm after the War and, with his new wife and small children, was sent out to India on a contract. After three years they tired of the heat and dust and unhealthy climate (they lost one child), and sensed also a growing hostility to the presence of the British. When the contract came to an end, they returned to England but could not settle. Then an unexpected legacy from a rich uncle gave them the chance of a new start. They came out to Kenya Colony in the mid twenties. It took them some time to find a plot of land for sale and they had to start from scratch.

'Just as well Geoffrey was an engineer,' said Doris. 'He knows about engines and pumps and that sort of thing.'

'And Doris, she is a farmer's daughter. Mind you, raising boran cattle is rather different from Aberdeen Angus, but we managed, didn't we.'

'Trial and error,' she said, 'not to say rinderpest. But we survived. Just as well the British Army likes beef.'

'Sunday lunch in the canteen would not be the same without it.'

Jane asked about the wildlife in the area, mentioning the antelope they had seen that morning.

'If they were bouncing on all four legs they were Grant's. They are quite common. If they have a black stripe along their flank they are Tommies. And if they have a red back they are impala. Doris will take you on a little safari this afternoon.'

After lunch messages were duly passed to the camp at Nanyuki and the Howarths. Michael changed into boots and Doris appeared in ancient jodhpurs. She carried a rifle.

'You never know.'

'Where are we going?'

'The river is about half a mile away. We'll walk along it then turn towards that small hill over there, which is one of the boundaries of the farm, though we don't have a fence, just a series of border markers. I suppose we have about three square miles, enough for two hundred cattle and some goats. At the back of the house are paddocks where they go for the night. Geoffrey and the herdsmen round them up in the late afternoon. It is easier to use horses than a motor. Most come to the paddocks here but some go to bomas around the farm. Ready?'

Doris set off at a brisk pace, the dogs leading the way. Along the river, the grass was longer than in the open bush, though it too was beginning to turn brown. Excited by all sorts of smells the dogs romped ahead and disappeared into a small copse. There was loud barking.

'They've found something. Let's pull back a little in case there is a buffalo in there.'

Jane took Michael's arm.

'What should we do if it is a buffalo? There aren't any big trees round here.'

'Their eyesight is not good. Get behind that rock there.'

The barking continued for a little longer and then the dogs emerged.

'Either whatever it was escaped them – could have been an otter or monitor lizard, or fox – or it was something bigger, and they beat a hasty retreat.'

They walked on. About twenty yards away to their right was a larger acacia.

'What's that, in the crook?'

They walked across. About ten feet up the trunk hung the remains of a bushbuck, its belly and hind legs chewed away and covered in flies.

'Leopards do that,' said Doris. 'They put their kills up a tree to store them.'

'Are there many leopards round here?'

'They used to be regular visitors to the paddocks, but poachers have been after them for their skins, and we don't see many these days.'

'Do you lose many animals to predators?'

'Goats are taken fairly frequently. We must lose about one in ten, but these Boran cattle are tougher propositions. They can fight back and they stick together to defend their calves. Besides, they have protection in the paddocks and bomas and a blast from a shotgun in the air usually deters hyenas and leopards, even lions. In the open bush, there are plenty of zebra to be had, and warthogs, too, both easy prey, so the cattle are usually left alone. We couldn't possibly keep lions off the farm. Much better to live in tune with nature than fight it all the time.'

They walked towards the base of the hill. On their way they came to one of the dams, fed by a stream from the hill. Two herdsmen were watering cattle which had tick birds perched on their backs. They greeted Doris with a wave and one came across. Doris introduced Jane and Michael.

The herdsman grinned and gave both of them an African handshake. He was grizzled and had only a few teeth; one eye was cloudy.

'Charles is one of our senior men,' explained Doris. 'He is very experienced with cattle.'

Charles called Michael and Jane over to inspect one of the bulls, a fine beast nearly five foot six at the shoulder. He spoke in Gikuyu. Doris translated.

'They are easy cattle to rear. They can resist parasites and have many calves.'

Jane was reluctant to get too close. Charles signed for her to stroke the beast. 'He is very gentle. His name is Nguvu, which means "strong".'

'Hello, Nguvu,' said Jane as she patted his hump. Nguvu snorted and thrust his snout towards her. Jane jumped back and the others laughed.

'I thought you were used to cattle,' said Michael.

'Naomi is. I am always a little wary when we are in the paddock at home. Anyway, this bull here is much bigger than the ones we have.'

They said goodbye to Charles and continued with their walk.

'Let's go and have a look for the cheetah.'

After twenty minutes of walking past termite hills and thorn bushes, Doris called the dogs in and tied them to a rock. Fifty yards ahead was a large acacia tree and below it two young cheetahs lay. Their askaris stood a little way off.

'They are orphans, brother and sister, about nine months old. We are looking after them for an animal charity. The askaris take them out during the day and bring them back to the farm in the late afternoon. In a few months we will let them go free, or rather they will choose for themselves when they go.'

'What do they feed on?'

'They love warthog. And small buck. They can outrun most things over a short distance, young as they are. Go and have a closer look.'

The cheetahs were lying half asleep. Jane went up and examined them. Their purr was deeper than that of any domestic cat. One sat up and allowed Jane to stroke its head and neck. It yawned and revealed a fearsome array of fangs.

'They are the most tameable of the big cats, but they mustn't become too reliant on us.'

'I wish I had a camera.' said Michael. 'Jane and the cheetahs, three beautiful creatures together.'

Jane blushed.

'He's right, you know,' said Doris.

On the way back Doris forged ahead with the dogs, Michael and Jane following a bit behind. They came to a track.

'Just carry on down and you will come to the house in about a mile and a half. Take your time. I must go on ahead to see to things.' She handed Michael the rifle. 'Have a good look around and if you can get a shot at a buck, we can always do with the meat. I'll send some of the men to get it.'

When she had gone, Jane said: 'Do you think she was being diplomatic?'

'You mean leaving us alone together in the middle of the African bush? Could well have been.'

'That's fine, but get me back in one piece. Every time I see a stand of trees or a clump of bushes I imagine some frenzied beast lurking there to charge out and tear me limb from limb.'

'Well, you will certainly make a juicy morsel.'

'It's not funny, Michael. I have been in Kenya for nearly two years but I have never been out in the bush on foot, without the security of a vehicle.'

He took her hand. 'There are two of us and we are armed, unlike most Africans who work in the bush.'

'They are used to it. Michael, am I being silly?'

'Of course not. As Doris said, we must live in tune with nature. Get used to it. Become an African. I find it exhilarating being out here under a huge sky. Makes a contrast with the forest where you can't see much beyond your own nose.'

'You are right. But don't let go of me, all the same.'

Jane wanted to press on but Michael insisted that they watch a herd of antelope grazing a hundred yards off. They were untroubled by the presence of humans.

'Look at those horns, bent back like handlebars on a bicycle. Long faces. And their backs seem to slope down, as though the rear legs are shorter than the front. We must ask the Unwins when we get back.'

They walked on and the track turned a corner and went down into a slight depression. At the bottom beside the track was a carcase being attacked by three vultures, inserting their scraggy necks into the belly of the victim.

'What is it?' she asked.

'Looks like the remains of a zebra.'

They had to pass within ten yards of the carcase; the vultures took no notice. The smell, sweet yet rancid, was appalling.

'God.' Jane took out a handkerchief and held it to her nose. At the same time some flies turned their attention from the carcase to Jane and Michael. She started to run.

When she had slowed down and Michael had caught up with her, she said: 'I thought I could cope with most things, but that was truly revolting.'

'Vultures are the dustmen of the bush, cleaning up after others.'

'Well, what useful thing do flies do, apart from annoying me?'

'They feast on smaller flies.'

'Like in the rhyme. That is as maybe, but I wish they would go away.'

'There's not much breeze to blow them away. Look up there.' He pointed to the sky where more vultures were gliding around in thermals. 'Those birds must be nine feet or more in wingspan. They may be ugly on the ground but they are so graceful in flight. Have a look.'

He passed over the binoculars. She watched them swirl around. Michael put his arm round her waist and she leant towards him.

'Let's go back, now. I have had enough encounters with Nature for one afternoon. But it has been fascinating.'

Arm in arm they walked on and met Geoffrey and two herdsmen on horses.

'Hello, you two. Have you enjoyed your safari?'

'Very much.'

'We're just off to bring some cattle back to the paddocks. They seem to have their own internal clock and start to come in of their own accord.' He looked over their heads to his right. 'Ah. There they are. The boys here will guide them in. I will go round the bomas to check all is well with the rest.'

Jane described the curious antelopes they had just seen.

'Hartebeeste. Some people call them kongoni.'

'They didn't seem to be alarmed by us.'

'Maybe you were downwind. They can outrun most things. If you had been any closer they would have been over the horizon like a shot. See you later.'

Meeting Geoffrey seemed to reassure Jane. 'You talked about being under a huge sky. I would find that frightening if I was on my own, but the knowledge that there are other people out there is comforting.'

'And I am sure they would come to rescue a damsel in distress.

Now you have me. I hope that will give you enough peace of mind.'

'Oh, you'll do all right.'

She turned and kissed him. With their arms round each other they strolled on and came to the paddock at the front of the farm house.

'I'm glad you didn't shoot anything, Michael. Ever since the raid I have been jittery around firearms.'

'I had forgotten all about the rifle. I was totally absorbed in you.'

'How sweet.' She suddenly broke away from him and sniffed her shirt.

'I don't know about you but I smell like…'

'A gorilla's armpit? I am the same. It's been so hot.'

'I hope we can get a shower, or better still a bath.'

On their arrival at the farm, this delicate matter was mentioned by Jane to Doris, who was not the least disconcerted.

'Easily done. There's the boiler.' She pointed to a large oil drum which sat on a brick pedestal; underneath it was a log fire, already glowing.

'I got the *watu* to light the fire in anticipation. And we will wash your clothes. Bring them over to the house when you have finished showering. They will be dry by this evening. I have put out something on the bed for you to wear.'

She showed them to a room in an annex. 'We use this for visitors. The shower is through there and towels are ready. Give the water fifteen minutes and it should be hot enough. I'll leave you to it.'

'Well,' said Jane, 'I didn't expect this.'

They examined the clothes. Jane had been provided with an old shirt and skirt which seemed to be about her size. Michael had a shirt belonging to Geoffrey but, as he was considerably taller, instead of trousers there was a kikoi. There were also two pairs of slippers.

'Michael…' Jane began, but he cut in.

'Don't worry. I will sleep in the chair.'

He went out and left her to shower.

* * *

Geoffrey came in just before dusk, having done his rounds.

'All tucked up, and all's well.' He looked at Jane and Michael sitting before a log fire with their garments draped over a clothes horse.

'Fancy dress, eh? Actually, Michael, that kikoi is very comfortable especially when it is hot. It allows a little ventilation up the Khyber Pass, as we used to say. And you have a safety pin to spare our blushes if it falls down. Let me refresh your drinks. We'll be eating soon. In honour of the occasion I have brought out some wine which we were given some time ago. A pinot noir. We don't have the opportunity to splash out very often.'

'That's very kind.'

'Michael, tell me about Burma. Jane, if you have heard this before, please bear with me.'

'Michael hasn't really talked about his wartime soldiering, so I would like to listen as well.'

Michael's narrative was mainly concerned with jungle fighting. 'What made things easier for us and much harder for them was the fact that very soon we had total domination in the air. We could drop supplies wherever they were wanted, and our wounded could be evacuated. And I think we were superior in numbers as well as equipment. The same applies to fighting the Mau Mau. We can drive them out of the forest, like beaters in a pheasant shoot. But the territory is vast and they have the advantage of surprise and rapidity of movement, and there is still quite a strong element of sympathy for them among civilians.'

'That is on the decline, or so I have heard,' said Geoffrey.

'What I am trying to do is to set up small units from my battalion to go into the forest and kill or capture the key men, in effect, to beat them at their own game. The High Command is a bit suspicious and has taken a lot of persuading but I hope we can go into action fairly soon.'

'Will you be going in yourself, Michael?' asked Jane.

'Sometimes, to see for myself how things are going.'

'I don't like the forest,' said Geoffrey. 'I prefer the wide open spaces.'

Doris came in and called them through to the dining room.

'Are you hungry, Jane?'

'Starving. What is the meat?'

'Zebra. Lean meat with a touch of sweetness.'

'Smells delicious.'

Over the meal Doris wanted to hear all about Britain, especially Queen Elizabeth. 'I saw her when she came out in '52 on her way to Treetops. We went over to Nyeri. Everyone turned out to see her and she stopped to speak to people. Such a charming smile she had. And the Duke was there as well, regulation two paces behind. Have you ever met her, Michael?'

'I haven't had that privilege, but maybe when I am promoted to Aide-de-camp, which will never happen, of course, because the King's African Rifles is not a fashionable regiment.'

'I'm afraid she will never come back to Kenya,' said Geoffrey, 'not the way things are going. The Africans loved her when they saw her, but the politicians regard her as a symbol of British oppression. When Kenya becomes independent, it will be as a republic. Pity, but I can well understand why.'

'Will you stay?' Jane asked.

'If at all possible. I have a feeling that Kenyatta will not wish to antagonise white settlers like us, especially in the early years. Anyway, another ten or fifteen years and we will be food for the worms.'

'You, maybe, Geoffrey,' retorted Doris, 'but I will be going on for ever.'

'I'm sure you will, love.' He got up from his chair. 'Michael, how about a night cap? Scotch?'

'Just a small one. I'm all in.'

'Jane?'

'No thanks. I'll help Doris clear away the dishes.'

For the first time Michael was able to have a good look at the watercolours on the walls, all depicting wildlife. He got up and walked around the room.

'These are wonderful. Who did them?'

'The memsahib. All of them are creatures she has observed on the farm. She has a wonderful eye.'

'Indeed. Would she be offended if I offered to buy one, or maybe commission one from her?'

'You can ask. She won't be offended, but she might refuse.'

'I'll take that chance.'

A few minutes later the women came through. Jane examined the clothes. 'They're dry.' She gathered them up.

'Time for bed, Michael.'

Obediently he got up and thanked Doris and Geoffrey warmly for their hospitality.

'Our pleasure. Sleep well. Breakfast tomorrow at seven.'

'We'll be there.'

When they got to their room, Michael said he would wait outside while she got ready for bed. It was distinctly chilly. He passed the time by looking at the sky. He has never really noticed it before but the stars were brilliantly clear. He thought it was another reason why the Unwins were determined to stay instead of going back to cloudy England.

When Jane called, he went in. She was in bed with the blankets up to her chin.

'Are you going to be a gentleman, Michael?'

'Of course. I always am.'

'The chair will be too cold. Come and join me.'

Chapter Eleven

The next morning Michael took Doris aside and, after thanking her profusely for her hospitality, asked if he could commission a painting from her, something he could give to Jane as a souvenir of their visit.

'I usually paint for my own satisfaction. Are you sure that I am good enough for you?'

'Of course I am. I will pay whatever you ask.'

'Don't let's worry about that just now. I have a charity that I support; a contribution would be most welcome. What animal would you like?'

'No doubt about it, the cheetahs.'

'That should be possible. I have been meaning to paint them while they are with us but have always got diverted. This will concentrate the mind.'

'Don't say anything to Jane, will you?'

'Mum's the word.'

After a colonial breakfast, enough to see them through the day, Michael and Jane bid farewell to the Unwins and set off for Nanyuki. Jane was to be picked up from the Sportsman's Arms later in the morning.

'I'll do some shopping.'

Michael went to his office and summoned Major Bright.

'Anything to report?'

'We have had this signal from Brigade, first thing this morning.' He handed over a sealed envelope.

'I'll look at it presently.'

'There is another matter, sir, which blew up yesterday, at least that was when it came to our notice. C Company. One of the platoons was patrolling in the Special Areas, the Kikuyu Reserve. Lieutenant Croxall.'

'Ah.'

'Not the brightest of buttons. That is why we gave him a British sergeant.'

'Let me see. Rawlings.'

'Yes. Rawlings and ten men were a little ahead of the rest. They stopped three Kikuyu. They were carrying *pangas* and explained that they were going out of the village to work at clearing some ground. They even produced a pass signed by the District Officer allowing them into the Special Area. Rawlings for some reason was suspicious and ordered the askaris to search them. Nothing untoward was found. Rawlings was not satisfied and started shouting at them in English and threatening them with his rifle butt. The men were obviously frightened and made to run away. Instead of telling them to stop or getting his men to chase them, Rawlings ordered his men to shoot. When they appeared reluctant to obey, he himself shot them in the back at close range. He examined the bodies lying on the ground. Two of them were still alive and so he shot them in the back of the neck. Then he took a *panga* and cut off their right hands. At that point Lieutenant Croxall came up.'

'How do we know all this?'

'Apparently there were two other Kikuyu from the village nearby. To escape the patrol they had hidden behind a rock. They could hear and see everything that went on. They reported it to the village chief, who told the local DO. He called us yesterday.'

'Can the story be verified?'

'Two of the askaris, Kikuyu themselves, reported the incident to Captain Symonds, the Company commander. He said that he would look into it. But he hasn't said anything to us yet.'

Michael lit his pipe. He got up from his chair and started pacing up and down. He went over to the window and looked out on the parade ground where a squad was being drilled.

Finally, he spoke: 'In a word. Bugger.'

'Bugger, indeed, sir.'

'This is far beyond my jurisdiction. I think it is a case for the Red Caps. I'll get on to Brigade.' He picked up the envelope. Major Bright got up to go.

Michael stopped him 'Let's just see what this is.'

He opened the envelope and read the contents.

'Just what we need.'

'What's that, sir?'

'Two Westminster MPs are on a fact-finding tour of Kenya and they want to observe operations. We have been chosen to explain to them our forest operations. They are coming next week, for two days. We have to afford them every courtesy and facility.'

'Who are they?'

Michael looked at the paper again: 'James Walker and Margaret Collier, both Labour.'

Bright chuckled. 'We could, er, take them into the forest and leave them there for a couple of hours, when it is raining. That might make them appreciate what our troops have to endure and stop them criticising us.'

'An intriguing thought. But…it says that we must submit to GHQ by the end of this week a detailed plan for their visit. Can you draft something today and we will discuss it this evening? I will deal with the other business.'

'Very good, sir.'

It took some time for Michael to get hold of the Brigadier.

His reaction was as exasperated as Michael's had been.

'Assuming that this story is true, and it sounds very likely, it is a direct infraction of General Erskine's directive. Here we are, trying to win the hearts and minds, and this destroys whatever trust with the locals we have built up in the last months. Was the General's directive explained to the troops?'

'I briefed all the officers and senior NCOs, as instructed. They were to brief their men. As our battalion is scattered I went round to every one over two days; it also gave me a chance to hear reports and inspect training and operations.'

'Very good. What about the DO?'

'Andrew Holmes. I have met him. I am going to ring him now.'

'Right.'

'I think this is a matter for the Military Police, sir. Way beyond my jurisdiction.'

'I agree. Look, I will speak to Major Prentice. Do you know him?'

'No. Fortunately we have not had anything serious enough to warrant his attention.'

'He will contact you today. By the way, where were you when all this blew up?'

'That was yesterday afternoon, sir. I gave myself a twenty-four hour pass. I haven't had one for some time. I was contactable by radio during that time. I was back here by 09.30.'

'I wish I could have a twenty-four hour pass. But Queen and Country call. One other thing. We must find out why the finger-print kit was not used.'

'I imagine because Lieutenant Croxall had forgotten to take it on patrol.'

'Who is his Company commander?'

'Captain Symonds.'

'Symonds? Didn't we have a little trouble with him a year or so ago?'

'He was officially reprimanded for ordering suspects to be rough handled. One of them was caned. It is on his record.'

'Some of the settlers have the same attitude. A clout across the ears or a caning is what they had when they were at school. That never did them any harm, so they say. The Africans are children and must be treated in the same way.'

'I have heard that myself.'

'And if the officers think like that, we can't expect the men to behave differently.'

'And Symonds told me that other units do it. I disabused him of the idea.'

'But I am afraid it was true back then. That was one of the first things that General Erskine had to deal with when he arrived.'

'Before you go, sir, the MPs' visit. Major Bright is drafting a programme and we will send it up to you in a day or so.'

'Very good. They are coming just at the wrong moment. Just keep them occupied and tire them out.'

'Sir, should I speak to GHQ about this?'

'General Erskine will certainly want to know about it, so that he is not caught unprepared. The Press is always on our backs. Wait until he calls for you and by that time you should have some positive action to report.'

Michael put the phone down. He summoned his corporal.

'Jenkins, I have a lot of business in the office this morning. Put the phone directly through to me. If necessary I will put it back to you if I am going out.'

'Sir. I have some papers for you to sign, usual stuff, and there will be some more coming in.'

'Just put them in the tray. I will come through and deal with them when I have a moment. I don't want to be disturbed just now. If World War Three breaks out, call Major Bright.

Michael made a note of his conversation with the Brigadier. Then he called Andrew Holmes, the District Officer. Fortunately, he was in his office.

'Andrew? Michael Charteris here. King's African Rifles. We haven't met for some time. You called us yesterday.'

'Yes.'

'A sorry business.'

'It won't help my work.'

'No.'

'What are you going to do about it?'

Michael paused, wondering how much to tell Holmes.

'I have reported the matter to the Brigadier and we agreed that this is a matter for the Military Police.'

'I think this is for the civil courts to decide, since civilians are the victims.'

'Not for me to say.'

'If there is a court martial it will be held in camera.'

'I can assure you that the same standards of jurisprudence obtain in military courts.'

'Perhaps. But you don't want the Army to be brought into public disrepute.'

'Andrew, we can argue about civil versus military till the cows come home. The important thing is to get hold of the facts. Can you identify the witnesses for us and confirm the names of those who were killed?'

'Your man mutilated the bodies.'

'He did. Therefore we probably have the fingerprints on record so we can identify them. Will you cooperate with us?'

'Very well.'

'I expect the Military Police will be in touch soon. They will want to take statements from the witnesses and the chief. Will you be on hand to translate if required?'

'I will. Sorry, Michael, to be so brusque. I am just very angry.'

'I understand.'

'We'll speak again soon.'

The call ended and Michael sat back and lit his pipe. He made out a list of other calls he had to make. Then he went through to the outer office and collected the papers waiting for him. He asked the corporal to bring him some coffee.

An hour went by as he read, noted and signed. He never skipped any papers brought to his attention, however trivial they might seem. Once, as a subaltern, he had missed something important and had been duly reprimanded by his colonel.

That chore done, he turned to the list of calls to be made. He was just about to pick up the phone when it rang.

'KAR. Charteris here.'

'Hello, KAR, this is Simpson.'

'Jane! Are you all right?'

'Of course I am. I am not being picked up till lunchtime and I am killing time at the Sportsman's Arms. So I thought I would ring you, and I got straight through.'

'There is a bit of a flap on. I have to be in direct touch.'

'Sorry. I won't keep you then. Just to say, Michael, thank you for, well, the last twenty-four hours. I had a lovely break. Lots of good things to remember. See you soon, I hope.'

'I was very happy too. It was a break that I needed but now I am back in the thick of it, with a vengeance.'

'I hope it is not too awful.'

'It is not pleasant. I can't tell you about it; it's all sub judice.'

'Sounds important. I must let you get on. Lots of love, Michael.'

'And to you, Jane.'

He put the phone down. His previous corporal had been in the habit of listening in, but this one seemed to be very discreet. Not that it mattered in this case. Nothing was revealed beyond the fact that the colonel had a girlfriend.

The phone rang again. It was Major Prentice of the Special Investigation Branch.

'Hello, Prentice. I am sorry but we have to call upon your services. Are you familiar with the case?'

'I have the outline, sir.'

Michael recited all the facts as he knew them.

'I see,' said Prentice. 'An immediate arrest upon suspicion is needed. The prima facie evidence is pretty clear. We will take statements and refer the matter to the Army Legal Services.'

'Will you want a statement from me or from anyone here at battalion HQ?'

'From you, yes. Just how you learnt of the offence and the action you took thereafter.'

'Apart from informing Brigade, and contacting the District Officer, is there anything else I should have done? It's only, what,' he looked at his watch, 'three hours since I found out about it. Should I go up to C Company myself and detain Rawlings pending your arrival?'

'No. Just send the Company commander an order to stand him down from whatever duties he is carrying out and confine him to barracks. Much better if you stand aside and allow us to get on with it. We have an established procedure.'

'Very well. I will signal C Company at once. When will you be able to get up there?'

'Tomorrow.'

'Please keep me informed of progress when you have something substantial to report. Or if you have any questions for me.'

'Very good, sir.'

* * *

After lunch Michael took a stroll around the camp to observe training in progress. For a few minutes he watched an inter-platoon soccer game, which involved a lot of running and shouting but not much skill. Further on, one platoon was being timed over an assault course in competition with another. Getting everyone across the twelve-foot wall and other obstacles required a team effort and the askaris were putting their hearts into it. After exchanging a few words with the CSM in charge, he decided to walk out to the range.

The solitary walk allowed him to put his thoughts in some sort of order; they were swirling around in his head after the morning's revelations. He reviewed his conduct over the Symonds affair. Should he have made an example of him, not just a reprimand? If he had, perhaps C Company might not have been tempted to vent feelings of frustration on defenceless natives. He remembered the military dictum often voiced at Sandhurst: 'There is no such thing as bad soldiers, only bad officers.' Officers and most NCOs in the KAR were seconded from regular home regiments; could Rawlings have been seconded because his previous regiment wanted rid of him? Perhaps that should be investigated by the Special Investigation Branch. And if the matter came to trial, probably he would have to appear and be questioned about his actions in command of the battalion. And always in the back of his mind was the memory of his time with Jane, only a day ago, but seemingly in another age. A Presbyterian ancestor might have said that such happiness was transitory and must be paid for. Well, transitory or not, he had been blissfully happy and was deeply thankful for it.

At the range he found Lieutenant Jamieson and askaris from his platoon. Sergeant Walters was conducting the range practice; sten guns at fifty yards, fired from prone or kneeling positions, or from the hip.

Jamieson drew him back from the firing point so that they could talk.

'I think these will be more useful than rifles in the forest, sir. Visibility is often poor and pinpoint accuracy is not necessary.'

'What other weapons do you use?'

'Two men in a squad carry rifles, in case a long shot is required. Each man has a combat knife, and a cord for securing prisoners. They have a torch. And we have developed our own system of hand signals.'

'That seems very sensible.'

Michael preferred to let his officers use their own initiative in working out their own operational methods, rather than directing them from above. After all, his expertise in jungle warfare was gained by trial and error as a young officer in Burma. Jamieson seemed to be on the right lines.

'I have something to tell you, Jamieson. Bit of a bombshell, actually.'

'Sir?'

'Soon we are to have a visit from two Labour MPs, a man and a woman. A factfinding trip. As you may know, there have been a lot of awkward questions asked in Parliament recently about the Army's conduct in dealing with insurgents. The GOC is concerned and he has the CIGS and Colonial Secretary on his back. So we have a hearts and minds operation.'

'You mean with the Mau Mau, sir?'

'Of course, as always. But this time I am referring to these two politicians. Can you talk to them about your role and then treat them to a little forest jaunt?'

'Will they be dressed for the forest?'

'We'll supply them with overalls. Take them on a forest patrol. Let them get wet and dirty and then we will fill them with gin and food in the Mess.'

'Sounds good, sir.'

'See Major Bright later today. He is drawing up a plan.'

Michael then asked how the men were getting on. 'I want them to be a special group, with lots of esprit de corps. They have to trust each other implicitly in facing the enemy at close quarters.'

'Berkeley and I are working on two groups of ten men each.'

'What about that ex-Mau Mau, Gichuchi? How is he getting on?'

'Very well. He is very strong. He can move silently and knows his jungle craft. The Mau Mau must have trained him well. He came out very well in the training exercise we had recently. Perhaps a bit serious, but calm and sensible.'

'Good. I think we should introduce him to our MPs. His English is OK?'

'Much improved. He is the best of those we have.'

'He can be an example of our humane treatment of erstwhile enemies.'

After his walk Michael returned to the office and dealt with more paperwork. When it was mostly done he filled his pipe and his thoughts were turning towards a restorative drink in the Mess when the phone rang. For a fleeting moment he hoped that it was Jane, but a gruff military voice asked:

'Colonel Charteris? This is the GOC's office. Major General Peters.'

'Charteris here.' Michael resisted the temptation to sit to attention. Instead, he lit his pipe as the General barked out a series of questions.

'Have you made arrangements for the MP's visit? Accommodation? What activities they will see? Transport?'

Michael took a long puff. 'Major Bright has been working out a possible programme. I have my own ideas as well and we will thrash it out this evening. We will send them to your office by 1200 tomorrow. However I have a number of questions before we can make any firm plans.'

'Oh? What are they?'

'How are they reaching us and when? Do they merit a guard of honour? What age are they? Are they fit?'

'What's that got to do with it?'

'Our plan could involve some walking, to observe some forest training.'

'I see.'

'Will the lady MP require any female escort, a lady-in-waiting as it were? Have they had any experience of Africa before, or indeed of the Army?'

'Why…?

'We want to present our forces and operations in the best possible light and also to make them understand the difficulties we face and the hard decisions that we have to make. We want them to go away with the right impression so that when they go back to England they will be able to give a sympathetic report. One final question, sir. Will they be accompanied by any GHQ staff?'

'Hm. I can't answer those just now. Make your plans, anyway. I don't think they merit a guard of honour. As to your other questions, we will reply as soon as we can.'

* * *

The Army Humber entered the camp at 10.30, having started early from Nyeri. In the front were the driver and Captain Lansdowne, the MPs on the back seat. Michael and Lieutenants Jamieson and Berkeley waited for them as they drove up to the Mess. Lansdowne got out and came over to Michael and saluted.

'Here they are, sir, at your disposal. When we have had coffee, I will leave them to you and come back for them tomorrow at 15.00.'

'Very good, Lansdowne. Any quick hints about our guests?'

'He served in the War, infantry, I think, and is quite relaxed. She carries a notebook and likes to inspect the ablutions.'

'Ah.'

The MPs looked around them and walked across as the driver carried their luggage into the Mess.

Introductions were made. Walker looked at Michael's shirt.

'Burma Star. I was in Italy. Hard fighting both.'

'Indeed, sir.'

Margaret Collier was clearly on edge. She kept looking around. Finally she spoke in a pronounced northern accent:

'I have a list of things I want to see, Colonel.'

'I hope we will be able to oblige you, Miss Collier. But first, some coffee after your journey.'

Over coffee, the lieutenants chatted to Walker about the Italian campaign.

'Don't imagine,' he said, 'that Italy was all sunshine and signorinas. In winter the Apennines were bloody cold and the locals kept well out of the way.'

Michael was careful to be attentive to Miss Collier.

'Before you give me your list, let me tell me what we have for you. It may well comprise what you want to see. This morning Lieutenant Berkeley will give you a talk about our forest operations and our strategy for dealing with the insurgency. After an early lunch we will go into the forest, so that you can experience conditions at first hand. That will take all afternoon. Before dinner there will be a chance to talk to other officers and later I will discuss with you our treatment of insurgents. Tomorrow after breakfast you will have a tour of the camp and then you go to the Sportsman's Arms to meet one of the local settlers. We will not be present at that conversation. Then back here for lunch and on your way thereafter.'

'Well, I expect I will still have questions.'

'Which we will endeavour to answer. We want you to go away from here with a better understanding of what the Army is doing, and why. Of course, you must draw your own conclusions from what you have seen.'

'Be sure I will.'

The morning's lecture by Lieutenant Berkeley was well received, both guests listening attentively. Walker asked a few questions about weaponry and air support. Miss Collier yawned loudly during this technical discussion. She apologised.

'I'm sorry, Mr Berkeley, but it was an early start this morning. I look forward to seeing your men in action.'

'Well, ma'am, be warned. They are a scruffy lot. For a few days before operations, they must not smoke, clean their teeth, shave or wash. In that way they start smelling like the Mau Mau and do not give themselves away. It is not a pleasant experience to undergo, I can tell you, but very necessary. And it is effective. As a result, Mau Mau and animals are not alarmed by the smells of civilisation.'

After lunch they were driven to the forest by Michael in a Land Rover; five askaris and Lieutenant Jamieson were in a lorry. The MPs were dressed in overalls, slouch hats and boots from the stores. Fortunately, Miss Collier was trim and easily fitted into male dress; Walker's waistline had expanded considerably since the war.

'This is an adaptation of an exercise we use to test forest skills,' Michael explained. 'Half a mile away is Sergeant Walters sitting in a small clearing. The objective is to reach him without being noticed. However, he will have put out sentries and maybe even a small patrol in the surrounding area.'

'Why are the men armed?' Miss Collier asked.

'We are reasonably sure that there are no Mau Mau in the vicinity. We carried out a check on foot and by air this morning. But to be on the safe side…and in case we meet any dangerous animals.'

'What animals?' asked Walker.

'Oh, elephants, rhino, buffalo.'

'I can't run that fast these days. In fact, I can't run at all.'

'Don't worry, Mr Walker, you will be all right. We'll see to that.'

'Do you shoot wild animals, Colonel?' Miss Collier asked.

'Not if we can possibly help it. In fact we have only killed one big animal, a buffalo, this last year, and it was injured. We try to operate with the forest, you see, not against it.'

She nodded approvingly.

'You will be led by Private Gichuchi, with two askaris. Mr Jamieson will follow behind. There are two things we insist on. Absolutely no talking and if you have to cough or sneeze you must do your best to stifle it. Sound can travel a long way in the forest. And you must follow instructions without question and immediately. Gichuchi, explain the most important signals.'

'Yes, sir.' He came forward and looked at them directly. 'I raise hand and that mean stop and freeze. And I point down it mean flat on ground. You have man beside you to help.'

'Thank you, Gichuchi. The siren will go at 1600. That is the end of the exercise. Wherever you are, break cover and come back to the track.'

They set off into the forest, following the path that Gichuchi had used before. He moved very slowly, much to Walker's relief. The altitude was taking its toll. Twice he raised his hand when the *ndete* birds started calling. But there was nothing significant. A little further on, the birds started calling loudly again and the colobus monkeys started screeching. A halt was called. Suddenly Gichuchi pointed with both arms to left and right and downwards. Miss Collier found herself on the forest floor and pulled into the undergrowth. The askari with her put his finger to his lips, pushed her head down into the soil and gently held it there. There came a loud snuffling, crashing of undergrowth and clatter of hoofs.

The askari beside Miss Collier whispered in her ear: '*Nyati*.'

The noise receded and she was allowed to raise her head. She could just make out Walker on the other side of the track. He saw her and smiled weakly.

Gichuchi gave the signal and they got to their feet and began to move on. There came a distant rumble of thunder and shortly afterwards a patter of raindrops on the leaves. It turned very cold.

Suddenly Gichuchi raised his hand. For a moment there was absolute silence. Then he gave the signal to hit the ground. A few seconds later came a burst of gunfire over their heads.

Chapter Twelve

'I have never been so scared in my life,' said Miss Collier later, 'not even before I made my maiden speech in the House. We lay there absolutely still. My askari had his arm over my shoulder, which was reassuring in a way. Insects started to crawl over my face and I was shivering with cold. Then he tapped my shoulder, pointed in front and to one side. I looked but at first I could not see anything, being so close to the ground. There was a rustling and then I saw a movement. It was a boot and trouser leg taking a step forward. My heart started beating very loudly.'

'Mine was going like a steam hammer,' continued Walker. 'We must have lain there for twenty minutes. I started to fidget but my askari gripped my arm firmly. The magazine of his sten gun was sticking into my ribs. Then I saw Miss Collier inch forward following Gichuchi. I was very stiff by that time and the going was painful. Fortunately there was no more firing and we emerged into the clearing to be greeted by Sergeant Walters with a flask of tea. Very welcome it was, too.'

Miss Collier went on: 'The sentries came in and Lieutenant Jamieson shortly afterwards. I asked him about the gunfire.

'"That was one of the sentries. He knew you were in the immediate vicinity and as instructed he gave a quick burst of fire to remind you to keep your heads down." Then the siren went and we walked back all together to the main track, and here we are.'

'So you survived,' said Michael with a smile. 'Back to camp and a hot bath.'

Nothing much was said during the journey back to Nanyuki. The MPs went to their rooms and Michael walked across to the office. There was a signal waiting for him from the Military Police, to the effect that Sergeant Rawlings had been arrested on a charge of murder and was in custody. Major Bright came to see him and they discussed arrangements for the following day.

'I think our guests got their money's worth this afternoon. You haven't spoken to them yet. They should be in the Mess at 18.30 so chat them up and see what you think of them.'

He passed over the signal. Bright read it. 'Well, sir, it shows that we are not brushing the matter under the carpet. But whatever the outcome, this will be a black mark against the battalion.'

'I am worried about the actions, or rather inactions, of Symonds and Croxall. The fact they did not report the incident suggests a conspiracy to cover it up, or connivance. Looking back on it, I am sure we followed the GOC's directive to the letter, so they can't claim that they had not been told. Do we face them with a charge of dereliction of duty?'

'I don't think we can jump in before the outcome of the trial of Rawlings. All we can do is to record our suspicions. If there has been connivance or a cover up, Croxall may turn out to have been guilty of perjury. Or he may have been following the orders of Captain Symonds. Learned counsel could have a field day debating the issue of obedience to illegal orders.'

'Very wise advice, Bright. Interesting that the askaris with Rawlings were reluctant to obey his order, if, that is, they are telling the truth. Look. We will make a note of the apparent negligence of Symonds and Croxall and that we have decided to await the outcome of legal proceedings against Rawlings before taking action at a battalion level. Seems a little pusillanimous, but to jump in with both feet would be prejudicial to the court hearing. Let us hope that it does not come out while the MPs are with us. I have a feeling that Miss Collier would seize upon it and forget all the good she has seen.'

Michael looked at his watch.

'Time for the Mess. I need a shower, so I'll see you there in a few minutes. I hope the chef has laid on something appetising. Damn, I forgot to ask if Miss Collier was a vegetarian. She is probably teetotal as well. All that non-conformist virtue. There, you have my prejudices in a nutshell.'

It turned out that Miss Collier liked a gin and tonic and she smoked a cigarette when it was offered to her. Walker had a pint. 'I feel I deserve it after the exertions and discomfort of this afternoon.'

The first one went down quickly and was replaced by another. When Michael joined them the atmosphere was relaxed. Major Bright was ensuring that the young officers engaged in conversation with the guests. Miss Collier, a little flushed, was talking to Jamieson.

'Mr Jamieson, at one point we were literally hauled off the track into the undergrowth and something crashed by quite close. My askari whispered to me; it sounded like "nasty".'

'*Nyati*. It means buffalo. They are short-sighted. Something must have spooked it and it was in a hurry to get away. If it hadn't been, you might have had an uncomfortable few moments.'

'I was uncomfortable anyway. How long do your men spend in the forest on an operation?'

'Anything from three days to three weeks. They carry all their supplies, as far as possible, but we can also supply them from the air.'

Jamieson described a previous operation he had led.

'We couldn't do it without the Africans. They are naturals in the forest, and easy to train. In fact, they train us.'

'So have I got it right?' said Walker to Berkeley in another part of the anteroom. 'You have three types of operation. There are the big sweeps through the forest, like beaters in a grouse shoot. It doesn't matter how much noise they make; in fact the louder the better.'

'Roughly speaking.'

'And then you have other forces around the forest to catch the Mau Mau when they emerge. These are at what, company strength?'

'Operating by platoons, so that we can cover a large area.'

'And the exercise we took part in today?'

'These are special squads, ten men at most. Their objective is to kill or capture Mau Mau leaders. Did you know that Gichuchi, the askari who led you today, was himself a brother?'

'Brother?'

'A member of the Mau Mau. He was captured during a raid on a farm and was persuaded to come over, to use his considerable skills on our side.'

'Are there many like him?'

'Not many that we can trust to the same extent.'

Dinner was called and they trooped into the Dining Room.

'Shepherd's Pie. Homely fare today,' Michael announced after inspecting the menu. 'Our cook likes to remind us of England. But all the ingredients are locally produced. A lot of vegetables are grown here.' He signalled to the waiter.

'Mohammed, bring us two bottles of the Burgundy. On my tab.'

Michael and Major Bright were sitting with the guests at one end of the table; other officers joined them further down. Jamieson and Berkeley ate their meal quickly and excused themselves: 'Duty calls.'

During the meal the MPs talked about their careers, but after coffee, when the other officers except Major Bright had gone, Michael returned to the topic of their tour.

'Mr Walker,' Michael asked, 'tell us what you have seen so far.'

Walker mentioned visits to Government House, an afternoon in the Nairobi Nature Reserve: 'We had only two hours but saw elephant, giraffe, a lion, and plenty of buck.'

'I had never seen animals in the wild before,' said Miss Collier, 'only in zoos.'

'Then we went to Thika,' Walker continued, 'to look at the detention camp. We weren't allowed to interview the inmates, and that fact will be noted. Then Nyeri. We were allowed to meet some local chiefs and inspected a couple of the new villages. We spoke to the Home Guard. A rough-looking lot they were, too. We had to have an interpreter and I am not sure if he was giving us an accurate version. They seemed to be boasting about how many Mau Mau they had killed. In fact they took us inside their little compound and showed us hands nailed up on the wall.'

'I asked if they had killed any women,' said Miss Collier. 'They said they hadn't but any they captured...our interpreter refused to translate, but they made it quite clear what happened to the women. Is that typical of African security forces, Colonel?'

'There are always bad apples, Miss Collier, and the Home Guard is not trained to regular military standards. It's a complicated matter. This is my own view. We have counter-insurgency operations in Malaya and Cyprus at the moment. Treasury restrictions mean that the number of regular battalions available to deal with the Emergency here is limited. Added to which, there is a very large area to cover. So these regular battalions are used for active operations against the Mau Mau, whereas protecting the loyal natives is devolved to local militias. They are supervised by the Army, but there are not enough British officers to go round and therefore the supervision is, shall we say, at arm's length. Therefore it is likely that there are some offences committed. I may be wrong in my analysis. You should take the matter up with GHQ. General Erskine has overall command of all security forces.'

'And the Police? We got the impression that the Africans are more afraid of the Police than of the Army.'

'Well, I suppose that is because they are more likely to have direct contact with the Police. Most of the constables are natives. I have only had dealings with Special Branch, who are basically an intelligence gathering organisation.'

'What about your own unit, Colonel? Do your askaris behave themselves? I have heard stories of askaris preying on weaker Africans, demanding bribes as protection money, and beating them up when they don't comply.'

'I know that those accusations have been levelled at the Home Guard and the Police. As I said before, our battalion is spread over several locations and often operates in small squads on patrol, which cannot be directly supervised in every instance. Investigating misbehaviour is always a messy and unpleasant business but it is essential that we don't brush things under the carpet. We have to be trusted by the Africans if we are to make headway against the insurgents.'

Michael hoped he did not sound too sanctimonious. He went on: 'We train them in correct conduct towards the Africans and we have strict rules of engagement. Whenever misbehaviour occurs we have powers under the Army Act to deal with it at battalion level. All offences have to be reported to Brigade or indeed GHQ and it is up to them to initiate courts martial for more serious offences, though we may well recommend one.'

'Have you had many courts martial since you have been here?'

Michael thought for a moment. 'Two for theft, four for drunkenness, one for indecency, two for desertion and several for other military offences, like sleeping on post or violence to a superior officer. No more than what you would expect in a unit of nearly a thousand men over a couple of years. Have I got the number right, Bright?'

'I would have to look at the records, sir, but that sounds about right.'

'What about Section 40 offences?' asked Walker.

'You mean, I hope I have got it right, "any act, conduct, disorder or neglect, to the prejudice of good order and discipline"?'

'That's rather a vague definition, isn't it?'

'Sometimes being vague can be useful.'

'But doesn't it give too much discretion to the military authorities?'

'That is what you will have to argue with them. I can only obey the directives sent down to me.'

'Have you had offences under Section 40?'

'Not so far in my time, but one can never rule it out in the future.'

He was not telling an outright lie, since no charges had been levelled at Symonds or Croxall, but he was conscious of equivocation.

Miss Collier got up and the men stood up as well.

'Colonel, interesting and important as this discussion is, I must go to bed. Otherwise I will be drifting off, which would be very rude of me. Thank you for an afternoon to remember and your hospitality. I am now beginning to understand the challenges your men face in the forest. Goodnight, Colonel, and Major Bright.'

With that she swept from the room.

Mr Walker was offered a nightcap, but he declined.

'Reveille at 0630, is it? I had better get my head down, too.'

* * *

After breakfast, Major Bright took the MPs on a tour of the camp. As well as inspecting accommodation and watching some training, they spoke to the askaris who had taken part in the exercise the previous day. Michael went to his office. While he was engaged in paperwork, a radio call came in from Patrick Howarth.

'What time do you want me at the Sportsman's Arms?'

'Say 10.30, for an hour and a half maximum.'

'Fine. There is someone who wants to speak to you.'

Jane came on the line. 'I am coming in with Patrick and bringing Naomi. Can we see you?'

'Of course, darling. I will introduce Patrick to the MPs and leave them to it. Then we will have an hour or so. What would Naomi like to do?'

'She says that she wants a ride in a tank.'

'Tell her we don't have any tanks, alas.'

'We'll have to settle for shopping. She can practice her Gikuyu.'

The MPs returned to the Mess at 10.00. Michael met them with a Land Rover and took them into town. On the way he asked them if they had any comments on what they had seen or heard in their tour.

'I see that dismantling and cleaning weapons has not changed since my day,' said Walker. '"Today we have naming of parts" and all that. I used to be able assemble a sten gun with my eyes closed. The men look a lot fitter that we were.'

'We have a daily routine of PE, weapon training and range work. We are trying to increase the number of wireless operators, but it doesn't help that we have a limited number of sets, and often they are duff. Perhaps you could raise this with the War Ministry back home. And we could do with better sleeping bags. The ones we have are pre-War issue. They are not waterproof and are very heavy when they get sodden. You can see how wet and cold it can be in the forest.'

'Surely the army should be able to provide you with decent kit,' said Miss Collier. 'After all, you are fighting an active campaign.'

'Budget restrictions, I should imagine. There is also the attitude that because there is so much kit available from the war, it should be used up before buying new. Elite forces have the latest stuff. Other troops, especially natives, have to make do with existing stock. And in the eyes of Whitehall, it doesn't seem to matter all that much if askaris get cold at night; they must be used to hardship, being black.'

'I will certainly have something to say about that when I get home.'

'Do quote me, but indirectly. Otherwise I might be guilty under Section 40. What did the askaris say to you?'

'They were very polite. They smiled a lot and I noticed that their teeth were usually very good. Their English was confined to military matters and when we asked something beyond, they looked for the interpreter.'

'We use English on formal occasions and we have regular English classes. The soldiers speak Swahili among themselves. It's a lingua franca in East Africa. You see, not all of them come from Kenya. The locals speak Gikuyu, but you can get by anywhere with Swahili and English.'

'The accommodation is a little rough and ready, Colonel. Some of the men are still in tents. And the ablutions are primitive.'

'That's segregation, Miss Collier. The British battalion has the huts and the askaris the tents. However, we have indented for more huts, but when they will arrive is anyone's guess.'

By this time they had reached the Sportsman's Arms.

'You are going to have coffee with Patrick Howarth, a big local farmer. His farm was attacked by the Mau Mau. My askaris came to the rescue. He'll tell you all about it, if you want.'

Michael took them into the lounge where Patrick was waiting. Introductions were made. He left them to it and went to look for Jane and Naomi. They emerged from the Ladies' and came into the lobby.

Jane and Michael kissed and Naomi offered her cheek to be kissed. Then holding hands together they went out into the sunshine, the girls wearing cotton dresses and straw hats, Michael in uniform and his slouch hat. He felt a little strange at the incongruity, but was just happy to be with Jane. 'I am nearly forty years old,' he thought, 'and I am like a boy on his first date.'

They walked to the main street and along to the *duka* for Naomi to buy some pencils and paper. Michael and Jane stood in the doorway, while she did business with Mr Hussein. He expected her to speak English but she had addressed him in Gikuyu.

'She is not backward in coming forward,' Michael remarked.

When she had made her purchases, Naomi led them back to an open space beside the river. There were makeshift swings hanging from a branch of a large fig tree. There were some other children there and Naomi waited for her turn on the swings, all the time chatting away. Michael and Jane sat on a bench, watching. Michael told her about the visit of the MPs; he had expected the woman to be a battleaxe but she had seemed appreciative of the hospitality and would dine out on her experiences in the forest exercise.

'I hope they will go away with a favourable impression of this battalion, at least.'

'What do you mean?'

'There have been many incidents of soldiers mistreating civilians, not so much now, but in the first year of the Emergency. Questions in Parliament. Hence the visit of the MPs. We have something going on just now, and I hope it doesn't come out until after the MPs have left.'

'Are you involved?'

'As CO, bound to be. I have been looking back over what I have done and I think I have done all the right things. But I am worried.'

She took his hand. 'Don't tell me about it now. Let's just enjoy this moment.'

'How much longer will you be with the Howarths?'

'Not sure. Naomi goes to Gilgil next year and none too soon. I feel that she is outgrowing me, which is perfectly natural. She needs more academic stimulus than I can give her. We still do lots of things together but she can be impatient.'

'Is she OK, after the raid? No nightmares or anything?'

'For a bit she kept asking questions and she took a long time to get to sleep. I had to sit with her, in case the bad men came again, but she seems to have forgotten about it. She goes to the school quite happily; she wants to be with her friends, not just boring old Simmie.'

'I don't believe you could ever be boring. Shall we go and find a drink?'

They called to Naomi, who came over with reluctance.

'Fancy a lemonade, Naomi?' Michael asked. 'You must be quite hot.'

'OK, so long as you and Simmie don't talk to each other the whole time.'

Michael looked at Jane, and grinned. 'I am sure you have lots to say to me, Naomi.'

They emerged onto the main street and were walking back towards the Sportsman's Arms when they met three askaris off-duty. At the sight of Michael, they braced up and saluted. 'Good morning, sir.'

Michael saluted back and wished them a good morning also. One of them was Gichuchi, and he recognised Jane and Naomi. He nodded slightly, and made as if to stop and say something, but changed his mind and hurried after his colleagues.

'What was that?' Jane asked.

'That was the man you shot at. He is now one of our best trackers.'

'I remember now. You said something about him at the time.'

'We weaned him away from the Mau Mau. He is a brave man.'

On the way into the Sportsman's Arms they met Hugh Frampton coming out.

'Ah, the fair Jane and the dashing soldier. I have just been speaking to those MPs. They have some weird ideas, but I put them right. Good day.'

They went into the garden at the back.

'I dread to think what he told them. I hope he doesn't meet Gichuchi. He used to work on Frampton's farm and Frampton beat him, which is one of the reasons why he fled to the Mau Mau.'

They all had lemonades. Naomi asked what Mr Frampton was doing.

'I expect he had to go to the bank and came in for a drink,' said Jane.

'His breath smells.'

'That, Naomi, is because he likes a drink, a proper drink.'

'Well, you and Mummy and Daddy like a proper drink.'

'So we do, and Michael does, but not in the middle of the morning.'

'When can I have a proper drink?'

'Not for a few years. Alcohol is not good for children. Besides, you would not like the taste.'

Naomi thought about this for a moment. 'Perhaps I could try, just to see.'

'That's up to Mummy and Daddy.'

'What's up to Mummy and Daddy?' said Patrick as he came into the garden.

'We were talking about alcohol,' said Michael.

'Well, I need a stiff one after those MPs. They were very polite and listened attentively until Frampton came in; he had been drinking. I had to introduce him and he went off on a tirade about weak-kneed politicians back home who did not understand the situation here - you know, the usual stuff. The African only understands force. The way to deal with them is to give orders and beat them if they disobey. As far as the rebels are concerned, every one should be shot on sight, and their collaborators with them.'

'What did the MPs say to that?'

'They soon got the measure of him and let him rant on. When he had finished he got up and left, much to my relief. They have gone for a little walk down the street. I gave them fifteen minutes. I had better be getting back. Ready, Jane? I'll see you outside in a moment. Come on Naomi.'

She dutifully followed her father to the jeep outside. Jane looked at Michael.

'When can I see you again?'

'Whenever I can wangle it, but it could be at short notice.'

'Don't worry. Patrick and Annabel are very accommodating.'

Michael took a deep breath. 'Jane, I have to ask this. Are we going somewhere, you and I?'

'Of course we are, wherever it takes us.'

They kissed and walked out into the street. Patrick and Naomi were sitting in the jeep.

'Come and see us soon, Michael,' said Patrick. 'By the way, I am having a telephone installed next week. Should make things easier.' Jane climbed in and put Naomi on her lap. She blew a kiss and Naomi waved.

Michael watched as they headed down the road. Five minutes later the MPs arrived, Miss Collier clutching a bag.

'What have you there?' Michael asked.

'We went to the market. I bought some *kangas* for my niece and nephew. And a carved elephant. I couldn't resist.'

'Are you ready to go back to camp?'

'We are,' said Walker. 'Otherwise Margaret will be tempted back to the market.'

'Well, one has to support local industries,' she replied tartly.

On the journey back, Michael refrained from asking them for their impressions of the morning. In the interval before lunch they went to their rooms to get ready to leave and Michael went to his office. There was a signal from GHQ. He opened it with trepidation. It was a directive laying down a new regulation for reporting accidents in training exercises. He read it and called through to his corporal.

'File this away, Jenkins. I shall be out after lunch, but will be back later on. If anyone wants me before that, leave a message on my desk.'

'Sir.'

Over lunch he could not resist asking the MPs about the morning's conversations. Miss Collier started in at once.

'Conversations? That Mr Frampton…'

'He wasn't invited by me,' explained Michael.

'…lectured us with extreme scorn for any point of view other than his own.'

'Margaret could scarcely get a word in edgeways, and that is saying something,' Walker quipped.

'To me,' she went on, 'he represents the worst, the most backward, the most racially prejudiced, the most benighted type of colonial. And he was drunk,' she added.

'He does enjoy a drink,' said Michael. 'He had probably been using his visit to Nanyuki to meet up with some old chums and have a break from his wife and the farm.'

Miss Collier snorted.

'I have only met him once or twice. Actually, I am told that he is an efficient farmer and runs a tight ship.'

'That is as may be, but his attitudes are disgraceful.'

'Perhaps. But not every settler shares his views. Mr Howarth is much more what you might call enlightened.'

'We certainly had that impression. A bit paternalistic, I would say.'

'If you mean by paternalistic taking care of his workers by building a school and a medical centre, and paying his workers a reasonable wage, then he is paternalistic. Perhaps you should have met Annabel, his wife, as well. She would have told you about the families on the farm and what is done for them. As a result they have a loyal workforce. Both of them are Kenya born and are very much aware of their responsibilities. This is their country, too.'

'They were very complimentary about your askaris when their farm was attacked.'

'We had established what we call a rapid-reaction procedure and it seemed to work quite well.'

Over coffee Walker asked Michael about the attitude of his askaris to the Africans.

'We don't have the potential for colour prejudice that a British regiment might have. Our askaris have pride in their regiment. They feel that serving in it gives them a leg up in civilian life, when they are demobilised. There is every incentive for them to behave correctly. For a start, they will get a pension which will help them set up a business or a *shamba*. To lose that would be a great blow and discredit.'

'Do they sympathise with the Mau Mau at all?'

'Not that I have heard, though I am obviously not party to their private conversations. I think they see the Mau Mau as gangsters, preying on an innocent population. They want an ordered society. The Mau Mau offers nothing but freedom from British rule. There is a general expectation that Independence will come anyway sooner or later, as in the case of other colonies.'

Further comment by the MPs was prevented by the arrival of Captain Lansdowne. While they went to fetch their bags, Lansdowne asked Michael how he had got on with them.

'Pretty well. I think they enjoyed themselves. We certainly showed them a thing or two in the forest. Are they going to any other battalions?'

'I don't know. I have to take them back to Nairobi and leave them at Government House.'

'No doubt they will make a report and it will be aired in the Press.'

'Sure to be.'

'So long as the report is based on fact and not on preconceptions.'

'Some hope!'

The MPs came to the car. They shook hands with Michael and thanked him for a most interesting visit. Miss Collier commented that he had given them much to think about; they now had a much clearer idea of what the Army was trying to achieve and the difficulties to be faced. Mr Walker said that as an old soldier he was impressed by the spirit of the battalion and wished Michael every success in his career.

Michael made suitable deprecatory noises and wished them a safe journey. Miss Collier waved to him as the car drove off.

He looked at his watch and reminded himself that he was due to inspect a platoon training exercise organised by Lieutenant Havers. He went inside to fetch his hat. His corporal accosted him.

'A phone call has just come in, sir. Will you take it or shall I take a message?'

'I'll take it.'

'Colonel Charteris? Prentice here, Military Police.'

'Hello, Prentice. Any news?'

'The case of Sergeant Rawlings has been examined by the Army Legal Department, and he is to be court-martialled on a charge of murder.'

'I see. When will this be?'

'Probably in a month.'

'Well, give me as much notice as you can.'

'Sir.'

Prentice rang off. Michael sighed deeply and hunted in a drawer of his desk for the manual on courts martial.

* * *

The following morning, Michael decided to telephone Patrick on his new line. The phone was picked up promptly.

'You are one of the first to ring me, Michael. Thanks. It is so much less cumbersome than the radio, but the trouble is that people might just start calling me for the hell of it and I will have no time to do other things. The tyranny of the telephone. But that is progress. Do you want to speak to Jane?'

'I would love to, but I expect she is busy with Naomi. Perhaps I could ring the evening.'

'I am sure that will be OK.'

'You and Annabel well?'

'We are as busy as ever, which is good. No time to swan around.'

'Good. Patrick, I wanted to talk to you about the MPs. They found your conversation most instructive. What did you tell them?'

'I talked about the farm and our methods. I made it quite technical – crop yields, production costs and so forth. At one stage I thought Miss Collier's eyes began to glaze over. Walker was more attentive and asked some sensible questions. She was more interested in social questions. Why did I not give the *watu* the right to buy their own plots? What role did they play in the management of the farm? I tried to be patient in my answers, but clearly her questions were loaded.'

'When I asked them about their morning she agreed that you were much more enlightened than Frampton, but she thought that you were paternalistic.'

'What did she mean?'

'That you looked after your people well but as the boss and owner you were firmly in charge and did not allow the *watu* any rights or representation.'

'What did she want? Workers' Councils? Trades Unions?'

'I think that is the policy of her party back in the UK.'

'Well, I suppose it might come to that with Independence.

Whether that would improve their lives is another matter. If it did come to it, I suspect that Frampton would sell out at once to some Indian businessman, who would probably be even harsher with the workforce.'

'They were appalled by Frampton. When they spoke to me afterwards they called him all sorts of names. Miss Collier said he was the most benighted type of colonial and his attitudes were disgraceful.'

'I don't warm to him myself but we settlers have to maintain a certain solidarity.'

'I quite understand. Which reminds me. When I first took over the battalion, I was at a reception for General Erskine and met James Ridout.'

'James? Ah yes. I haven't seen him for some time. He was always a level-headed chap. Unfortunately, not all farmers appreciate his wisdom.'

'We had a brief chat. He was emphatic that Independence would come sooner or later. He said that of one the casualties of the Emergency and the way we have dealt with it is the loss of trust between us and the Africans.'

'He's absolutely right. Once trust is gone, it is very hard to restore it. I have bent over backwards to earn the trust of my workers and it has cost me a lot of effort and money, but it has been worth it for their loyalty. I couldn't manage my farm in any other way. That sounds pompous, but it is true.'

'Never mind what Miss Collier says. It is all too easy to pontificate from a London standpoint. There is another matter. Are your security arrangements still up and running?'

'They are still in place, but we haven't had a drill recently. I must get round to it. Actually life has been pretty smooth these last months; no alarums and excursions. Fingers crossed.'

'Well, I won't keep you. Please tell Jane that I will call her tonight.'

'Will do.'

Michael put the phone down. It seemed an awfully long time to wait until the evening.

Chapter Thirteen

In the event, it was six weeks before the court martial of Sergeant Rawlings began and a further fortnight before a verdict was reached. One reason for the delay was a lengthy debate between the Deputy Attorney-General for Kenya and the military prosecutor as to whether the case should be heard under military or civil law. In the end the Governor of Kenya, advised by London, ruled that the trial be held as a court martial, on the grounds that the Army would be severely hampered in its efforts to bring the Emergency to an end if every soldier who fired a shot might be the subject of a judicial enquiry of some sort. There was a firm of lawyers in Nairobi which, in the interests of civil liberty, exploited every opportunity to attack the conduct of the Army. A court martial would be no less stringent in its procedure than a civilian court. Furthermore, a prosecution before a civilian court would take a very long time and would engender unwelcome publicity.

The case was held before five officers, chaired by a Major General, who was assisted by a Deputy Judge Advocate. In view of the seriousness of the charge, Rawlings was defended, not by an officer of his battalion, but by an officer from the Army Legal Department.

The burden of the case against Rawlings was the evidence of the askaris who had been with Rawlings at the time, and of the two Kikuyu who had witnessed the incident. Andrew Holmes, the District Officer, confirmed that the villagers had informed the chief, who passed on the information to him.

Captain Symonds, when asked why he had not reported the matter to his commanding officer, said that, in his experience, testimony from Africans was generally worthless, since they would say what they thought would please the listener, and they had little concept of the truth. He had interviewed Sergeant Rawlings, who said that he had reason to suppose that the three Kikuyu were up to no good. They had produced a bit of paper which they alleged allowed them to work in the Special Area; however, they were armed with *pangas* and when approached behaved in a shifty manner. Then they had become abusive and he had to threaten them. They started to run away and disregarded his order to stop. Because the askaris were fumbling with their weapons, he himself fired the shots, because the men would have escaped otherwise. Symonds did not doubt Sergeant Rawlings' word, since he was an efficient and reliable NCO. When asked why the information had come to him via the askaris and not from Lieutenant Croxall, he replied that Croxall was not on the scene at the actual moment, as he was leading another squad some distance away. He had heard the shots and came as quickly as he could. He had inspected the bodies and approved of what Rawlings had done. Unfortunately he did not have the fingerprint kit with him, since it had all been used up and a new kit had not been provided; therefore there was no option but to cut off the hands of the dead men to make certain of their identity.

The prosecutor then drew the Court's attention to the previous reprimand that had been administered to Captain Symonds by his commanding officer for ordering the beating of a suspect. That reprimand had gone down on Captain Symonds' official record. The defence pointed out the information gained on that occasion had resulted in the location and destruction of an insurgent gang. Furthermore, the general situation was such that only firm measures had any chance of success when dealing with Kikuyu, most of whom were supporters of the Mau Mau.

Lieutenant Croxall was questioned. He did not doubt Rawlings' account of the episode and denied the accusation that he had been browbeaten by Rawlings into conniving at maltreatment of suspects. It was alleged by the prosecution that Croxall was a young officer, not long in Kenya, and Rawlings was a considerably older man, who had seen service in Palestine, and therefore had much experience of dealing with insurgents amid a potentially hostile population.

Although Michael had been summoned to appear as a witness to the reprimand he had given to Captain Symonds, he was not called to testify, and he had not heard the evidence given by the askaris and the other officers. He had seen Symonds and Croxall but had not spoken to them. He returned to Nanyuki after a day kicking his heels in a waiting room; all he could do was to wait for the verdict.

Over the next three days he tried to put the matter out of his mind, but it kept cropping up. At last he received a call from the Secretary to the Court Martial, who informed him that he would receive a copy of the verdict, when it was delivered. Another two days passed and Major Prentice rang to tell him that Rawlings had been acquitted of murder, on the grounds that he had good reason to suppose that the men were members of the Mau Mau. Against the evidence from the askaris and the two Kikuyu witnesses, it was found that the men were shot while attempting to escape. The mutilation of the bodies was regrettable but there was no other way of establishing their identity. The hands were taken to the Company HQ but in the event were thrown away without being fingerprinted. Lieutenant Croxall was deemed negligent in not having a fingerprint kit with him and not reporting the incident at once to Captain Symonds. The possibility of collusion between Croxall and his NCO was dismissed outright. However, it was recommended that both men be transferred to other units. It was acknowledged that Captain Symonds had been remiss in not following up immediately the askaris' report to him, but no disciplinary action was to be taken against him.

'What do you think, sir?' Prentice asked.

'I am appalled.'

'So are we in this office, but there is nothing we can do about it. The verdict was political. Rawlings had to be acquitted so that the Army could not be charged with the indiscriminate murder of civilians. Never mind the facts of the case, which to my mind was open and shut. I wonder if the judges got their orders from above. Sorry, sir, it is not my place to comment like this but I am angry.'

'I share your feelings.'

The following day a copy of the judgment arrived in the office. Michael read it and called Major Bright.

After reading it Bright asked if he might sit.

'Of course. Sorry, should have invited you at once. And have a smoke. I need one to calm my mind.'

'There are a number of issues here,' said Bright, 'if we accept that the askaris are telling the truth. First, their reluctance to shoot showed that they were unhappy with the order. But the general rule is that orders must be obeyed promptly at all times, although soldiers have the right to protest afterwards that the orders were inhumane or unjust.'

Michael replied: 'At Nuremburg it was established that obedience to orders is no defence for inhumane conduct.'

'It's a dilemma for them. But the matter was taken out of their hands by Rawlings doing the shooting himself. Secondly, there is a practical reason for acquitting Rawlings. In combat or patrol work, decisions of life or death have to be made in a split second. Assuming that the three men really were insurgents engaged on some dastardly scheme, Rawlings would have been remiss in letting them escape. And it might well come to this: if it meant that every time an African was shot, the soldiers concerned might be subject to a criminal enquiry, then they would be reluctant to fire even when it was necessary. And that is a situation which places undue stress on the individual soldier and must be avoided.'

'I suppose the corollary would be that there is bound to be collateral damage; you cannot make an omelette without breaking eggs. A few innocent men killed is a small price to pay in the ultimate defeat of the Mau Mau; hard luck on those men, but that is war.'

'That argument can be used to justify anything.'

'There is a difference between strict logic and the exigencies of operations.'

'We all realise that, sir. And no matter how strictly the rules of engagement are drawn up and applied, they cannot cover every eventuality.'

'Naturally. Which is why the obiter dictum at the end upsets me. It implies that there was a lack of supervision by senior officers in the battalion, as a result of which junior officers and NCOs acted as they saw fit. I have gone through in my mind all the steps we have taken to inculcate the rules of engagement and I cannot see what more we could have done. I officially reprimanded Symonds. I have always made the point that we must earn and maintain the trust of the Africans. This verdict has undermined all our efforts in that direction.'

Michael drummed his fingers on the desk and went on: 'I don't think we can leave Captain Symonds in charge of C Company. I know the court's comment was that no action was to be taken against him. But his removal would be a salutary reminder to other officers that we mean business about hearts and minds. I want him back here under my watchful eye. Who is our senior Lieutenant? Havers, isn't it? He's a sensible chap. We will give him a field promotion to Acting Captain and he can take over the Company. Have you any suggestions as to what to do with Symonds?'

'I notice, sir, that the Camp Commandant here is due for a long leave soon. Symonds could work with him and take over during his absence. A boring desk job will fill the bill nicely.'

'A good idea. I will brief Havers. He can have RSM Tickell with him, at least for a few weeks, to sort things out in C Company. Draft the orders and let me have them tomorrow.'

* * *

News of the acquittal of Rawlings soon spread by bush telegraph among the lower ranks of the battalion and was received with indignation, not so much at the unlawful killing of the three men but at the fact that the evidence of the askaris was ignored and that of the white officers preferred. A garbled version, to the effect that the askaris were to be punished for giving evidence against a white man, gained credence. There was an undercurrent of resentment in the battalion. Gichuchi's brother Njeru soon heard the rumour and accosted him about it; they had not spoken for some months.

'How do you feel now, being ordered about by *Wa Johnny* who lie to save their skins?'

'You're talking nonsense as usual, Njeru. I have no complaint about my officers. They have been fair to me. I am grateful that they saved me from detention camp and gave me, well, self-respect.'

'But you broke your oath and deserted the Mau Mau.'

'Do you know what being in the Mau Mau is like, living in the forest, being cold and hungry, no women? Not very comfortable, I can assure you. Have you seen what the Mau Mau has done to Africans? During the raid in which I was captured, the *watu* were shot, their *bandas* burnt and one family hacked to death, including young children. I dare say you have passed on to the Mau Mau bits of information. Yet you are quite happy to take *wazungu* money by working in their camp. You have money for a drink and a smoke and a woman to cuddle at night.'

Njeru had nothing to say to this. Gichuchi changed the subject.

'How is our father?'

'I haven't seen him for a long time.'

'Why not? He is not far away.'

'Just haven't got round to it.'

'Well, I will go and see him when I have some leave. I must be due some soon. And our little brother?'

'Karumbi? He is much too grand to acknowledge me, now he is working in the District Surveyor's Office.'

'I will go and see him. It must be nearly a year.' Gichuchi took his brother's arm. 'Look, Njeru, I have now saved a little money. I will help you have treatment for your eye.'

'I don't want your money.'

'But your eye will only get worse if it is not treated. I dare say Father would help as well, and even Karumbi. Don't be stubborn. As a family we must stick together and support each other. Do think about it.' He offered his hand. 'Come on. Don't let's part on a sour note.'

Slowly Njeru put out his hand too. They parted without another word.

A few days later Gichuchi walked into town with three colleagues. He left them to shop and with some difficulty located the District Surveyor's Office. He knocked on the door and eventually it was opened by an elderly white woman.

She took one look at his uniform and made to close the door. 'You have come to the wrong place.'

'Does Karumbi work here?'

'Yes. Why do you ask?'

'He is my brother.'

'Oh. Wait here. Don't attempt to come in.'

After a few minutes the District Surveyor himself appeared and looked him up and down.

'What unit are you?'

Gichuchi pointed to his shoulder flashes. 'KAR.'

'Based here?'

'Yes.'

'Who is your commanding officer?'

'Colonel Charteris.'

'And your name?'

'Gichuchi, son of Njoka.'

Karumbi had been working in an inner office but the door was open and he heard the names and looked up. He could not see Gichuchi but recognised his voice. He came through and spoke to the Surveyor.

'He is my brother, Mr Sandford. I haven't seen him for quite a long time. Can I have permission to go outside and talk to him? Please, sir.'

Sandford nodded. 'But not too long. I want that work finished today.'

'It will be, sir, even if I have to stay late.'

Karumbi came out and the brothers embraced.

They walked down to the river. Karumbi was smartly dressed in dark trousers and white shirt and wore a straw hat. Gichuchi towered over him. On the bench by the swings they sat down and at Gichuchi's prompting, Karumbi talked about his job.

'I am really enjoying it. Mr Sandford is strict but he has taught me a lot. I have learnt to read maps and building plans. I can draw elevations and estimate costs. Now I am eighteen, he is going to put me forward for professional exams.'

'That is very good. I am sure you will go far.'

Gichuchi asked him if he had seen their father recently.

'No. I should have done but other things have cropped up. I play football at weekends and I go to church on Sundays.'

'And do you have a friend?'

'A girlfriend? No such luck.'

'I met my Mary in church. I do miss her very much, but I have plenty of other things to think about.' He described his time with the Mau Mau.

'They are thugs, Karumbi. All they can do is to kill and destroy. They will never be able to beat the British Army.'

'But aren't they fighting for freedom from the British?'

'They say they are, but I wouldn't trust them. I know nothing of politics - that's more your line, Karumbi – but the British will give us up in due course, I am sure of that.'

'What are you doing in the Army, Gichuchi?'

'I can't tell you that, but I have learnt a lot about discipline, and I am proud of what I do.'

They fell silent for a moment until Karumbi said: 'When I was at the *duka*, the Mau Mau seemed to me to be heroes. But now, working in the Office, I realise that there is a lot more to life than shooting and killing. I read the newspaper every day. When we become independent, I want to be somewhere in the government. That is why I must get qualifications.'

'And I will be a general in the new Army.' They both laughed.

'Tell me, Gichuchi. You took the Mau Mau oath and broke it. Were you not afraid that something awful might happen to you or to us, your family?'

'What I saw in the Mau Mau convinced me that the oath was an evil one. I went through another ceremony which released me from the oath. So I have no fears on that score. It's all superstition, anyway. I am glad to hear you have changed your mind about them.'

'Have you seen Njeru recently?'

'He works in the camp but I saw him for the first time in ages just a few days ago.'

'How is he?'

'At the moment he seems happy just to exist cleaning latrines and doing odd jobs. No ambition. But we must not ignore him.'

'I think he was passing on information to the Mau Mau. I don't know for certain.'

'I agree. I challenged him and he did not deny it.'

'We must give him something to look forward to. I offered him some money to have his eye treated. He refused, but I told him not to be so stubborn. It will help him to read better, and so get a better job. I hope he will find a niche for himself.'

Karumbi replied: 'I'm sure you are right.' He looked at his watch. 'I had better be getting back.'

'I'll walk a little way with you. I've been thinking. If I can get a day pass, shall we go together to see Father?'

* * *

A fortnight later, Gichuchi obtained a pass, and he and Karumbi caught the bus; Gichuchi was in civvies. They walked up to the farm and came to Njoka's *banda*. He was sitting in the sunshine beside a woman.

'My word, I don't see my sons from one year's end to the next and now two arrive at once. My cup overflows.'

He introduced them to the woman. 'When you all went off I began to feel lonely and Miriam here was on her own. I knew her through church. So we became friends.'

Miriam got up and went inside the cottage, leaving the men.

'Now, you two, what are you up to?'

Karumbi told him about his work and his aspirations. Njoka nodded enthusiastically.

'When you are President of Kenya, you won't forget your old dad?'

'Of course not. I will make you Minister of Agriculture.'

'Glad to hear you are getting on so well. What about you, Gichuchi?'

'It's a long story, Father. I went to the Mau Mau.'

'I have heard about the raids on farms. Were you involved in one?'

'Yes. And I regret it. We killed no *wazungu*, only a dozen or more *watu*. We did very little damage. Pointless. But now I am in the British Army, King's African Rifles.'

'You look well on it, strong and healthy. Have you got a woman?'

'No, Father. I still weep for Mary. But perhaps I will find someone. At the moment I am too busy. The training is very hard.'

Njoka chuckled. 'A thought has occurred to me. What would Mr Frampton say if he found you here? He beat you and ordered you off his farm. I would like to see his face if you meet.'

'I would be very polite and tell him that my commanding officer is Colonel Michael. He knows Mr Frampton.'

'Mr Frampton is not popular, to say the least. I know he was unkind to you and he is very strict with his workers. He calls us all sorts of bad names and uses his stick more than he should. But he runs a good farm and will listen to advice from me and his other supervisors. He pays well and regularly, which is more than can be said for some.'

'So you are happy to go on working here?'

'I doubt I will ever have my own land again. But who's to say? Thank God, I have a job, I am in good health and Miriam will look after me if I am not.'

'Are you, er, together?'

'You mean, do we share a bed? I may be over sixty years old, but I am not past it. I find her a great comfort.'

'I suppose we all need that,' said Gichuchi. 'Take Colonel Michael. He has a girlfriend. It is common knowledge in the battalion. I have seen her. She is very beautiful.'

'Lucky man. Now how about something to eat. Miriam!' He called out loudly.

She stuck her head round the door and waved.

During the meal Njoka did most of the talking and the others listened respectfully. Miriam said nothing, but smiled all the time. Afterwards, Karumbi went for a walk and Njoka had a nap while Miriam cleared up. Gichuchi offered to help but it was refused. So he sat and watched her. He asked if she had any family of her own. She shook her head. Then she held up three fingers and let them fall slowly and clenched her fist. Gichuchi was puzzled and asked her to explain. So she put her hand to her mouth and shook her head again. Gichuchi suddenly realised that she could not speak.

'You had three children but they are dead?' he asked.

She nodded.

'I am very sorry,' he said. 'I hope Njoka is kind to you.'

She nodded again and went into the back behind a curtain

where Njoka was dozing. He heard his father grunting and went outside.

The little plot outside the *banda* was neat and tidy with vegetables and maize growing. Miriam's work, no doubt. An unkind thought occurred to him. It would suit Njoka very well to have a woman round the house and in his bed, doing all the housework and tending the plot, and yet unable to say anything. Poor woman. But otherwise she would be living in the direst poverty and at the mercy of everybody. He judged her to be rather younger than Njoka.

He decided to take a walk around the farm to see if anything had changed since he went away. He noted the tidy fields and well-kept ditches, some of which he had dug himself; fences were in a straight line. A few people were working but he did not accost them. He turned a corner and found Mutahi sitting under a tree with another man. He could not avoid the encounter.

'Well, Gichuchi, I hear you are serving Her Majesty.'

'And are you still recruiting for the Mau Mau? You are content to sit here, nice and comfortable, while the fighters suffer great hardship in the forest. Men are deserting all the time or are in captivity and yet you are still trying to persuade them to die in a lost cause.'

'You broke your oath.'

'A piece of nonsense which cost me fifty shillings.'

'Don't be so sure about the nonsense. Retribution will come. You will always be looking over your shoulder. People have long memories.'

'That works both ways, Mutahi. I wouldn't be surprised if the Police have kept an eye on you. I have heard that they have a short way with prisoners.'

Mutahi was about to respond but Gichuchi had already turned away.

When he got back to the *banda*, Njoka was talking to Karumbi and Miriam was working in the plot. He told him about his meeting with Mutahi.

'He has always been a trouble maker. Why Mr Frampton has not sacked him, I can't imagine.'

'He warned me about retribution on those who break their oaths.

I am not worried for myself, but he might decide to take it out on you.'

'I can look after myself. I have done so for sixty years.'

'Very well, Father. But all the same, beware of him.'

'Will you two be going back this evening?'

'I think so. I have to be in camp by 06.00. tomorrow.'

An hour later they bid farewell to Njoka and Miriam and walked down towards the bus stop. Gichuchi was telling Karumbi what he had discovered about Miriam when Mutahi and two other men came out in front of them from behind a large tree.

'That's him,' said Mutahi.

The two men were armed with sticks and a *panga*.

'Run, run,' Gichuchi shouted to Karumbi, who retreated into the wood.

Now was the time to apply his training in unarmed combat. He picked up a stone and hurled it with full force at the man with the *panga*. He was slow to dodge the missile which caught him on the side of his head; he dropped the *panga* and staggered back. The other man ran at him, raised his stick and made to bring it down on Gichuchi's head. Gichuchi replied by charging at him and blocking the blow with one arm, stepping in close and hitting him with his fist above the heart; he collapsed on the ground. It was all over in seconds. Gichuchi picked up the *panga*. The two meni lay groaning; one was bleeding heavily from his ear. The other tried to get up. Gichuchi kept out of his reach and pointed the *panga* at him.

'Stay down, and don't move. If you do, I will come at you with this.'

Meanwhile Mutahi had remained at a safe distance. When he saw his colleagues on the ground and Gichuchi picking up the *panga* he turned and ran as fast as he could back towards the farm.

Gichuchi was tempted to shout an insult at him but instead called Karumbi back; he had been watching from the wood. Together they ran down the road. Fortunately, they did not have to wait long at the bus stop. When it came, Gichuchi threw the *panga* into the bushes.

'That was good fighting, brother,' said Karumbi in admiration, when they were on their way. 'Why didn't you kill them?'

'I had no reason to. I had no quarrel with them. They were just thugs hired by Mutahi.'

'Have you ever killed someone in a fight?'

'No, but I have been taught to. You don't have to be strong but you have to be quick.'

'You are strong and quick.'

'I have also been taught that you only kill as a last resort, when no other way is possible. If I had been attacked by four men I would probably have had to kill or badly wound one to discourage the others.'

'How would you kill?'

'Depends on how I am threatened. You, Karumbi, are small but I expect you can run fast because of your football.'

'Yes, I can.'

'That is your best defence. Don't try anything fancy. Just get away as fast and as far as you can. Don't be a hero.'

Chapter Fourteen

Michael was due a few days local leave. He had put it off for several weeks, but there was a lull in operations coming up and nothing that could not be left for subordinates to deal with. He spoke to the Brigadier, who readily agreed with his request.

'Will you be going far?' he asked Michael.

'Um…I was hoping to go down to the coast for a few days. I have never been there before.'

'Good idea. Taking that girl with you?'

'Er…well, yes. I haven't asked her yet.'

'I'm sure she will jump at the chance. Good luck, Michael.'

Sooner rather than later Jane would be going back to England to see her parents before doing anything else she had in mind for her future. Without her presence, twenty miles away, soldiering in Kenya would be much duller. Indeed, there were moments when he resented the time his military duties kept him from her. That he had come round to the idea of marrying her was not in doubt. But she was considerably younger than him and he had only known her away from home. Was theirs just a holiday romance? Yet she had given every sign that she wanted their relationship to deepen. Would that be the same after a week by themselves? It would be a good test.

Michael raised the matter with Patrick, who gave it his blessing. Then he asked to speak to Jane, and put it to her directly. As the Brigadier had surmised, she was delighted with the prospect.

'Of course I'll come. It will be something new to both of us. Can't wait.'

Two days later, Patrick called him. 'Michael, I have the offer of a house for you. It is at Vipingo, about twenty miles north of Mombasa. It belongs to the Framptons. They are more than happy for you to borrow it. There will be no charge, just tips for the servants. When do you want to go?'

'As soon as possible.'

★ ★ ★

Michael drove Jane down to Nairobi. The road was in need of repair after the recent rains and the journey of one hundred and fifty miles took most of the day.

'Is it like this all the way to Mombasa?' Jane asked. 'I looked at the map. It's over three hundred miles to Mombasa and Vipingo is another twenty miles north of Mombasa.'

'Don't worry.'

'Are we going by train?'

'Contain your impatience. I have my magic carpet waiting.'

They turned into the Muthaiga Club.

'The Military have visiting rights. Let's enjoy a bit of luxury. You can have the hottest and longest bath in Kenya.'

'God, I need it after today's journey. All that dust. And you do too, Michael.'

'I'll have a quick shower and leave the bathroom to you. I have one or two things to sort out before tomorrow.'

'What things?'

'All in good time.'

'You are infuriating.'

'I know.'

Some time later, Michael was waiting in the lobby for her. Some heads turned as she came in.

'You look a million dollars. Isn't that what the Americans say?'

'And worth every penny. I haven't worn a dress for months. The bath was heavenly.'

He led her into the lounge.

'I can't take you into the bar; gentlemen only.'

They sat down in armchairs looking out on the lawns. A white-jacketed waiter took their order. When the drinks arrived, Michael held up his glass.

'To us.'

'To us. And a happy week ahead.'

They sipped contentedly.

'Can I ask now? Where is your magic carpet?'

'At the West Aerodrome.'

'Really?'

'Being in the Army has its compensations. There is a plane going down to Mombasa tomorrow morning to pick up some brass hat. I've hitched a lift for us. It is a civilian plane in RAF colours.'

'How exciting! I have never flown before.' She thought for a moment. 'Will I be airsick?'

'The pilot will not be doing aerobatics. There will a steward who will serve us coffee and biscuits, or something stronger if you want.'

'Luxury indeed.'

They were about to get up and go to the dining room when an elderly gentleman came over, leaning on a stick.

'Colonel Charteris?'

Michael got up.

'James Ridout. We met at Bobby Erskine's inauguration. Must be nearly three years ago.'

They shook hands.

'May I sit down for a moment,' said Ridout. 'My leg is playing up.'

When he was comfortably settled he refused Michael's offer of a drink.

Michael introduced Jane.

'Ah. You work for the Howarths. I haven't seen Patrick and Annabel for a while. How is their daughter getting on?'

'Naomi. She is a very bright girl and mostly a pleasure to deal with, but, as with all little girls, there are times when I could cheerfully strangle her.'

'I have a granddaughter like that. How is the battalion?'

'I think we are doing a good job, for the most part, Mr Ridout. My askaris are coming on well and we are going after the Mau Mau, rather than waiting for them to strike. I have a couple of ex-Mau Mau whom we captured and have turned around. They seem to be loyal and their information and jungle skills are very useful.'

'That is the way; hearts and minds, and beating the buggers at their own game.'

'Are you still President of the Farmers' Association?'

'No. They retired me. And I was glad to go. There are still too many who won't acknowledge that times are changing and I am fed up with arguing with them. They are a millstone round the neck of the Government. And my wife is not very well. But she lets me come for a drink and a round of geriatric golf. And what brings you here, if I may ask?'

'We are going down to the coast for a spot of R & R.'

'I am sure you both deserve it. I haven't been there for years. Too damned hot.' He got up with difficulty.

'It has been a pleasure to meet you.'

* * *

At eight o'clock they took the Muthaiga taxi to the airfield. Waiting on the tarmac was a de Havilland Dove.

'I haven't been in one of these before,' said Michael. 'I'm looking forward to it. There are big windows so that you can have a good view.'

They walked across to the aicraft and a porter brought their baggage up.

The pilot introduced himself: 'Flight Lieutenant Kennedy, Ma'am. And this is Pilot Officer Wood. It will be a lovely morning for a flight, not too bumpy at this time of the day. We are not in a hurry, so we can fly around a bit and show you the sights.'

'Thank you, Mr Kennedy. This is my first trip in an aircraft and I will enjoy every minute of it.'

There were no other passengers.

Fifteen minutes later they were airborne. Kennedy took them due south over the Athi plains. His voice came over the speaker.

'Look to you left, Miss Simpson, as we turn to port. You will see Mount Kenya.'

The twin peaks stood out with crystal clarity.

'And now to your right. The white dome is Kilimanjaro. It is a hundred miles away and higher than we are now.'

The aircraft turned south east. 'We now follow the road and railway for a bit. We will descend and throttle back so that you can have a look for wildlife. Would you like some coffee? Flight Sergeant Wallace will bring some.'

Jane was too rapt in the view to drink much of her coffee. The country was mostly scrub with an occasional *shamba* and here and there a small pillar of smoke.

'What's that?' Jane asked.

'Charcoal burning, probably,' replied Michael and handed her the binoculars.

Kennedy came over the speaker again. 'If you look to your right, Miss Simpson, you will see the Kyulu Range. All those cones along it are volcanoes, and quite recent ones at that, just a few hundred years ago. The black amidst the vegetation is the remains of the lava flows.'

A few minutes later Kennedy announced that they were over Mtito Andei at the entrance to the National Park and would be turning due south. Once away from the town, the plane descended to a few hundred feet as they flew over the bush. In a short space of time they saw elephant at a water hole, buffalo in herds and antelope of various kinds.

'Look, Michael, a giraffe with its *toto*.'

'This is the Tsavo,' said Kennedy. 'There has been recent rain, so it is very muddy. However, look out for hippos. They congregate to wallow in the shallows.'

The plane turned to follow the river. Sure enough there was a pool full of large brown backs, with some heads raised in huge toothy yawns. Another turn and more open plains lay below them. Herds of zebra roamed and through the binoculars she could see a pride of lions asleep on a small outcrop of rock.

Michael tapped her shoulder. 'Over there. By those trees.'

'Rhinos. Three of them. Ugly brutes. White or black?'

'Can't tell from up here.'

'This is Voi coming up,' said Kennedy. 'If you are travelling to Mombasa by car, here is where you fill up with petrol. Or change your tyres; the road can be pretty bumpy. One day they will get around to laying tarmac. Miss Simpson, would you like to come to the cockpit?'

Jane looked at Michael, who nodded. Pilot Officer Wood got up from his seat.

'From now on we follow the road. Another twenty-five minutes and we will be there. Would you like to fly the aircraft? Two hands on the wheel. Now pull it gently towards you.'

The aircraft rose.

Kennedy pushed forward the throttles a notch. 'We need to be a little higher for Mombasa radar.'

'Very good. Now turn the wheel to the left and press the left pedal…gently now.'

The aircraft banked smoothly and continued to climb.

'Now get us back to level flight.'

Jane reciprocated her previous action and pushed the column forward. The aircraft flew straight and level. Kennedy took her hand in his and eased the throttle back.

'There. Now you have control. Say "I have control".'

'I have control.'

'Follow the road. Climb a bit more if you like.'

Jane climbed, banked left and right, descended and resumed course.

'I'm surprised how light the controls are,' she observed.

'With a little help from hydraulics. And I notice that you have not looked at the instrument panel once. You have a natural feel for the aircraft. If all else fails, you could become a pilot.'

Pilot Officer Wood returned to the cockpit.

'We are starting our approach to Mombasa.'

Jane got up and thanked Kennedy for her little adventure.

'A pleasure, Ma'am.'

'Well done, Jane,' said Michael on her return. 'You didn't manage to crash the plane.'

'Don't be cheeky. You were entirely safe in my hands.'

Ten minutes later they arrived at Port Rietz Aerodrome. On the tarmac Michael and Jane thanked the crew and their bags were carried to a car, a Morris Oxford. Michael inspected it.

'Looks in good nick. And it is clean. Jump in. We'll head for the beach.'

⋆ ⋆ ⋆

The house at Vipingo was built on an old coral reef set back a few yards from the beach. There was a good view out to sea from the verandah. On the landward side there was a carport and a shed. Bougainvillea bushes and flame trees provided splashes of colour amid the green of palms and the dusty ground. Yellow and black weaver birds had made hanging nests in the trees. Steps led down to a sandy beach along the sweep of the bay. In the distance, out to sea, a line of breakers could be seen, marking the reef. Anchored a little way off shore were two dugout canoes. The nearest house was several hundred yards away.

Jane unlocked the door with the key she had been given and followed Melanie's instructions about switching on the electricity and water. The refrigerator started to hum and the fans came on. The heat inside was overpowering, so she opened the shutters and all the doors to allow onshore breezes to circulate. Michael announced that he was going down to the *duka* to buy supplies. Jane unpacked and hung up clothes and made the bed. Instead of her khaki slacks she took out a *kanga* and wrapped it around her waist; much more suitable for this climate.

Michael had brought some tinned stew and fruit salad with Carnation milk.

'Basic fare for our first day.'

There was a cardboard box with bottles of gin, tonic, whisky, beer and some wine.

'May as well spoil ourselves.'

Jane filled a tray with compartments for ice cubes and put it in the freezer.

There was a knock on the door.

'I'm Betty, Ma'am. Missus Frampton said you were coming. I am the maid. I come every morning to clean the house and prepare food for your supper.' She brought a bag with bananas and papaya.

'Thank you, Betty. I am Jane. I will be grateful for your help. The colonel is away just now, but he should be back any minute. One thing, Betty, I can't seem to find any…paper for the lavatory.'

'Ah yes, Missus Jane. I will show you.' Betty took her to a cupboard beside the kitchen.

'There you are. Anything else you want. Just tell me. The local fishermen come round most days, with very good fish. Just fry them in oil or butter.'

During lunch on the verandah a vervet monkey jumped down onto the table and tried pick up scraps of food. Michael shooed him away.

'We mustn't leave any food out, otherwise the whole family will descend on us.'

They went for some Egyptian PT under the mosquito net and ventured forth later in the afternoon. The tide was out but between the coral of various colours were pools of clear water. Jane and Michael explored these, poking the creatures gently with a stick to see them move. There were starfish a foot across, sea urchins with long spikes and hermit crabs. Tiny fish swam in between. Jane tried to memorise the sea birds they saw, to identify them in the bird book back at the house.

Over drinks before supper they made plans for the next few days, or rather, agreed to have no plans save for a visit one day to Mombasa and lunch at the club.

'This will be the longest time we have spent together,' said Jane. 'I don't want to share you with anyone. The big question is: can you put up with me for the next few days?'

'I will try. I'm in a job where I am always having to deal with people and making decisions about them, very important decisions and sometimes ones involving life and death. I have to harden my heart, not something in the Sandhurst curriculum, and I worry about it. So I am more than happy to let life take us where it will for a few days. Quite apart from the delights of your company, there are books to read. I never have time normally.'

'I am going to keep a note of our week, what we have done and birds and animals seen. Otherwise I will forget.'

Michael raised an eyebrow.

'Everything?'

'Not quite, darling. Just stuff children can read without blushing.'

Jane cooked the meal that night. She brightened up the stew with herbs she found in a cupboard and added fresh bananas to the fruit salad. Michael poured some wine. Even when it got dark the temperature was in the high eighties. While they were eating, a dragonfly flew into the room; its wings were a hand's breadth. They watched helplessly as it immolated itself in the blades of the fan. Another visitor was a hornet-like insect about three inches long. It flew in and out again without taking any notice of them.

'My theory is this,' said Michael. 'The bigger the insect, the less harmful it is. You have to watch out for the tiny ones that buzz in your ear when you are trying to sleep. There are a lot more down here than in the Highlands. We mustn't forget to light the coils.'

After supper they took a torch and went for a walk along the beach. They watched the ghost crabs scuttle down from the undergrowth across the sand in an effort to reach the water, only to be driven back by the incoming surf.

'The tide should be in tomorrow morning. Let's go for a swim before breakfast.'

Despite the heat they slept reasonably well and were up betimes. After a swim and a shower they were hungry for eggs and fruit, the papaya that Betty brought.

The morning passed effortlessly. Jane made a list of the birds seen and wrote an account of their journey down to Mombasa and a description of the house at Vipingo. Michael began to read Churchill's volumes on the Second World War, which he had been meaning to tackle for some time; he was disappointed with the lack of space devoted to the Burma campaign. They retired to bed after lunch and later walked along the beach before another swim. Then they had drinks and Jane cooked fish as Betty had suggested. An hour after supper they were yawning and went to bed. Despite heavy rain on the roof they slept for nine hours.

'We had a lot of catching up to do,' observed Michael.

A day passed in blissful idleness.

The following morning they were up at dawn. It seemed cool at seventy degrees. After a swim and breakfast they smartened themselves up and drove into Mombasa. Roadside stalls sold fruit, rice and fly-blown chickens. Having queued up along with traders' carts of all sorts for the bridge and paying two shillings for the toll, they made their way along to Fort Jesus, a relic of the original Portuguese occupation. While walking along the parapet they saw, out to sea, a dhow with a huge lateen sail making its way towards the harbour. They could feel the onshore breeze in their faces.

'Trade winds,' said Michael. 'Arab sailors have been using them for centuries.'

From Fort Jesus they plunged into side streets looking for trinkets to buy. After much deliberation Jane chose an elephant hair bracelet encased in silver. 'Looks good,' she remarked, 'even if the silver is not silver and the hair belongs to another animal.' Michael bought a new watch strap.

As the heat grew, they headed back towards the shore and found the Mombasa Club. Michael signed themselves in using his military rank. They sat down on the verandah and ordered drinks. Jane looked at the menu.

'I have never had avocados. Must try some.' She asked the waiter for chicken curry ('not too hot, please'), saffron rice, and ice cream and strawberries to follow.

'I'll have the same,' said Michael.

They caught each other's eye.

'Jane, I have been thinking…'

'So have I, Michael.'

'We have known each other for some time, years, even, but these last few days I have come to wonder why I waited so long for us to get together like this.'

'Well, you have had other things on your mind, like commanding a battalion, for instance. And I have had responsibilities, too. Thank goodness we have been only a few miles apart.'

The salad course arrived.

'We have never discussed your future, Michael. Are you going to stay in the army, become a general?'

'I have been thinking about that. I don't suppose I will get much further in the service of Her Majesty. Besides, higher rank would mean less direct action and more management at second hand, in short, being tied to a desk. You have no idea how much bumph the Army generates.'

'What might you do otherwise?'

'Big question. I have been a soldier since I was eighteen. I had a good war…'

'You never told me about your Military Cross.'

'Sometime I will. It wasn't pretty. The thing is, I have no skills apart from soldiering. After the war I watched men come out and become salesmen or even clerks. Only those with connections landed good jobs with big companies. My brother is a civil servant; he is far too moral to put in a word for me in the right quarters. We keep in touch, but I haven't seen him for some years. So, whatever I do, it will be an entirely new venture.'

'Does your brother know about me?'

'I have mentioned you once or twice en passant.'

'Only en passant? I would have expected an essay describing my charms.'

'I hope one day he will see for himself. What about me and your parents?'

'A gentle hint has been dropped from time to time, but I have played it down, since my mother would worry in case I was being carried off to a fate worse than death. She didn't like me going to Africa in the first place. And the idea that we share a bed would appal her.'

The curry and rice was brought to their table.

'I can type and I can look after children,' Jane went on. 'Basically, I am a girl from the suburbs and provincial suburbs at that. But I have a sense of adventure, which is why I came out here. My horizons have been expanded. If there were opportunities here I would prefer them to living in England. Maybe it's an unrealistic pipe dream.'

'Perhaps, but worth dreaming all the same.' Michael shook his head. 'I wish I had a more positive idea about the future. Could we begin somewhere else, do you think? Could you face being an Army wife, uprooted every three years?'

'Is that a proposal, Michael?'

'I just want to know how you feel. There's another matter. I am over ten years older than you.'

'If I marry you, I will be marrying you as you are, not as you will be twenty years hence. Who knows? The Russians may drop a bomb on us and that question will be academic.'

Michael said nothing to this and Jane carried on.

'I will be finishing with the Howarths in due course and I really must go back to England to see my parents. But I needn't stay for ever. You will have to go back sometime. We may be separated for a few months, but we will be in a better position to plan for the future.'

'You are wonderfully practical, despite your dreams.'

'Well, we have to be. Michael, don't propose to me just now. Let's enjoy each other as we are. And when you feel the time is right, you can be assured of the right answer. Just as well it isn't a leap year; otherwise I would have proposed to you myself.'

The subject having been shelved, they spent the next days pottering, reading, swimming and making love. Jane walked to the *duka* every morning, and Betty cleaned and tidied the house. They chatted while she gutted fish brought to the door and chopped vegetables. Betty had had eight children and had buried three. Her husband worked a *shamba* and took casual work wherever he could find it. He was often away. She earned a modest amount working as a maid, occasional cook and babysitter in the houses along the shore.

Betty had examined Jane's left hand. 'Are you and the Colonel married, Missus Jane?'

'Not yet, Betty. Soon, I hope. We have so little time together in the ordinary way. This is a little holiday for us, away from his duties.'

'He seems a fine man, Missus Jane. And you are very beautiful. He is a lucky man.'

'I am lucky, too.'

'But you should get married. I know you love each other, but you must have God's blessing. Otherwise you fall into sin.'

'It doesn't feel like sin, Betty. I am sure God will forgive us in due course.'

'I have sinned, Missus Jane, and I have had my troubles, but God saved and helped me.'

'I'm afraid I haven't been to church for some time, but I would like to be married in church. My parents will want it. They are back in England.'

'Will you be going home?'

'In a few months. And the Colonel will be moving to a new posting. So let's hope that this time next year we will be man and wife.'

* * *

The day came, all too soon, when they had to go back to Nairobi. Michael had been unable to get a flight and he had booked berths on the train.

'First class, of course, Jane.'

They had to get up very early for the morning train; a substantial tip was left for Betty. The car was left at the station, to be picked up by an RAF Corporal. They boarded just in time and were shown to their compartment. Once the train was moving, they were called to the Dining Car for breakfast. Michael happily tucked into eggs and bacon, but Jane picked at her food.

'Sorry, darling, I still haven't woken up.'

Instead of looking at the countryside and wildlife, Jane dozed for most of the morning. When they came to the bridge over the Tsavo, where two lions had killed Indian coolies during the construction of the line in the 1890s, Michael told her the story but she merely blinked and shook her head.

'I am going to lie down. I don't feel very grand.'

Michael became very concerned. He sat beside her and watched her shiver. Her forehead was burning and she couldn't find a comfortable position to lie. She asked to be helped to the lavatory where she vomited and had violent diarrhoea.

'What Matron used to call OBE,' she whispered.

'OBE?'

'Open Both Ends.' She managed a smile. 'God, I feel awful.'

Michael went to the steward at the end of the carriage and asked him to find out if there was a doctor on the train. By the time Dr Mackintosh arrived, Jane was barely conscious.

'Malaria, a classic case. Keep her well hydrated. Water, so long as it has been boiled. Cold tea will do. We just have to let it take its course, I'm afraid. Still, she looks a fit young lady. Has she been taking her pills?'

'As far as I know, yes.'

'Mombasa is well-known for being malarial. In the last century the British used to die like flies there. Is she pregnant by any chance?'

'Oh God…She can't be, surely.'

'Mm. Shouldn't matter, but you never know. When we get to Nairobi have her checked at the hospital.' He looked at her closely. 'Better still, at the next stop, I'll make a call and have an ambulance waiting.'

Michael thanked the doctor profusely. Jane continued to shiver. The steward brought a flask of boiled water from the Dining Car and Michael gave her sips from a spoon. After what seemed an age, the train arrived at Nairobi and to Michael's relief there was an ambulance waiting. Jane was carried to it on a stretcher and Michael climbed in afterwards with the luggage. At the hospital an Indian doctor examined her.

'The next twelve hours will be crucial. On balance of probability, you know, I think she will come through. There may be a problem with recurrent fevers, but equally she may not suffer any long term effects. Come back first thing tomorrow. Fingers crossed, eh?'

Despite the late hour, Michael found a room at a hotel. After an early breakfast he went back to the hospital. He was shown to a side room to wait but he could not sit still and paced up and down. After an hour, the doctor came in and gave him the thumbs up.

'All very good. Her temperature is coming down fast. She needs a few days under observation in case of a relapse. But all goodie good.'

'Thank God, Can I see her?'

'She's all yours.'

Michael went into the ward and approached her bed.

'Hello, Michael,' she said weakly. 'Sorry to be such a nuisance.'

He kissed her and she sat up a bit. She was very pale, with dark rings under her eyes.

'They have been pumping me full of stuff. I feel as though I have been hit by a bus. But the headache has gone.'

'Well, that's good. The doctor says that you must stay for a few days.'

'I don't feel like going anywhere. I just want to sleep.'

'The more the better.'

'Will you stay in Nairobi? Do you have to get back to the camp soon?'

'The Army can do without me for a few more days.'

'It is such a shame, my getting ill like this. We had a wonderful time. I was happier than I have ever been and it has ended up with me in hospital.'

Chapter Fifteen

Michael stayed for some days in Nairobi, during which he received a message to report to GHQ, East Africa Command. His uniform was still in Nanyuki and he had to arrange for a driver to bring it down. He had spoken to Major Bright who assured him that the battalion was in good heart and behaving itself; operations were confined to routine patrols and training.

'And Miss Simpson, sir?'

'Still in hospital under observation, whatever that means. She has taken quite a knock.'

'Well, give her our best wishes.'

'Thank you, Bright.'

He visited Jane in hospital as often as he was allowed. One day he found her sitting in the garden in a dressing gown. She looked much better and had had her hair done.

'Now you are here,' she said, 'let's take a walk around the garden.'

'Are you sure you are up to it?'

'I shall get sores on my backside if I sit down any more.'

She took his arm. She was moving confidently.

'They say three or four days more and then I will be able to go back to the Howarths. It's all been a question of getting the antibodies to work. I have had so many pills that they are rattling around inside me. But they are having an effect. So long as I take care over the next month, I should be fine.'

'I should have asked earlier. Do you need any money?'

'I can cover the hospital bills.'

'No you won't. I will.'

'But..'

'Now we are one flesh, even without the Church's approval. So no argument.'

'You know, Michael, when I was really ill, I thought I was going to die. But you stayed with me and I didn't want to let you down by dying. So I told myself not to die. And I didn't.'

'Oh, Jane.'.

They embraced, and then burst out laughing.

'Melodramatic, but true,' she said. 'Can we be practical for a moment? My clothes need washing. Can you take them to a laundry? I don't want to go home smelling of unmentionables.'

'Would you like a new outfit?'

'That can wait. Take my bag. If you deal with it now, it should be ready for tomorrow.'

He went off, suddenly embarrassed about carrying a bag full of underwear and shirts. Being an officer, he had a servant who dealt with such matters. But he told himself that marriage means running errands like this as well as fond kisses. Not far from the hospital he found an Indian laundry and left the clothes there.

* * *

Michael could not help but wonder why he had been summoned for a meeting. He was directed to the office of the GOC, General Sir Gerald Lathbury. He had to wait in an anteroom for half an hour, which did not help his nerves. Like a schoolboy summoned to the headmaster's study, he went over in his mind all the things that he had done or omitted to do which might have earned criticism. At last he was summoned. He went in, saluted, doffed his cap and was invited to sit.

'Charteris, we haven't met, but I have been acquainting myself with your career.'

Michael said nothing.

'You have had command of your battalion for three years or so. You took it over when numbers were well down and you successfully brought it up to full strength. You organised a rapid reaction procedure which was tested in action in dealing with a raid on a farm near Nanyuki. You instituted a programme of training for forest warfare, based on your experience in Burma, which is being followed by other battalions and indeed the Police.'

He rang a bell and ordered coffee.

'I see that there has been a court martial in your battalion relating to the treatment of civilians and prisoners.'

'This business was not covered up, sir, but subject to the due process of law. I didn't agree with the verdict, but perhaps that is not for me to say.'

'I have read the report of the trial and I have my own opinion, which I have no intention of sharing with you, by the way. But I do understand your view.'

He played with a pencil in front of him.

'Now, Charteris, there are also people reading reports of trials and courts martial, people back in London, who are not aware of the difficulties we face out here and will ignore our very positive achievements. I understand that there are certain newspapers in London, who have their correspondents in Nairobi and are intent on blackening the British Army's role in Kenya. And there are politicians who have suspicions of our operations. I think you did a pretty good job of showing two MPs what is really involved in counter-insurgency. Nevertheless, questions are being raised. I have the War Office and the Colonial Secretary on my back. I am a Para and therefore a fighting soldier, not a politician.'

At this point the coffee arrived. Sir Gerald was about to resume when the telephone rang.

'Not now,' he barked.

'I think you should take it, sir,' said the secretary.

'Very well. Lathbury here.'

'I have Mr Lennox-Boyd on the line, sir.'

Sir Gerald covered the mouthpiece and whispered to Michael 'Colonial Secretary' and added 'bloody nuisance'.

Michael go up to go. Sir Gerald nodded. Michael left the room and was invited to take a chair by the secretary.

'Had your coffee?' she asked.

'I had to leave it in there.'

'I'll pour you some more. Have a biscuit.'

'The General,' she continued, 'doesn't like phone calls from London. London always goes on at considerable length and often is not au fait with the latest intelligence. And calls invariably come when he is in the middle of a meeting. He would much rather be out in the field away from the telephone.'

Half an hour passed. The door opened and the general stuck his head into the office.

'Sorry, Charteris. Come back at 14.00.'

'Sir.'

After lunch he collected the laundry and returned to HQ just before the appointed time.

'The General is ready for you.'

He went in and saluted.

'Sit down, Charteris. Where were we? Oh, yes. The Minister's call indirectly affects you. We discussed the changing roles of the Army and Police. This has been in the air for some time. Special Branch has been taking over more of the operations to capture Mau Mau leaders. They have been quite successful with their deep penetration squads. We believe that when the heads are cut off, the remainder will surrender. Already things are getting difficult for them. The corollary is that the Army will be concentrating on routine patrols. This will not come as a total surprise to you. In view of all this, I have been ordered by the War Office to reduce some battalions to company strength. I am afraid your battalion is one of them.'

Michael could not help looking dismayed.

'This is absolutely no reflection on your conduct as commanding officer. You would be due for replacement anyway within a year. What I want you to do, in consultation with the Brigadier, is to keep the best men and demobilise the rest. Not a pleasant task. The officers and British NCOs will be reassigned and I will need your recommendations. When are you going back to Nanyuki?'

'I hope to go within two days, if the hospital releases Miss Simpson.'

'How is she?'

'Very much on the mend.'

'Good show. I want you to get started on this straight away and have it done within three months. The sooner the better. Formal orders and notification of procedure will be issued in due course.'

'Sir.'

Michael rose to leave but the General waved him to sit down again.

'There is another matter, Charteris. Your future in the Army. Normally this would not be any direct concern of mine, but I think you deserve better than having your battalion removed from you and leaving you hanging in the air. I believe that you have shown more appreciation of, shall we say, the African point of view than most of my commanders. And I hear that you are fluent in Swahili. Times are changing, Charteris, and sooner or later we will have to bow out. But we want to keep our military link with Kenya and I believe that is what a future Kenyan government will want. I think there is a role for you in this. Is that something that you could envisage for yourself?'

'I must go, sir, wherever the Army directs me.'

'Of course, but a willing horse is better than a conscripted one. I can tell you, Charteris, that you will not get another regimental command, because, despite its many virtues, the KAR does not rank high in the Order of Battle.'

'That had occurred to me, too, sir.'

The General looked at his notes.

'I see that you are due some long leave. Take it when you have finished sorting out the battalion. After your leave, why don't you come back here in a new capacity. If I am no longer here, I will make recommendations to my successor. Or will you want to retire from the Army?'

'There are many things I have to take into consideration, not least that I am hoping to marry Miss Simpson as soon as possible, back in England.'

'Quite understood. Colonels should marry.'

* * *

As can be imagined, Michael's mind was reeling as he walked away after the meeting with the GOC. He regretted the approaching end of his command but was excited by the prospect, indefinite though it was, of a change in direction, not only in his personal but also his professional life. He mulled over the situation and decided that whatever the future might bring his priority was to marry Jane. Whether she would really want to come back to Africa was another matter.

He went to the hospital with the laundry and was greeted by the news that Jane was to be discharged immediately. He booked a room at the Muthaiga Club while she changed into fresh clothes. She had obviously lost some weight but her eyes were bright. Over dinner she talked about her treatment and the nurses.

'All Africans or Indians, except for the Ward Sister, who was a bit of a battleaxe. They were very gentle and chatty. They wanted to know all about "the Colonel" and when we were to be married.'

'I hope you did not reveal any military secrets.'

'I don't know any.'

'I have some military secrets to tell you, but not here.'

'That is exciting.'

'It's rather complicated and depends on a lot of factors. Can we talk about a wedding?'

'Gosh. We are moving fast. I don't even have a ring yet.'

'You told me not to propose until I felt the time was right and I think that means when I can see a clear way ahead. But I think we can still make tentative plans. I will be having a long leave coming up soon. It will last for three months. Can you talk to the Howarths about coming home? It might be a bit earlier than they were anticipating.'

'I'm sure they will not object. Naomi is ready for boarding school, anyway. I hope we can go home together. We will have to do the rounds of relatives so that they can have a good look at us. I think we have some writing to do. And making lists.'

'And finding somewhere to live. Do you fancy Chez Nous in leafy Surrey?'

They talked about this and other matters for some time. Jane did not eat much and she refused a pudding.

'I am totally whacked. I must go to bed. You carry on.'

'I won't be too long myself.'

Although they started early, the journey back to Nanyuki took all day. They stopped at Nyeri for lunch to give Jane a rest from the bumpy road. On their way into the town they passed a small group of people standing on some open ground. They were chanting in Gikuyu and holding up banners saying in English “Kimathi will never surrender”. They were being watched by three nervous policemen, but no one else.

They made their way through the crowds milling round the *dukas* lining the street. At the edge of the town they turned into the Outspan Hotel.

‘Hungry, Jane?’

‘Ravenous. I suppose that means I am on the mend.’

Over lunch Michael told her about his interview with the General, the changes he had to make in his command and how it reflected grand strategy.

‘Are you upset about losing the battalion?’

‘In the Army you have to be stoical about what is handed down from above, whatever you really think of it. He did hint that there might be a role for me later. Yes, one half of me is upset, but there are other things in Army life and of course there is you.’

‘Me?’

‘I can’t make a decision without consulting you.’

‘That’s very thoughtful. I am quite happy to be a camp-follower, you know.’

‘Would you be happy about coming back to Africa and, dare I say it, possibly bringing up a family here?’

‘Why not? Other people do.’

‘Or I might be posted to some other colonial battleground, like Cyprus or Malaya, and be separated from you. Or it might be Salisbury Plain, or Germany.’

‘Dull. Though I wouldn’t mind Germany so much, at least for a bit. But I know more Swahili than I do German.’

‘Would you mind coming back to Kenya?’

‘We have talked about the Africa bug. Now I have got it in both senses.’

‘Sorry, I can’t be more definite. All I can say is that in six or more months time I will have to report to wherever Her Majesty is pleased to send me.’

'Michael, I am not a child bride. I will accept your proposal with a clear head and I know that marriage to an Army officer has its penalties. Let's face it. You don't really want to come out of the Army.'

'Not at the moment but the time will come.'

'Besides, you once implied that you have no civilian skills. But you do have – what do they call it? – man-management skills.'

'I am used to giving orders which have to be obeyed. I am not sure how good I would be at persuasion, when I don't have military sanctions behind me.'

'Well, you haven't done badly at persuading me. Tell me, is there something that might tempt you to leave the cocoon of military life?'

'There is, actually. A pipe dream, a flight of fancy, call it what you will.'

'Go on.'

'Ever since I first came here, nearly four years ago, I have been taken with the idea of having a farm, like the Howarths', but not so big. I was very impressed with the Unwins.'

'Well, we would have to be self-sufficient. I have never seen you do anything mechanical. And it could be lonely, stuck out on some remote estate. I have seen it in the Howarths. Weeks go by without them seeing another European, and the farm is forty minutes from Nanyuki. What do you know about animal husbandry?'

'Not much. I would have to learn fast.'

'I can see two major snags. First, do we have the capital to buy a farm and maintain it, putting in a manager, perhaps? And you say that Kenyan Independence will come sooner or later. Might we be evicted? And would we have to take out Kenyan citizenship? Sorry to put a damper on the idea.'

'As usual, Jane, you are being realistic. You did ask me about my dream. If it is to come to pass, I would have to have a rich relative who will conveniently die and leave me pots of money, and secondly, I would have to go and learn about farming in the Tropics. Oh yes, and I would have to find a farm already in operation and in the right place; I don't fancy breaking new ground out in the bush.'

'That is a lot to ask.'

'I have no such relative, I am not too keen about going back to school and I doubt there are many farms available. As far as I can see, they tend to be passed down in the family. As for Independence, no one really knows what is actually going to happen, not even Kenyatta himslf, I suspect. No point in speculating too much.'

He sighed. 'So, all in all, my dear Jane, my dream will remain a dream.'

'Michael, I am sure something will turn up for you, one way or another, and I will be there with you. It will our joint adventure.'

'Jane, I have something in my pocket, burning a hole in it. I bought it when we were in Nairobi, just in case. If ever I thought there was a right time, this is it. I hope it fits.'

He produced a small box with a ring inside it.

'Will you become Mrs Charteris?'

Jane said nothing at first but took out the ring and put it on her finger. She got up and walked round the table to kiss him.

'Yes I will, Michael, with all my heart.'

She held out her finger for inspection. 'It's beautiful, Michael. Thank you.'

Michael did not know what to say. Eventually he found words.

'Well, Mrs Charteris, let's start our joint adventure by getting back to Nanyuki.'

'Whose the practical one, then? Before we go, can we visit Baden-Powell? It's on our way.'

They drove off to see B-P's grave.

'Were you ever a Scout, Michael?'

'No. I was too busy with rugby, cricket and the OTC, though I was a Cub at prep school. What about you?'

'I was a Brownie and Girl guide, with lots of badges. For a townee, like myself, camping in the countryside was a novelty, and character building. I remember one camp in the Mendips when it rained most of the time. Our parents came to visit us and we had to push their cars out of the field. We were soaked and covered in mud. And we made wasp traps out of jam jars. Singsongs around the camp fire, and all that. I hope our children will have as much fun as we did.'

Having paid their repects to B-P, they continued their journey. By the time they reached the farm, Jane was very tired. Patrick and Annabel fussed over her and Naomi hugged her. She noticed the ring.

'Simmie, that's a new ring. Are you…?'

'Yes, Naomi, Michael and I are engaged to be married.'

'How romantic!' she gushed.

Patrick shook Michael's hand.

'We are very pleased for you both,' said Annabel.

Michael did not stay long and returned to the camp. He went to the Mess for a drink and answered urgent questions about Jane's health. He asked Major Bright to see him first thing the following morning, to catch up with current business and to tell him of changes to come.

* * *

Despite the euphoria of his engagement Michael had little time to revel in it. He was immediately summoned to a meeting of battalion commanders at Brigade HQ; a member of Special Branch was also present.

'As you know,' said Special Branch, 'the government has been working on surrender schemes. Through back channels letters were distributed to known Mau Mau leaders, suggesting points where people could surrender, provided they carried a green branch. They would be taken to reception centres and finally put into detention camps. Guarantees of safe conduct were given and an amnesty, free from prosecution, for all crimes committed before the start date. At first only a few came in but then, when the government appeared to be keeping its promises, we had a rush, several hundred in fact. But all of these were poor bloody infantry. No leaders. Nevertheless they kept coming in and we had quite a job to process them. Then, very recently there was a major setback. A considerable body of men was coming out of the forest into the mile strip, carrying green branches as well as their weapons. One unit, not represented here, came across them and decided that they were hostile. A firefight broke out and thirty Mau Mau were killed. Thereupon the surrenders ceased abruptly. The GOC was not pleased and the fruits of many months of hard work to establish trust with the insurgents had been nullified. So we were back where we started. A Mau Mau commander, calling himself the Brigadier, was captured when Colonel Charteris' unit scotched a raid on a farm not far from Nanyuki. His name is Njirami Watui. He was kept in custody for several months and intensively interrogated. The information he provided was useful, up to a point. To encourage him to open up further he was allowed a visit from his relatives. He then revealed what he knew of the Order of Battle, you might call it, of the Mau Mau in the Mount Kenya and Aberdare areas. Inevitably, the information was somewhat out of date. Nevertheless we reckoned that it was adequate for us to use in a new initiative to obtain surrenders after the debacle. We took him on a tour round some areas of the Reserves where we thought the militants were especially strong. This was to show that he was being well-treated, as an example of the Governor's clemency, and to encourage others to come forward and surrender. He was not booed off the field. And so we decided to make further use of him. He agreed to go back into the forest, make contact with the leaders there and present them with a new set of proposals. He was required to return to us by a particular date. That was about three weeks ago. He has not returned and we have no information as to his whereabouts, or what has happened to him.

'I think we can take it that, if he is still alive, he has broken the terms of his release and therefore must be treated as hostile. He must be punished as an example of what happen to people if they break their word.'

The Brigadier thanked Special Branch for his presentation and turned to Michael.

'Charteris, you have been training up forest squads and your unit is nearest to Mount Kenya. Can we rely on you to bring this scoundrel to book? Better if you captured him alive so we can parade him in chains, or, if we have to kill him, make certain there is a photographic record of his corpse, so that we can publish it in the papers and leaflets. Liaise with Special Branch. Meanwhile the rest of us will continue our sweeps in the reserves and forest fringes. Any questions?'

There being none, the meeting was dismissed. The Brigadier kept Michael back.

'The GOC has had a letter from Mr Walker and Miss Collier, the MPs. They are not happy with the way the Army is dealing with civilians. They say that there is insufficient control of the Home Guard and that British soldiers are not given clear guidance as to their conduct. The result is excessive violence not subject to full legal process.'

Michael was about to respond but the Brigadier held up his hand.

'All these matters were discussed with the GOC and the Governor. The letter goes on to say that having talked to soldiers face to face they were impressed by the straightforward comments they had received and now they had a better appreciation of the problems facing soldiers in the field. They received a rebuff from some officers and did not have complete cooperation everywhere. However, they singled out for praise the twenty-four hours they spent with your battalion of the KAR. The officers and men were most helpful and courteous and they enjoyed the hospitality of your Mess. The highlight was the exercise in the forest, an experience they will never forget. Their meeting with the two farmers was instructive, in all sorts of ways. Good show, Michael.'

'I must confess, sir, that I did point out to them the inadequacy of some of the equipment provided for our askaris. I suggested they might like to take the matter up with the War Office. I hope I haven't committed a military offence.'

'Don't worry, Michael. Other people have bent their ears on the subject as well. Look, while you are here, have a drink.' He pulled a bottle of Scotch from a drawer. He poured a generous measure and passed it to Michael.

'Have there been any repercussions among the men after the acquittal of Rawlings?'

'There was some muttering. Obviously the officers and I couldn't speak to them about it, as that would undermine discipline, but we made sure that everyone was kept busy. I think they would relish some action now.'

'Good. I'm sure the grumbling will die out. The verdict was political and misguided, but we can't say that openly. Just patch things up and carry on. The GOC was furious, by the way. Rawlings was very much the old soldier and no wonder a weak vessel like Croxall was under his thumb. I see you have transferred Symonds. A good move; he couldn't stay in command of C Company. Havers and RSM Tickell will do a good job, I'm sure.'

'Both are very capable and have my fullest confidence, sir. They will take a firm line and will sort out any nonsense. Men like to be led; it gives them confidence to face tricky situations. It is one thing to have an enemy in front of you, quite another to have civilians who might be insurgents under cover.'

'That is a dilemma we all have to face out here.'

'I was a little miffed, sir, by the final paragraph of the judgment which suggested that closer supervision of patrols could have averted the incident. I have followed the GOC's instructions to the letter. I don't see what more I could have done.'

'Twenty-twenty hindsight is a wonderful thing. Don't let it bother you. There are more important things to worry about. Top up?'

'No, thank you, sir. I have to get back to Nanyuki.'

'Oh, well. I'll have a small one all the same.' He poured another generous measure.

'I gather you have a young lady in tow.'

'Yes...we are engaged to be married.'

'And I gather she is a beauty.'

'Well, yes, but she has many other qualities as well.'

'I'm sure. Let me tell you that the battalion is very proud of you. Not every man can – what is the term? – pull a girl like that. None of my business, but don't keep her under wraps. To see her with you will be good for morale.'

'I'll bear that in mind, sir.'

Chapter Sixteen

Deep in the forest of the Aberdares, a ceremony was taking place in a large hut with the surviving leaders of the Mau Mau. Field Marshal Dedan Kimathi had been chosen as the first Prime Minister in the Kenyan African Parliament, and his appointment had been ratified by the drinking of beer and anointing with sheep's fat, blood and honey. Kimathi stood up, holding the staff and flywhisk that had been presented to him, and facing Kirinyaga prayed that he might fulfil the trust that had been placed in him. He then went round the assembly, shaking the hand of each man and greeting him in Gikuyu: *Wanyua wakine*. He bade everyone sit and invited Njirami to speak.

'I am here,' he said, 'not to urge you to surrender, as my captors wanted. I have no intention of fulfilling the terms of my release. Instead, I urge you to continue the struggle. It will be difficult. We have to accept that the high hopes with which we embarked on this great venture have been somewhat dashed. The people who used to support us have been herded into villages which are watched closely by the Home Guard. It is shameful that our supporters are beaten up and tortured by lackeys of the British. We are confined in the forest and supplies cannot reach us. Our ammunition is only enough for maintaining a defence and killing for food. Those of us who have surrendered, but not me, have given precious information to the enemy and some of them have joined the British in tracking us down.

'If we give up now, all our previous efforts, the sacrifices we have made and the lives that have been lost, will have been in vain. We will have broken faith with our gallant fallen comrades. Now is the time for resolution. We are the true representatives of Gikuyu and Mumbi, and, confident of their blessing, we must draw on our resources of courage for a final effort. Attack is the best form of defence. I, for one, will continue the struggle to the last bullet, and then with *pangas*, fists and even teeth. I cannot bear to live in a country in which its own people are serfs. I hope you are all of the same mind.'

His remarks were received with applause by all who were present. Kimathi thanked him for his inspiring words. Others spoke in the same vein. However, Kagiri, a leader who had operated round Kiambu and had been forced to take refuge in the forest, made another point:

'Comrades, I am not here of my own volition. Not that I am at variance with you. Very far from it. I am here because I was betrayed and barely escaped with my life. I had loyal followers but there was also a Judas who gave us away to the British. Many of my men were killed. I know who that Judas was. When we have driven the British out of Kenya I will seek this man out and wreak my vengeance on him. He broke his most solemn oath. Therefore, comrades, I propose that we all take another oath that we will carry on the fight as Njirami has so eloquently described, so that our hearts will not fail us when danger comes.'

This speech was also applauded. Kimathi indicated his agreement and said that arrangements would be made to administer the oath the following day.

Another leader commented on the absence from the meeting of Stanley Mathenge, a prominent leader and a decade and more older than Kimathi.

Kimathi replied with some irritation that Mathenge no longer accepted his leadership and had left the country, taking many of his men with him. In doing so, he had abandoned the cause and his name would no longer be mentioned.

This provoked shouts of disapproval among those who admired Mathenge and recalled his fighting qualities in the Burma campaign. He was a man who had direct experience of jungle fighting against a formidable enemy. Kimathi by comparison was an amateur. One man stood up and said that he had been in touch with Mathenge recently and it was certainly not the case that he had deserted. Perhaps Kimathi resented his popularity and was anxious to silence him.

This remark brought an angry response from Kimathi's supporters. The shouting increased. The meeting, which had begun with a show of concord, degenerated into a bout of accusation and counter-accusation. At last, Makahe, the oldest man present, seized Kimathi's staff and banged it on the floor. The gesture commanded silence.

'Brothers, comrades, we must not let personal differences distract us from our task. Please think. We will never defeat the *wazungu* unless we are united. Despite the difficulties and the desertions which have been mentioned, we must coordinate our efforts and follow one leader. Otherwise our cause is lost.'

The clamour had died down and Kimathi invited Makehe to continue.

'Very well, Field Marshal. Njirami mentioned the shortage of ammuntion. This is serious. And I know that some groups have been hoarding their supplies, not for use against the enemy but for a factional fight between us that may erupt at any time. This shows grossly bad faith. What use can we be to the new country that we all hope for if we are fighting amongst ourselves? Think on, comrades, and remember, the cause is greater than any of us as individuals.'

Despite the exhortations of the *mzee* the meeting broke up without a binding resolution. Kimathi commanded the obedience of a number of the leaders but not a few ignored him and went away to their encampments to pursue their own projects. There was no oath-taking.

Njirami went to Kimathi and told him of an idea that he had been brooding on for some time. For this he did not need anymore military supplies and he reckoned it could be accomplished with just a few men. Kimathi gave him his cautious approval but warned him that he would be forever a marked man.

'I am that already. If I succeed, it will be a victory, a small one, but which may lead to other ventures of a similar kind, which will show the *wazungu* that they are vulnerable everywhere, even in the country clubs and military camps, even in Nairobi itself. We don't need large forces, just the dedication of small units, and basic equipment. We can strike effective blows out of all proportion to our numbers.'

Kimathi nodded. 'Very well. And may Ngai bless your endeavours.'

Njirami went away and after three days of dodging British patrols he reached his camp in the forests of Mount Kenya.

* * *

Michael sat in his office with Major Bright discussing the way in which they might proceed with reducing the battalion to company strength. They had already broached the matter with company commanders and had received the names of askaris that they thought might be worth keeping on. As Michael had expected, these were too many for a single company. They looked through the names and decided that they would consider them at another time. It was near the end of a hot afternoon and both men were flagging. Michael poured them a glass of whisky.

'Let's talk about something else. The most recent opinion in GHQ is that the Mau Mau is losing impetus, very much on the back foot. There are rumours of division in the high command and the number of desertions has started growing again.'

'Well, if true, that is good news,'

'Yes, but we must still be on our guard. I am sure that there is an African proverb about a sleeping lion.'

'Lion?'

'Jackal in this case then. A lesser predator, but still one to be reckoned with.'

'Indeed, sir. What do you make of Lathbury?'

'Good fighting record. Commanded 1st Parachute Brigade in Tunisia and Sicily. Wounded and captured at Arnhem but escaped. Doesn't wave his rank around. Considerate. Believes in small unit operations, which he sees as the ultimate weapon against Mau Mau leaders. The right man for the job.'

'Good.

'I am sure he will come and visit us soon.'

Michael topped up their glasses.

'Bright, when first we met you mentioned that you enjoyed wildlife photography. You have never shown me your work. No reason why you should, but I am interested. I know we have kept you pretty busy these last few months and especially while I have been away, but I hope you have not abandoned it.'

'As you say, I have been pretty busy. I am very happy to show you some of my albums.'

'I would love to see them, when we have a moment. Tell me. I expect you have the big five and a lot more besides, but do you have any cheetah?'

'Cheetah? No, alas.'

'I know where you could find some.'

He related his visit to the Unwins' ranch and seeing the young cheetahs.

'Why don't we slip away and go and see them? I have to visit the Unwins anyway, to collect a painting from Mrs Unwin. How about next Monday?'

'Suits me, sir.'

'Things should be quiet in the camp, and the officer of the day can cope. That's what he's there for. I will leave radio contact details in the office.'

After dinner in the mess, Michael phoned Patrick and asked to speak to Jane. She came on the line.

'Hello, you. Have you been frightfully busy?'

'I'm sorry to be ringing so late. I have become a *deskwallah* these last few days, spending my time at meetings or on the telephone.'

'So I am last on your list of calls.'

'Last, but by no means least, darling.'

'Well, that's comforting to know. I have been busy, too. Naomi has decided that she wants to throw away her old clothes and have more fashionable things. No more slopping around in old dungarees. She has been besieging Annabel these last few days so I have been appointed to sort things out.'

'I expect you were just like that as a girl.'

'True. I see a lot of myself in Naomi. Sometimes I think we spend too much time together. Patrick and Annabel are very loving but they are so busy with the farm and everything that they only really see her at breakfast and at her supper. It also means that if she is a bad mood I am in the front line.'

'I am sure you are patience personified.'

'There are times, when I am sorely tempted to...but I suppose every parent and nanny has these moments. Do you remember her calf, Lakme? Now she is in calf herself. It can't be too long now and Naomi is very insistent that she attends the birth; I have to explain what is going to happen. I am not a vet. Patrick has given me an old book full of diagrams. One thing you can say about this job is that there is never a dull moment. And I have to give her some extra tuition in Arithmetic as well. Her English and reading are very good but sums still present a problem.'

Michael told her about the forthcoming visit to the the Unwins.

'Do you remember the cheetahs? Major Bright wants to photograph them to add to his collection. We are going over next Sunday. Would you like to come? Bring Naomi.'

'I'd love to, but she has a test paper to do for Gilgil that day.'

'Pity. I'll try and come up to the farm as soon as I can. In the meantime, duty calls.'

'Don't I know it. Take care, my love.'

'You too.'

Michael put the phone down and sighed. If only he could be with her in person. Just a few miles separated them but at times it seemed as though they were on different continents. But he was counting the days until he could bring her the painting, a reminder of one of the happiest days he had ever spent.

* * *

Michael had forewarned the Unwins and they were invited to lunch. When they arrived Geoffrey immediately took Bright out into the bush.

'The cheetahs grow up fast and it will soon be time to release them. You should be able to have a good sight of them after their morning run and they will soon be resting because of the heat.'

Doris offered Michael a coffee. She led him into her studio to inspect the painting. It was beautifully executed in watercolour, showing the two cheetahs prowling in the open bush near acacia trees, with Mount Kenya in the background.

'This is amazing,' said Michael. 'Such detail. And you have caught their arrogant stride: "Look at me. Aren't I beautiful?" What is this creature in the corner?' He looked more closely. 'It's a warthog running away.'

'And well he might unless he wants to be their lunch. I have taken the liberty of putting it in an old frame. If you want something posher, I am sure that there will be someone in Nairobi who could provide you with one.'

'Certainly not. It will do fine.'

'Let me wrap it up for you to take it back safely.'

'I am very grateful, Doris. I am sure Jane will like it. You mentioned a charity.'

'Yes. An orphanage in Nyeri. Run by the Catholic Church. I am not of their persuasion but they do very good work and I have supported them for a number of years.'

Michael pulled out his wallet but Doris told him to put it away.

'You can pay it into the bank at Nyeri. This is the account number.'

She handed him a slip of paper. 'And how is Jane?'

Michael told her of their visit to the coast and her bout of malaria.

'She seems to be fully recovered, though I suppose there may be long-term effects. But the other news is that we are engaged to be married.'

'Well, I thought there was something in the offing when you visited. It didn't need much woman's intuition. I am very pleased for you. When is the day?'

'I will be going home on long leave soon. If we have a plan at all, it is that we go home together, meet parents and people, and have a church service. After that, who knows? Jane will be leaving the Howarths anyway, when Naomi goes to boarding school, and I may be posted, well, anywhere. Depends on Her Majesty. But whatever happens I hope we will come back to Kenya sometime and keep in touch with folk here.'

They took a turn round the paddocks and met Geoffrey and Bright coming back.

'Some excellent shots,' said Bright, 'including two close-ups. They will have an honoured place in my album. I shall pretend that I spent weeks in a hide to capture the exact moment, when in fact they let me get right up close. Thank you, Geoffrey, and thank you to your askaris.'

'A pleasure. One thing, Major. Don't give away their precise location. There are people who would abduct them or kill them for their skins, which could fetch a lot of money.'

'My lips are sealed.'

'Good. Time for lunch, Doris?'

'In a moment. Drinks first.'

After a convivial lunch they drove back to the camp. Michael went to his office. He worked there until just before seven. He was about to leave and go to the Mess for dinner when a radio message came through. It was Patrick Howarth.

'Patrick, what's up?'

'I had to use the radio since the telephone wires have been cut and I couldn't get hold of the Police. It's Jane and Naomi. They have disappeared.'

'What? This afternoon?'

'We have searched the farm. Annabel and I are frantic. Can the Army help?'

'I'll come at once.'

* * *

Annabel was in tears and Patrick looked grim.

'When were they last seen?' asked Michael.

'They were going to the Dam for a picnic. Naomi likes to play in the water. She deserved a little outing after her test paper in the morning. We expected them back at about four, but when they hadn't appeared I drove up and found the picnic basket and Naomi's wet bathing costume and a towel. We immediately organised a search of the farm, as thoroughly as we could. When it was getting dark we rang the Police but the line was cut.'

'That suggests collaboration somewhere.'

'After all we have done for our people,' wailed Annabel. 'It must be Mau Mau.'

'We can't expect all of our staff to have resisted the blandishments of the Mau Mau,' said Patrick. 'What are we going to do, Michael?'

'Wait and hope. Not very helpful, I know. I must think.'

His mind was whirling and he had to force himself to be rational. 'I am sure Jane would not do anything irresponsible. Therefore her absence is not of her own volition. Who knew that they were going to the Dam?'

'Apart from ourselves, well, a number of people saw them going up the track. The *watu* are used to seeing them around the farm.'

'Do they go up to the Dam often?'

'Now and then. Usually it is with us, but today just the two of them. It was Naomi's idea.'

'Hm. If it was an abduction, I think it had been planned and that implies a Mau Mau agent among the *watu*. I suspect there were men waiting in the forest for an opportunity for mischief and they were tipped off.'

'Bastards,' said Patrick.

'Have you received any messages from them? Any demands or threats?'

'Not so far.'

Michael looked at his watch.

'I must get back. I have some arrangements to make. I will be back tomorrow. I think this is an Army matter. I will call you at seven in the morning.'

On his return to camp, despite the late hour, he summoned Major Bright and Lieutenants Jamieson and Berkeley. The last two were dirty and unshaven.

'This is a job for A Company. Not an exercise but a vital mission and a matter of urgency.'

He explained the situation.

'I think we can take it that it is a Mau Mau stunt. We have to act promptly since the news of the kidnapping will soon be all over the place. We have to be very careful as they have hostages.'

'Sir, I have to ask,' said Jamieson. 'Is there any room for negotiation?'

'I doubt it. I am sure that the Governor would not sanction anything that looks like caving into Mau Mau demands. Major Bright and I will be drawing up plans and I want the Forest Squads ready to move at 08.00 tomorrow. Plan on seven days in the forest. I will be liaising with Special Branch to find out what is the latest intelligence about Mau Mau camps. This is very important. The men must regard this as an exercise until a final briefing in the forest itself. Not a word of its real purpose must leak out.'

'Will you be taking part, sir?'

'I will be in radio contact at all times. Anyway, I have been shaving, smoking and cleaning my teeth. I must declare a personal interest, as Miss Simpson and I are engaged to be married. Your primary aim will be the rescue of the hostages, especially the child. If you can destroy the gang so much the better. Any intelligence you gather will be useful. Any questions?'

'We await your briefing tomorrow, sir.'

'Very good. 06.00. Thank you, gentlemen.'

The lieutenants went out. Michael kept Bright back.

'Bright, join me in a smoke. This will be a three-pipe problem.'

By the end of an hour Michael and Bright had worked out a tentative plan, a search for the gang using three squads commanded by Jamieson, Berkeley and Sergeant Walters.

'We must assume that the gang will be based in the northern sector of Mount Kenya, since they will not be able to go far and fast with the hostages. We will approach from the west, north and east. It is a large area to cover, but I hope our trackers will pick up the scent.'

Bright then drew up an inventory of supplies and transport arrangements while Michael phoned Brigade. After some pressure he persuaded the signals officer to fetch the Brigadier.

'This had better be good, Michael.'

He gave a succinct account of the situation and the arrangments he had made.

'We must move fast, sir. Not only for my personal reasons but because we cannot allow the Mau Mau to pull off a stunt like this.'

'Agreed. I will inform the GOC. Go ahead and keep me up to date with progress.'

'Sir, it is remotely possible that Jane and Naomi will return to the farm during the night. I would much rather that happened and our preparations were not needed, than we have to swing into action. I don't mind having raised a false alarm.'

'Whatever the outcome, you have my backing, Michael.'

'Thank you, sir.'

Michael then tried to get hold of Special Branch but without success.

'We'll give them an early morning call.'

Michael and Bright had a final conference at two o'clock in the morning and then went to bed. Michael did not sleep much, his mind going over all the dangers that Jane and Naomi might be facing and how generally helpless he felt. At five he got up, cooked himself some breakfast in the Mess, roused the steward and told him to prepare rations for himself and Bright.

At six he and Bright briefed the lieutenants and Walters.

'One thing we must not do is launch search parties from the farm itself. This will alert the watchers that the Army is involved. We have made your start points at some distance from each other and you will converging from different directions. I will be contacting Special Branch for their latest information on the gangs; I tried to get hold of them last night, but they weren't answering. Brigade had given its approval for the operation and I hope there will be back up from the RAF. But in essence you will operating as individual units.'

Bright then gave details of logistics and communications.

Michael concluded: 'My thanks in advance for the very delicate task you have to undertake. There is more at stake than the fate of the two people involved.'

By late morning the Forest Squads reported that they had reached their start points and had been briefed on the true nature of their mission. Michael stayed in the office. At last he got hold of Special Branch who promised to supply him with the information he wanted. The Brigadier called and Michael told him of the plans that had been made. These received his approval. Not long afterwards the GOC himself came on the phone. Michael repeated what he had told the Brigadier.

'Very well. I will inform other units so that there is no interference with your operation.'

'One of my officers, sir, asked about negotiation with the kidnappers. I said that in my view the Governor, or indeed you yourself, would not countenace any deal. I hope that is correct, sir.'

'I think you can take it that that is the case. This is not a political situation. We cannot possibly negotiate with criminals. It would be very hard luck on the hostages and their families, but in the overall scheme of things...Has there been any communication with the kidnappers?'

'I haven't heard so far. I am going up to the farm as soon as I can.'

'Right. Another thing. We must keep this matter out of the press until it has been resolved. We will have about forty-eight hours before the news breaks.'

With that General Lathbury rang off.

Special Branch rang with the latest known positions of Mau Mau camps. This was bound to be out of date but nevertheless Michael sent the information to the squads. Special Branch also had some thoughts to offer from Police experience in kidnap situations.

Michael held his head in his hands and prayed that the two were still alive and he had been doing the right thing in the crisis. After a further conference with Major Bright he set off for the farm with Corporal Harun, his radio operator.

Chapter Seventeen

Naomi had her swim and had changed back. The sun was warm and Jane had closed her eyes while Naomi was building a little tower of stones. She looked up and saw five men approaching from the direction of the forest. They were coming directly towards her. She nudged Jane awake. She stood up and took Naomi's hand. The men surrounded them.

'What do you want?' Jane asked with a tremor in her voice.

'You are to come with us. If you resist and shout out you will suffer.' The man who spoke waved a *panga* at them. Another tied Jane's wrists behind her back. A rope was put around Naomi's neck.

'Now we go.'

Within a minute or so they were in the forest following a narrow track. The pace was gentle but steady. Once or twice Jane slipped and she was hauled back to her feet.

Naomi started whimpering.

'Simmie, can we go home now?'

'Naomi, we have to do as the man says. Then we will be all right. We have to be very brave and patient.'

'Simmie, I want a widdle.'

Jane asked the man who seemed to be in charge to stop so that they could relieve themselves. 'Let the girl go.'

'She can do it here.'

'Well, let her go behind a bush. You can keep the rope on her.'

Naomi went out of sight of the men.

'Now it's my turn. You will have to untie me.'

The man refused at first.

'Look, I'm not going to run away while you have the girl.'

Grumbling, the man released her and she went a little way into the forest. She could not prevent herself from weeping but composed herself so that Naomi should not see. On her return, her hands were tied again and the march resumed; but she had won a little victory.

After an hour Naomi said that she was very hungry and felt faint. It was also getting cold.

'Not far now,' said the man.

They came to a small camp in a ravine beside a stream. There was a cooking pot on the fire which a woman was tending. Jane and Naomi were untied and given some water to drink. It was ice-cold. Both were now shivering. Nothing was said to them, but the woman gave them a couple of blankets which they wrapped around themselves. It was beginning to get dark. They were each handed a gourd full of goat's meat stew. It did not look very appetising but Jane insisted that Naomi ate it all up.

'Use your fingers. We don't know when we will eat next.'

When they had finished they were put into a tent with a rough rug on the floor. They could see the woman and the men sitting around the fire. Jane put her arms around Naomi and covered them both with the blankets. Naomi started to sniffle.

'Simmie, will I see Mummy and Daddy again?'

'Of course you will. I am sure people will come and rescue us. It might not be for a day or two, but we must be brave and look after each other. Agreed?'

'Yes, Simmie.'

'Now there is something you can do. You are much better at understanding Gikuyu than I am. I want you to listen carefully to what they are saying and whisper it to me when you get the chance. But you must not reveal that you know what they are saying. Can you do that?'

'Yes, I can.'

'Good girl. Let's try and sleep.'

Naomi soon dropped off, but Jane lay there sleepless. She could hear the men talking and smelt *bhangi*. She felt vulnerable as she had never felt before. The transition from lazy afternoon to captivity had been so swift that she had had little time to collect herself. She had never been religiously inclined, but now she prayed for strength to endure whatever might happen; above all she had to protect Naomi. Several times the child stirred, kicking off the blankets, and had to be covered up again. At last Jane managed a few hours fitful sleep and awoke just before sunrise. She looked out of the tent and saw that the woman had already kindled the fire and was preparing *posho* porridge. The woman nodded to her but did not say anything. The men were lying on the ground wrapped in blankets.

Jane woke Naomi and they both went to the stream to wash. The morning was very cold and when they came back they wrapped themselves in blankets again. The woman handed them a mug of tea which they had to share. It seemed very bitter to Naomi but Jane told her to drink up; it would warm her.

After breakfast, the men took down the tent and gathered up the cooking pots. The fire was extinguished and a pile of stones laid on top. While the men and the woman were busy, Jane tore her handkerchief in two and put half behind a stone. When all was ready, Jane was told to carry the blankets and take Naomi's hand.

The man who seemed to be the leader spoke to them:

'You are now in the middle of the forest. If you run away from us, we will not come after you. You will die of hunger or of cold, or a *nyati* or *kifaru*★ will trample you. So there is no need to tie you up. If you do as you are told, you will be OK.'

They had to pick their way through tree ferns and a mass of fallen bamboo. Even their captors gave a wide berth to giant nettles, 'fire leaves'. For a short distance they followed a beaten path strewn with dung and marked by the rounded three-toed prints of a rhino. After an hour and a half, they were allowed a rest. The men started talking and laughing among themselves. Jane nudged Naomi who listened carefully. When it was time to move on, all the men, except the leader, went ahead. Jane and Naomi were escorted by him and the woman. At one point a loud-hailer aircraft flew over and circled round. Jane and Naomi were told to lie down and not move. The aircraft's noise covered their whispers.

'What were the men saying?' Jane asked.

'I am not sure, but they said that they hoped that the Brigadier – is that the right word? – would be pleased and that they liked you,

★ rhinoceros

thought you were beautiful. They wouldn't mind having you. What did they mean by that?'

'I'll tell you another time. Anything else?'

'Not yet. But I will keep my ears open.'

'Good girl.'

Jane left the other half of her handkerchief where they had taken cover.

They reached the main camp which was in a small valley. A stream ran through it and the canopy of trees concealed much of it from the air. Jane and Naomi attracted interested looks as they were led into the camp, but no one approached them. The woman took them straight to a tent beside a larger one. It had two coarse mats on the floor on which were a couple of pullovers, two tin mugs and plates. There was a flask of tea and a bowl with rice and pieces of meat.

'You are to stay here until you are told to come out. You will not go round the camp.'

'How long are we staying here?' Jane asked.

'That is for the Brigadier to decide.'

The woman went away and left them to eat. Naomi at first turned up her nose at the food, but Jane insisted that she eat a good portion.

'You must keep your strength up.'

After the first mouthful Naomi eagerly ate up the rest and drank some tea, which was now lukewarm. Then she showed Jane some insect bites on her legs and tummy.

'I have been bitten, too. I know they itch. Try not to scratch. We don't want to get dirt into the bites. And somehow we must clean our fingernails when we are allowed to wash. Naomi, whatever happens we must look after ourselves and each other. Do you understand?'

Naomi nodded, then asked:

'Tell me, Simmie. Do you love Michael?'

'Of course I do, and he loves me. We are engaged to be married.'

'Does he love you enough to send the Army to rescue us?'

'I have no doubt he will. But, Naomi, you must not let on that we know someone in the Army. Just say, if asked, that you live on the farm with Mummy and Daddy.'

From the door of the tent they were able to look out onto the centre of the camp. There was a lot of coming and going. Jane told Naomi to count the number of different people she could see. After an hour or so, she reckoned about forty. It appeared that the large tent next to theirs was used by women only, half a dozen of them. On the opposite side of the camp was a cookhouse and beside it what appeared to be racks for rifles. By sticking their necks right out, they could see a large tent, like a small marquee, decorated with an arch of foliage and a curtain of skins drawn across the entrance. From time to time this was pushed aside and men went in and out. When the noise of an aircraft was heard, everyone rushed under the trees and averted their faces. Jane was tempted to get up and wave but judged that the risk was too great. All this activity kept Naomi's and Jane's attention for most of the afternoon. Jane tried to remember every detail and encouraged Naomi to do the same. Later on they compared notes.

'We can tell Michael all about this. It will be useful information for him.'

When they had eaten another meal of rice and goat's meat they were called from the tent and taken across the camp to the marquee. Both were wearing the pullovers; Naomi's reached down to her knees. They were told to wait outside. Then the leader of the men who had kidnapped them came out and signalled them to go inside. They went past two men armed with *pangas*, and stood near a table. The man sitting behind it got up and came round to greet them. He was well over six feet tall and wore a khaki jacket with crowns crudely sewn onto the epaulettes, and khaki trousers. He had a pistol tucked into his belt. There was a livid scar across his forehead and he sported a bushy black beard. When he spoke, his voice was deep and loud.

'Naomi Howarth and Jane Simpson. Welcome to the forest.'

'Who are you?' Jane asked.

'I am Brigadier Njirami Watui, commander of the Fighters for Freedom in the forests of Kirinyaga. You are my guests. I hope my people are looking after you. Is there anything you want?'

'I want to go home to Mummy and Daddy,' Naomi blurted out.

'Alas, my dear, it is not possible just at the moment, but when the time comes you will be allowed to go.'

Naomi's eyes filled with tears and she clung onto Jane's hand.

'Why are we here?'

'Miss Simpson, Naomi, look at me. You see this?'

He pointed to the scar along his forehead.

'I got this when we attacked your farm. It is still painful.'

'So you are keeping us here out of revenge.'

'Not at all. We want to make the point that all white settlers, so long as they occupy land that should by rights belong to Africans, are vulnerable. No matter how many soldiers they have, they cannot protect all their people. The only safety they can have is to give Africans full rights or leave our country altogether.'

'But I am an African,' Naomi cried out. 'I was born here and I live here. I have never been out of this country.'

Njirami ignored her. 'We will release you when Mr Howarth makes a public declaration of support for our cause. And no harm will come to you.'

Jane received this statement in silence.

'Do you understand, Miss Simpson?'

'I understand that we are hostages. So why don't you allow Naomi to go home and keep me here? She is just a child.'

'She is a child who will inherit the land that her ancestors stole from the Africans. If we release anybody, it would be you. You do not matter to the Howarths as much as Naomi.'

'I will never leave Naomi.'

'I know that. You will look after her as you do on the farm.'

'What will happen if Mr Howarth does not make this declaration?'

'We will have to wait and see. If he is wise, he will make it.'

With that, Njirami went back to his desk and sat down. The attendants signalled for Jane and Naomi to leave.

'He frightened me,' said Naomi as they went back to the tent.

'Me, too.'

'Such a big, ugly man.'

They were taken down to the stream to wash. By this time it was nearly dark. They got ready for bed. The mats were hard but they provided insulation from the cold ground. Naomi nestled up to Jane under the blankets and was soon asleep. Jane was grimly aware that pressure would be put on Patrick not to make any declaration. She tried not to think what might happen to her and Naomi if he didn't, but all sorts of ghastly scenarios floated into her mind. Eventually she drifted off to a troubled sleep.

Some time later she woke with a start. Someone was crawling into the tent. He smelt strongly of drink. He seized her legs and began to pull her out of the tent. Another set of hands groped for her skirt. She screamed as loudly as she could but a hand closed over her mouth. She used her fists but stopped when she felt the point of a knife at her throat. Naomi woke up. In the darkness she could not see anything but realised that something was very wrong. She too screamed. By now Jane's skirt had been pulled up and her legs were being forced apart. One of the women from the next tent came out, saw what was happening and, seizing a stick, began to beat the men about the head. Other women came out, shouted for help and attacked the two men. Men also ran up, grabbed the two and flung them on the ground, holding them down. Jane was sobbing uncontrollably and one of the women helped her to sit up and covered her with a blanket. The noise and shouting reached Njirami and he and his attendants came across with torches. He was told what had happened. He kicked the men on the ground several times and ordered them to be frogmarched out of the camp. Taking Jane's hand, he raised her up.

'You are safe now. I am very sorry this has happened. The men will be punished.'

He turned to his attendants. 'Take the ladies to my quarters and give them a warm drink. I will be there in a moment.'

He checked his pistol and strode into the forest. Soon four shots were heard, two and two.

Njirami brought his woman from the back of the marquee and told her to make up beds for Jane and Naomi. He apologised again for the attack.

'For the rest of your stay you will sleep here and Ngina will look after you. My guards will protect you.'

Jane and Naomi were taken into the back, an area curtained off from the rest. Rugs were laid on mats. Naomi lay down and was soon asleep. Jane covered her with a blanket and sat on a chair. She shivered and wrapped herself in a rug. She was given a mug of tea and to her surprise it had sugar in it. Although her hands were shaking she managed to get it down without spilling. Cautiously she examined herself. Her legs and arms were bruised and her lips were sore from the rough hand that hand covered them. Where the knife had been held to her throat there was a trickle of blood, but the wound was superficial. Gradually her heartbeat returned to normal. She lay down on the rug and curled up beside Naomi.

* * *

On the second morning after the disappearance, Michael returned to the farm. Patrick and Annabel were grey with worry and exhaustion. Patrick handed him a letter. It was neatly typed out on clean paper, with no smudges on it, or visible fingerprints.

'Where did you find it?' Michael asked.

'We found it pinned to the front door. We had left it open in case they should come back and again we sat up waiting. But we did not hear anybody. We must have dozed off.'

Michael read the letter.

> Dear Howarth,
>
> Some time ago my forces raided your farm and were beaten off with loss of some of our warriors. Your success did not mean that you had won. On the contrary, our determination has not been dimmed but has grown stronger. Afterwards you raised a memorial to those who died and praised the loyalty of your people. Your trust in them is misplaced; some work for us. Many of them want the same things as we do.
>
> All we want is to form an African government which will end all discrimination and will extend individual freedom in movement, press and speech, give better pay and conditions to the workforce and, most important, eliminate Europeans' selfish-

ness and pride. We do not hate the white man's colour, but we cannot tolerate seeing a foreign settler with 50,000 acres of land, most of which only the wild game enjoy, while thousands of Africans are starving in their own country. Nor can we accept the white man as a master and the African as a servant.

Your only alternative is either to cooperate with the Africans as equal human beings by creating friendships and good relationships, which your guns and bombs will never achieve, or to quit Kenya and leave the African to manage his own affairs. The more you fight the African the more you endanger your future in Kenya. You cannot kill ideas by killing people.

We have your daughter and her ayah. They will be cared for. They will remain with us until you make a public statement endorsing our demands as set out above. If you refuse to do this or if you enlist the help of the Police or the Army, then I cannot answer for the consequences.

Your New Kenyan,
Brig. Gen. Njirami Watui,
January 1955.

'Do you think that we should make the statement they ask for?'

'I must tell you,' said Michael 'that my superiors will not agree to any general acceptance of those terms. They say that they will not negotiate with criminals.'

'But if we make that declaration we are not committing the government to a course of action.'

'No, but you will be giving the Mau Mau a propaganda coup. You will be alienating most of the settlers and many Africans who don't think very much about politics but regard the Mau Mau as dangerous thugs.'

'Surely people will recognise that we will do anything to get our daughter and Jane back.'

'They will understand, but not approve of, concessions. They will just give thanks that it is not their own daughter who has been kidnapped.'

'I don't care what other people think,' said Annabel. 'I would go down on my knees to this Njirami.'

Michael took her hand. 'I quite understand. I have been talking to Special Branch about their experiences of kidnapping. We have to consider this point. If you make an approach to Njirami, there is no guarantee that he will keep his word. He might intend to, but others might steal Naomi and Jane for their own purposes. Perhaps to drive a harder bargain, such as a demand for money.'

'We would pay any sum.'

'Or they might make an example of them.'

'You mean…?'

'Yes, I do.'

'Oh God.'

'That is why we have to move fast and trust that our men can rescue them before worse things happen. There is also a danger that when they are cornered they might use them as a human shield or even kill them as a final act of defiance. I am sorry to spell it out in such brutal terms. But I think my men are capable of carrying out this delicate operation. I see no other alternative.'

Patrick and Annabel digested this in silence for a few minutes. Then he asked if they should call in the Police to question the *watu* to find out who might have been collaborating.

'My advice would be to leave the matter for the time being. The priority is to get Naomi and Jane back. Maybe the loyal *watu* will come up with a name. And the less obvious Police activity, the better. Remember what the letter said.'

Patrick agreed with reluctance.

'What will you be doing today?' he asked.

'I must go back to the office soon.'

'Will you stay for some lunch?'

'No, thanks. My radio operator and I have our own rations. Patrick, Annabel, please don't expect any news in the next twenty-four hours. I know it's hard. The waiting is awful. But be assured that my men are already in the field. I will let you know as soon as I have anything to report.'

Michael asked Corporal Harun to drive; he was too preoccupied with his thoughts. It had been with a great effort that he had managed to speak with the Howarths rationally, when inside he was as sick with worry as they were. At least he had a task to carry out, rather than having to sit waiting for a call which might well be bad news. Quite apart from their safety in the hands of a terrorist, he was afraid that Jane might not have thrown off her dose of malaria fully, and she might have fallen ill again. And there were all the dangers of the forest, the damp, the cold, wild animals and the sheer difficulty of moving round. However, from his own experience he knew that a body of men of any size was bound to follow paths rather than cut their way through virgin jungle, and therefore the chances of tracking them down were improved. And the passage of people was bound to leave traces which a skilled eye could pick up. He had confidence in his squads but there was always the strong possibility that they might be too late.

From what he knew of Jane, he reckoned that she would be resourceful; it would help her that she had Naomi to look after, someone to divert her, even slightly, from her own predicament. He remembered their conversation when she started to improve after the crisis of malaria.

'I didn't want to let you down by dying. And I didn't.'

He hoped that she was showing the same spirit in her captivity.

Chapter Eighteen

Midmorning, the woman, Ngina, woke Jane with a cup of tea and in halting English asked how she felt. Jane replied that she had bruises but nothing too serious. She wondered if she might have some delayed shock from the attempted rape, but a long sleep had refreshed her, and there was too much to deal with in the present without brooding on the past. She suddenly noticed that Naomi was not beside her and had a moment of panic. Ngina smiled.

'The girl was hungry. She is eating. Come and see.'

Jane got up and found Naomi in the main tent sitting at the table with a bowl of porridge.

'Are you all right, Naomi?' she asked.

'I'm fine,' she replied and took another mouthful. 'What really happened last night, Simmie?'

'I was attacked. I screamed and you screamed but fortunately people came to my rescue.'

'I remember now. They were very nasty men. Where are they now?'

'They have been punished and...will not be troubling us any more.'

'What are we going to do today? Isn't it time we went home?'

'I hope we will be going soon.'

'Why don't we just run away?'

'Well, for a start, I don't know where we are. And the forest is very dangerous.'

'I can be brave.'

'I know you can. But we have to be sensible. After the attack my legs are bruised and I couldn't walk very far, let alone run. And if other men found us wandering in the forest, they might well do us great harm. I'm afraid that we must stay here until we are allowed to go.'

Naomi was not convinced but changed the subject.

'Simmie, you said you will tell what those men meant by saying that they wouldn't mind having you.'

'It's difficult to explain.' She took a deep breath. 'They wanted to have sex with me.'

'Oh. Does having sex mean attacking people?'

'No, Naomi. Sex should be a loving act when both people want to share it.'

'But you didn't want to have sex with those men.'

'No. Certainly not.'

'As you love Michael, do you have sex with him?'

'You are a persistent girl. Some things are private. Please don't ask any more.'

'OK,' said Naomi, a little resentfully. 'Do you think I could go out and play in the camp?'

'We must ask Ngina.'

Ngina brought two bowls of warm water for Jane to wash herself, which helped to sooth her bruises and remove the touch of the men's greedy hands. Then she said that she wanted to go outside and stretch her legs. Ngina did not understand the idiom and looked puzzled.

'Can I speak to Njirami?' Jane them asked.

'Wait.' Ngina went to consult the guards at the entrance to the marquee. She came back shaking her head.

'He is away. But he will be back later today. Now you must stay here.'

For a few minutes they sat glumly, not saying very much. Then Jane got up and went to the table. She saw some blank sheets of paper and some pencils.

'Here, Naomi. Why don't you draw me some animals?'

Happy to have something to do, Naomi sat in the chair and got down to work. Meanwhile, Jane tore a sheet into smaller pieces and wrote on them:

Please rescue us. J and N.

She tucked the pieces into her bra and knickers.

At midday they were given a bowl of goat stew. During the afternoon they played games, sang songs and did some physical exercises. When these activities had run their course they sat silently, even Naomi, with a kind of mental numbness. Towards evening Njirami came in, followed by his guards, and shouted for Ngina. He sat down at the table, sighed and noticed them in a corner.

'Hello, Jane and Naomi. Are you well?'

'Yes, thank you,' said Naomi.

'I hope you have found things to do. I am very sorry that we can't let you outside. For your protection, of course.'

Ngina came in with a mug of beer. Njirami drank deeply, wiped his lips and told Ngina to take Naomi into the back.

'Now, Jane,' he resumed when they were alone, 'there has not been a statement from Mr Howarth. This is most regrettable. I hope he understands the seriousness of your position. I don't want to frighten you unduly but we will have to take steps if we do not hear from him soon. I have sent him a message which says that he has another twenty-four hours.'

'How will you know that he has made a statement?'

'The newspapers will tell us. I have told him to publish it in the *African Standard*.'

'So we stay here for the time being?'

'Yes. There is no alternative.'

After supper they were taken to the stream to wash. When it was dark they went to bed, there being nothing else to do, and they were not supplied with a torch. Jane told Naomi stories until she fell asleep, but lay awake herself for a long time, thinking about what Njirami had said. If the *African Standard* did publish a statement, it coud be a day before the news was brought to Njirami. It was likely, therefore, they would be spending two more days in captivity, even if they were to be released. With these thoughts she drifted off to sleep.

Well before dawn she was woken up as Ngina rushed in and shouted at them.

'Get up! Get up! We have to go!'

Jane started to ask what was the matter but was cut short by the noise of gunfire. Naomi was shaken awake. Jane wrapped her in a rug and picked her up. Ngina took them to the back of the marquee, opened a flap and ushered them out.

'Follow me.'

Ngina ran into the forest and led them to a bush. She pushed it aside and uncovered a foxhole into which she jumped, beckoning Jane and Naomi to join her, putting a forefinger to her lips. Naomi started to whimper but Jane whispered in her ear and she fell silent. Meanwhile the noise of firing increased and there was the louder explosion of a grenade. Through the foliage Jane could see flames coming from the tents. There were shouts and screams. She covered Naomi's head with the rug. Her own heart was racing. After what seemed an age the firing died down, apart from individual shots. They heard footsteps outside and Njirami's voice.

'Are you all right?'

Ngina looked at Jane, who nodded. 'We are OK.'

'Good. Stay there for the time being. Until it gets light. We need to check the perimeter of the camp. Ngina, you stay there, too.'

For the next hour there was more shouting and the occasional gunshot. Then they heard Njirami's voice again.

'It's safe to come out.'

Feeling very stiff and still carrying Naomi, Jane emerged from the foxhole. Many of the tents were burnt down, including the marquee. Bodies lay on the ground, some motionless, others groaning and writhing. In the middle of the camp was a group of men sitting on the ground, tied together, and two armed guards with rifles cocked. Jane and Naomi were told to wait at the edge of the clearing while Ngina fetched tea and a bowl of stew left over from the previous day. Jane forced Naomi to eat some of it and she had a little herself. She was filled with foreboding because she thought that the Army had attacked the camp and had failed. But while they were eating, the guards took one of the men and tied his hands behind his back. He was led to a tree. A rope was thrown over a branch and one end tied round his neck. With horror, Jane realised what was going to happen and took Naomi away into the bushes so that she could not see what was being done. She wriggled.

'Keep still.'

'Why?'

'Because I say so.' She pushed her down and covered her with the rug.

She ventured to look over her shoulder. The man was lifted off the ground and the rope was tied to a tree root. He kicked his legs violently, but not for long.

When she looked again, the man was being cut down. The others had been removed.

Ngina brought them back into the clearing. Njirami, his arm in a sling, came across to them.

'That man was not worth a bullet.' He sat down beside her. 'We were treacherously attacked by another group of freedom fighters. They wanted to get hold of you two so that they could make a bargain with the government. They would have sold you for cash, several thousand pounds. Their leader, the man we hanged, used to be my friend and colleague. We also suspected him of having given information to the Army in the past.'

He noticed that Naomi was staring at the red patch on his sling, which was growing in size.

'Yes, Naomi, my arm does hurt. Very much. I must wash it in the stream and have it bandaged. We will be moving camp soon.'

'Where to?'

'Not far. To a small camp we have used before.'

'Have you lost many men?'

'Three killed and seven wounded, but none badly. The enemy, for that is what I must call them, had six killed, several wounded and we captured the men you saw.'

'Are you going to hang them?'

'No. they will be burying the dead and then will be our porters.'

Jane offered to help with the wounded but her offer was declined.

'You must keep an eye on Naomi. She is very precious.'

Jane and Naomi played I Spy and told stories. Jane had used up most of her repertoire on previous occasions but Naomi didn't mind repeats. Jane was wondering how long she could keep this up when she saw that the porters were lined up with their loads and that a column was being formed. Jane and Naomi, with Ngina, were assigned a place near the rear. Behind them were three armed guards.

Jane remembered the pieces of paper she had hidden in her bra and knickers. Without being seen, she managed to leave two pieces at the campsite. Not long into the march Naomi complained of being tired and Jane carried her for a while. When she had had enough she put her down and Ngina said that she would carry her. Naomi accepted this offer and Jane was able to drop more pieces at the side of the path. Occasionally she turned round and saw with relief that the guards had not noticed them. When she begged to relieve herself, she took off her bracelet and left it hanging on a twig. She had two pieces of paper left. One she left a little further on and the another she tucked into her shoe. A mile or so further on, she stopped to retie a shoe lace and left the other.

Soon they reached the new camp. Shelters were being constructed but Jane and Naomi were assigned to one of the surviving tents. After a few mouthfuls of cold stew for supper, they lay down. Ngina joined them and Naomi was quite happy to cuddle up to her. After two disturbed nights, Jane was exhausted and fell asleep quickly.

⋆ ⋆ ⋆

'Why haven't your men found them?' Annabel had asked Michael crossly on the morning of the second day after the abduction. 'With all the resources you have, and the RAF, surely they must have been located by now.'

Michael chose his words carefully. 'Annabel, you know what the terrain is like. We have three squads searching an area of nearly three hundred square miles.'

'Why haven't you sent in the whole Army?'

'We have found that it is easy for the Mau Mau to evade the large sweeps we have taken through the forests. Yes, we have caught a good many, but by no means all. The gangs don't reveal their presence by attacking our troops and they can retreat into the remote recesses of the forest. Don't forget we have to rescue Naomi and

Jane without putting their lives at risk. That is our priority. The destruction of the gang comes second; we can deal with it later.'

'Yes, I understand that, Michael. But how will your men rescue them?'

'They are trained to follow tracks through the forest and engage the enemy at close quarters. When they have located their captors then they have to get Jane and Naomi away in one piece. How they will do that is for the officer to decide on the spot, as he reads the situation. We have regular reports from each squad and we can exchange information.'

Michael forbore to mention that the radio sets were pre-War models and anyway reception in the area was notoriously unreliable.

'We will let you know immediately of any significant developments. Please trust us.'

'That is all I can do.' She wiped away a tear. 'Sorry, Michael. I just feel so helpless, and when I think of all the terrible things that could happen to them… Patrick won't leave the radio and the telephone; thank goodness our line was restored yesterday. We have hardly slept for days. The *watu* don't like to bother us and just get on with things. At the school they said prayers for Naomi's safe return.'

Patrick came in. 'I have just had a call from the Governor's office. Soothing words, but no mention of any concessions to the Mau Mau. What I expected. Other people have been in contact, including James Ridout.'

'Ah, yes. I have met him twice. The last time was at the Muthaiga before we went to Mombasa.'

'A nice man. Head screwed on the right way. Knows Kenyatta from way back. He was very supportive.'

'One thing occurs to me,' said Michael. 'I am not an expert on these matters, but if a number of people know about the situation, you might well find reporters from the newspapers sniffing around. Be careful of what you say to them.'

'Such as…?'

'How about "We are terribly anxious for our beloved daughter and her governess and hope that they can be found as soon as possible. We are too upset to say anything more"? Whatever you do, don't say anything about the Police or the Army.'

'That sounds very sensible,' said Patrick.

'I would rather not speak to anyone,' Annabel said. 'I would probably collapse in tears and become incoherent. I don't want anyone to see me like that.'

As he drove away from the farm, for the umpteenth time Michael recalled his last conversation with Jane and the warmth of her voice. Like the Howarths, there was nothing he could do now but wait. He hit the steering wheel in frustration amd swore loudly. To collect himself he pulled off the road and filled his pipe. He was about to light it when Corporal Harun at the radio called his attention to a message coming through. Harun listened on the headphones and then asked the caller to repeat. He handed the head phones to Michael; he heard the voice of Lieutenant Jamieson.

'This is Echo Foxtrot Juliet. Have picked up a trail and found recent campsite, with half a lady's handkerchief. Over.'

'Good work, Juliet. Call base at 18.00 unless you have more news before then.'

* * *

Lieutenant Berkeley's and Sergeant Walters' squads, at a considerable distance from Jamieson, had to move slowly. They followed several tracks for some miles but found nothing. Walters thought that he had discovered evidence of recent passage by the Mau Mau but he was drawn too far to the south and retraced his steps. Berkeley's progress was impeded by elephants, which not only barred their way for some time but destroyed any evidence of Mau Mau presence. Both parties made camp and reported their approximate position. The corporal at the Battalion office marked them on a map with a circle; the map showed little detail of the terrain and therefore their positions were approximate. Michael considered their relative positions and decided that for the time being they should pursue their own searches rather than coordinate their efforts. The following morning Walters had gone about a mile or so when he encountered Mau Mau in a bivouac. He spread his men around in concealment for some time in case they had Jane and Naomi. Eventually they moved off; Walters followed them for some way but decided that they belonged to a different group and were not the kidnappers; he left them alone.

Jamieson's squad, having reported the find of the handkerchief, spread out to identify a likely track from the campsite. Several leads looked promising, but all of them fizzled out. They regrouped at the campsite and made a bivouac a little distance away. About three o'clock in the morning Gichuchi awoke to hear the sounds of distant gunfire. He immediately alerted Jamieson and they listened carefully. Jameison took a bearing on the direction the sound came from. They broke camp and moved off soon after dawn. Gichuchi, now his best tracker, was in the lead. Suddenly he gave the sign to take cover and freeze. The *ndete* birds and Sykes monkeys became active and noisy. There was a crashing in the undergrowth.

'*Nyati*.'

Three buffalo approached. Instinctively the men flattened themselves against tree trunks. One man began to cock his rifle but Jamieson signed to him not to fire. The animals stood on the alert for several minutes, as if aware of an alien presence but unable to locate it. At last they headed off, but Jamieson kept his men hidden until he was sure that the buffalo would not turn back and stalk them. One of the men showed him a torn handkerchief he had picked up. It was covered in mud from where the buffalo has trampled it but it was clearly the other half of the one they found the previous day. Jamieson showed the two halves to the squad and gave them a thumbs-up. Unfortunately the buffalo had churned up the ground and it took them some time to find the right track. But it was not long before they picked up the smell of burning. Jamieson gave the sign to spread out and wait. He and Gichuchi moved forward to the edge of the clearing. They watched for signs of movement, but could not see anything. Jamieson waited another few minutes and then got up and entered the clearing. He walked round and across it. He put down his rucksack and his men came out of the undergrowth with their weapons at the ready. They searched the site. There were charred remains of tents and blankets.

Embers in the fireplace still smouldered. In one place they found the remains of a chair and several bits of scrumpled paper that had escaped the fire. Jamieson examined them and found one with a child's drawing of an elephant. He folded it and put it in an inside pocket. At one side of the clearing was a pile of recently turned earth. Jamieson told two men to probe it and bodies were found.

'Leave them for now. We can come back and examine them later. We must rescue the two girls first.'

He told them about the child's drawing.

'I am sure we are on the right track. But we must be very careful. If the girls are still alive, they will be closely guarded. Absolutely no firing unless I give the order. Use your knives if necessary. Now fan out and see if we can find the direction in which they have gone.'

Jamieson reported by radio the discovery of the abandoned camp and its approxinate position. Michael immediately replied with an instruction to find the new camp, if there was one, and keep it under observation, but not to attempt a rescue unless he was absolutely sure of a successful outcome. He also instructed the other two squads to make their way to the area as soon as possible. 'Report at dawn tomorrow unless there is something significant before that. Over.'

Before long Jamieson discovered the path the Mau May had taken. There had been little attempt to disguise their passage, and the pieces of paper which Jane had dropped were picked up. Gichuchi, who was leading as usual, spotted the bracelet that she had left hanging in a twig. The camp was found in the late afternoon. Jamieson withdrew his squad for half a mile to bivouac, leaving Gichuchi and another askari to observe from a vantage point on a small rise adjacent to the camp. Although the undergrowth was thick they had a line of sight for most of the camp. A rough count revealed thirty-five men and six women. After about an hour, just before sundown, they had a glimpse of Jane and Naomi being taken from a tent. Gichuchi told his colleague to remain on watch while he went back to report the sighting. Jamieson radioed the news and gave the location of the new camp. This was duly passed on to Berkeley and Walters. Jamieson decided that the camp should be kept under observation the whole night. He himself took the pre-dawn shift.

No movement was observed during the night. When Jamieson was relieved he went back to the bivouac and radioed in. He was told that Berkeley and Walters were within two hours march of the camp and he was instructed to wait until they arrived, so that the camp could be totally surrounded. He moved his whole squad up to the perimeter of the camp at a distance of thirty yards and spread them out ten yards apart, so that they were in visual range of the camp and could keep in touch with each other. That left the other half of the perimeter unguarded, the intention being that the other two squads would cover the remainder. While the men were getting into position, one of them surprised a sentry. He was sitting against a tree stump, dozing. His throat was cut before he could give the alarm and his body rolled into a hollow and covered with a branch. This was reported to Jamieson by hand signals.

The morning wore on. Someone must have noticed that a man was missing and Jamieson could hear shouting. He saw the tall figure of Njirami standing in the middle of the camp and heard him ordering his men to search the surroundings. Jamieson was plunged into a quandary. There was now a strong possibility that the squad might be discovered, and even if not, the dead sentry might cause an alarm. There was no sign of Jane and Naomi. If he attacked, it was possible that they might be used as a human shield or killed outright. He decided to wait on events.

As it happened, the body was not discovered and the searchers did not stumble on any of Jamieson's men, such was their skill in concealment. Njirami still appeared agitated, shouting at his men to go back and look again. At that moment his attention was called to a disturbance in the forest at the opposite side of the camp. He ordered his men to take up defensive positions. Jamieson was sorely tempted to launch an attack from their rear but he held back because he could still not see where Jane and Naomi were.

Nothing happened. Njirami eventually stood his men down and called them to the centre of the camp, where he addressed them. He was speaking in a loud voice, so that all should hear and be in no doubt of his message. Jamieson was able to follow most of what was said, even though he was speaking in Gikuyu.

'I don't know where our brother has got to. Perhaps he has deserted and if we catch him he will suffer for it. As for that other alarm, did any of you hear or see anything?'

No one volunteered any information.

'Well, must have been an animal.'

He then asked for a report on food supplies. It turned out that they were down to the last of their rations and they had to go and forage soon if they were not to starve.

One of the men asked why they were feeding two extra mouths. 'Wouldn't it be better to get rid of them?'

'I gave my word that I would look after them.'

'Has there been any statement from Mr Howarth?'

'No. The messenger I sent out has not come back.'

'The *wazungu* will not give in,' the man continued. 'I think the best thing to do is to kill the two and leave them where they will be found. Just to show we mean business.'

Njirami shook his head. 'Brother, we are warriors, not barbarians. If we kill them we will prove to the *wazungu* that we really are terrorists, unfit to be a government for the people of Kenya. Whether you like it or not, the *wazungu* will not go away without a fight. Therefore we have to negotiate from a position of strength, and that means keeping the two safe. Their lives are our biggest asset. Do you understand?'

The man nodded resentfully.

'Very well. I will kill anyone who harms them, as I did the men who tried to rape the woman.'

He glared round at his men. No one met his glance.

'I have an uncomfortable feeling,' he went on, 'that we are under observation. I don't know how. But we haven't seen any of the RAF planes for the last two days. They usually fly over morning and afternoon with their loudhailer. And our brother has disappeared. I don't believe he deserted. He was always a loyal man.'

Jamieson crept back to his radio operator to see if any message had come through from Battalion HQ or the other squads.

The operator shook his head. 'Just crackling, sir. There is considerable interference.'

Jamieson swore in frustration. 'Just when we needed to be in contact.' He did not know where the other squads were. He had about two days' rations left. By itself, his squad was outnumbered three to one. His men were getting tired and vigilance could slip. There was no knowing what state Jane and Naomi were in. Taking all these factors together, he decided to attack and was on the point of giving the order when there was a crack of thunder and it began to rain heavily. By signs he called his men to close right up to perimeter of the camp. After an hour the storm passed on and the sun came out. The Mau Mau were emerging from their shelters, some of them very bedraggled.

Jamieson did not hesitate. He gave the sign. Following the drill they had practiced many times, his men picked out individuals in their sights and fired. A number of men fell and a second volley accounted for some more. The squad broke cover and charged. Those who attempted to resist were shot. Others saw in an instant that discretion was the better part of valour, dropped their weapons and put their hands up. They were told to stand in the centre of the camp and were guarded by two men with sten guns. Meanwhile captured weapons were gathered together and emptied of their ammunition. Most of the magazines were empty or with just a few rounds. Knives and clubs were removed. Shelters were demolished and anyone hiding was forcibly removed. A head count was taken: seven men had been killed, there were five more gravely wounded and four walking wounded. Twelve men and four women were under guard. Of Njirami, Jane and Naomi there was no sign.

Jamieson was in a dilemma. It was unlikely that they had gone very far but he could not afford to detach men to go after them. He summoned his radio operator and, to his relief, contact was established. He gave a brief report.

'Very well, Juliet. Stand fast for the moment. Tango and Lima should be close. Over.'

Berkeley's squad arrived in half an hour.

'We heard the firing and came as soon as we could.'

Jamieson explained the situation. 'I must go after them, but we had better wait for Walters. I assume they went that way, since we had this side covered. Can you and Walters look after this lot?'

'Of course.'

Sergeant Walters soon arrived with his squad, and now the prisoners were outnumbered. The dead were searched for identification. In what had been Njirami's tent several papers were found which were in due course handed over to Special Branch. A burial party got to work. The wounded were given rudimentary first aid. A message from Battalion announced that the Colonel would be bringing up transport as close as possible to the camp.

Jamieson's men had had a quick brew and had spread out into the forest to find the path taken by Njirami and his prisoners. Gichuchi came back within fifteen minutes holding a ring which he had found hanging on a branch.

Chapter Nineteen

Jane had woken early and felt better. Naomi slept on. Ngina had left the tent and was preparing food. She offered Jane a mug of tea and a small bowl of porridge.

'What about food for Naomi?' Jane asked.

'That's all we have. You will have to share it.'

Jane was feeling ravenous but she went back to the tent and woke Naomi. The child, usually bright at this hour, was listless and said that she wasn't hungry.

'You must eat something.'

Jane took a spoonful and put it in Naomi's mouth but she shook her head. Jane put a hand on her forehead and it felt hot.

'Well, you must drink this tea.'

Naomi grudgingly accepted it and eventually drank most of it. Jane continued to offer her mouthfuls of porridge but she refused. In the end Jane finished it all. Naomi lay back on the mat.

Jane put another blanket over her.

'Never mind. Just go back to sleep. I will stay here with you.'

Ngina came back.

'I think the child has a fever,' said Jane. 'Go and tell Njirami.'

An hour later Njirami came to the tent. He had a look at Naomi.

'You will have to let her go,' said Jane. 'Otherwise you will have a very sick child on your hands. She will be no use to you if she dies. Keep me, if you must.'

'I cannot let either of you go until I have heard from Mr Howarth. We will give her some of our medicine.'

'No. Just plenty of boiled water.'

Njirami grunted and said he would tell Ngina.

Sometime later Ngina came with a can of very hot water. When it had cooled, Jane woke Naomi and forced her to drink. Her forehead was still hot but she seemed a little more alert. They heard Njirami speaking to his men.

'What's he saying?' Jane asked her.

'I'm not sure. Something about no RAF planes flying over. He thinks we are being watched.'

'Let's hope it is the Army.'

They looked out of the tent. They saw Njirami talking to Ngina. She came over and told them to get up. Jane hauled Naomi to her feet, wrapped a rug around her and took one for herself.

'We must go,' said Ngina. 'Come. Be quick.'

They slipped out of the camp along a path, Ngina leading, then Naomi and Jane in the rear. Jane realised that she no longer had any scraps of paper to drop, and no handkerchief. There was only one thing for it: she would have to leave her engagement ring. With great reluctance she took it off her finger and, letting Ngina get a little bit ahead, hung it on a branch at head height at the side of the path. It felt like a betrayal of Michael, but there was no other way she could mark their passage.

They had not gone far when there was a clap of thunder and it began to rain heavily. Ngina took them to shelter beneath a rocky overhang; they were damp but not soaked through. Naomi was shivering and her teeth were chattering.

'Why did you tell us to leave the camp?' Jane asked Ngina.

'Njirami, he thinks that there will be a fight. Much better you are away, out of danger.'

'But what is to happen to us? There is no more food and Naomi is sick. Surely we must be allowed to go home.'

'He will not let you go until he has what he wants.'

'You mean a declaration from Mr Howarth. He will never give it, even if he wants to; the Governor will not let him. Don't you see that?'

'I just do what I am told. My job is to look after you.'

'Like us, Ngina, you are at the mercy of other people. Why don't the three of us just walk away? We can't be too far from a road.'

'I don't know where we are, so I don't know which way to go. And Njirami would punish me if I took you away. He is my man, you see. I have to do what he tells me.'

'How did you come to know him?'

Ngina gave a long sigh. 'I had lost a child and was burying him. I had used all my money to pay for a priest. Njirami found me weeping by the road and took care of me.'

'Are you his servant?'

'I have become a servant. But he has been kind to me, and I have nowhere else to go now.'

Jane knew that the life of Kikuyu women was hard by any reckoning; they would be glad to have someone to protect them.

'When the soldiers catch up with us, I will be arrested and put in prison.'

'I'm sure you won't. The Police might talk to you but they will not harm you in any way.'

Jane suddenly realised that she was not quite so sure if that would be true. African policemen were not noted for their gentle treatment of prisoners. She resolved to put in a good word for Ngina if they were rescued.

The rain eased off and the sun came out. Naomi stopped shivering.

'I'm hungry, Ngina,' she said.

'I have no food.'

'Just be patient,' said Jane; she was relieved that Naomi has recovered her appetite. Her forehead was cooler.

'Where do we go now?' she asked Ngina.

'We wait here till Njirami comes.'

Suddenly there was the sound of firing. Ngina crossed herself. Jane prayed that it was the Army.

The firing did not last long. They could hear shouting in the distance, then all went quiet. After what seemed an age there were footsteps approaching and Njirami and another man came up. Njirami was clutching his arm which was bleeding again.

'We must move on,' he said. He looked at Naomi who standing beside Jane.

'Naomi is sick and hungry,' she said. 'It is dangerous for her to walk any distance.'

'Very well.' He signed to the other man to carry her.

'No!' shouted Jane and tried to interpose herself, but was pushed aside. The man picked up Naomi, who started kicking and screaming.

'Tell her to be quiet,' Njirami ordered.

Ngina offered to carry her, but Njirami strode ahead with the man close behind him. Jane and Ngina followed as fast as they could. They had not gone far when Njirami tripped and fell on his injured arm. He lay on the ground and groaned; his sleeve was now soaked in blood.

The other man still had Naomi in his grasp.

'Keep hold of her,' Njirami told him.

Jane could see that he was in great pain.

'You can't carry on,' she said. 'Just let the girl go.' She moved forward.

Njirami with his good arm brought out his revolver and pointed it at Jane.

'Stay where you are.'

Naomi continued to wriggle for a bit, but the man's grasp was too firm and she stopped.

There was silence apart from gentle forest noises. Jane kept her eyes on Naomi; she was quite still. And then she moved her head slightly forward and seemed to be listening carefully. Then she turned her head and nodded in a theatrical gesture. Jane followed her glance and saw for a fleeting moment a green uniform in a bush to one side and behind Njirami. The *ndete* birds suddenly began their clamour.

Jane felt a hand on her back and Gichuchi gently pushed her aside and came towards Njirami. He held his arms out to show that he was unarmed.

'It's over,' he said. 'Let the child go. You are surrounded.'

Njirami recognised him. 'You. I thought you were dead, killed at the farm. So you have joined the *wazungu* to do their dirty work. You broke your oath.'

'It was a worthless oath.'

'Nevertheless, you will pay the penalty.' Njirami pointed the gun at him.

'Shoot me if you like. But hand over the girl first.'

Gichuchi stepped forward towards the man holding Naomi. 'Give me the girl.' The man was about to refuse but he felt the muzzle of a rifle at the back of his neck. He let Naomi go and she ran towards Jane. Gichuchi realised that she about to cross Njirami's line of fire and he hurled himself at him. Njirami, in an automatic reflex, fired. Gichuchi took the bullet in the throat. It hit an artery, and he collapsed bleeding heavily.

Jane took hold of Naomi. She pulled her away and ran into the arms of Lieutenant Jamieson. 'Thank God we have found you. Lieutenant Jamieson, Ma'am. I am from Colonel Michael's battalion. Are you all right?'

Jane did not reply but buried her head in his shoulder and burst into tears.

Meanwhile the squad had rushed in and pinioned Njirami on the ground. The other man stood still with his hands raised. Ngina knelt on the ground sobbing.

Ngina and the man were tied up and marched swiftly back to the camp. Njirami was also tied up and none too gently hauled to his feet and dragged away. Jamieson went to Gichuchi, who was now unconscious, and stuffed whatever he had to hand into the wound. But he died within a few minutes.

* * *

Over the last two days Michael had been monitoring the operation by radio reports. When rescue appeared likely within a day, he organised two platoons to relieve the men in the field. In addition, the lorries had rations for the prisoners. Michael and Major Bright came in Land Rovers. The position of the camp was reckoned to be about three miles from a track that was accessible by vehicle. When they reached the rendezvous, Corporal Harun called the squads and was informed that Jane and Naomi were safe, but that Gichuchi had been killed. Michael set off with the platoons into the forest; it took an hour and a half to reach the camp. There he found the prisoners under close guard. He wanted to look for Jane but he spoke to Jamieson first.

Jamieson gave a brief report.

'Our men have done pretty well, sir.'

'You have indeed. When we get back to Nanyuki we must have a thorough debriefing with everybody, not just the officers. And Jane and Naomi. She can speak Gikuyu.'

'Really?'

'Yes. Quite a sharp little madam is Naomi.'

'What are your orders for the prisoners, sir?'

'Have them escorted to the lorries. Tell them that there will be food for them when they get there. That should deter them from trying to make a run for it. I want Njirami and the woman kept separate for the others. I have forewarned Special Branch and they can collect him from Nanyuki. He broke his parole, you know. Apart from kidnapping, he had several *watu* killed in the raid on the farm and there must be other crimes he has committed. I hope the judge will throw the book at him. Not our concern, fortunately.'

'And the woman?'

'Don't know. I'll ask Miss Simpson about her. She will have to go to the cells for the time being.'

Michael went over to the men who were bringing in Gichuchi's body. It was laid on a stretcher and covered with a groundsheet.

'A pity about Gichuchi. One of our best men.'

Jamieson explained how he had come to be killed. 'He saved Naomi's life. Njirami was clearly unstable and could have fired wildly at anything. I don't think Gichuchi suffered for long, which is a mercy. I want to put him up for a medal.'

'Well, that is as may be. Ah. Here they are.'

Naomi and Jane were led into the camp.

Suddenly Michael found himself wondering how he should greet Jane in front of the men. With an embrace? A chaste kiss? He had no idea of what she was feeling and how she would react to a gesture.

One look at her face told him that she was deeply shocked. He put his arms around her, but she did not make any response. He kissed the top of her head and let her go. She went and sat by herself. While he checked that everything was in hand for the evacuation of the prisoners, the askaris provided Jane and Naomi with some food and water. When they had had a little refreshment, he told Berkeley and Walters to take their squads to the RV point. He went ahead with Jamieson's squad and Jane and Naomi, who was carried on an askari's back. The path was narrow and he could not take Jane's hand. She said nothing. At the track, Corporal Harun was waiting in the Land Rover.

'Radio the Howarths and say that we will be there with the girls in an hour.'

When the askari put her down, Naomi turned to him.

'*Nindauga ni wega*,' she said.

'*Niwega*,' he replied.

'*Tigwo na wega*.'*

'Don't mention it.'

* * *

Jane went to say thank you to Jamieson.

'Ma'am, I have some things for you.'

He held out the bracelet and her engagement ring.

'We found these and your handkerchief and notes. Without them we would not have found you so quickly.'

'You have been very brave,' said Michael.

Jane gave him a weak smile.

'Perhaps,' she said. 'I am very tired and very dirty. And I have been very frightened. Just let me absorb being free. We will have a long talk later.'

'Understood. Jump in.'

Michael drove in silence. Naomi took Jane's hand and kissed it; Jane put her arm round her.

'Looking forward to going home, Naomi?

'You bet. But it has been quite an adventure, hasn't it?'

'Not one I want to repeat.'

'I'm feeling better now.'

'Good,' said Michael. 'Give your parents a big kiss, Naomi. They have been desperately worried about you.'

Patrick and Annabel were waiting in the yard in front of the house.

* 'Thank you very much.' 'You're welcome.' 'Goodbye.'

They had been joined by some of the *watu* who clapped enthusiastically when Jane and Naomi got out of the Land Rover. Naomi rushed to her mother who wept copiously. Jane lingered by the car for a moment and held up her finger with the ring back in place.

'Thank you, Michael, and all your men.' She put her head against his chest. 'I have so much to tell you, but it will take time. Please be patient with me. You have had plenty of practice at that when I was ill.'

'Just relax, now that it's all over. You don't have to worry any more.' He kissed her. 'I will have to go back to Nanyuki, but I will come over tomorrow.'

'I must go to Annabel and reassure her that Naomi has not been harmed.'

Patrick came over to Michael and shook his hand. He began to express his thanks, but Michael cut him short.

'We did our job. I'm just glad it went well. I'll see you tomorrow.' Michael waved as he drove off.

When he got back to his office he drew up a list of things to do. It was long, but at the head was a note in capitals:

DON'T FORGET PICTURE FOR JANE.

The next item was a call to the Brigadier.

'Jolly good. What a relief. Any casualties on our side?'

Michael explained about Gichuchi. 'Jamieson wants to recommend him for a medal, but I don't see how that can be done given his unofficial status.'

'Not directly, though. Has he a widow?'

'Not as far as I know.'

'But there are ways round this. He must have relatives. I'll get back to you in due course. What is your next step?'

'I will be having a debriefing of everybody, tomorrow morning. I will get Special Branch to sit in. They can also interview Jane and Naomi, who will have very useful information for us, I'm sure.'

'Very good. By the way, the Press have got hold of the story. Tell your men not to speak to reporters and don't say a word yourself.

Just refer them to the GOC's office. I will ring the General and tell him the good news. He may wish to contact you in due course. What is happening to the prisoners?'

'There are fifteen or so. Tonight they will be in camp under guard, but I want the Police to remove them as soon as possible. I have kept Njirami separate and I hope he will be off my hands tonight; he is badly wounded, by the way, but not by us.'

After several other calls, Michael sat down to write his own account of the day. After an hour, Major Bright reported after putting Njirami and Ngina in the cells. Then the Forest Squads arrived and Michael went out to greet them. Having praised them for their efforts, he ordered them to shower, shave and make themselves presentable. There would be no more forest duties for them in the near future.

* * *

The debriefing of the Forest Squads took most of the following morning. Major Bright and a Special Branch officer made notes while Michael asked the questions. At the end he addressed them all together and congratulated them on a job well done, a model, he hoped, for future operations. They were not to talk about it to anyone, especially not the Press. The askaris were dismissed but Jamieson, Berkeley and Sergeant Walters he kept back for a private talk. They had nothing significant to add to what had already been discussed, save some complaints about equipment and recommending some askaris for promotion.

'I think we can give them all a stripe.'

Michael asked them whether the prisoners might have any cause for complaint about their treatment, and was assured there had been no need for any rough stuff; they had been willing to cooperate. Jamieson said that they were exhausted, hungry and tired of a fugitive existence; some of them had not seen their families for a very long time. The wounded had received treatment.

Major Bright asked what should be done about the woman, Ngina, now that Special Branch had removed Njirami.

'Keep her in the cells for now, but see that she is protected; give her some clean kit and feed her. I will let you know in a day or so.' An idea was forming in his mind.

'What are we going to do about Gichuchi, sir?' asked Jamieson. 'We must bury him soon.'

'We must also find if he has any relatives.'

'I think he has a brother who works in the camp,' said Bright. 'Um…Njeru is his name. A slovenly character. I'll speak to him today.'

Njeru did not show much emotion about the death of his older brother but told Bright about his younger brother, Karumbi, who worked in the District Surveyor's Office, and his father on the Frampton's farm. Jamieson was despatched to break the news to them and offer a lift to the burial service.

That afternoon Michael drove up to the Howarths'. He was very anxious about Jane. From his experience in Burma he knew that after a traumatic event people generally reacted in two ways. Either they could not stop talking about it, to get it out of their system, and he suspected that Naomi belonged to that category, or, like Jane, withdraw into themselves and only start talking after some time. And there were a few people who never got over it and were reduced to a catatonic state. He was fairly certain that Jane, so eminently sensible and level-headed, would not be like that. All he could do for her was to be patient and support her until she could put the episode behind her.

When he arrived he found Patrick and Annabel sitting on the verandah.

'Come and have a seat, Michael. Coffee?'

'Yes, please.'

Patrick poured. 'Your men did very well. Must have been quite a tricky operation, to rescue them without putting them at risk. And finding them in the first place.'

'Tracking requires practice and experience, and our programme of training seems to have worked. These askaris are naturals. Unfortunately, the Mau Mau are quite good at it, too. But they become careless. And however careful you are you cannot disguise the passage of large numbers. That is why we prefer to operate with small squads.

And we were helped by the fact that a rival gang attacked Njirami's original camp in an attempt to steal the hostages, or so we think. We will have confirmation of this when we speak to Naomi and Jane.'

'Are you asking them to relive their experiences?' said Annabel. 'Isn't that rather cruel?'

'There will be an officer from Special Branch coming here to talk to them. They could be a valuable source of information. Don't worry. He will be very gentle. I will suggest to him that he talks to Naomi and Jane together. But I would also suggest that you don't sit in on the interview. It will be better if you don't know all the details.'

'Well, a mother has the right to...'

'What Michael says is true,' said Patrick. 'Knowing Naomi, it will all come out anyway. Much better not to inhibit her.'

Annabel sighed. 'I suppose you are right. I have been so wound up these last few days, I haven't been able to think about anything else. And now that they are safely back, I still can't relax. But I do see that it may be better if a mother does not know everything.'

'You can't live her life by proxy,' observed Patrick.

'I am not sure if you know,' said Michael, 'that one of my men was killed in the rescue. When Njirami was about to fire he threw himself between the gun and Naomi and took the bullet in the throat. He died very soon after.'

'O my God,' exclaimed Annabel. 'Poor man. Does... er...Naomi know about this?'

'I'm not sure. We will find out soon.'

'Does he have a wife, or relatives?' asked Patrick. 'We would want to do something to help.'

'Leave it for the time being. I will perhaps make a suggestion in due course, when we know a little more clearly what the situation is. Now, what about the *watu*? What do they think about this business?'

'Difficult to speak for everyone, of course,' said Patrick, 'but, whatever they thought beforehand, after the raid on the farm and now the kidnapping they deplore the violence of the Mau Mau and they reckon the rebellion is failing. The Mau Mau have been cooped up in the forests and they have been shown to be vulnerable there.'

'It's not over by any means, but we are getting there. Did you find out who might have acted as a spy for the Mau Mau, telling them when Jane and Naomi were up at the dam?'

'No. I don't want the Police nosing around. It will only stir things up; people will think that we don't trust their loyalty. Most of them have been with us for years. There are some who come and go after a short time, but that is the same on any farm. I suspect that they will find out who was responsible and deal with him in their own way.'

'Probably the best course. And how are Naomi and Jane? I should have asked earlier.'

'Naomi? A hot bath and cream on her insect bites and some home cooking seems to have restored her. She did cry out once in the night but she was asleep again when I went to her. This morning she said that she had had a little nightmare but she was all right.'

'Where is she now?'

'She went with Ephraim to look at Lakme's new calf. We told her not to be long.'

'And Jane?'

'She has been very quiet. She came down for breakfast and had some toast and coffee and went back to her room. She hasn't appeared since. We don't want to disturb her. But you go up.'

Just then Naomi came bouncing back onto the verandah.

'Hello, Michael.'

'Colonel Charteris to you, Naomi,' said Annabel sternly.

'Hello, Colonel Michael.'

'Hello, Naomi. How is the calf?'

'Taking its milk. It's only a few days since I last saw it and it is growing fast. Have you seen Simmie today?'

'Not yet. I think she is very tired and sleeping.'

'That is good for her. I had a long sleep last night.'

'Well done. Now, Naomi, a man from Special Branch will want to talk to you. He will be very interested in your experiences; you will have a lot of useful things to tell him. And you understand Gikuyu. Will you help him?

Naomi looked at Patrick, who nodded.

'Good girl,' said Michael. 'Now I must go and see if Jane is awake. Can you show me her room?'

Naomi led the way upstairs. She pointed to the door.

'Thank you, Naomi.'

Naomi was rathe reluctant to leave, no doubt curious about what would transpire between Jane and Michael.

'Off you go, now.'

With a flounce she went downstairs.

Chapter Twenty

Michael knocked. There was no reply. He knocked again. There was still no reply so he opened the door slightly and peeped in. Jane lay on her back moaning quietly. He called her name several times and then went to the bed and took her hand.

With a start she woke up and seized his wrist.

'Oh,' she said, when she realised who he was. 'It's you, Michael. Thank goodness. I was having this dream.'

'A bad dream?'

'Yes, a bad dream, but…only a dream.'

She sat up. 'Don't ask me if I'm all right. I am getting there gradually. At least I hope so.'

She lay back again. 'But all the better for seeing you. Come and sit down.'

She patted the bed.

'Give me a kiss.'

Michael asked her tentatively if she would join Naomi in an interview with Special Branch.

'I am sure there are things you don't want to remember, but it would help enormously if you could.'

Jane sighed. 'You are right, there are things I don't want to remember, but I suppose I must, and it may help me as well to get the whole business out of my system. There is one thing that I don't want Naomi to hear all over again. At the time I was able to brush it off but…you can imagine it was quite a shock. And I would rather not tell anyone else, not even Patrick and Annabel. You see, one night two men attempted to rape me. I have the bruises on my legs to prove it. And a little cut on my throat from a knifepoint.'

Michael did not know what to say.

'The men dragged me out of the tent. Fortunately the women in the next tent heard my screams and started hitting the men. Njirami came across with his guards. The men were taken into the forest and shot. Then Njirami took me and Naomi into his tent and we were given a space at the back. His woman Ngina looked after us very well. The thing is, Njirami would have no bargaining power if we were dead or injured. That is why he took care of us.'

'No wonder you don't want to relive that episode.'

'There was something else. The following night the camp was attacked by a rival gang. Ngina took us to a hiding place until it was all over. The leader of the attack, who had been a friend of Njirami, was hanged. I saw what was going to happen and so I took Naomi away and covered her up. You know what she is like. She wanted to see what was going on but I had to hold her to stop her looking.'

'She seems to have bounced back. At least so far.'

'I'm sure. Don't tell her, but looking back on it I think she was very brave. Once she realised we were prisoners, she did what she was told and didn't complain. When she got home, she cried a lot and insisted that her parents bathe her and feed her and wouldn't let them go until she fell asleep. Reverting to babyhood, I suppose.'

'Now you wouldn't know she had come through such an ordeal.'

'Bless her. I wish I had her insouciance.'

'But you have been very brave, too. And thinking ahead, dropping your handkerchief and those slips of paper, the bracelet and your ring.'

'I had to do something even if it was but a faint hope at the time that they would be found. And I was very sad to take off the ring, but I had no choice. It was wonderful that it was found.'

'The man who found it, Gichuchi, was one of my best trackers. You have met him before, during the raid on the farm.'

'The one I shot at?

'Yes. He came over to us afterwards. And he was the one who was shot by Njirami, saving Naomi's life.'

'Poor man. It all happened so quickly and we were hustled away immediately.'

'He died within a few minutes.'

'That's quite a thing to think about,' she said, 'to have one's life saved by someone who was killed in the process.'

'He was doing his duty, a cliché, but askaris like him have a keen sense of honour.'

'I hope he will be buried decently. I would like to come to the service.'

'It will be very soon, tomorrow, perhaps.'

'You must take me.'

He got up. 'I have something for you in the Land Rover. I'll be back in a moment.'

He returned with the picture that Mrs Unwin had painted of the two cheetahs.

'This is in memory of a very happy day we spent together. Unwrap it.'

Jane got up and took it to a table. She untied the string and folded back the brown paper.

'Oh, Michael. How lovely!' She looked at the signature. 'Doris. I knew she liked painting wildlife. Gosh. Proud animals. She has caught them wonderfully. And a little warthog. Mount Kenya in the background. This will have an honoured place in our dining room.'

She came over and kissed Michael. 'Thank you. I feel so much better already. Go down while I tidy myself. Can you wait a bit?'

Michael went downstairs to Patrick and Annabel and told then that Jane was on the move. Naomi was reading a book, sitting on a swing in the garden.

'While you were upstairs I had a call from Inspector Davies of Special Branch. Know him?'

'I met him after the raid on your farm.'

'He wants to come soon and interview Naomi and Jane. I said that I hoped he would be gentle with both of them because of their ordeal. He assured me he would be.'

'What are your plans for the next few days?'

'Catch up on farm business I have neglected. And I would like to thank your men in person for the rescue.'

'It was a team effort by a lot of people.'

'Well, perhaps just the squad who found them and brought them back.'

'That can be arranged.'

'Good. Just five minutes. It would mean a lot to Annabel and me.'

Jane came down, looking fresh, but still with dark rings under her eyes.

'How are you, dear?' asked Annabel.

'Better, thank you. Ready for the world again, almost.'

'Come and sit down. Coffee?'

'Please.'

'I'll go and make some more.'

Patrick asked if she would be able to speak to Special Branch.

'I've discussed this with Michael. And yes, of course I will. And I want to get back to things right away. No mollycoddling.'

'Business as usual, then.'

'Michael has given me the most wonderful present. It's not connected with recent events but it came at just the right time. One of Doris Unwin's pictures, specially commissioned. I'll show you later.'

'No. Bring it down now. I have always admired her work.'

Jane went up to her room and fetched it.

'Wow! Look at this, Annie,' said Patrick. She was bringing in the coffee for Jane.

They both admired the painting.

'Can I hang it downstairs?' Jane asked. 'It seems a pity to keep it to myself.'

'But it is special to you.'

'Only Michael and I know how special. I want others to enjoy it, too. And in the future it will be a vivid reminder of my time in Kenya.'

Michael stayed a few more minutes.

'I have to go, alas. Say good bye to Naomi for me.'

Jane came with him to the Land Rover.

'Jane, darling, we have some serious talking to do.'

'We do, indeed. As soon as we can.'

* * *

Gichuchi was buried in the small cemetery at the camp. The priest of the church he had attended conducted the service. Njoka, Gichuchi's father, and his brothers were present; each of them threw a handful of earth on the coffin. Michael, Jane and members of the Forest Squad were there. Patrick and Annabel stood a little way back and afterwards he spoke to the askaris to thank them for the rescue of Naomi and Jane. He noticed that they were all wearing a lance-corporal's stripe.

'Very well deserved, I'm sure,' he said.

Patrick and Annabel were taken to the Mess for coffee and Michael put a proposition to them. The Special Branch had finished with Ngina and had found no reason to bring charges against her. She was homeless; Jane had already asked if something could be done for her. Patrick and Annabel, after some persuasion, agreed to take her on as a housemaid for a trial period.

* * *

When the Howarths had gone, taking Jane with them, Michael returned to his office. He had just settled into some paperwork when the Brigadier came on the line.

'We have a problem, Michael. The *African Standard* has been sniffing around. In today's paper they report that Mau Mau prisoners have been beaten up in Nanyuki camp.'

'What? I saw them when they came in and inspected the security arragements. I admit I haven't been down there since. The Camp Commandant, Captain Symonds, had immediate responsibility for them but I suppose the buck ultimately stops with me.'

'It does.'

'I must say that the Police were very slow to deal with them. It took till yesterday before they were on their way to the detention camp at Thika.'

'Well, look into it and report back.'

'Sir.'

He called Major Bright and told him about the Brigadier's call.

'Come along to a meeting with Captain Symonds in half an hour.'

At the appointed time Symonds arrived. Michael was sitting behind his desk and Bright was at a side table with a pad of paper in front of him. Symonds was not invited to sit.

'Captain Symonds, it has come to my notice that the Mau Mau prisoners were beaten up. Is this true?'

'Well, sir, there was a bit of a set-to.'

'Set-to? When did this happen? Must have been two days ago at least. Why was I not told before? Makes me look pretty foolish if I have to hear it from someone outside the camp or read it in the newspapers.'

'Sir, you were very busy and I thought it best to handle the matter myself.'

'But a matter of this sensitivity surely merited my personal attention. You know how careful we must be, as the GOC has ordered.'

Symonds said nothing.

'Who are the men responsible?'

'I'm not sure, sir. I think it was some men from D Company. They had custody of the prisoners.'

'Have you got a list of their names?'

'No, sir.'

'But you must have had a list of the men detailed for the job.'

'I can't seem to put my hands on it.'

'Surely it must be in your office somewhere? What about your clerks? Have you checked with them?'

'No, sir.'

'Do this as soon as you leave this office. I want this list on my desk first thing tomorrow morning. Have you taken any action against those responsible?'

'No, sir. As I don't know who they were.'

'So there was no list.'

Symonds said nothing. Michael just stared at him. Eventually Symonds spoke.

'I just…just took the first detail I could get hold of at short notice.'

'I inspected the prisoners when they came and I noticed that Corporal Singh was in charge of them.'

Michael called through to his clerk: 'Have Corporal Singh brought to me straight away.' He turned back to Symonds.

'What injuries were inflicted on the prisoners?'

'Nothing serious, sir.'

'Did you inspect them as they were taken away?'

'No, sir.'

'You seem to have been remarkably casual about the whole affair, Captain Symonds. We have a duty of care towards our prisoners, just as much as to our own men. Tell me about this set-to, as you describe it. What actually happened?'

'I don't know exactly. I wasn't there at the time.'

'So how and when did you find out that there had been a set-to?'

'Er…Corporal Singh told me.'

'When did he tell you?'

'Some time afterwards.'

'What action did you take upon receipt of this information?'

'Action, sir?'

'Yes. Seeking out and punishing those responsible, for example.'

'Well, sir, now that the prisoners have left the camp and no longer our concern, I thought it best to let sleeping dogs lie.'

'But you have been caught out. In fact, we, as a battalion, have been caught out, because the Press has got hold of it. By your negligence we have been brought into disrepute.'

Michael picked up the phone and rang the Mess.

'Have Lieutenant Berkeley brought to my office at once.'

Then the clerk rang through and said that Corporal Singh had arrived.

'Tell him to wait outside.'

Symonds began to shift uneasily from foot to foot. Michael continued to stare at him and Major Bright said nothing but wrote notes.

Five minutes later, Berkeley arrived and saluted.

'Berkeley, escort Captain Symonds to his room and bring to me his service revolver.'

He turned to Symonds. 'You are confined to your room until further notice. Meals will be brought to you. On no account are you to communicate with brother officers or men. Is that understood?'

Symonds was about to say something but changed his mind. He gave a slack salute and preceded Berkeley out of the office.

When he had gone, Michael lit his pipe.

'It's like boarding school,' he said, as he puffed, 'when the housemaster is investigating a broken window in the dormitory. Very tedious. But it has to be done. Whatever actually happened, we have to be seen to have dealt with the matter swiftly. I am very angry with Symonds but he mustn't become a scapegoat. Let's see what Singh has to say.'

Corporal Singh came in and saluted smartly.

'Corporal Singh, I am concerned about reports that the Mau Mau prisoners were treated badly. I understand from Captain Symonds that you were in charge of them.'

'Yes, sir.'

'What happened to them when they arrived?'

'I don't know what you mean, sir.'

'If the reports are true, they were beaten up while they were in our camp. Is that the case?'

Singh did not answer at once.

'Come on, man,' said Michael.

'Er...some of the prisoners attempted to escape and had to be restrained.'

'Escape? When they were inside the cage? When there were armed guards at the entrance? When they were tired and hungry? How did they try to escape?'

'I'm not sure, sir.'

'Not sure? But they were in your custody. Did you see them attempting to climb the barbed wire fence?'

'No, sir.'

'Did they try to rush the entrance?'

'No, sir.'

'Were they digging a tunnel to the outside?'

'No, sir.'

'This story about an attempted escape is nonsense, isn't it?'

Singh was reluctant to answer. Michael said nothing for a few minutes; he was turning over the pages of the file in front of him. Bright drew animals on his notepad. Singh looked increasingly uncomfortable but still said nothing.

Michael broke the silence.

'I have your service record in front of me, Corporal Singh. It is a good record. No black marks against your name. In fact, you earned an early promotion to Lance Corporal and a second stripe not long afterwards. "Good NCO material", the record says.'

Michael paused. There was no response from Singh save that he blinked and a tear started to roll down his cheek. Michael affected not to notice.

'Now the ancient Persians, Singh, taught their boys two main things. Do you know what they were?'

Singh shook his head.

'They taught them to shoot straight and speak the truth. What is the truth of this matter, Singh?'

Singh took a deep breath to collect himself. 'I didn't want this, sir. When the prisoners were in the cage, and you had gone, I was told to teach them a lesson. I asked what he meant by that.'

'Who was "he"?'

'Captain Symonds, sir.'

'Go on.'

'I was ordered to have the prisoners beaten up. I protested but Captain Symonds came and directly ordered my detail to go into the cage. Some of the men were reluctant but Captain Symonds shouted at them.'

'What did he say?'

'He said that these were the men who had kidnapped and tortured a little girl and Miss Jane.'

'What happened then?'

'They went into the cage. The prisoners were hit with rifle butts and beaten with sticks. When they were on the ground they were kicked.'

'Was Captain Symonds present?'

'He watched for a few minutes and then shouted at the men to stop.'

'Where were you at this time?

'I was standing outside the cage. Captain Symonds ordered the men not to say anything.'

'So you maintain that the prisoners were beaten up on Captain Symonds' orders. Will members of your detail corroborate that?'

'You can ask anyone, sir.'

'Is there a list of men in your detail?'

'I wrote it down just after.'

'Why?'

'Because I knew there would be trouble after what had been done.' He produced a paper from his inside pocket.

'You realised that there was bound to be an enquiry into this affair?'

'Yes, sir. And I am deeply ashamed to have been part of it, but I had no choice.'

'Very well. Major Bright, I want the men on this list on parade in half an hour.'

'Sir.'

'Corporal Singh, I want you to wait in the outer office. You are not to speak to anyone. Dismiss.'

Singh saluted and went out.

It took a bit of time to assemble the askaris. Meanwhile Michael took down his manual of Military Law and studied the clauses relating to the collection of evidence before a court martial. So far, it seemed, he had been following the book. When all the askaris were present, he told Corporal Singh to leave by a back door out of sight of the others. Berkeley had been summoned to keep watch on the detail. One by one, the askaris were summoned and questioned by Michael, with Bright as witness and record keeper. All agreed that Singh had protested at the order and that it had come from Captain Symonds. Michael did not ask whether they agreed with the order or not. However he did ask what they had actually done to the prisoners and it emerged that the blows had been delivered to the arms, legs and shoulders and not to the head.

'They did not resist, sir, and we did not need to hurt them too much.'

Then Michael asked if they had told anyone about the beating. Most said that they had not, but one confessed to having spoken to a civilian worker, who happened to be passing at the time.

'What is his name?'

'I don't know, sir, but I have often seen him around the camp. A scruffy looking chap.'

Michel made no comment. When the askaris had been dismissed he pulled a bottle from a desk drawer and poured a drink for himself and Bright.

'I think we deserve this. Cheers.'

'Cheers, sir. Not a pleasant business.'

'No, indeed. Remember when we talked before when the case of Sergeant Rawlings came up. We discussed obedience to orders. If it is true that Symonds gave the order over the head of Corporal Singh, then Singh is in the clear. He seemed mortified to have been associated with the business.'

'I agree.'

'Can I have your notes? I will write up a report tonight and take it to the Brigadier tomorrow. It will take some time, since my typing is so slow. But I can't let anyone else see it. Then, if he approves, I will send it to the Legal Department.'

* * *

Michael's discussion with the Brigadier was not a comfortable one. On the desk was a copy of the *African Standard*.

'This sort of publicity is exactly what the GOC does not want. Added to which, it has tarnished your rescue operation, which was a great success and was favourably reported in the papers. How could you let this happen?'

'In my report, sir, I have described every step I took to deal with the matter. Major Bright was present at all the interviews. I followed procedure to the letter.'

'I'm sure you did. You told me that you inspected the prisoners and the security arrangements when they arrived, but then did not go near them.'

'That is correct, sir.'

'So where were you?'

'I had to visit the Howarths the day after about matters arising from the kidnap, and there was other battalion business to attend to.'

The Brigadier nodded.

'One matter I had to deal with was to arrange and supervise the burial of Gichuchi and a visit by the Howarths to thank Lieutenant Jamieson's squad. I was also in contact with Inspector Davies of Special Branch.'

'Why did you put Captain Symonds in charge of the prisoners?'

'He was Camp Commandant. He was the officer in charge of their accommodation, food and security.'

'And yet he was reprimanded for negligence in the supervision of his company.'

'That was some time ago.'

'And there was the court martial of Sergeant Rawlings, where he showed a marked disinclination to exercise his responsibilities.'

'Rawlings was acquitted. But I removed Symonds from his Company. The post of Camp Commandant needed filling and there he has stayed. Actually, as far as I can see, his administration has been reasonably efficient. I haven't had cause to complain.'

'There will also be the question why you did not monitor the prisoners' treatment more closely yourself. It might also be said that you have spent rather a lot of time in the company of Miss Jane Simpson. Are you engaged to be married?'

'I don't think that is any business of the Army. As for the first point, sir, any commander has to let his subordinates get on with things. He cannot be everywhere. Indeed, it is contrary to the spirit of the Army, as I was taught, for a colonel to do a lieutenant's, let alone a captain's, job. How else can officers learn to take responsibility for their actions?'

Michael paused, but the Brigadier did not say anything.

'As for Jane,' he went on, 'we are engaged to be married. Of course, I would like to spend more time with her, especially after her ordeal, but I have never neglected my duties because of her. Whenever we have been out together I have always informed

Battalion HQ and ensured I could be contacted. Jane fully understands my commitments. Do I need to say more, sir?'

The Brigadier leant back in his chair and took out a packet of cigarettes. He offered one to Michael.

'No, thank you, sir.'

'There is no doubt,' said the Brigadier between puffs, 'that Captain Symonds will go before a court martial and might well be found guilty. The atmosphere is very different now from the trial of Sergeant Rawlings, who was acquitted despite the evidence of the askaris. We have learnt to evaluate properly the testimony of all members of our Armed forces, whatever their skin colour, and not simply dismiss it, as in the past. This is not a doctrine that appeals to many of the settlers, and some of our personnel. But the GOC is adamant on the matter – no more political verdicts. Your report of the incident is straightforward and counsel will have difficulty in shaking it. However the questions I have put to you might well be raised in a plea of mitigation. I seem to remember an obiter dictum in the judges' verdict on Sergeant Rawlings that there had been inadequate supervision of patrols. It did not specify who had been failing in this respect but anyone reading that would infer that the Commanding Officer had been negligent.'

'It is easy to say.'

'But very hard to prove a negative. And the damage will have been done. Now the papers know about this, they will make the most of it. It is unlikely that the Governor will slap a D Notice on it.'

'Well, so be it.' Michael shrugged his shoulders.

'It may not come to anything. I just wanted you to be aware of the possibility.'

Chapter Twenty-One

The court martial of Captain Symonds was held a month after Michael's interview with the Brigadier. This time the evidence of the askaris was accepted and the judges did not take long to reach a verdict. Symonds was sentenced to dishonourable discharge from the Army for conduct unbecoming an officer. In the record of the judgment there was no reference to the possibility of inadequate supervision.

Michael was relieved at the verdict. At the same time he felt a pang of pity for Symonds. He also had been a professional soldier: Army family, public school, Sandhurst, a good record in the last years of the war. Something had gone wrong. Perhaps he had found the transition to peacetime soldiering hard to manage, had chafed against inaction and the lack of the stimulation of wartime and therefore had volunteered for service in Kenya. Perhaps he had been eased out of his previous posting and had been told to find employment elsewhere. Such files as Michael had on him were not very informative. He was in his mid-thirties and with no immediate prospect of promotion to Major. For whatever reason, he had vented his frustrations on Africans. Perhaps it was just racial prejudice, which he shared with many of the settlers and some brother officers.

This speculation promoted thoughts about his own career. His battalion was to be reduced to company strength. He had commanded, in Burma and Kenya, what in England would be called 'native troops'; it was not much consolation that the Duke of Wellington himself had been despised by Napoleon as a 'sepoy general'. His service with the KAR would not carry much weight with regiments who had fought in Korea or were facing the Soviet Bloc across the Iron Curtain. Counter-insurgency was unfashionable.

So after Kenya? Commanding a Jungle Warfare School or, irony of ironies, Commandant of some depot back in England, the fate of superannuated half-colonels? Of course, there was the possibility of a course at Staff College with a War Office appointment to follow, travelling up to London every day from a small house in Surrey to sit at a desk. Was that what Jane would want for them?

* * *

The battalion held its Standing Down parade at Nanyuki; it was Michael's last official act as colonel. The GOC, several other senior officers and a representative of the Government were there, sitting on the Saluting Base. Local dignitaries and their wives, among them the Howarths, the Framptons and Andrew Holmes, now Senior District Officer, watched from a small stand. Michael had insisted that there were chairs laid out for any Africans who cared to come and watch. These were soon taken up and more chairs and benches brought out. For the townsfolk of Nanyuki, whatever their views on the British military, it was an opportunity for a show and a change from routine.

Jane was walking around the Parade Ground and recognised Njoka and Karumbi slipping into seats. On an impulse, she went up to them and introduced herself.

'We know who you are, Miss Jane,' said Njoka.

'Gichuchi saved our lives. And Colonel Michael thought a great deal of him.'

'Colonel Michael saved him from bad ways, and we are grateful for that.'

Karumbi chipped in. 'He showed me that the Mau Mau were no more than thugs. We joked that when we had won Independence I would be President, father would be Minister of Agriculture and he would be General.'

'He was a very brave soldier, and very skilful.'

'We hear that you are going to marry Colonel Michael,' said Njoka.

'As soon as we can when we get back to England. He has yet to meet my family, and I have never met his family.'

'Ah. That is very important. Marriage is the meeting of two families, not just two people. Out here, we don't always remember that.'

Jane was not sure how to reply, but Njoka carried on.

'We hope you will be very happy together and have many, many *totos*.'

Just then a bugle sounded to announce the start of the parade. Jane hurried to her seat near the Howarths.

She had never seen Michael in Number One uniform, complete with sword. She watched him standing with a group of his officers while RSM Tickell made a final check on the alignment of the ranks. Tickell came up to Michael and snapped a smart salute. Michael then marched across to below the Saluting Base and in a voice that everyone could hear reported to the GOC.

'Battalion ready for your inspection, sir.'

The GOC accompanied by two staff officers came down and walked along the ranks. Michael introduced the officers as he came to each company and platoon. The GOC sometimes talked to an askari. Meanwhile a military band, brought up from Nairobi, played martial airs. After some twenty minutes the GOC returned to the Saluting Base and the battalion formed up for the March Past. Although the askaris' skills in the forest were well-honed, Parade Ground drill had not been a priority in their training; nevertheless in a short time RSM Tickell and Sergeant Walters had licked them into shape. Michael marched ahead of the battalion with Major Bright close behind and the askaris kept their ranks reasonably straight at the 'eyes right'. Instead of marching off the Parade Ground, they were wheeled back in front of the Saluting Base. The GOC came to the microphone hurriedly placed before him.

'Men of the King's African Rifles, you have played a vital part in countering terrorism and ensuring that Kenya can be at peace. Your skills in the forest are impressive and you have carried out your tasks, whatever was given to you, with courage and devotion to duty. It is with much regret on my part that your battalion, as a unit, will be decommissioned, but a number of you will continue in the Service of Her Majesty. However, it is to be hoped that those who will be leaving will continue to serve this country in other ways, building a new society…'

'Does he mean Independence?' Patrick whispered to Annabel.

'Shush…'

'The task is not yet fully accomplished,' the GOC went on, 'but you can look back on the your time in the battalion with justified pride for…' he hesitated for moment '*kazi iliyofanywa vizuru*…a job well done.'

The spectators applauded politely. The battalion came to attention. Michael saluted and gave the order to march off. Jane had never seen military ceremonial before and was duly impressed. Michael had looked tall and commanding and yet at ease with himself. She wondered whether he really wanted to leave the environment in which he had spent more than half his life. She realised that there was little in service life to match the responsibilities and rewards, and exhilaration, of commanding men when you knew every one by their names and had trained them to carry out difficult tasks. Higher rank brought heavier responsibilities without the personal involvement. She doubted that he would be really happy manning a desk back home. But the uncertainty of their future was also in its way exhilarating. As for herself, she had chosen to follow the colours and it was her duty to support him, wherever that might lead.

The GOC and the dignitaries made their way to the Mess, where tea had been laid on. Michael came over to her.

'I though you looked splendid,' she said.

'I haven't worn Number Ones for ages.' He took her arm. 'We must go and thank the General for his inspection and talk to our guests.'

'Do you want me as well?'

'Of course. This whole show was put on for your benefit, my love, never mind the brass.'

When they entered the anteroom, they were soon accosted by the General himself.

'Good show, Charteris. The men did you proud. It will be a pity to lose some of them, but you will not have to worry about that.'

'I would like to think, sir, that they would be treated well, gratuities and so forth.'

'I hope so, too. But we have to argue with the War Office and they have to argue with the Treasury.'

He turned to Jane. 'Miss Simpson, how rude of us to be talking military shop in front of you. How are you? Have you recovered from your ordeal?'

'Pretty well, thank you, General. I am very grateful to all those who helped to rescue us. Michael says that it was a team effort.'

'Indeed it was, Miss Simpson. The Army responded to the challenge efficiently and effectively, which it must be admitted, doesn't happen every time.'

He looked at Michael with a twinkle. 'Only generals are allowed to say that and then only in private.'

'Sir.'

'When are you going home, Charteris?'

'In about a fortnight, sir. Jane and I will go together, meet our respective families and then be married as soon as possible.'

'Good show. Why wait? There is one thing, though, Charteris. When we talked before I said that there might be something for you back here. That is still the case. In the meantime, however, enjoy your leave.'

'Sir.'

'Miss Simpson.'

He nodded to her and went to talk to the District Officer.

Jane wanted to ask Michael what the General had meant, but they were accosted by other visiting officers who did not show the same scruples about military chat as the General. Jane excused herself and went over to the Howarths.

'I am very pleased for Michael,' said Jane.

'Now, Jane,' said Patrick, 'Annabel and I have been thinking. You can't er…spend the night with Michael in the Mess, but we think that it would be nice for you, and for us, if he came and stayed the weekend before you go. There will be just the four of us, and Naomi, of course. And then we can all take you to the airport.'

'That would be very kind. Will you speak to him yourself? He has quite a few things to sort out before he goes.'

In a round of farewell visits round Nanyuki, Michael made roughly the same short speech, thanking people for their help during his time in command and wishing them well; he was careful not to mention Independence. He spoke individually to as many of the NCOs and askaris as he could. At other times he was closeted with Major Bright, who was going to take over what was left of the battalion. In spare moments he packed up what he wanted to take home and left the rest. Jane was doing the same at the farm. She managed to pack everything into two suitcases, wrapping the picture carefully and padding it round with clothes. At a farewell dinner in the mess she sat next to Michael. After the Loyal Toast Lieutenant Jamieson said a few words, as did Major Bright. Then Michael rose to speak, thanking them and wishing them well in their future careers. He concluded by saying that he would be leaving with many happy memories of Africa, though there had been some difficult times (he did not need to expand on this point). He would be travelling light, he said, with just two cases, but what were material possessions in comparison with the woman who had done him the honour of becoming his wife? This remark was greeted with loud applause and banging on the table. He concluded by toasting the King's African Rifles. Major Bright, who had slipped out after his own speech and was now standing at the side of the room, came forward with a parcel which he presented to Jane.

'Well, thank you,' she said. 'Can I open it now?'

She unwrapped it. Major Bright had given her an album, beautifully bound, of his wildlife photography, with a note of the date and location of each shot. She looked at it for a few moments.

'This is lovely,' she said. 'Thank you so much.' She gave Bright a kiss which was warmly applauded by the company.

At the end of the evening the young officers, already well-oiled, repaired to the bar, where Michael had left a tab for them. Michael and Jane made their final farewells to Bright and walked over to the Land Rover where Patrick was waiting. There was a small Guard of Honour standing by and they presented arms; Michael saluted them. Then they got in and were driven away.

* * *

After doing the rounds of relatives, Michael and Jane were married, by special dispensation, in St Mary Redcliffe, Bristol, and had a brief holiday in Scotland before returning to London. They rented a house in Surrey, not far from Camberley, and Doris' picture had pride of place in the sitting room. In the remaining weeks of Michael's leave, they caught up with friends they had not seen for several years. Jane wrote once a month to the Howarths. At first she received enthusiastic replies from Naomi, but once she had gone to school at Gilgil, the letters ceased. Annabel, however, was a conscientious correspondent. Michael attended two courses at Staff College and was then posted to the War Office in London, commuting every day. Jane gave birth to a daughter, whom they called Katherine Naomi, Katherine after Jane's mother. Gradually memories of their time in Kenya were superseded by fresh experiences, not least the care of a toddler and the imminent arrival of another child. Michael had been promoted to full Colonel and was working with colleagues from the other services on strategic planning. This was totally outside his previous experience and he found it very absorbing. Within eighteen months they had produced a report which was duly passed up the line and then put on a shelf where it gathered dust. Thereafter Michael was given various routine assignments which caused him much frustration. The birth of a healthy boy was a welcome diversion.

In 1959, as he was walking along a corridor in the War Office, he saw a general coming towards him. He duly stood to one side at attention. The general stopped.

'I know you,' said Sir Gerald Lathbury, 'Michael Charteris.'

'Sir.'

'You have crossed my mind recently. Come and see me tomorrow, Director of Military Training.' He turned to a staff officer. 'Make a note: Charteris 09.00.'

With that he swept on.

Michael returned to his desk, his mind whirling.

The following morning he was ushered into the General's office. Lathbury asked him how he had fared since leaving Kenya and Michael told him briefly of his new family and of his current malaise.

'I feel becalmed, sir, but that is part of Army life. I can't really complain.'

'No, you can't. However I have been attending meetings with ministers about the future of Kenya Colony, and it is recognised that now the insurgency is pretty well over steps should be taken towards self-government and possible Independence. That is the tide of the times. Many things are up for discussion but there is one matter upon which HMG insists and will, I think, be welcomed by a new adminstration out there. We want a military presence to be maintained, not just for strategic reasons but also to keep the new country in the Commonwealth. They, whatever has happened in the past, will need us to provide military training. I was asked whom I thought might be useful in that regard, and I remembered you. You established good connections with settlers and were much respected by your askaris. What do you think about returning?'

'I would welcome the change. I would like to discuss it with my wife first.'

'Yes, of course. How is Jane? No after effects of the kidnap?'

'She is well, thank you, sir. I think she has put it behind her.'

'Good show. I'll put your name forward in the appropriate quarters.'

* * *

At the end of 1960, Michael, Jane and the two children flew out to Nairobi. They were given a house in Langata, complete with houseboys and an ayah. He reported to the new GOC, who gave him an outline of the tasks ahead of him.

'The principal one just now is to expedite the commissioning of African officers and their training, which will be at Sandhurst for the foreseeable future. One of your colleagues will be looking at the provision of weapons and equipment. The RAF have people doing the same sort of thing. It is also vital that the armed forces of Kenya are drawn from all tribes in the country, not just the Kikuyu. Otherwise it will become an element of political control. You must try to persuade future ministers of the importance of this. But whatever you do, don't get into the politics. It's thorny enough as it is without people like us commenting from the sidelines. Kenyatta is being released very soon, following the Lancaster House talks. He wants to be the Father of his country, but he has rivals, not only from other parties, but also in his own party.'

Michael was very busy over the next year but he and Jane made a point of catching up with old acquaintances and friends. He sought out the wisdom of James Ridout, but the old man had died while Michael was in London. As soon as they were able they made the journey to Nanyuki. They had lunch with the Unwins. Doris was very taken with the children; she had not seen her own grandchildren for some years. They spent a week with the Howarths. Naomi was spending her last holiday at home before going off to boarding school in England. She too was much taken with the children and insisted on removing them from the ayah and playing with them and reading to them.

One afternoon, when the men went out to shoot for the pot, Annabel took Jane aside for a chat.

'You look well, dear. Marriage and motherhood suit you.'

'It hasn't been all sweetness and light but we have come a long way together. Provided Michael is busy, he is happy. Since we have been back here, he has put on weight – all those lunches he has to attend – but he is doing important work.'

'Did you want to come back to Kenya?'

'When I went home I knew that it was only a matter of time before I came back. Michael's contract is for two years with the possibility of a third. We will have to go home sooner or later - children's education and both our parents are getting long in the tooth. Besides, Michael is thinking about coming out of the Army then. He'll have a decent pension and be young enough to make a new start.'

'What might he do?'

'One obvious possibility is a School or College Bursar, but who's to say? He wants to keep physically active as long as his old wound doesn't play up.'

'Is that becoming a problem for him?'

'Not so as you would notice straightaway but when he tires he starts to limp a little.'

'I have a favour to ask. Could you keep in touch with Naomi when she is at boarding school? She will have an official guardian but it would be nice for her if you were to take her out on occasion and be a sort of long stop?'

'It would be a pleasure for us both. I was hoping you would ask us to keep an eye on her. After all that we went through together, I have grown very fond of her.'

Michael was indeed limping as he and Patrick, with a bearer, walked through the bush in search of small game. Already they had shot a guineafowl and a small buck and were looking for something the bearer could take home for himself.

'Let's go up there, Mike,' said Patrick, pointing to a small kopje, 'and have some lunch.' They sat under a tree in the shade. The bearer sat a few yards away and nibbled at a piece of chicken that Patrick had given him.

'Coffee?'

'Please.'

Michael told Patrick about his work. 'A fair number of former KAR are keen to sign up, especially as they are being offered officer or senior NCO status.'

'Any whites interested?'

'One or two, but I have been told not to encourage them. I can see why, but their expertise will be missed. Quite a few British officers stayed on in India for a few years after Independence. I have also been drawing up plans for a Kenyan Army, gazing into my crystal ball and trying to work out the sort of forces it will need. I have been talking to all sorts of people. One thing, though. The Indian community here is not keen to participate.'

'I think they fear Independence as much as most of the Europeans. The chief bogey man is Kenyatta. He was imprisoned because he was seen as the instigator of the Mau Mau and every atrocity they committed subsequently was blamed on him. The trial was controversial, to say the least. Many Europeans are convinced that he will take his revenge by driving out the whites, and then he will assert the primacy of the Kikuyu. He is aiming for a one-party state.'

'What do you think?'

'We have in effect a one-party state with British rule. Kenyatta is the only Kenyan with international status and there is no one else we can hand the country on to. Whether he will govern wisely is another matter. I have read that many whites are starting to emigrate; 700 a month, some say. I think that the new Kenya will need us for quite a few years. White farmers provide most of the country's exports and the country needs stability before dogma. I hope Kenyatta realises this. What I fear is that younger radicals, men like Mboya and Odinga, will force the pace.'

'Will you stay?'

'Of course. Whether Charlie or Naomi will stay with us…one half of me hopes they will but I do recognise that there is wider world out there for them. Charlie has been making noises about going to university in England and so far he has shown little interest in farming. As for Naomi, well, she'll make a mark whatever she does. I can't see either of them letting the grass grow under their feet.'

They fell silent, contemplating the view. Michael was about to remark about how hard it would be to leave with country like that on their doorstep when Patrick spoke again.

'There is one thing you could do for us back in England, if you don't mind my asking.'

'Not at all. Carry on.'

'Annabel and I are thinking of buying some property back in England. Just a small house somewhere not too far from London. Something for Charlie in future years, perhaps, and a bolthole for us if things go badly wrong here. Can you find us a suitable agent, who can keep an eye on it and let it out to tenants in the meantime?'

'Of course we will.'

* * *

A meeting of white farmers in Nakuru in mid-1963 was addressed by Kenyatta, now the First Minister in waiting. The farmers were despondent and hostile. Kenyatta concluded his speech thus:

> 'Many of you, I think, are just as good Kenyans as myself. I think some of you may be older than me a little bit. I am seventy-three myself and I have my age-group among you…I think some of you will be worried – what will happen if Kenyatta comes to be the head of the government? He has been in prison, maybe he has given trouble. What is he going to do? Let me set you at rest. That Kenyatta has no intention whatever to look backwards. Not at all. I want you to believe what I am saying now, that we are not going to look backwards. We are going to forgive the past and look forward to the future. Because if we start thinking about the past, what time will we have to build the future?'

Kenyatta, the *Mzee*, as he was now known, was enthusiastically applauded. In other speeches he urged Harambee!, all pull together. As Elspeth Huxley wrote in *Out in the Midday Sun*:

> 'The night of the long knives – or the sharpened *pangas* – never happened. Wild-eyed "generals" with matted hair emerged from the forests, and "rehabilitated" oath-administrators with "Jomo beards" from the detention camps, to mingle with "loyalist" home guards and stalwart Christians and turn back together into ordinary citizens. Harambee worked…'

On December 12th 1963, in the presence of Prince Philip, the Union Jack was hauled down and the flag of the Independent Republic of Kenya was raised in Nairobi.

First published in Great Britain by:

Ashgrove Publishing

an imprint of:
Hollydata Publishers Ltd
21 Ewen House
Caledonian Road
London N1 0SH

ISBN 978 185398 204 0

First Edition

Book design by Brad Thompson

Printed and bound in England